this is fine

ALSO BY POORNA BELL

FICTION

In Case of Emergency

NON-FICTION

Chase the Rainbow

In Search of Silence

Stronger

poorna bell

this is fine

C

CENTURY

1 3 5 7 9 10 8 6 4 2

Century
20 Vauxhall Bridge Road
London SW1V 2SA

Century is part of the Penguin Random House group of companies
whose addresses can be found at global.penguinrandomhouse.com

First published by Century in 2024

www.penguin.co.uk

A CIP catalogue record for this book is available from the British Library.

ISBN: 9781529901214

Typeset in 10.6/15.11 pt Palatino LT Pro by Jouve (UK), Milton Keynes
Printed and bound in Great Britain by Clays Ltd, Elcograf S.p.A.

The authorised representative in the EEA is
Penguin Random House Ireland, Morrison Chambers,
32 Nassau Street, Dublin D02 YH68

www.greenpenguin.co.uk

For my sister Priya, the lioness. I grew up encircled by your love and protection; now we stand side by side and face the world together.

1

It is deeply unfair that time is linear – that you can't just borrow moments from other parts of your life when it's casually sloshing about, doing nothing at all. Standing at a bus stop. The circle of doom buffering on your laptop. Waiting for your mother at the supermarket. I would gather all those moments like sticky bath pearls and cram them into the space before my boyfriend Wallace placed the doctor's letter down on the kitchen dining table.

The letter is the thumbtack between the before and after parts of our relationship. In the before, I knew our life together. For the better part of ten years, I planned new meals or comfort food for the weekend depending on the weather and my mood, spent hours in the market checking how firm the fish was, picked up my spice order. He would work at his private GP practice half of Saturday, select a boxset for the evening, and we'd drink a glass of red wine while we ate dinner. Sunday mornings were spent with me, the *Sunday Times*, a pain au chocolat and a coffee before meeting his friends for football.

But the after is now, as he crosses his arms and pulls his lips inwards, like sandbags holding back whatever emotions are threatening to flood through. 'You know how I feel about this, Padma,' he says with the kind of clipped coldness he reserves for his patients. 'I've made it quite clear how I feel about having children.'

In a long-term relationship, you sieve out much of what your partner says, for your own sanity and because life is short. At the beginning, there is endless patience to watch them compete at sport, pretend to like ska and listen to their work problems. As time goes on, you know that hobby number 52 is unlikely to last beyond the next tax quarter, and that the work grumbles are always an iteration of the same thing. Had Wallace made it quite clear about children? Had I accidentally filtered out his views on fatherhood alongside proclamations about the shrinking size of sandwiches in Pret and the state of the NHS?

He jabs a finger accusingly at the piece of paper that has thinly sliced our life in two. The letter that tells us what our chances are of having a baby.

*

A few years ago, while taking the 355 bus from Brixton to Tooting to get my weekly fix of masala dosa at the imaginatively titled Masala Dosa World, I'd sat with a dreamy smile on my face. I was thinking ahead to the dramatically large, golden and crispy crêpe-like roll, tiny stainless-steel pots of coconut chutney and yellow cubes of potato flecked with curry leaves. I let out a small laugh at the thought of Shivdas, the cranky, elderly waiter, who always heaved a long-suffering sigh when anyone asked for more curry.

'She's the cutest, isn't she?' I heard a woman's voice saying, winching me back into reality. I looked over to see a thirty-something mother smiling at me, her pram wedged in the space in front. The contents of said pram were looking at me and gurgling, chubby cheeks barely contained in a furry hood. I looked at the mother, realisation flooding in. She thought my laughter was from delight at seeing her child.

Judging from previous encounters, this was the point where I was supposed to make a cooing noise, or say how cute she was and punctuate my sentences with an 'Aww!' But I couldn't do it. Not because the baby wasn't cute – she was Boden-catalogue beautiful, capable of shifting rompers by the dozen. But because it felt false. I didn't get that molten feeling most women presumably do when encountering a baby in the wild. And I felt affronted because this exchange was not expected of the rangy, forty-something man next to me with his neat navy loafers and V-neck grey sweater. I wanted to correct her, tell her that I was actually excited to be going for dosa, but feared that sounded like the kind of thing a maniac would say.

In the absence of any reaction from me, the mother's face fell, her brow wrinkling in mistrust as she curled herself protectively around the pram.

I could hear her thoughts clearly: *What kind of woman can't compliment another woman's baby?* Maybe over time, I thought, I'd get better at complimenting other people's babies. Or maybe it would be different if I had my own. If you're able to have kids, you're supposed to want them, aren't you?

*

A couple of months ago, Wallace, who played five-a-side football every Sunday at the pitch on Villa Road, was hit in the testicles at considerable velocity by the ball.

Although he was a doctor, it hadn't occurred to him to get himself properly checked out – in the same way that many of his doctor friends still smoked and sank concerning amounts of expensive whisky. An older male friend on the team suggested he have a proper check-up, and given the area that had been impacted, advised him to get a fertility test. Wallace expected to be given green lights all the way because he'd never had anything significantly wrong with his health. Instead, the doctor said something about sperm motility and added: 'If you want to start trying for children, now is the time.'

He lay in bed agonising over it for days. Could we have children? Had we left it too late? Although I murmured along to soothe him, I thought the discussions were mainly hypothetical. When he asked me to get a fertility test done, I agreed because he seemed so anxious about it. 'I've set everything up for you,' he said, 'my friend Marta works in the women's hospital in Marylebone and she'll look after you.' The test was seamless, I got a free Murray Mint afterwards, and forgot about it.

Until the results arrived a week ago. The letter told me my hormone levels were great, my ovarian reserves excellent for a thirty-nine-year-old woman. That I am not just able to have children, but apparently my fertility equipment is the Vitamix of baby-making. I had planned to tell Wallace about it, but the day the letter arrived he'd been working late.

The next evening he went out for client drinks, and the rest of my week was taken up with job hunting. After being let go three months previously, my dwindling bank balance had spurred me into action because I did not want to be financially reliant on Wallace, or worse, my younger sister Daisy. But if I didn't find something soon, a conversation would have to be had. These things seemed far more important than a letter telling me about my fertility. Babies weren't exactly cheap from what I'd heard, and I needed to sort out my ability to pay my bills before adding anything else into the mix.

Then it was the weekend. I didn't want to ruin it with heavy fertility chat. But today, when he was looking for spare shoelaces ahead of his Sunday football session, he found the letter stuffed in the drawer with the takeaway menus. I was accused of 'hiding it' from him. He was not amused when I said if I had really wanted to hide it from him, I would have put it in the cupboard with all the cleaning supplies.

'Why didn't you tell me?' he asks. I know it's a serious conversation, but he's wearing his football kit at the table, and it's like being interrogated by a PE teacher.

'I didn't . . .' I start to say as my gaze crosses that of Wallace's elderly cat Winston, who has consistently showed signs of a well-nurtured hatred for me ever since we first met. He steadily licks his white fluffy fur while maintaining eye contact, as if to say: *You're lying. I'd say you're better than this but we both know you're not.*

'I didn't mean to,' I say defensively. 'You were out, I put it away for us to discuss and then I sort of forgot about it.'

'You forgot about it?' says Wallace in disbelief, rubbing the close-cut shave of his head. 'You know how much I've been worrying about this for the last few weeks and it's not something you wanted to text me about?'

'I just didn't think it was that big a deal,' I reply. 'When did having kids become such a thing in our lives? It's something we've never really discussed.'

'Padma, I didn't think it was something we *needed* to

discuss. We've been together for ten years. I've never hidden the fact that I want a family. When we see our friends, I've said how much I want what they have. And these tests recently – what the doctor told me – it really clarified what I want.'

'Which is?'

'TO HAVE KIDS!' he bellows. Wallace doesn't have a temper, so for his cool, calm, reserved mask to drop, it must be something upsetting him deeply. He presses his hands over his face to steady his breathing and calm himself down. 'Look,' he says eventually, 'I love you, I do. But I'm forty-one. You're thirty-nine. If we want to have kids, we need to be having them now. And if you don't want kids, I need to know that.'

'But what if the answer is no?' I say, perplexed. I felt our relationship was the engine of our lives. Now, from what he is telling me, it has merely been a temporary structure for something bigger. 'What if I don't want children?'

In what is very unfortunate timing, the scratch of a record player next door indicates only one thing. Usually we are both out of the house on a Sunday at this time, but not today. Loud Trinidadian choral music, courtesy of our elderly neighbour Ettie, floods through the wall, strong and uplifting. The sound of such unity washing through our kitchen feels too much to bear as realisation sets in that we are standing at the peaks of two different mountains. Neither of us willing to climb down.

Then Wallace says something I do not expect.

'If you don't want children,' he says, 'then I don't know if we have a future.' It shocks me, the electricity crackling through his words. I thought this was a discussion, a conversation around compromise, but somehow we've arrived at an ultimatum. And in no universe did I expect him not to choose me.

What signs did I miss? Or had Wallace expected me to guess how strongly he felt about children? One thing is evident. He means what he says.

As the music rises to a crescendo, my heart sinks so fast, I barely register the depth. He's saying that if I don't want children, we have to break up. The thought of my entire world being snatched away is too much to comprehend, the portion size of heartbreak too big to digest. 'But it's not the right time to start trying, Wallace,' I say, doing my best not to cry. I'm not upset, I'm overwhelmed at how some vague conversation in the past about a friend's cute kid has accelerated the potential end of our relationship. 'I'm still looking for a job, and I need money.'

'It's never the right time,' he says matter-of-factly. 'I put this off for so long because I didn't want to pressure you . . .' He pauses, and I know what sits in the trench of that silence: Wallace's concern about my mental health because of what lay in the past. 'I was setting up my own practice. Then it was always one thing after another. And for what? Who am I building this for, if not my own children? And I have money. You wouldn't have to work if you didn't want to.'

I thought we were building our life together, and that would be enough. But it's clear that for him, it is not. It makes me wonder how differently we feel about the last ten years, if I've been unaware of such a treacherous undercurrent and happy that our relationship mostly works, while he's been viewing it as a holding space for something bigger. It is unsettling, that he has spent years building a career and is so fiercely independent, and considers both things to be vitally important, yet expects me to give up both, to be financially reliant on him.

'Can I think about it?' I say desperately. I want him to reach across the table, to hold my hand. To give me the softness I need, a reassurance that it will be okay. No matter what has happened in the last ten years, including losing my job, especially with my health, I have always been able to reach out and feel his love for me. But now it feels closed off, sealed behind his eyes.

'I don't believe there's anything to think about,' he says. 'You either know or you don't. How can you not know after all this time?'

'Please. Just give me some time.' This can't be happening.

Winston jumps on his lap, and the presence of his warm little cat heart is an instant anchor for Wallace, releasing something tight and unyielding. He holds Winston to his chest and closes his eyes. When he opens them, he says: 'If I don't do this now, I don't think I ever will. I think we should take a break.'

*

When you are between jobs, a lot of your online life is spent going down random tunnels of information. One minute you're looking up the job requirements for a lighthouse manager on the Orkney Islands; the next you're learning about sinkholes. The first article I read began with: 'The best way to survive a sinkhole is by not falling in one.' It also tells you there are signs – water pooling on the ground, cracks forming in the walls. I imagine many people ignore them, make excuses. The water is an errant hose that wasn't turned off; the cracks a sign of bad building work. Then – whoosh! – the ground opens up beneath your feet, and the damp earth closes over your mouth.

'You're saying your relationship is like a sinkhole?' my friend Delilah says as she places a beautifully puffed croissant in front of me, as if I'm a toddler in need of placating. She wipes her hands on her apron and takes a seat opposite. Everything in her presence is calm, grounded and rooted to a core that stretches miles below the surface. Her sturdy forearms, bright pinny and no-nonsense manner make me feel safe, as if I can be myself around her. I don't have to squeeze my true thoughts inside me like a Swiss roll.

After announcing we were on a break, Wallace left for football, while I remained at the kitchen table, unable to move. My phone lay near me, blank, empty, quiet. I kept waiting for a message from him to say it was a mistake. When it was clear it wasn't forthcoming, I wanted to crawl into bed and go to sleep, and perhaps I'd wake up to a different reality, but Ettie's choir continued with relentless cheer.

We live in the two-bedroomed house Wallace inherited from his formidable grandmother Clementine, who had passed long before I came along, and she and Ettie had grown up together in Trinidad. Asking Ettie to 'turn it down' would be tantamount to declaring war and provoking Clementine's ghost to haunt us forever. On to Delilah's café then, where I normally spent my Sunday afternoons talking to her about life, food and everything else, in between her serving customers. Her pastries are faultless: glistening Danishes cradling stewed fruit, and fat little sugar-dusted doughnuts. Being Australian, she has incorporated the best of Aussie café culture without succumbing to hipsterism. Her mother is Aboriginal and her art lights up the walls with deep swirls of ochre, green and burnt orange.

'I'm not saying it's exactly like a sinkhole, it's just that I didn't see it coming,' I reply. 'And it's not as simple as Wallace seems to think, us taking a break. I live there. In his house. And I don't have a job. Where am I supposed to go while we figure this out? The relationship stuff is bad enough, but all the other things make it so much worse. I feel like my entire life has collapsed with that one bloody letter.'

Beyond the doorway of the café, summer has arrived, with newness and warmth on its breath. It is blue sky and contrails, pink and yellow blooms. It is hummus tubs and Prosecco picnics, dogs sniffing out waterholes. My life collapsing at the start of the most energetic season feels wrong, like something that has wormed its way into the world from a different dimension.

'The good news,' says Delilah, handing me salt and pepper shakers to refill, 'is that baby mathematics being what it is – Wallace knows that it's better for you guys to go on a break rather than breaking up completely and him finding a new partner to impregnate.'

'Wow, thanks, Delilah.'

Her afro is halo-shaped against the sun and gives her the appearance of an angel making a proclamation. She smiles and squeezes my arm in apology, but she's never one to sugarcoat things. 'The bad news,' she continues, 'is that some people think breaks are just postponing the inevitable, which may be true if you know you don't want children.'

Delilah is a rare friend in that she always meets me where I am at rather than projecting what she would do in that situation. She doesn't like Wallace much but she knows he has always been there for me, especially when I experienced what we loosely call my 'health' issues – a particularly entrenched bout of depression at the start of our relationship.

Part of the reason our bond grew so quickly was her willingness to talk honestly about her life back in Australia and growing up as a foster child. There is a softness and compassion that comes from living skin to skin with a certain kind of darkness, and although it had been years since I had experienced anything approaching a bad spell, and Delilah now had a life she loved, we both lived with the spectre of it every day.

'What if I'm making a mistake?' I say, pouring salt into a shaker. 'If having a kid is the way we stay together, is it really that bad? I mean, sometimes people have children for worse reasons.'

Delilah looks shocked. 'I heard how that sounded,' I say. 'It's bad, isn't it? It's just – this whole thing has blindsided me. I hadn't realised how strongly he felt about it. And now that it might be the end of our relationship, I'm not sure how I feel about it all.'

'I think it's fair enough that you take your time thinking about it,' she says. 'It's a lot to take onboard. And maybe he's pushing you to see how far you'll go. Going on a break is very different from a break-*up*, Padma.'

'Yes, but what happens at the end of the break if I don't change my mind? I'm about eighty per cent for not wanting kids.'

'Well then, there you go! Twenty per cent is still a respectable number to work with.'

'Yes,' I say gloomily, 'but not enough to start trying for kids, which he wants to do *right away*. Even the thought of it makes me feel sick. Not babies – just the quickness of it all. I still haven't come close to finding a new job. I checked my bank balance and it's down to double digits. I just thought I'd have more time to figure things out.'

'I could give you some hours working here,' she says. 'People loved your Indian street snacks.'

To give myself something to focus on during a particularly bleak spell when I had no interviews and HR departments refused to reply to any of my emails, Delilah let me help out in the café a little bit. I was playing around and created a croissant and samosa hybrid called a cramosa: little cubes of potato, brightly coloured yellow with turmeric, peas and small lightning bolts of green chilli hidden within buttery folds of flaky pastry.

When she tried one, I saw the surprise and pleasure on her face. She had let me into her kitchen as a kindness, but until that moment hadn't realised I could actually cook. 'I'm sorry for the surprise,' she said, 'but when people say they can cook, it's usually a spaghetti Bolognese or a curry that just happens not to be shit. This is something else, Padma.' I was terrible at taking compliments so just mumbled a *thank you*. But while I was busy cleaning up in the kitchen out back, Delilah started selling them – and they were gone within the hour. People kept asking when they were coming back, and it went some way towards healing the damage caused by losing my job, which had knocked my confidence.

My last job had been working behind the scenes as a researcher, caterer and all-round dogsbody on a food YouTube channel for an influencer named Lanky Pandey, whose real name was Majid. After he 'borrowed' one of my recipes, which then went viral, I'd asked to be credited. Not even paid, just given a mention. He'd told me not to be silly, and that it was something he'd been working on for weeks, and the only reason it was successful anyway was because of him and *his* fans. 'Do *you* have fans, Padma?' he'd scoffed.

The next day, I'd been let go on the grounds that my role would be filled by one of his cousins. 'Cost-of-living crisis, Pads,' he'd said with a nonchalant shrug, then pretended to take a phone call so he didn't have to deal with my reaction. The same loose approach he had to recruitment – he didn't mind that I'd had no credentials beyond HR temp work – was now acting to my detriment. I had no reference, no severance pay and no real sense of what I wanted my next job to be.

I am grateful for Delilah's offer but it isn't enough. I need more than a few hours of shift work. Majid didn't pay me well enough for me to stash away any savings, but it was enough to pay my share of the bills and leave me a bit of disposable income to buy books and cooking supplies. Our home was mortgage-free thanks to Wallace's grandmother, which had always been a relief. But now – thanks to this unwanted break – I would have to find three months' rent as a deposit for somewhere else, as well as deal with the potential collapse of my relationship.

I tuck my head into my arms, as the magma of panic that has been slowly rising since my conversation with Wallace comes to the surface. It's about to push through when I feel the calming, steady pressure of Delilah's hand on my shoulder.

When I eventually look up, she says, 'I know you're going to say no, but what about . . .'

'Don't say it.'

'. . . asking your sister for help?' she finishes.

I emit a long, tortured sound like a whale in distress. Then, as if somewhere in the universe a cosmic beacon picks up the noise and sends it hurtling back to Earth, my phone starts ringing. It's Daisy.

Delilah arches an eyebrow and heads back behind the

counter to take a customer's payment. I stare at the phone until it rings out.

*

Daisy is three years younger than me, but when she had my niece Myra at the age of twenty-one, she auditioned for the role of the older sister and got the part. Motherhood closed a gap she'd been trying to fill all through our childhood, a void created by our absent father and the death of our mother. I tell Daisy very sparing details about my life because if she senses there is something she can do or suggest to make it better, a barrage of texts and emails and introductions swiftly follows. It's well-meaning but exhausting, and carries the faintest whiff of condescension, especially if you don't accept her help. Although she is a lawyer, she also has a Master's from the school of I Told You So.

I would have kept news of the firing from her, had she not asked whether my fifteen-year-old niece could do some work experience with me. The flurry of questions upon hearing that I was out of a job was unrelenting. *What's the severance package like? What do you mean, you don't have severance? We should take them to a tribunal. Have you been applying for other jobs? Why don't you come over and we can practise some interview role play. If you don't get serious about this, Padma, you only have yourself to blame!* To keep her at bay, I told her about helping out Delilah, embellishing slightly. That prompted a renewed onslaught – this time trying to get me to apply to the catering school Leiths so as to get a proper set of credentials. Wallace said she reminded him of a hydra; I said she reminded me of why you shouldn't throw water on a gremlin.

I know Daisy is calling to see if I've received her email about her knowing someone at Leiths. I have seen the email but haven't the energy required to staple restrained politeness to my voice. Not when everything is imploding at home.

But then she calls again. And again. No text to explain why she is calling – which is unusual. Normally she would send an all-caps text saying: **PADMA WHY AREN'T YOU ANSWERING YOUR PHONE.**

I pick up on her fourth attempt. 'Yes, Daisy – what's up?' I say, borrowing some of Wallace's coldness because I know she's going to make comments about what else I could possibly be doing. She believes that because I don't have children, my life must be so much less complicated than hers.

Immediately I can tell something is wrong. Normally she bellows down the phone, but there's a pause and I hear an intake of breath, dense with tears, like a cloud holding in rain. 'Daisy?' I say a bit more softly. 'Are you okay?'

'Padma,' she replies, gulping out the words, 'it's Myra.' She starts crying so hard then it's impossible to make out the next few words. The sound is disconcerting because Daisy is not a crier. Whatever this is, it must be bad.

'It's okay,' I say soothingly. 'Take your time. What happened?'

'We're at the hospital,' she says. 'She's had alcohol poisoning – she's unconscious. She collapsed at the front door. Her friends just dumped her there. I called the ambulance . . .' The sound of her crying pools into my ear. I know what exists in Daisy's past – and mine – that makes all this horribly familiar. The fabric of time pinches the past and present sharply together, and old ghosts step over from their world to ours. Myra is only fifteen. She should be making summer plans, playing video games, watching daytime cartoons – whatever it is that teenagers do.

'I'm on my way,' I say. 'Text me where I need to come.'

Even though I've probably told the bank manager at Barclays more about my life in the last year than I have my own sister, I say the four words that every younger sibling needs to hear, when they look to you as the closest thing they have to age-old love and safety. 'It will be okay,' I tell her.

2

Just as I was about to step on the bus to go to Kingston Hospital, Daisy asked me to stop by their house to pick up a few things. In contrast to mine and Wallace's well-loved, mildly ramshackle home in Brixton, Daisy lives in a smart two-storey Wimbledon townhouse, just off the Common, surrounded by high hedges and framed in late-blooming wisteria. Although we can afford it, Wallace doesn't like to get things fixed or throw them out unless they've deteriorated to the point of no return. It's a trait he inherited from his grandfather, Eustace, and it explains why the cold-water tap in our kitchen sink sometimes needs to be turned on with a wrench, and the lock on the back door is fortified with a plank of wood.

Although I had never before been to the townhouse without anybody being there, I could hardly refuse. After punching in the code for the front door lock, I halt at the sight of Myra's school backpack askew in the hallway, surrounded by a sheaf of legal papers scattered ominously like feathers under a tree. Daisy must have dropped them the moment she saw Myra on the ground. I tidy the papers and place them on the console table; put the backpack in the hallway cupboard. Daisy hates mess and everything has its assigned place – from her husband Henry to the monthly copy of *National Geographic*.

The interiors of her townhouse are decorated in tones of blue, white and grey. We come from a people who paint our lives in marigold yellows and fuchsia pinks, so this small rejection of our culture is fitting, given that she changed her name from Dhara to Daisy when she went to university, shortly after our mother died. We have no one older than us to gently guide us back to where we came from, our father being absent for all of Daisy's life and his whereabouts unknown. It wasn't difficult, then, to rip out her entire root system and replace it with something she deemed more palatable.

Being in a house when the owners aren't present is like walking around a museum, examining the fragments, piecing their lives together. What I know about them is from spending time with them, which isn't much, and what Daisy tells me. I have only ever come to this house when there is a reason to: a birthday, an anniversary. It is something else altogether to observe the spaces in between, to add colour, shade and dimension to who they are as people from the type of milk they drink, the books on their nightstand. Who Myra is. Since I heard the news about her, I've been trying to come to terms with what has happened and why. But I've also been struggling with my own guilt. I see my niece so infrequently, know so little about her, that I don't know the distance between who she once was and who she is now.

I remember her being a sweet child around the age of eight or nine, and then she seemed to become progressively more angry. Maybe some of her angst comes from sitting in two continents and never feeling as if she fully occupies either. Her skin is a pale cream colour in the winter, and then the moment the sun comes out, her Indian genes flip her skin tones to a deep brown. If she was so inclined, with her face and angular limbs, she could be an Instagram model but she's 'grossed out' by the idea of people looking at her body. 'I don't want to be a booty bitch,' she once said, referring to her peers who would wear Gymshark leggings and pose bum-first to the camera. Instead, she wears oversized T-shirts, tailored black and white shirts with long strips of fabric dangling from the arms, leather girdles, vinyl leggings and Doc Martens. Her fingernails are coated in chipped black polish; her eyes are ringed in kohl. Like other people her age, she believes she is the first person to dress like this.

Daisy's relationship with her in recent years has seemed fraught, in the way that some mothers and daughters do constant battle. She talks a lot about how Myra never behaves, never does what she is asked, and is a 'fucking nightmare', but because she always couches it in a tone that implies 'your life must be so much easier because you don't have children', I've only half-listened to her complaints. Their inordinate amount of wealth has also made me assume that, however difficult Myra is, they could just buy their way out of it. Now I feel guilt, not just for my neglect of Myra, but of my sister too. Perhaps I haven't been there for her as much as I should have been.

I'm heading upstairs, feet digging into the plush grey carpet, when a wall of recently framed photographs draws my attention. There are photos of Myra with a gappy smile at a waterpark. The three of them sitting atop an elephant on the Serengeti. Daisy blowing out the candle of a Mother's Day cupcake in bed. I'm observing my sister's life through a window when I should be alongside her.

I follow the photographs up the stairs until an image of our mother halts me in my tracks. The ones in my possession are kept in a battered Dolcis shoebox that I only bring out on the anniversary of her death. I'd forgotten this version of her; before the drinking began to puff out her face and turned her eyes to glass. She's in a scrubby little garden, laughing. People are sitting around in plastic chairs, drinking out of mismatched cups. Her hair is a Farrah Fawcett flick and she's wearing a pale pink kurta top with little mirrors sewn around the neckline. She almost looks like the kind of mother who makes idlis on Sundays, buys Ferrero Rocher for our birthdays and tucks us into bed at night. Almost.

*

I make the mistake of sitting on the top deck of the bus to Kingston Hospital, so that by the time I arrive in reception, I am thoroughly microwaved by the summer sun. The oversized T-shirt I've stolen from Wallace has changed a Pantone number due to the amount of sweat watering my body like a hydroponic garden. A lady in her late forties, standing behind me, remarks helpfully: 'Cor, I thought I was sweaty, love, but you're like the Niagara!'

I follow a blue line on the floor all the way to the ward, and when I get there, Daisy is sitting by the front desk, hunched over her YSL bag. Her Sunday casualwear is still better than anything I'd wear on an evening out. Chanel slippers with interlocking embroidered Cs, slightly crumpled brushed linen shirt and £300 Victoria Beckham jeans. She presses her hands against her eyes, as if trying not to cry. So much has changed between Daisy and me, but this moment is such a Dhara gesture, the gleaming fin breaking through the surface to let me know she is in there somewhere. That although my sister is all angles and bone, I once used to cuddle her on the sofa when her face was puffed with crying, when she'd sit with her knees pulled up to her chest. Something about the way her small, insubstantial hands wrap around herself makes me rush over to give her a hug.

The moment she catches sight of me, she starts wiping her face furiously with a tissue, and rearranges her countenance into something hard and resilient.

'What took you so long?' Daisy frowns – or attempts to through the Botox she's recently begun experimenting with. It is a struggle to imagine that somewhere inside her, like a ring within a tree trunk, is the little girl from Rochester in a Teenage Mutant Ninja Turtles T-shirt, eating Frazzles while applying nail polish she's stolen from my make-up tray.

When she goes to her job as a lawyer in the City, she favours tailored suits. She is the kind of person who considers Breton stripes daring, and flip-flops to be a sign that someone has given up on life. Her jewellery is understated and expensive, much like her body, and she stopped eating carbs when she turned thirty. Looking at her body, with barely any trace of extra flesh, it's hard to believe she birthed Myra. She catches my gaze, which lingers a little too long on the unnaturally smooth space between her eyes.

'The bus was late,' I sigh, knowing how Daisy feels about people who take the bus. She thinks people choose to do so for entertainment versus necessity, that they are not serious people who respect punctuality. It is yet another observation I must tuck behind my teeth that Daisy herself used to be a bus person; that she wasn't always one of the drones who drive all-terrain SUVs in the city to do their weekly shops and make the school run.

'Are you okay?' I say, taking a seat next to her. She just

shakes her head because she can't allow herself to break down. 'Is Henry here?'

'No,' she says tiredly. 'He's away on a business trip. But he's on his way back now.'

'How is Myra?'

'They've pumped her stomach. She's stable.' Daisy's face is drawn with worry. Even she can't wallpaper fully over the grief and fear that mark her. Some of it is new, some of it old, a haunting. 'But still asleep.' She points to the side room Myra occupies.

'I'm just going to look in on her, okay?'

Daisy nods, and I squeeze her shoulder.

Myra is asleep, and without the weight of the waking world, her face has taken on its true form: young, vulnerable, peaceful. The softness of her youth, the raggedy friendship bracelet around her wrist, makes the sight of her IV drip and the oxygen tube in her nose almost unbearable. Although she is a near-exact mix of Daisy and Henry, she has the same high cheekbones as our mother – which neither of us inherited. There is such a sharp sense of longing when I look at her, remembering who wore those cheekbones last, that I wonder how Daisy bears it.

By the time I come out, my sister's usual hard veneer has disappeared under a fresh bout of tears, which she hurriedly tries to hide again. 'We need to talk,' she says, her eyes ringed in tiredness, the kind that has been going on for a while.

*

Our mother, Ashwini Alva, was a respected doctor in her field of cardiology. She wasn't just clever, she had charisma and gravitas. When she spoke to her patients and other parents at school, she came across as knowledgeable and also soft, funny and wise. Everyone loved her. They thought she was 'so much fun' because they didn't notice the overly bright expression in her eyes, the brittleness that sometimes entered her voice. The intensity with which she needed to get home, to lock herself behind her door.

Her alcoholism wasn't gregarious. It was mostly conducted through the miniatures I found stuffed down the side of her desk, bottles of wine hidden in the bin under rolls of kitchen towel, a morning mug of something added before Daisy and I came down for breakfast. 'It's not a problem' and 'stop worrying' and 'who's the adult' and 'everyone does it' were phrases used on rotation by her to deflect queries daily.

When I've told partners that my mother was an alcoholic and also a doctor, their first reaction has been one of disbelief. One even said to me: *Are you sure?* As if I had somehow misunderstood an entire childhood. My mother wasn't negligent as a doctor – she was always sober when she worked – but the hardest part of her condition was that any time she did have outside of her surgery was spent with a bottle rather than with us.

The anger I feel about that still burns in me. I believe it's at the heart of why I have never wanted children. Even though I'm not an alcoholic, there are still ways in which I could mess them up, and the responsibility of that feels dark and enormous. While Wallace and I hadn't explicitly had a conversation around children to the point of it being a clear deal-breaker in our relationship, the subject had come up a few years ago.

We'd visited one of his friends who held a baby shower in

Streatham that turned into a mini-rave, with all the men trying to relive their youth by taking coke behind the garden shed, while the women stayed inside drinking Prosecco and exchanging birth horror stories. I'd had to leave after the third mention of mucus plugs.

'Most women *want* to have kids,' Wallace admonished me afterwards when I'd railed about never wanting to be a mother.

'Just because you own an oven doesn't mean you have to bake a cake,' I'd replied.

'That is one of the stupidest things I've ever heard,' he laughed. 'I don't understand why you don't want them. You'd make a great mother.'

I tried to tell him why – explaining that the idea of looking after someone in the same way I'd had to look after Mum and Daisy made me feel as if someone was wringing out the air from my lungs. It sounded perverse, but I told him I didn't think my mother should have had children, if she wasn't going to look after us the way we needed to be. That I didn't think it was okay that I'd had to role-play motherhood when I was still a child.

But he didn't listen. He didn't see how deep the feeling ran within me, or maybe didn't want to.

And now Myra. Was her drinking just a case of teenagers being teenagers? The circumstances were disturbing. That she had consumed so much she'd had to be hospitalised. That her friends cared so little about her they'd just abandoned her to save their own skins. All of it pointed to someone who was fragile, who could shatter at far too early an age. The question was why? And how fixable was it?

Daisy and I have never spoken about our mother's drinking. Not directly. She can't say the A word. Instead she says things like 'Mum was difficult' or 'unreliable'. I wonder if she thought that by never talking about it, she could leave it in the past. I wonder how she feels, seeing flashes of it reappearing in her present.

*

'What actually happened?' I ask once Daisy and I are seated in the hospital café. She looks down into the dark portal of her coffee, as if it is the gateway to a distant land she might escape to.

I thought I had done a good job of protecting Daisy from the consequences of our mother's drinking. But in the harsh fluorescent light of the hospital, every ridge of her worry is visible; she's just been hiding it under the life of a different person. Even in death, our mother was like a larger planet who exerted a gravitational pull so strong, it influenced our own trajectories.

'Myra was out with friends on Saturday night,' she says brusquely, as if she is relaying facts in a court case. 'We thought she was spending the night at her friend Lana's place. She texted all was fine. Then this morning, the doorbell rang and . . .'

She pauses, trying to gather the parts of herself that are fragmenting because it's too hard to maintain this artifice. 'She was lying there. They'd just dumped her there like a garbage bag. She was struggling to breathe and seemed to have a seizure . . . and then I don't really remember.' She taps the side of her head as if trying to dislodge the memory, confused as to why it isn't accessible. Daisy is someone who remembers every detail, down to whether you forgot to put a label on her Christmas present, or if you cancelled a dinner less than twenty-four hours ahead of time. 'I must have . . . called the ambulance, then the paramedics came.'

We don't really do hugs any more, so I reach for her hand. 'It's okay,' she says, pulling it away, as if she can't bear any sort of kind gesture. 'I'm fine. Honest. They said she had alcohol poisoning.' She spools her emotions back into herself and crosses her arms. The hardness returning to her face. I have to reach out, say something, before she walls herself back in.

'Daisy,' I say softly, 'I am so sorry you had to go through that.' When she doesn't answer, I get up and go over to hug her. Fear spikes on her face as if to say: *No, please don't*. But she is my little sister, the only other one called into being in the same body. I had helped feed her milk from a bottle. She holds her feeble bird-like arms up to push me away, but I scoop her into an embrace anyway. I hold her close, all of her. It's like hugging a pile of coat hangers. Even though she struggles like a sparrow in a shoebox, eventually she softens and lets go. Presses her face into my T-shirt and starts to cry in big, whooping sobs. It seems impossible someone so small could make such a noise. 'Oh, my god,' she says, mortified that she's cried in public, and covers her face with her hands. 'I can't believe I just did that. What are other people going to think?'

'Well, one person in here is on an IV drip so I'd say they have bigger problems, and the other is more concerned with stealing packets of sugar. You're good.'

She folds her hands, a vein feathering in her jaw. 'She could have died, Padma. Do you know that people can die from it? And if I hadn't been at home . . . and I'm not normally at home on a Sunday. I usually play tennis but my partner cancelled. If I hadn't been . . .'

'But you were,' I say, pinching the end of her spiral and snuffing it out before it catches fire. The memory of Myra's face, wan against the hospital pillow, flickers before my eyes for a moment. 'You were home. Now she's here, and she's being taken care of. And one day this will all feel like a bad dream.' My phone buzzes. Wallace.

Finished footie. Going for a beer with the boys.
See you later.

Even if we are angry with each other, which isn't often, we'll always sign off our messages with a kiss, even when it's wildly passive-aggressive. The lack of a kiss, the business-like tone, feels like a punishment, a withdrawal of love because I can't give him the answer he wants. But I don't have time to think about Wallace right now, not when this feels more important.

'Sorry,' I say, 'Wallace.' Daisy rolls her eyes as she always does at the mention of his name. When we'd started dating, she'd been so impressed he was a doctor, and relieved that I was dating someone with a Proper Job – unlike the man who sold used vinyl from his living room or the gym receptionist who didn't own a pair of full-length trousers. But Wallace was sometimes distant with people he didn't know, and he wasn't glamoured by Daisy and Henry's wealth. After the one and only visit she'd paid to our house, she'd remarked that he'd seemed more affectionate with his cat than with me. He'd overheard.

'Things have been bad for a while,' Daisy says, returning to our conversation. 'We've been yelling at each other a lot – she doesn't listen to anything I say.'

'But you both normally yell at each other, don't you? I mean, every time I see you both, you're fighting like cats and dogs.' Which, in retrospect, is the wrong thing to say.

'I don't yell at her for no reason, Padma,' says Daisy, glaring defensively at me. 'You don't know what it's been like. You're not . . .'

'A mother,' I say wearily, finishing her sentence. She looks taken aback because normally I act like an armadillo, retreating into silence when she gets hot-headed, waiting for her to cool down.

'Well, yes,' she says uncertainly. 'Look, I'm not being unfair. Over the last year, she's made some new friends and I'm not a fan. I couldn't ban her from seeing them because they also go to the very bloody expensive school we pay for her to go to, and their parents are . . . influential. But she's been in trouble several times over the last year – vodka bottles at school, and sometimes she comes home drunk and then denies it. She misses her curfew. Nothing we say gets through. When she's at home, she spends all her time in her room playing video games or watching Netflix. She says she doesn't want to do A-levels let alone a university degree. We're at our wits' end.'

'She's a teenager though, right?' I say, trying to be reassuring. 'They're supposed to be difficult at this age – aren't they?'

'I wasn't. You weren't,' she says flatly. That was true, but we had a very different upbringing from Myra's. When you have to parent your own parent *and* your sibling, there is precious little time left to be a child.

But it sounded like Daisy had been really struggling with Myra. Our mother was a first-generation immigrant. We were raised with the very clear understanding that the world was stacked against us, and we needed to be grateful for whatever we were given. The idea of purposefully sabotaging your chances, or disobeying your parents, was inconceivable. I am almost envious of the privilege in which one must be raised in order to be so careless with it.

'Can't you just – you know – give her a good kick up the pants? Show her the Way of the Chappal?'

At this, Daisy starts laughing. Hysterically. It is so loud it finally makes the other people in the canteen look over. 'Way of the Chappal,' she says, wiping a tear of laughter from her eye. 'I *wish*. You know what I realised as a parent, which we didn't know as kids? If they don't want to do what you ask them to do, there is fuck all you can do about it. You can't lock them up. You can't even take away their phone because you need them to have their bloody phone so you can call them! Henry and I both have busy jobs – we can't even ground Myra, because we aren't around half the time to enforce it.'

'What does Henry think of all this?'

She taps her nails on the table, drumming out her frustration. 'I love him but he's useless when it comes to this sort of thing. He parents like a hippy. His rationale is that if we talk to her like an adult, she'll behave more maturely – and clearly that hasn't bloody worked! When I threaten to cancel our holidays or take away her PlayStation, he just softens and relents. If we had relatives in India that we still talked to – believe me, I'd ship her off in a minute.'

I twist an empty sugar wrapper guiltily. I'm one of her relatives, and I haven't done very much to help or even been aware of what's going on. If I had been, might things have been different? But then, Daisy has never asked. She's never said, *Talk some sense into your niece*, and part of me has always wondered if the reason is that my sister doesn't want Myra to take advice from someone like me. That her constant suggestions for how I should improve my life do not stem from some over-zealous fixer-upper mentality, but because I would fit into her life a whole lot better if I went to Leiths or lived somewhere 'less stabby'.

Her phone pings. 'Henry,' she says, relief flooding through. 'He'll be here in a few hours, Hugo is going to drop him from the airport.'

'Who's Hugo?'

'You remember Hugo – from our wedding! Henry's cousin?' she says, and starts texting him back. Why do people insist on referencing weddings as a time when you *must* have met someone? Given the volume of people, copious alcohol, the sheer number of things happening at any one time, from cake-cutting to first dances, it's the most inopportune landscape in which to have any meaningful or memorable experiences with other guests unless you sleep with them. Which I didn't.

'Which of the ninety-eight white people present was he?' I say sarcastically, knowing that Daisy and I represented all of the diversity at her wedding, which had taken place sixteen years ago.

'Well,' she says, looking up from her phone and arching an eyebrow, 'he remembers you.'

'Stop right there,' I say firmly. Daisy had a bad track record for trying to set me up with Henry's toff friends before I met Wallace. There was a Nigel, a Pravesh and a Ulysses, and they were all terrible and united in their goal to make as much money as possible. They believed people who blamed things like class and race for their poverty or lack of success just weren't working hard enough.

'I'm only teasing. He's just moved back from Brazil after years out there, which Henry is delighted about. Anyway, if you want to go, you can. Myra isn't awake and I can work through some emails. I'll walk you to the bus stop.' Although I feel worried and sad with all this new information to take in, part of me is relieved to be dismissed. The day is only two-thirds done and it already feels like it has lasted a thousand years.

*

As we walk to the bus stop, I tell Daisy I'll come back tomorrow but that if she needs anything, to text me. It's the most sustained contact we've had in years. Usually after seeing each other, the intensity of it requires a lie-down and some distance.

'Ten minutes,' I say, squinting at the board. When I look at Daisy, her eyes are filling with tears again. 'Or I could stay?'

'Padma, I feel so guilty for not stopping it,' she says, a fresh wave of emotion washing through. 'So ashamed. I don't know what to do.'

I hug her and this time she doesn't push me away. 'It's not your fault, you know that.'

'I'm her mother,' she sobs into my shoulder. 'If it's not my fault, then whose is it?'

I think of what it must be like to be a mother, to know your heart sits inside the body of another person, to feel the terror of that every single day, but to know that you are the beacon on the hill. The one they call home, the singular point of safety, the one who cannot bend or break, even when the storm rages overhead.

Maybe this isn't about our past, but about how she perceives she has failed Myra. 'I don't know what to do,' she says, blowing her nose. 'I can take a few days off but not much more than that, especially now that I've made partner. Henry's schedule is a nightmare – he's flying all over the place. I don't know how we're going to manage it.'

'Look, whatever you need, just let me know. I'm here,' I say, even though it's a page from the book of hollow platitudes. I love Myra, and I want her to be well and happy, but what do I know about raising children? I also have pressing problems of my own.

The bus arrives and I feel relieved at the prospect of being alone. But when I get on the bus, the card reader beeps red. I tap it again. And again. 'You don't have any money, love!' the bus driver says exasperatedly, gesturing at the passengers who have already paid, and who I'm preventing from reaching their destination. I tap it again, just in case. *Beeeep*. I remember too late that the payment for the electricity bill would have just gone out, leaving my account empty.

'Padma,' Daisy says from the pavement, making me jump. 'What's going on?' This is my nightmare. Having the truth of my situation laid bare for her to witness.

'My card isn't working for some reason,' I say, holding it up. The bus driver lets out another annoyed huff.

She looks at me, and there is understanding in her eyes. 'That happens to me too,' she says. Even though I know the last time Daisy got public transport, Tony Blair was still Prime Minister.

She hands me her Amex Black. 'Here. Give it back to me tomorrow.' I have no choice but to take it.

3

On the bus journey home, I try to drown out my thoughts with an eighties mix playlist, but even Wham! can't dispel the image of Myra's face floating in front of me. Alcohol poisoning. She will be okay physically, especially now that she is in hospital, being monitored. But mentally, the work ahead sounds serious.

Teenagers misbehaving might swig from a bottle or two on the weekend, but this seems like more than that. This feels like it has been going on for a while. I know that cracks exist in any life, ready to swallow someone whole if they aren't held tight and supported by their loved ones. Maybe if I visit more, take an active interest in her, I can ask a bit more about her life . . . get to the bottom of whatever is driving this.

But the closer I come to Brixton, the more my new reality sets in. It squeezes the breath from my body. I am not going back to the familiar comfort of my old life. That thought makes me nostalgic for yesterday when my biggest worries were around what to cook for dinner, and whether Wallace and I would get to go to sleep together at the same time or if he'd have to stay up working late. All I want is to wake up feeling loved and ready to start a new day. As the bus pulls up to my stop, I try to convince myself that perhaps he didn't mean what he said, that he was acting out of anger and haste. *It'll be fine, he loves you,* I tell myself. *I'll cook us a nice dinner, we can talk about things.*

When I get home, Wallace still hasn't returned. I text him, asking if he has eaten, but he doesn't respond. I haven't messaged anything about Myra or Daisy because it feels too big to summarise within a text, but I start to miss him. I want him to come home so I can absorb whatever comfort he can give me, even if it's just crumbs.

I start cooking because the only time my brain slows and focuses is when I'm making food. Yesterday I'd picked up a fresh and gleaming, blue-and-silver mackerel from Harry Otto's, wondering how much longer their business would last. Brixton had been dealt a deadly blow a decade ago with the arrival of a Foxtons and the creep of food chains. The market is still what it was in parts; some small business owners have been there for years selling fabrics, spices, local art, handmade lotions, dumplings, saltfish and ackee, Japanese pancakes, books that are gateways to worlds forgotten by mainstream bookshops. But it can't hold on forever. I pat the fish in semolina, chilli powder, turmeric and lemon juice, and listen keenly for the point at which the oil is hot enough to start frying.

Once I've eaten and the dishes are done, the sound of a key in the door and a grunt as someone pushes against the warped wood indicate Wallace is home. Winston shoots towards him, thirstily demanding attention. Wallace dumps his football kit in the hallway and comes through to the kitchen. 'It absolutely reeks of fish in here,' he says, sounding irritated, before throwing his keys in the misshaped bowl I made for him during pottery class years ago.

'Wallace, I have to tell you something,' I say, hoping he'll be able to smooth the roughness of the day.

'Oh?' he says, raising his eyebrows. 'Have you changed your mind?' It is worrying how quickly his expression softens as a reward for what he thinks I'm about to say.

'No, it's not that. Myra ended up in hospital. I've just come back from seeing her – and Daisy.'

'Is she okay?' he says, alarmed but also trying to shelve his disappointment. 'What happened?'

'She had to have her stomach pumped. Alcohol poisoning. She'd been out with friends and had drunk too much. Daisy says she's been acting out for some time – apparently they've had a lot going on.'

Wallace fights to keep the contempt from his voice; his mind snags on the part where it is self-inflicted, the wasted medical resources. But I can see he is also reframing the level of sympathy he needs to show in order to be a good boyfriend. 'Oh,' he says, 'I'm sorry to hear that. But don't worry – if she's in hospital and stable, she'll be fine.'

'I'm going back there tomorrow,' I say, hoping he will offer to come with me.

'I would come,' he says defensively, 'but I have such a full day of work. You'll keep me posted as to how she is?' I nod and let out a sigh of relief as he comes over to hug me. Even if his words aren't warm, a gesture of affection is sorely needed. But instead of holding me, he announces he needs to have a shower and the rejection sends me sagging back into the sofa. The sharp edge of Daisy's credit card in my pocket pokes against my thigh, reminding me that my more immediate concern is that I have no money. Asking him for it now would be humiliating, because for the first time in our life together, I am not sure what his answer would be.

*

When Wallace comes out of the shower, the scent of mint carried on a crest of steam, he sees me sitting on his side of the bed, but doesn't say anything. Eventually he starts rubbing scalp oil onto his head and, seeing that I'm not moving, sighs. 'What is it?'

'I hate this,' I say, struggling not to cry. 'How can things change so much between us so quickly just because I'm not sure if I want children?'

'I'm not doing this to punish you,' he says, vigorously rubbing behind his ears. 'But I've become very clear about what I want. I would be a good dad, you know.'

He says it so earnestly, but even if I believed him – which I don't because I have yet to see any relationship in which the man does more or an equal share, unless he's specifically a house husband – what I feel about absent fathers is too big to put into words.

'But,' Wallace continues, 'if you don't feel the same, then I do need to know.'

'And then what? Is it really that easy for you to call time on our relationship? After all we've been through?'

Guilt flashes across Wallace's face because he knows what I'm referring to. He knows what parts of our past, my past, make this even more difficult. 'Don't you think I'm aware of that, Padma? Your health issues? Why do you think I've waited so long to have this conversation?' He sighs and starts rubbing cocoa butter on his body, muscles gleaming as he works his way up. Although outwardly Wallace looks like a cross between a software engineer and a librarian, underneath his clothes he's quite wiry and lean.

'I'm not saying we're breaking up,' he says, pulling on his pyjamas. 'I'm just saying I think it will be good for us to take a break while you figure things out. And I need time too. I love you but this is important to me.'

'But what does that mean . . . we're on a break?'

He sits down on the chair opposite me. 'It means that we take some time apart. It would be best if you found somewhere else to stay. Temporarily. So that we can have some proper space.'

'And we don't speak during that time?' The thought of not being in Brixton, not being able to see him every day, makes me feel as if my entire body is plummeting into a dark, depthless space.

'I think that's for the best, don't you?' he says, trying to be kindly though it comes across as somewhat patronising. 'Look, Pads, we're not breaking up, we're just giving each other space. Loads of couples do it and get back together. My practice manager, Becky – her sister just got back together with her partner and they are better than ever.'

I can't bear to be in the same room as he continues his bedtime routine. I head downstairs and take the bag of fish guts out to the bins, spending a moment in the scrubby front garden, hearing the sounds of Brixton around me. Faint fragments of music, the throaty growl of traffic going by.

I'm not ready for dividing up our spoons; learning to sleep

in the middle of the bed. I don't want to go on those dating apps I've overheard people talking about in Delilah's café. I don't want to know what ghosting or cocaine dick is – although the last one seems self-explanatory. But neither do I feel able to say yes to the idea of having children. But while I'm fairly sure I don't want them, it isn't the same as being *absolutely* sure. Do I want to throw away an entire relationship when the answer isn't one hundred per cent obvious? On the other hand, this version of Wallace worries me. I don't feel inclined to agree to something as enormous as having children with someone who doesn't seem to be concerned about where I might stay during this break or how I will financially support myself. I have always felt safe within our relationship but now, for the first time, I don't.

By the time I go back upstairs, he has his earphones in and his eye mask pulled over his face. The equivalent of a 'Do Not Disturb' sign. He looks peaceful, as if he hasn't just blasted my world apart, and the fury I feel almost knocks me off my feet. I could talk to Daisy about it but I don't think she will understand.

She will say what they all say. *You'd be a great mum. Once you have them, you'll see what we mean. You might regret not having them.* But maybe some of us cannot bear the weight of it. Maybe some of us have parents who taught us that being a parent didn't default to being good at it. That some of us will carry the marks of that forever, and perhaps we don't want to be the indelible ink in another person's life.

*

Daisy texted sometime in the early hours of the morning to say Myra has woken up and is doing well. I text back with one eye cracked open, to say I'll be coming just before noon. Wallace must have left earlier than normal, because I didn't wake up to the clink of his cereal bowl or the soft thud of the front door. The house feels empty, and not just of its occupants – including Winston, who has gone to sexually harass the silver-haired Russian Blue next door. Our future, which includes our home, has been hollowed out and replaced with uncertainty.

Although I still have Daisy's Amex to get me to the hospital, it isn't a long-term solution. I check my banking app while on the bus, which tells me I am £100 overdrawn, and the anxiety spiral around money begins in my chest. On impulse, and slightly panicked, I text Majid with gritted teeth. Even though he is a recipe thief, I am desperate enough to ask. **Hi Majid. Hope you are well. Just checking in to see if you have any part-time work available?** The message flips to read but no reply. As he's done with my last two.

The stagnant hot air of the bus combined with my rising panic mean that by the time I get off at my stop, I am yet again sweating. I attempt to gather myself on a bench.

'Fan?' someone says in a cut-glass British accent, holding out a battery-operated hand-held fan. It's incongruous to see a man proffer a device I usually associate with pregnant and menopausal women. He's a similar age to me, with blue eyes and a button nose. He's easy to overlook at first, maybe because he is dressed in a white T-shirt, navy jeans and the type of trainers you might see on an elderly person doing the rounds outside a retirement home. But his features are kind; his pepper-and-salt beard renders his face teddy-bearish. And he's surprisingly tall.

'What?' I say irritably, ruffled by the heat.

'Honestly, take it,' he says. 'I already have a few at home.'

'A few?' I raise an eyebrow as I take it from him. 'What are you, a hoarder?'

'No,' he laughs. 'Ex-girlfriend left them behind. It's nice seeing you again, by the way.'

Maybe it's the heat or the suppressed annoyance at my conversation with Wallace, but I snap at him. 'Again? What do you mean, again? We've never met.'

He looks confused. 'Of course we have. When . . .'

'Oh, I see. Let me guess. You met a random brown lady. And so I *must* be her, because we all look alike, is that it? Nice.'

'No, honestly . . .'

I get up and hand him back the fan. As he gingerly takes it from me, I hear Daisy yell my name. Aha! Now he's in for it.

'Daisy, you'll never guess . . .' I start to say, and then trail off in surprise as she moves in to hug the man sitting on the bench.

'Oh, Hugo,' she says, 'it's so lovely to see you.' It is a good thing we are at a hospital because I am about to die from embarrassment. Hugo looks at me apologetically even though I'm the one who has behaved badly, and somehow, it makes me feel like even more of a donkey.

*

Henry comes to greet us in the ward reception area to avoid overwhelming Myra in her room. 'They're discharging her later today,' he says softly, his white-and-navy polo shirt looking uncharacteristically crumpled. I have seen Henry get more emotional at the cricket than he does towards human beings, so I'm surprised when he gives Hugo a deep hug, both arms wrapped around him like an elastic band. Hugo, Daisy tells me later, isn't just Henry's cousin – he's like a brother to him. They went to boarding school together, and although Hugo has spent most of his life living and working abroad, he's the only person Henry ever gets emotional about, apart from herself and Myra.

Although I've never given Henry a hug before, I feel this time the occasion merits it. He leans in and exits awkwardly like a shirt trying to break free from its hanger. Even though I've always found him to be a bit of a drip, I am glad he is here. He curves his body around Daisy's small frame, the scent of old cologne indicating he made it here straight from the airport and stayed the night. It's such a contrast to how they normally look: Henry like a pink, bespectacled, freshly washed seal, and Daisy so crisp she looks like she's just unfolded from a dry-cleaning bag.

I am still mortified about Hugo, and although I have apologised several times between the bench, the lift and the ward, my face still burns with embarrassment. He says it's fine, but I don't know if this is the British version of fine, which means it is far from fine, in fact it's biblical. The men step away to have their own whispered conversation.

With both of them gone, Daisy's true countenance returns and it's clear she's angry and upset. 'How is Myra?' I ask.

'She's so . . .' my sister begins, and then makes a stifled noise of frustration. 'I'm so happy she's okay. I can't begin to tell you – but she's *fucking impossible*. Since she woke up, she's shown no remorse, no sense that what happened was wrong. If anything, she seems angry at me. *At me!*'

Her voice rises so high and loud, it's likely Myra has heard her on the ward. 'Why don't we get a coffee?' I say. 'Not that awful hospital coffee, but at the local caff down the road?'

As we walk into the outside world, a middle-aged man with no shirt on stomps down the opposite side of the street with 'I Hope You're Happy You Voted For Brexit!' written on his body in thick black Sharpie. Daisy doesn't notice. She is so angry she can't see anything. Not him, not London in bloom, not the driver of the scaffolding truck who toots his horn at her in appreciation. Daisy has always been pretty, while my beauty requires a suffix. I'm a pretty-if. In the way that a woman's beauty requires a caveat if it doesn't meet the eye of the beholder, I would be pretty if I lost some weight, pretty if I wore brighter colours, pretty if I stood up straight.

'She's upset her friends have ghosted her. Blocked her on social media. I had one of the mums call me last night, and rather than apologising for her child dumping mine on the doorstep, it was to inform me that we are no longer invited to their summer soirée. Fuck their soirée and the canapés they rode in on!'

'That doesn't make any sense. Why—'

'And then I tell Myra that something has to change. That she's going to therapy, and that we are going to find a summer camp for her to attend because she's not going to be sitting around the house all day playing video games while we're at work. Some discipline and routine. And you know what she says? She says if we do that, she is going to – quote – "run away and likely get sex trafficked" . . . and then it will be all our fault. What kind of child says that? How did she come from *me*?'

Usually, I listen more than I talk. People say I'm understanding, or they can 'tell me anything' as if I have some witchy ability to extract their innermost thoughts, but really, it's just not saying much. But it's hard when it's your family, and some of your history is in the same chapters as theirs, and the future of a family member might rest in the space between what you did and didn't say. I knew that pressing a boot against Myra's neck was not the way to treat her. That how Daisy reacted now would inform whether or not her home remained the place Myra would return to over the years. I wasn't a parent, sure. But did that mean I shouldn't say anything? Wasn't that what aunties were supposed to do? To broker peace and be a channel of communication when opposing sides refused to engage?

'In any case, most of the summer camp places are already booked,' Daisy continues. 'The holidays have already started. And the only place I managed to find was some military prep school that just had a dropout. And I have to say, I am tempted.'

I am alarmed to hear her speaking like this. Daisy could not unleash on her daughter the unresolved, repressed anger she felt towards our mother. By being heavy-handed now, she might end up pushing her daughter towards the very future she was trying to warn her against. When I say as much, she retorts: 'But I told her! I told her that if she didn't fix her ways, there would be consequences.'

'Right,' I say gently, 'but she's a child. Not a puppy. They don't always know what consequences are. And look at the way she was found – her friends dumped her there, which was a mean thing to do. They didn't even know if anyone was going to be home. What if you hadn't been there? Myra's probably feeling really messed up about that. And the drinking – it's worrying but it seems like a cry for help more than anything.'

Daisy's eyes stare straight ahead, glazed over at a memory. A different year, a different ambulance. A different person, but the only other person she knows through blood, and love, and amniotic fluid. The ghost of our mother takes shape between us. I put my arm around her shoulders and say quietly: 'She's not Mum. It's not the same, Daisy.'

'Of course it's not the same,' she snaps. 'I know that.' We walk back to the hospital in silence.

*

When we get to the ward, Henry looks at me apologetically and asks if I'd mind waiting while the three of them go to have a chat. A dark flash of rejection snakes through me – what is it they'll be discussing? Why am I not involved? But instead I nod my head and say it's fine, no problem, and that I'm going to look in on Myra.

Henry looks at me gratefully. 'She'd like that,' he says.

I push through the door and see her propped up in bed. She looks fragile, like a wisp of smoke about to slip through the crack under the door, yet her green eyes burn with such fury. She isn't pretty or a pretty-if, she is beautiful. Even when her face is sweaty and pale, her hair tangled and spread haphazardly against the pillow, like a cat that has been blasted with a hose. I'm unsure of what to say. We haven't spoken much at all in the last few years beyond monosyllabic grunts. I couldn't tell you what music she listened to or what her favourite subject was in school.

'Hey, kid. How are you?' I say awkwardly, hovering at the foot of the bed. I don't want to be here any more than she likely wants me to be. When I brought her birthday cake over the previous year, she'd told me that chocolate was no longer her favourite flavour, and hadn't I heard of red velvet? It was so sharply rude that I almost left along with the cake, until Daisy bustled in with a dress that looked like the remains of an assaulted swan, and I realised the reason for Myra's mood was perhaps because she was being forced to wear something she didn't want to.

'I know you probably could do without talking to anyone,' I say tentatively. 'For what it's worth, I want you to know that I'm here.'

She stares at me a long while before saying: 'I know you're an agent of Satan. So tell her I'm not going to that fucking summer camp. I'm a fuck-up. I get it.'

'Wow, I don't remember you ever swearing this much,' I laugh, to try and lighten the mood. But Myra's stare evaporates anything light enough to enter her atmosphere.

'I don't think you're a fuck-up,' I say slowly, unsure of whether or not I should swear in front of her, but she started it. 'I think you fucked up, but that's different. We all make mistakes. What can I do to help? *Is* there anything I can do?'

She looks at me with those enormous green eyes, new and unlined but somehow also ancient and old. 'Can you make my friends text me?' she says. 'Can you make them unblock me on their phones? Can you make those Judas bastards tell their parents it wasn't me who bought the alcohol? Can you talk some sense into Mum?'

'I can't do anything about your friends, but I can try with your mother.'

She snorts a laugh. 'You don't have the ballbags to go against Mum.' Myra is infuriating because technically she's right. She's never seen me stand up to Daisy, ever. But there was a time when my word was God, and Daisy listened to everything I had to say.

'No, I don't have the ballbags,' I say to Myra. 'Because I have something stronger. A vagina. All right?' Myra's eyes become even larger and I can tell she wants to laugh but isn't allowing herself to. The ferocity of that stare lessens, and for a moment I wonder if a speck of something I said got through.

'Please, just leave me alone,' she says, and closes her eyes. Or maybe not.

*

Come to the café, Daisy texts about an hour later. An hour of wondering where they were and what time they were coming back. By the time I get there, they look as if they are still locked in an intense conversation. It's strange seeing Henry somewhere other than his house. Given that my interests don't extend to investment art and I don't work in finance, our exchanges are almost always perfunctory. He usually asks me what I'd like to drink, then their housekeeper, Sue, fetches it and that's the extent of it.

'Padma,' Daisy says, pulling out a chair for me, 'we think we might have a solution.' Although she still looks exhausted, there is something new in her eyes: hope.

'Wait a minute,' says Henry. 'I'm not entirely sure . . .'

'Henry,' she says sharply. 'You haven't offered any other solution. Unless you're planning to cancel your next two business trips and stay at home with Myra, what else do you suggest?'

He drops his head, chastened. I smile at the memory of how disapproving I was about him marrying my sister. Daisy was only twenty and I felt no one should be getting married at that age, let alone to someone eleven years older than her. I didn't care about Henry's wealth, his banking job or his private education. I only cared about Daisy's future, and saw it all being placed in his hands, where I feared he would crush it. But over the years I've watched as he has made room for all of Daisy's dreams and given her the life she always wanted. If the worst thing about him is that he is soft in his parenting style, it isn't all bad.

'Myra can't stay in London,' she continues. 'She just can't. It's not a good place for her to be. Hugo has very generously offered us his seaside home for the summer so that Myra can rest, recover a little bit. Isn't that wonderful?'

I look at Hugo, who is stirring his coffee intently as if he's trying to read his future in the grounds. I see something else in Daisy's eyes. Hesitation. It's noticeable because it's new. She is always sure of herself, and even when she isn't, she is an expert at making it seem like she is. While Henry looks embarrassed – like when you have to ask for a big, awkward favour, such as asking someone to help you move house and the contents include a corner sofa and twenty boxes of books.

'That *is* wonderful,' I say, cautiously.

Daisy puts everything she has into her next words. 'But I can't take time off work and neither can Henry. All our leave is tied up in our family holiday at the end of the summer. So . . . we have something to ask you. How do you feel about spending the summer with Myra?'

Her words tighten my chest. The responsibility of it rushes quickly into focus, the sheer scale of the request. Daisy rushes on with more information. She tells me they will pay me £2,000 a week because she knows I need money and it's a big ask.

That Myra will have weekly therapy sessions and Daisy will come and visit. That Hugo will be on hand for anything that might go wrong in the cottage. That it will be for six weeks only and the time will fly by. The more she talks, the more her words take up space in my lungs, leaving me no room to breathe.

It's not just what she is asking me to do, it's the thought that the three of them have been discussing my finances, and now Hugo, almost a complete stranger, knows I am struggling for money. The shock of what I am being asked, coupled with the shame of being exposed like this, makes me dizzy. If I say no, I am the selfish one. If I say yes, I feel like the opportunistic greedy one. I cannot win either way.

'Padma, I'm worried about her,' Daisy says pleadingly when she realises I haven't said yes to her, like I normally do. 'I know this is a lot to put on you, but I trust you. I know you can do it. I know you can.'

I stand up so quickly I almost lose balance. Their three concerned faces look up at me.

'I need a moment.'

*

While I'm hyperventilating by the bus stop, a middle-aged white man tells me to: 'Smile, it won't be so bad.' Something breaks in me then and I yell, 'FUCK OFF, JUST FUCK OFF!' I have never yelled at anyone like this before. 'Get help, love,' he says with a scowl and walks off.

I couldn't possibly take this on, could I? Myra is a teenager with issues. She seems deeply unhappy. She might have substance abuse problems. If Drew Barrymore could have a drinking problem aged eleven, why not my niece? I'm good at cooking. I can tell when a mackerel isn't fresh. I know how to grow mint and coriander. I listen to people's problems. None of this has prepared me for taking care of a child, even if she is toilet-trained.

And yet, the alternative. No money, no job and potentially no relationship unless I agree to grow another human inside of me. Where am I going to live? How will I scrape together the rent and deposit? What am I going to do?

But you've done something similar before, a little voice says, struggling to get through an epidermis of negative talk. And I realise with a jolt that it's true, I have. I took care of Myra when Daisy wasn't able to, when she was in the deep throes of post-natal depression.

*

We were on strange terms at the time, given that I was so vocal about what a terrible idea it was marrying Henry so young, and even more aghast at the news that she'd be taking a year off uni because she'd fallen pregnant. That was back when being an older sister still brought with it some measure of authority. After I'd yelled at Henry for ruining her life, Daisy assured me she'd go back to university straight after giving birth.

Despite our less than cordial relationship, a few weeks after Myra was born, Henry called and asked me to come over. *Please just come,* he said, when I asked what was wrong.

I knew something was up the moment I entered the room. Burgundy velvet curtains blocked out most of the light. Clothes were strewn all over the carpet, and there was a sour smell, as if Daisy was leaking unhappiness through her breast milk. But the worst thing was the expression in her eyes. Vacant. She seemed to be lost in a landscape far away, unable to find words that made sense of her version of motherhood.

Seeing my sister, who was barely twenty-one, looking so lost and detached from herself, filled me with dread. I couldn't lose her too. Henry loved her, I saw that clearly. But ours was womb love, the love of sisters connected by the umbilical cord that stretched back in time through our mother, to India, to rivers and earth and belonging. I put aside our complicated history. I told Henry I was going to stay for a few weeks, expecting him to fight me. Instead, he looked relieved. I knew nothing about babies, but I could clean, look after Daisy, cuddle Myra and be there.

Daisy didn't question my presence, she just absorbed me into her life without comment. After a couple of days, it was as if I had always been there. Myra glowed with new life, dipping in and out of the long sleep of newborns, opening her big eyes and staring at me. I wondered what she saw and felt. I looked at her and felt the potential and vastness of her life, but also the disassembling of Daisy's. All I had to do was hold on to both of them, until they reached the same place and could hold on to each other.

Henry had an air of defeat. He would go out to work – shared parental leave not being a thing back then – and return exhausted. He'd kiss Daisy on the cheek, hold Myra for a bit and then say, 'Right then, well', and disappear to his office.

By the fourth week of my stay, Daisy's eyes looked clearer, and by then Myra and I had already established a little routine. I'd finally mastered changing her nappy without muttering about how gross it was, and she'd gurgle from her basket as I sang to her while washing the dishes. I told her where she came from, the little I knew about the Alva clan back in Karnataka.

By the start of the fifth week, Daisy was able to do more. She was able to bear brushing her hair and started to shower again. She talked more to the baby. When the three of them went for a walk around the block, Myra giggling in her pram, I knew it was time for me to go. Daisy cried when I left, and said *thank you*, while Henry asked me if I needed anything – a taxi, some money. *Anything*, he said, imploringly.

When I visited the following week, Henry and Daisy had gone back to being a unit. Daisy was fussing around Myra, and I seemed to get in Henry's way. I felt awkward, like an interloper. I held back and waited to be asked over, which wasn't until a month later. And then that stretched out into longer and longer chunks of time. We never spoke about it, ever again.

*

By the time I come back to the café, Hugo is gone and Daisy's look of hope is extinguished. Henry is stress-eating a sorry-looking cherry Bakewell, crumbs spilling on his shirt. They both look up at me, resigned. 'Padma, it's okay . . .' Daisy starts to say. I see the rest of her words ready to form. *Don't feel guilty. We shouldn't have asked. We'll figure it out.*

I'm worried I won't be adequate, that I'm in over my head. I worry I won't be able to keep Myra safe. But I also know when we were growing up, I wished someone from our family had come to save us. Not just when Mum was struggling, but after she died, too. And no one did. And although taking money from them feels grubby, I have no other option. 'I'll do it,' I say.

And then, in the murk of doubts, a beam of light cuts through as Daisy hugs me. A proper hug. Not that weird half-hug where only the tops of your shoulders touch. She wraps her arms underneath mine and pulls me to her. It is the first time she has hugged or thanked me since the end of that dark period in her life.

4

I have never been on a summer road trip, but I assume it involves singing loudly to songs, eating fistfuls of sweets and playing I Spy with the limited inspiration of a British motorway all around. It is not meant to be the prison-van energy currently rolling through the BMW I've borrowed from Daisy to make the trip from Wimbledon to our destination. While I battle with the car's manual gearbox, Myra is tightly sealed inside her oversized black hoodie, looking like a moody Kalamata olive. Her eyes are ringed in eyeliner, a new pair of chunky black Chloé boots sprouting from her feet. Presumably a bribe, one of many in the last few days since being discharged from hospital. It's the longest we have ever spent alone together since she was a baby. And there's the rest of the summer ahead.

'Are you okay?' I ask her. 'Want me to turn down the aircon?'

She immediately puts in her AirPods. When Daisy and Henry hugged her goodbye, she remained motionless, arms at her sides, like a plank of wood, unwilling to give them anything, even her anger. But her deep resentment at being excommunicated cannot be contained. After a time, it leaks from her pores, potent enough to fill the car. It is a strange thing, to be able to feel her fury, but also sense the fragile, broken parts that lie behind the wall she has built around herself.

I put on some music to lighten the heaviness of her silence and try to focus on the road. We are driving towards an unknown where so many things are held in balance. The sky is a cornflower blue, and in the distance are hills and meadows ablaze in sunlight. Caught in the windscreen, a contrail to the left and the searing white glow of the sun to the right.

Our journey is relatively straightforward. Once we escape the morning football and brunch traffic surrounding Wimbledon, we find ourselves on the M25, working our way towards the M2. Despite the whooshing white noise of the cars zipping past, I periodically glance at Myra to see if she is all right. She seems to have two settings. One, in which she checks her phone, scrolling, scrolling, presumably to see if her friends have sent any messages. Daisy warned me about this. *They're still giving her the silent treatment because she got them in trouble with their parents.* When she sees she is still blocked, she angrily pockets her phone.

The second is more disquieting. She gazes out of the window, her eyes empty. It is like watching someone step out into the black cosmos in a spacesuit, their expression unreadable, barely tethered. I know that look. It isn't of someone staring at the stars, it is of someone being pulled into darkness. I ask her again if she is okay, yank on the cord connecting her to Earth to remind her I am here. But she is too far away to hear me. Something in the inky black has caught her gaze, is pulling her towards it. I recognise it because it has pulled me too.

*

Our destination is the seaside town of Harkness, where Hugo had inherited a property from his great-aunt Rosemary. I had mixed feelings about returning to Kent after so long, given that it was where we grew up. We had lived in a small three-bedroom house in Rochester, with horrible 1970s wallpaper and shag carpeting from a previous owner. Since South Asians in the eighties didn't really believe in interior design, and that extended to keeping anything that wasn't actually on fire or broken, our house sat incongruently against a backdrop of Tudor houses with their black-and-white criss-cross exteriors, little tea shops in narrow brick streets, and the spire of the cathedral standing watch.

In Kent, seaside towns tended to go one of three ways. Either they became golden-oldie towns for retirees, depressed little enclaves with empty arcades and pound shops, or they tried to push towards modernisation, art and hipster coffee shops, like Whitstable and Margate. Harkness had ambitions towards the latter, Hugo said, but the town council was made up of disparate characters who couldn't agree on anything, and so progress had been slow.

It lay on the stretch of south-east coastline between Rochester at the westerly end, and Ramsgate, Broadstairs and Margate, which jutted out into the sea like a thumb, on the other. Most immigrant families who didn't have the funds to travel overseas knew places like this well. These towns were the ones we could afford to visit on day trips, their residents bemused as we'd unpack tandoori chicken legs, rice and dal in the middle of the park. We'd sit on a concrete wall facing the sea, wrapped in big coats, our mothers trying to search for home in the watery expanse ahead, but finding nothing familiar in the greyness, nothing that resembled coconut trees, snakebirds or sand the colour of burnished gold.

*

About an hour in, the playlist switches to Air Supply, 'All Out of Love'. It makes me feel mournful about Wallace, summons up emotions so big they have no room in the car, not with Myra already taking up space.

When I told him I was leaving for the summer, I'd hoped it would be the moment he realised he'd made a terrible mistake, call off The Break and beg me to stay.

He looked surprised, but in the manner of someone realising their life would be made easier. 'We were going to take a break anyway,' he said. 'Maybe this is for the best.' I knew Wallace compartmentalised his emotions thanks to his strict grandparents, but I wanted to know where he'd parked the angst. Where was the part of him that was going to miss me? I asked him, and he frowned. 'Padma, of course I am going to miss you terribly. That goes without saying.'

'Sometimes,' I replied, 'it needs to be said.'

But he had never been great at validation or comfort. Wallace found it hard to understand why someone might get upset, because he felt as long as he'd explained a situation clearly, that was all there was to it. It was a startling lack of empathy that sometimes made me wonder whether his patients liked him, or whether their treatment came with all the personal touch of a vending machine. 'Look, if you need to call or text me,' he said, 'you can. But just to be clear: there's no expectation on my side that you should do so, no designated day for us to chat. Does that sound okay to you?' It did not, but I agreed anyway.

I don't want to obsess about Wallace when I am sure he is just carrying on with his day. I try to change the playlist to something more cheerful, whereupon it shuts down Google Maps. The only thing that could make this trip worse would be getting lost, so I make a sharp exit to a service station after clocking the little M&S logo. The motion jangles the contents of the car and knocks Myra's phone out of her hand and into the crack of doom between the car door and the seat.

'Stop the car!' she yells, the first words she's uttered. Although I've reduced my speed to enter the car park, we are still in motion when to my horror, she tries to open the door. 'Myra!' I yell. 'What the hell are you doing?'

'Stop the car! Stop the car!' she howls, with such anguish, I'm tempted to do an emergency stop, if it wasn't for a white van tailgating me. 'Hang on,' I yell, hoping she doesn't do anything stupid, as I pull over into an empty space.

The moment we stop and the doors automatically unlock, she pulls it open and scrabbles frantically around like someone digging for an earthquake survivor. My heart hammers so hard against my chest, I feel like I'm about to be sick. Not a great start. While I compose myself, she retrieves her phone, and when she doesn't see whatever it is she is expecting, her eyes fill with tears. 'Myra,' I snap, as she opens the door and goes to sit on the grassy bank separating the edge of the car park from the Days Inn motel. I know she's upset but so am I. At what might have happened had the internal locks not been switched on. 'What the hell was that?' I say, angrily. 'You could have hurt yourself, or someone else.'

'You ruined it,' she says miserably. 'Lana was typing and now it's stopped.'

'Who's Lana?' My upset segues to confusion. 'Is it a friend of yours?'

She buries her head in her knees, her long, dark brown hair cascading like a curtain. I've never felt as if I've had the solutions to everything that happens in life, but when I reach back into my mental locker to figure out how to handle this, there is nothing.

I'm tempted to turn around and drive back, but Daisy's words still echo in my head. Before we left London, I had to ask her one last time. 'Daisy . . . listen, what do I know about raising or looking after a child? Why are you and Henry trusting me with this?'

All she said was: 'Because I just do.'

Maybe I don't know what it's like to be a parent, but maybe rather than trying to think like one, I need to think about what I would need and want if I were in Myra's position. I want her to understand the severity of what she's done, but maybe this doesn't need to be a teachable moment.

'I don't know what's going on,' I say, exhaling a deep breath. 'but if this person wants to text, they'll text. Maybe they just got called away and will do it later. It happens to me all the time. One minute I'm texting your mother, and then . . . I don't know . . . the cat will bring in a dead mouse and I have to take care of that. And then your mother goes: PADMA WHY AREN'T YOU TEXTING ME BACK? And I'm like, hey, I'm trying to deal with dead Mickey over here.'

I nudge her knee to make her lift her head, to see if a smile is somewhere underneath all that pain. It isn't, but some of the raw upset has at least been smoothed out of her face. 'Listen, I need to go to the shops to get some proper snacks,' I say. 'Your mother has packed a horrible collection of protein bliss balls and kale crisps and I don't know what the shop situation is like in Harkness. Want anything?'

She wipes her nose on her hoodie and looks at me, properly, for the first time. As if trying to work out what shape I fit into, what kind of person I am. When I don't yell at her, she considers for the first time that I am not just an extension of her mother. 'No,' she sniffs, and goes back to checking her phone.

*

When I return with a bag full of crisps, sweets and fizzy cans of Rubicon, Diet Coke and Fanta, Myra is back in the car. 'Mum doesn't allow that stuff in the house,' she says, looking at my haul.

'And?' I say, opening a bag of Hula Hoops (salt-and-vinegar-flavoured, of course). I stick them on each finger of my left hand and waggle them at her. She looks at me aghast, as if she can't believe she is related to such an embarrassment. 'What, you've never done this? Even as a kid?' She rolls her eyes and retreats back into her hood, whatever warmth was briefly generated between us evaporating into the summer air.

*

At some point, as if the chaos and drama had never happened, Myra falls asleep, her face warmed by the sun overhead that is cleansing the car with pure light, smoothing her furrowed brow. When she emerges from her nap, forgetting she has applied kohl, she rubs her eyes into dark raccoon circles. For a moment as she wakes, the veil of childhood covers her and then is gone, replaced by something in between, grumpy and resistant. 'Where are we?' she asks.

'We are currently stuck in traffic,' I say, grateful for the working AC of Daisy's car, although the hot sun is burning my forearms. 'It's the first week of the summer holidays.' To our left, a lady with bright red arms and flax-coloured hair plastered to her forehead is fanning herself with one elbow poking out of the window. In front of us is a family of four, their bicycles strapped to the luggage rack.

'What the hell is this?' says Myra, referring to the music. It's Fleetwood Mac, 'Dreams'. A song that feels to me like liquid sunlight and soft naps. It is impossible not to hum along to it.

'You don't know who Fleetwood Mac are?'

'No, I'm fifteen,' she says, voice dusted with salt.

'So? I know the Beatles, Led Zeppelin, the Carpenters – and they were all before my time.'

After about thirty minutes of inching forward half a metre at a time, I try to make conversation by asking Myra if she knows what her name means.

'Yeah, yeah,' she says gloomily, 'I know it's the name of a serial killer. The dickheads at school remind me often enough.'

'You weren't named after her though, were you? I'm talking about what your name *means*.'

'Dad is a massive Latin geek,' she says, staring out of the window, 'and as he's told me a thousand times, my name means "behold", apparently.'

'It's also a Sanskrit word,' I say.

'What's Sanskrit?' says Myra, using a little rubber band to secure the end of one of her many plaits.

If we weren't in traffic, it would have been the moment in a movie where someone slams on the brakes. 'Are you serious?'

'Yes,' she says, bewildered. I file away my outrage with Daisy for a later point, because Myra doesn't need to feel the shameful heat of not knowing. But still, I look at the colour of her skin – a caramel latte brown that will deepen into a dark chestnut with enough sun – and feel as if something big has been denied her.

'Well, Sanskrit is one of the oldest languages in the world – about 3,500 years old. It comes from South Asia – where you are from, and me and your mum. Your name in Sanskrit means "beloved, admired".'

'Oh,' she says, turning over this piece of information. 'I had no idea. Well, I'm also English.'

'Yeah, but English as a language is just over 1,000 years old. And in English your name is shorthand for a serial killer. So that's something else to think about.'

*

About an hour later, we move deeper into the Kent countryside. We drive from the M20 onto the M2. To the west lies Rochester, and further east is Harkness. Miles of countryside and farmland are ahead of us, and the metal barricades of the motorway cut away to wide fields, stalks of bright yellow rapeseed catching the wind and whispering it across the hills that stretch into the distance. Eventually it broadens to a patchwork of green fields, trees shaking the fullness of their foliage in the breeze, and tiny brick houses in the distance. The convergence of the landscape, the warmth of the day and the sound of Oasis on the radio make me think of sunlight and orange squash, ham sandwiches, sitting on a blanket and reading a well-thumbed book. The roundabouts move us through the tributaries, flowing into smaller streams, each road growing narrower than the last until we pass Whitstable, where people cluster for oysters and British fizzy wine, then Herne Bay with its Victorian and Edwardian houses and long promenade, and finally Harkness.

Before we left, Hugo had texted and asked if I wanted to

meet up to discuss anything I needed to know about the house and the local area. For some intangible reason I hadn't felt comfortable inviting him over to our place. Not just because the ever-increasing list of the house's ailments meant it was embarrassing if someone needed to use the toilet (the flush was operated by a coat hanger), but because it felt odd to have a man come over while Wallace was at work.

Instead, I made him come to Delilah's. I was already on her public liability insurance, and sometimes after-hours she let me experiment in the kitchen where she had fancy mixers and bowls that weren't contaminated with cat hair. When I told her I was leaving for the summer she gave me a long hug, and said she thought it would be a good thing.

'What if Wallace realises he's better off without me?' I'd said.

'And what if you realise you're better off without him?' she replied.

Hugo came in while I was prepping a test batch of Nutella dosas – thin, papery rice pancakes with a gooey chocolate filling. Some were spiked through with chilli, others sprinkled with roasted almonds, and the third and final batch had caramelised bananas, their edges burned to give a hint of smokiness beneath the richness of the chocolate.

'You cook?' he said with raised eyebrows.

'Why do you look so surprised?'

'You're different from Daisy, that's all,' he replied. 'Can I try some?'

I hesitated. In my world, there were two types of cooking. There was the cooking I did only for loved ones. If I made food for you, I put all of myself into it, my love, my care and my hope. My food was marked with the lines on my hands that were given to me by my mother. It wasn't just food, it was legacy. I would never cook for a solitary man unless I felt something deep and beautiful for him. But technically, seeing as I'd be leaving these for Delilah to have for breakfast, it wouldn't hurt to let Hugo try some.

As the chilli Nutella did its work, searing the lining of his tongue with fire and sweetness, he said: 'Thank you. Incredible. The one and only time Daisy ever cooked for me, she made a curry the day they asked me to be Myra's godfather. I didn't know it was possible for food to taste like that. It was as if she had cooked the world's oldest sheep in just water and salt.'

'Wait – you're Myra's GODFATHER?' I said, my voice rising. 'WHO is her godmother?'

'Well, you, of course,' he said nonchalantly, as if this was common knowledge. When it wasn't. I hadn't received a phone call. They hadn't cooked me a curry – not even a terrible one.

Hugo started to tell me about Harkness. It was an odd place, he said, but his great-aunt had loved it and so had he, during the summers he'd spent there. She'd bought it as a home to retire to at the age of sixty, expecting not to live much beyond seventy, given that she'd had breast cancer twice and a heart attack. She ended up living to the age of ninety-four, to the great chagrin of her daughter Agnes, who'd hung around, waiting decades for an inheritance. Then the lawyer declared Rosemary had left the property to Hugo, who'd brought life and youth and tadpoles into her home all those years ago.

Now Harkness was making attempts at a revival, as people

were starting to get priced out of Margate and Whitstable. Rent was relatively low and the local council had tried to attract rich Londoners looking for a different lifestyle, and it was working. Slowly, a small creative community was emerging, though they met with some resistance from locals who wanted the money they injected into the area but didn't actually want to deal with outsiders. The widening disparities in wealth exacerbated a simmering tension that dated back decades.

In the early noughties, a terrible investment was made by the then head of the council, John Reed, funnelling town funds into building a pier that was to serve as an expensive arts venue and restaurant, expected to draw in the kind of tourists who'd visit Whitstable. When it was nearly finished, the town's railway station was shut down by South Eastern Rail, which cut off vital access – the nearest stations were five miles either side. At first, people visited from surrounding areas – Minnis Bay, Faversham – just for the novelty of something new. But slowly the numbers dwindled, and anyone walking by would see the candyfloss machines lying idle, dusty unoccupied tables laid with linen and silverware, deep-fat fryers promising 'authentic fish and chips' drained and silent. Locals could not afford the rent of the inflated units, nor did they need to with enough space going begging in the interior of the town. The arts development was eventually flypapered over as artists abandoned it in favour of Margate's busier scene.

A tourist visiting for the day might never see it, but stay any longer than a weekend and you'd notice the difference between the houses, the intangible sense of something brewing, the feeling that after 5 p.m. you might walk down a street and not emerge from it again.

*

Eventually we pass the sign that says 'Welcome to Harkness!' The road is lined with a scattering of houses, small purpose-built pebble-dashed bungalows. Set behind a strip of yellowing scrubby grass is a string of shops – a rundown corner store, an off-licence called Booze! and a garage called Monty's: We Fix Any Car. The road widens to accommodate modern, bigger houses with well-maintained lawns and hanging baskets of red geraniums and bright purple petunias speckled with white spots. The closer we come to the old centre of Harkness, though, the buildings become smaller, older and more beautiful. Pastel Victorian frontages with freshly painted white trellises. Window boxes and pots on steps overflowing with dahlias with their compact, intense ball of colours, roses of white, damson, yellow and bright pinks lining the fences.

A sweet-faced elderly lady looks up from under her floppy pink hat and glares at us as we drive past. I remember my mother saying that just because a place was green and beautiful, it wasn't any indicator of tolerance – an important thing to remember in the 'garden county' when the P-word was being yelled at you from a double-decker bus. A small frisson of worry fizzes through me.

Ahead there is a patch of blue – our first sighting of the sea. Although it should be straightforward, the satnav is doing that infuriating thing of not matching the directions to the route ahead.

'Myra,' I say, 'can you direct me, please?' She continues to ignore me and tap on her phone, so I slam on the brakes. 'OW!' she says. It doesn't bode well that I've already had enough of her. The fury I felt when she tried to open the car door to find her phone hasn't entirely dissipated.

'I am not your chauffeur. I am not your mother. I am in this situation *with* you, I have not done this *to* you. Okay? I am not expecting you to have sunshine Rainbow Briting out of your bum, but when I talk to you, I expect you to treat me like a human being and respond. Got it?' The last time this version of myself was aired was in 1998 when Daisy missed her curfew and our mother hadn't noticed.

Myra rubs her neck with a scowl, but something filters through and she picks up my phone and zooms in on the map. The narrow one-way street opens into a wide road that is the start of a long bay curving around to the right and jutting sharply into the sea. There's a concrete walkway beside it and, while it isn't pretty, the view is.

The tide is out, pulling back a long sheet of water to reveal an expanse of dark golden sand, the surface brushed clean, little rivulets of water catching the light as they snake towards the sea. The doomed pier occupies the far side of the bay, and while there is a defeated, dilapidated look about it, the main stretch of shops and cafés that directly face the sea looks promising. A tiny shop selling rock has a cluster of sticky, eager-faced children around it. Next to it is a modern-looking café, more East London than East Kent, with black-framed floor-to-ceiling windows to allow an uninterrupted view of the sea. A few doors from that, a little boutique that sells only white and navy clothing.

'What's Rainbow Briting?' says Myra, breaking the thick coils of silence.

'I'll show you a video,' I reply, trying not to smile.

Rosemary's house is further down on the far side of the bay, beyond the old pier. As we drive along, we pass older women walking dogs of the small and fluffy variety, a few younger people sedately pedalling along on bicycles with wicker baskets.

Along the pier, some of the fishing tenders are arriving from a day out at sea. A middle-aged man with grey hair and well-muscled arms hauls crates onto the concrete walkway, catching my eye as we slowly drive past. We get stuck behind what passes for rush-hour 5 p.m. traffic in Harkness – three cars waiting for a learner driver to complete a three-point turn.

Myra tells me to take a left with such dourness I get nostalgic for the satnav's robot tones. Rosemary's house faces the sea, according to the map, but we can only access it through the back roads, and it isn't obvious exactly where the turning is.

The house sits on raised ground, hemmed in by a retaining wall made of compacted stone. Curved around one side of this is an old, gnarled apple tree, and the sight of that new life pressing through the old bark, the rising sap and light green leaves bearing the glow of newness, makes a measure of hope rise within me. Despite the idyllic location, the house is being eaten up by ivy, thick and unruly, woody branches so bedded in that they obscure some of the windows. To the left is a large patch of neglected land, strewn with weed-filled raised beds, and an empty chicken coop merges with the woodland to the far left. To the right, in the direction of the town, is another house of similar size in much better condition, with a tidy garden and plantation shutters at the windows. Several wind chimes and dreamcatchers are hanging off the porch, and the deranged-looking gnome sticking out from a flourishing bed of ferns has a bindi stuck to its forehead.

I open the door to Rosemary's house and it wedges halfway against something. I keep pushing; suddenly it gives way and I almost topple through, a stack of books falling to the ground somewhere behind. As the door widens, Myra says: 'Fucking hell.'

'Language,' I murmur, but my heart isn't in it. What awaits us inside looks like a landfill site. Boxes piled high to the ceiling, piles of loose paper rustling in the breeze flowing straight through the house where ivy branches have broken through glass, rusted cookware, towers of newspapers extending all the way to the back of the house. Rosemary, it appears, was a hoarder.

5

'Hugo,' I say as calmly as I can on the phone, 'when was the last time you visited your great-aunt's place?'

'Probably about ten years ago,' he says. 'Why – is everything okay?'

'And you didn't think it would be a good idea to visit it, say, any time after she passed away?'

'Not really,' he replies. 'She died about two years ago and I had plans to come and sort the place out, but I was in Brazil. One of the locals offered to turn off the water and lock the place up so I thought it would be fine. What's wrong?'

I take a deep breath. I know not all men etc., but there was something infuriating about the male lack of consideration around anything domestic that might require forward thinking. I tell Hugo about the state of the place, including the dead rodents we found. After Myra had given me a withering look when I screamed at the sight of them, I was impressed she'd been brave enough to gather them up and deposit them outside. Hopefully she would show the same stoicism towards insects.

'I am so sorry,' Hugo says apologetically. 'I had no idea how bad it had got. Look, do you want me to come over? I should probably help.'

The amount of clutter in Rosemary's house makes me uncomfortable for reasons I can't tell Hugo about yet, if ever. It reminds me of the fallout from my own bad days, when even the smallest action such as getting out of bed or having a shower seemed impossible – let alone washing my dishes or throwing away the rubbish.

If we are to stay here, I need to tackle it immediately. And I don't want Hugo over during the time when I'm meant to be getting Myra settled.

'It's okay,' I say, 'I can make a start on it. Is there anything you want me to keep or should I just throw things out?'

'I'd keep anything you think might be useful, and maybe any photos, but get rid of anything else. I'll arrange for a skip to be delivered.'

'You want me to get rid of *everything*? There's nothing you want to hold on to?'

He sighs. 'What would I be holding on to? Besides, I want you both to feel settled and comfortable there. You can't do that if you're living like mole people.' It's considerate of him, and I don't always find men considerate. Some of them push ahead of me to grab a seat on the Tube, finish the last of the milk, bellow at a volume that pierces the noise-cancelling ability of my headphones. I'm not sure what to make of Hugo.

*

It occurs to me for the first time that although I'm tired from the drive, I need to make sure Myra is settled and fed before sorting myself out. And that it will be like this for the next six weeks. Every day. How do parents do it without screaming into a void? After managing to clear enough space to make up our beds, and plug the kettle and fridge in, I plate up some of the food Daisy packed for us, made by Sue the housekeeper. Her obsession with low carbs means there is no bread or pasta. Things I require for comfort at the end of a long day.

Instead, there is quinoa salad and grilled fish; the latter has not survived the car journey either in texture or smell. After picking at her food, Myra heads upstairs, relieved to be somewhere she can close a door between herself and the outside world. 'Goodnight!' I say to silence but for the sound of crickets chirping outside in the grass. I text Wallace to tell him we've arrived, to receive only a thumbs-up emoji. I tell Daisy we've arrived in the hope that she at least will fill in the quiet with a torrent of questions, but she doesn't.

*

The next morning, while making tea, I look outside the window and there is something reassuring about finding the sea in my line of vision. Ever since a mini-heatwave mid-July, the days have been long and hot, sun baking the earth into terracotta, flies finding a way through the small holes in the windows. I wonder whether the water will be warm enough for a swim, and whether I feel confident enough to wear my swimsuit given the last time was at Brockwell Lido a decade ago.

I go for a short explore around the grounds. Rosemary's house was built during the early 1900s, during a time when Harkness was still mostly fields, and the promenade wasn't as long as it is now. As a result, the configuration is odd. The back of the house is actually the front, as it's the part accessible by the gravel drive. And the front of the house – if using the sea as a marker for the definition of the front – is actually the back. Although there is a fence and a sequence of gates that sections off the left side of the house, leading to the veggie beds and garden, the right shares a thin alleyway with the neighbouring house, leading to the coastal path that runs towards town. A long deck stretches out from the back, and beyond that is a boundary wall to keep foxes and badgers from coming in and doing whatever they do for fun, such as having loud, painful-sounding sex and pooping.

Myra doesn't get up for hours. Not at 10 a.m. or 12 p.m. Not unusual, I think, remembering back to when Daisy was a teenager and used to sleep in until midday at weekends. Unthinkable now.

A quick tour around the house makes it clear that there is a lot of work ahead. The upstairs is divided into three bedrooms; the master is mine, with an en suite, and the second room, Myra's, is a mid-size that fits a double bed and a wardrobe. The third is a box room that has a single bed and is crammed with so much miscellaneous garbage, I close the door and pretend it doesn't exist.

Around 2 p.m. I crack open Myra's door to check if she's awake, but all I see is a mound of bedsheets rising just perceptibly with her breathing. Worry starts to spark in me. I don't want to wake her but this doesn't feel right.

I'm not ready to call Daisy. Yet. To distract myself, I get to work. I remove everything that is easy to dispose of and doesn't require checking with Hugo – the stacks of newspapers, rusted saucepans. The kitchen is the space I need to access most urgently, and after being plugged in overnight, thankfully the fridge appears to be working fine. I clear most of the boxes off the counter-top and the kitchen table, which has a vinyl tablecloth patterned with yellow flowers. I spray everything with bleach and lemon juice, and after a couple of hours, it starts to look clean and presentable, especially when I give the ivy a haircut and allow some more light into the house.

Songs from the nineties play while I unpack some of the things I've brought for the kitchen – a pressure cooker to make dal, my spice dabba – the little stainless-steel tin with six compartments filled with chilli, turmeric, cumin, mustard seeds, black pepper and garam masala. A stash of curry leaves, smelling like spice and earth and the peninsula of India, are contained in one small box. The fragrances make me feel homesick, some of it for the home I knew before Wallace came along. Food is my anchor and it doesn't exist here yet. Not with Daisy's rabbit food as our only supplies. I want to do a big shop but don't feel comfortable venturing further than the garden when Myra is in such an uncertain state. Instead, I give in to using Daisy's Deliveroo account to order groceries, and while I feel guilty about the money, it soothes something in me to see the fridge full.

By dinnertime, the house in the half-light of dusk feels gloomy and strange. I turn on every light to dispel the feeling of displacement, and hum as I continue to clean. Daisy pings a message asking if we're free to chat, but I fob her off by saying Myra has gone to bed early. **Tomorrow**, she texts. Eventually I decide I'm too tired to cook and a ham sandwich will do. I cut the thick sourdough loaf, layer on ham and chunks of Cheddar. I always carry a little bottle of Encona chilli sauce, and sprinkle that on liberally.

Usually my favourite thing to do is watch Netflix on my laptop with it balanced on my chest while I'm wrapped in a blanket, but given how warm the house feels, and the lack of fans, I have to make do with sitting in my underwear and propping my laptop up on a pillow. My mind wanders to Wallace. I wonder what he's having for dinner. Is he eating properly? I catch myself in the ridiculous double standard of it all. Whatever the current direction of Wallace's thoughts, I know he's not thinking about what I've had for dinner.

*

The next day, the door to Myra's bedroom is still closed. At some point in the night she must have woken up and eaten, because I find teeth-marks in the cheese and some of the loaf is gone. Ten a.m., 12 p.m. and 2 p.m. pass by without any movement from her. Finally, unable to withstand any more waiting, I go into her room with a glass of water and try to wake her up. Her eyes open and close again as she wraps the blanket tightly around herself. Beyond physically shaking her awake, I don't know what else to try.

Daisy and Henry had not prepared me for this. Surely they must know how bad things are? They had mentioned that they'd sat down to talk to her about her drinking. They declared an amnesty on any bottles of alcohol hidden in her room, and while horrified by the number of vodka miniatures, resolved to start afresh, commending her on her honesty. As there was no evidence of any harder drugs, they seemed convinced her behaviour was purely connected to the friends she was hanging out with. Myra would have weekly therapy sessions on Zoom, and they must have felt that would be enough. It explains why they were so optimistic her sabbatical to Harkness would work.

I feel out of my depth already but I am due to chat to Daisy when she finishes work today. She will have to figure it out – she's the mother after all. I continue to clean and take some measure of comfort from the way the living room is starting to take shape. Everything is exactly as you might expect in the house of an older lady: cream linoleum, 1970s cupboards in plywood, fussy little dolls on the mantelpiece. Dust plumes into the air once I lift a mound of net curtains to reveal the sofa – a squashed cream pillow of a thing. As I wipe it down and stuff the curtains into bin bags, my phone rings. Daisy.

'I'm still at work,' she says. In other words: keep it snappy. 'How's it going? Can I speak to Myra?' I tell her she's asleep, and then hesitantly mention she's been in bed since we arrived.

'Is that normal for her?' I ask.

'She sometimes does that,' Daisy replies, 'but she usually snaps out of it after a couple of days.'

'How often does she do it?'

'I don't know, Padma – I mean, from time to time. She's a teenager, they sleep a lot. If she isn't up by this afternoon, shake her out of bed and make her have a shower.'

Something about Myra and the *way* she is sleeping seems off. I remember being a teenager and wanting to sleep in, but that was different from staying in bed all day. The sense of putting my day on hold also pulls me back to the past – to hours spent waiting for my mother to get up, for our day to start. Realising it would never start, that whatever she was sleeping off was not going to release her from its grip.

'You don't think something else is going on?' I ask anxiously.

'Honestly? No, I don't, and it's only been two days. If you're finding it too much though . . .' That passive-aggressive tone summons up years of past comments about how I don't understand how hard it is to be a parent.

'No, it's okay. But you said she's got a session with a therapist, is that right?'

'Yes – Wednesday morning. By Zoom. Make sure she doesn't skip it. And look, I will come and visit. Make sure everything is okay with her. Hang on . . . BERNARD, BRING ME THAT FILE NOW! Padma, look, I've got to . . .'

'Wait – before you do.' Something has been bothering me. 'Is Hugo Myra's godfather?'

'Yes – and?' she says impatiently.

'Then who is her godmother?'

'You, of course. Why are you asking me such stupid questions?'

'But you never told me!'

'I don't have to *tell* you. You're my sister. I thought it was a given? Look, I really have to . . .'

'Go. Don't worry, I'll figure it out,' I say, and put the phone down. Although I am miffed that I didn't get a sash declaring I was godmother, or even a phone call, there is something strangely nice knowing Daisy automatically assumed it would be me. As for Myra – I want to believe this behaviour is just her being a teenager, but I suspect we might have something in common.

*

I was prone to difficult interludes as a teenager, but I always assumed this was because of our mother, and the burden of her drinking, and the chaotic storm that came with it. But it wasn't until Mum died when I was twenty, and I started working my first job in telesales, that I realised it was more than just feeling tired, disconnected or moody. In the early years of temping to pay the bills, going out with work colleagues almost constantly, I buried the growing evidence of who I was under other distractions. It was when I was in my first long-term relationship, at the age of twenty-three, that I realised something wasn't right.

It would start as a tickle around my neck. I would feel its fingers gently press against my throat. My eyes would pucker with tiredness that prevailed no matter how much sleep I had. The part of myself that normally sat front of stage would recede further and further into the back, until one day I would wake up and find my emotions, my ability to think, sealed away behind a sheet of solid glass. I could see them, I knew they were there, but I couldn't touch or connect to them. The washing-up would build up in the sink, boxes would pile up on the table and clothes would form into mounds on the floor. When I didn't feel well, I would simply take a few days off from temping. Sometimes it would last weeks, but the nature of temping meant that no one was paying close attention.

When I met Advaith, or Addy as he liked to be called, an older divorced man who was from the same state in India as our family, I found something resembling home in his dark brown skin, broad nose and statuesque shoulders. I had dropped out of university, but he encouraged me to pick a job that offered training and benefits. Eventually I started working in HR because a corporate company offered free healthcare and a fast-track entry scheme, and several months in, it looked as if my life was taking shape. Until the creeping darkness visited me again. This time it was bad. Perhaps because I tried to ignore it, especially because with Addy in the mix, I was terrified he might leave me if he found out. I didn't have the vocabulary to explain what I was experiencing when I didn't fully understand it myself. It didn't seem normal that one day I'd be enjoying a coffee in the sun, and the next I wished for an asteroid to smash into me just so that I didn't feel so raw and awful. Even opening the post felt like doing an Ironman.

The way Addy responded was the way they all did. Concerned at first, then irritated, then detached, and then: 'I don't think this is working.'

I lost jobs because I couldn't leave my bed to get showered, let alone pass through the front door. Managers assumed I was calling in sick because I was either lazy or had been partying too much. I spent days, weeks, ignoring Daisy's messages because I couldn't tell her why I was finding life hard. The more she kept trying to upcycle my life with fresh career suggestions, the harder it became for me to explain why I couldn't engage. But then came Wallace when I turned twenty-nine.

He was the one who made me see my GP to ask to be prescribed meds. My condition had a name: depression, he said. I remember feeling taken aback. Depression felt like something that happened to other people, a sense of feeling sad, whereas I felt nothing at all. Wallace never made me feel as if I was behaving that way 'to get attention' and he didn't pressure me, but he also never stopped asking if I wanted to do things. Walks, the cinema, visiting friends. Sometimes he would sit with me and work on his laptop while I lay hidden in my blankets, staring out through the window, watching the stars pull into view. When my medication took hold and stabilised my mood, I was slowly able to pull my life together. I couldn't bear clutter, or certain foods that reminded me of that time. I still can't eat fishfingers and oven chips, or chicken Cup a Soups – which at one point was what I survived on.

As I was coming out of my last big episode at the age of thirty-one, I was able to think about what I wanted, versus what I needed to survive. I knew I hated HR and loved working with food and experimenting. It was why a couple of years after that, I felt confident leaving temp life for good and working for Majid. Although he was a terrible boss, it was better than the sterile environment of the corporates I'd worked in. And I made friends there, one of whom was an Indian middle-aged expat named Rekha who still texted me about goings-on in the office.

The medication meant that, mostly, the depression was isolated and locked out. But sometimes I felt it gathering strength, drawing from all the things in my past that continued to play on a loop, and it would bang a fist hard against the wall. I wonder if that is what is happening to Myra, and we are searching for any kind of explanation for her behaviour other than the one that is evident and has shown itself in our family time and time again.

*

On the third day, I'm torn between getting Myra up, and not wanting to make her feel guilty about not getting up. When I was ill and someone suggested that a walk would make me feel better, if I'd had the energy I would have choked them until they went away. The answer to my present dilemma, however, awaits me when I look into her room. She is sitting upright, still wrapped in a blanket, smoking a cigarette. Her AirPods are in so she doesn't notice when I come over, grab the cigarette out of her mouth and throw it out of the window.

'Hey!' she says, outraged.

'Are you kidding me?' I say, picking up her cigarette packet. She glares at me but doesn't attempt to snatch it back. Although it's unbelievable she's smoking, part of me is glad she's awake.

'Today's the day,' I say. 'I'd like you to get up in the next hour, have a shower and come with me into the town.'

'I don't want to,' she mumbles.

'I know, but if you don't,' I say, trying to make light of it, 'I will have to disconnect my internet hotspot, which will mean no TV or streaming and then you'll have to take up knitting to pass the time. Rosemary has hoarded about a hundred balls of yarn so you'll have plenty to do.'

'I don't care,' she says, pulling the covers back over her face. I feel wretched and powerless. I can't physically force her to leave her room, but the prospect of spending six weeks like this is horrible. I don't think it's good for her, and while Daisy is paying me to be here, I don't want to play nanny.

Part of the reason why I want her to get up is because I need something, anything, to distract me so that I stop obsessively checking Wallace's Instagram for signs of what he has been up to. He's terrible at posting, so I check his friends' accounts, searching their social media to piece together his whereabouts. Since we've arrived in Harkness, it has become a compulsion, and part of me understands why Myra reacted the way she did in the car when she dropped her phone. So far, the only glimpse of him I've had was in a video posted by his local football team. I've held off on messaging, but he hasn't messaged either, and part of me wonders how he is so completely fine with us not being in touch when we have spoken to each other every day for the better part of a decade.

*

On the fourth day, I wake up having made the decision to broach the subject of a return to London with Daisy. I feel out of my depth and can't keep roaming around the house trying not to go mad thinking about Wallace while Myra holes up in her room.

A strange sense of peace envelops me as I walk around the garden with a cup of tea, taking inventory of the overgrown flowers, the woody and gnarled hebes, the parsley gone to seed and the rusted rakes and spades propped up against the shed, dusty in the stark sunshine.

I take a photo of a knobbly carrot that has an end shaped like an enormous bum and send it to Wallace with the caption **Baby (carrot's) got back!** Just as I'm about to chew another nail out of nervousness, I see him typing. He responds with a laughter emoji. At least it isn't a thumbs-up. But his bare-minimum response is almost worse than no response. And yet, consumed by the need for his love and validation, I think maybe what the situation needs is yet another message. As I type out the words **I miss you. How are you? Do you miss me?** the doorbell rings in the distance before I have the chance to send it.

A willowy red-haired woman stands on the doorstep. She has blue eyes so bright they look like topaz, her long, ectomorphic limbs clad in a flowy yellow pyjama set.

'Namaste!' she says, looking delighted to see me. Her voice is soft and hushed, as if I've just arrived for a spa treatment. 'My name is Esme and I'm your neighbour.' She gestures at the house over to the right. Even without her pointing, I know the bindi-wearing gnome belongs to her. I would be willing to bet on Myra's life that she has done yoga teacher training, there is likely a massive crystal geode in her hallway, and she's going to tell me all about her trip to India. 'On behalf of the Om Shanti community in Harkness, I wanted to give you a warm welcome.'

'The Om Shanti community?' I say, puzzled.

'You don't know of Om Shanti?' she says, frowning. Does she assume I should because I'm Indian?

'Regretfully not,' I reply.

She rallies quickly. 'Well, I must have you over to talk about it in that case! It's nice to see the cottage being opened up – no one's lived here for years.' She pauses, looking at me expectantly, waiting for me to fill the gap with who we are, and why we are here. In a matter of hours, the information will be telegraphed to the entire town.

Eventually I relent. 'I'm here with my niece for the summer – she is Hugo's god-daughter. Hugo is – was – Rosemary's great-nephew.' It feels like a safe amount of information to relay.

'Oh, yes, we know all about Hugo!' says Esme excitedly. 'I'm sure you'll both love it here. And in the meantime, if you'd like to do a sound bath or some tarot, or even join my women's group for some socialising and mandala drawing, we'd love to have you.'

'That's very kind of you,' I say, backing away. 'I'd better get ready – I'm just heading out for a walk.'

She looks tentatively at me as if she's struggling to hold something in. Eventually the thought is released from her, like a helium balloon to the sky. 'I just want to say how excited I am to have you here. My trip to India was the best experience of my life. I would *love* to talk to you about your experiences. I was there doing a teacher-training yoga course at the Maharishi centre in Kovalam – have you been there?'

As a brown person, I have always been fearful of the English countryside. It contains some of the most staggeringly beautiful scenery, but anyone with even the smallest amount of coffee in their complexion is almost always stared at in the street, whispered about in the local pub. When I've tried to tell white friends about it, particularly if I took their recommendation of a place to visit, they've asked if I wasn't imagining it. It became too exhausting to say I know the difference between a cursory look and a stare as if you are an attraction in a petting zoo.

What I hadn't expected was to encounter this particular subset of willowy middle-aged white lady who's discovered yoga, spirituality and life coaching. In London, she normally resides in Richmond or Chelsea and I rarely enter those areas. I don't have a problem with it per se – if yoga, crystals and a little sage smudging is your thing, who am I to judge? It is the conversations I have a problem with, where they assume that because I am Indian, I must be the repository of all spiritual knowledge. I must also love turmeric (I do, but only in a curry) and be a vegetarian, because that was what they experienced that one time they visited India (despite the majority population being non-vegetarians). I must understand everything about the place, including its geography and customs, despite it being a country with over twenty-two national languages and thirteen times bigger than the United Kingdom. Perhaps I am touchy because my deepest shame is that I've never even been to India. To me, Kovalam might as well be Coventry.

'I don't know the centre, I'm afraid. But it sounds lovely.'

'If you both want or need your energies cleansed, I would be happy to do it,' she says earnestly.

My phone rings, saving me from having to answer. Daisy. I excuse myself and take the call.

*

'What do you mean, you think you should come home?' Daisy says irritably. 'You just got there.' I don't understand my sister. Aren't parents supposed to be angsty about being separated from their kids?

'I'm not sure this is the right thing for her. Wouldn't the best place be with you and Henry?'

'Padma,' Daisy says, using the placating tone of voice I imagine she adopts when telling criminals they can expect to be jailed for longer than they've anticipated, 'we've discussed this. I would love to have her at home. But Henry and I have to work and we can't take extra leave until the end of August when we're going away with her to Greece. Besides . . .' she trails off, slightly embarrassed. 'Her therapist says it might be good for her to have a break from everything. Including us, apparently.'

'It just feels like something bigger is going on here, Daisy. She's been in bed for days, and won't leave the house, which means I can't either.'

'Why? She's not a toddler. She's fifteen.'

I don't understand parenting. One minute Daisy is on Myra's case, wanting to send her to a camp, and the next it's a shrug and: 'What am I supposed to do about it?'

'Look,' she says, 'you need to give her boundaries and also

structure. And if you can't do it, then fine. Come back here and we'll find somewhere else for her to go.'

Just as I'm about to make a renewed attempt to return Myra to sender, my phone pings with an automated update from my banking app. **Your bank balance is £1,899.** Daisy and Henry's direct debit.

The relief that floods through my body makes me realise how heavy the stress of worrying about money has been. It is like cool water poured over the hot, anxious knot in my stomach, and releases some of the pressure I've been feeling around Wallace and my reliance on him. Although I try to tell myself that we will be okay, I am concerned at how precarious my situation is, not realising how much power I had devolved to him.

I saw the house in Brixton as our home together. But he clearly didn't and the realisation has almost broken my world. The only reason I haven't fallen apart is because of Myra and needing to take care of her. If I can stick it out for another five weeks, I will be in the kind of financial position I have only ever dreamed of.

When I get off the phone to Daisy after agreeing to see it through, I have a renewed sense of optimism, albeit with an undercurrent of guilt that Myra doesn't know I'm being paid to be here. That guilt evaporates, however, when I realise I can reinstate the direct debit on my phone bill without having to ask Wallace for money.

Although Myra hasn't left her room, she *is* awake. I'll give her a day's grace and then we'll start the real work. Over a cup of tea, I make a list of what needs to be done in the next week – not just around the house, but projects Myra could be getting on with to keep her occupied. If she thought she'd be staying in bed all summer and watching TV, she was about to discover otherwise. There is plenty to get done around the house. Plenty to distract her from her friends and vodka and smoking.

I wanted to finish clearing the house and then, if Hugo approved and paid for it, I would buy some new outdoor furniture so we could sit outside and enjoy the sun without always having to go down to the beach. If I had time, I wanted to paint the living room and buy some new kitchenware. There was a list of things for which I needed a handyman, such as replacing some of the windows, fixing the leaking bathroom tap, changing a few fuses, but hopefully I'd find someone in town. As for Myra, the garden seemed like a good project for her to take on.

With the list done, I reward myself by making one of my favourite dishes: poori bhaji. Small round discs of dough fried in a big saucepan of oil. The dough needed to be perfectly rolled, without any bubbles or holes in it, so that when it hit the hot oil, it would puff up golden and crisp.

As always, cooking allows my mind to drift to a place of lightness and calm, a nothing place. After a time, I am aware of being watched.

'What's this?' Myra says, sitting on the stairs in an oversized T-shirt, peering through the banisters, wrinkling her nose at the potatoes frying in onions, turmeric, black mustard seeds and tomatoes.

'Poori bhaji,' I say, trying not to show my delight and relief she is out of her room.

'OMG – are you sprinkling in leaves?' she says, referring to the curry leaves on the counter.

'Have you never seen Indian food before?' I laugh.

'I mean, Mum doesn't normally make this kind of food.'

'What does she make?'

'Well, she doesn't. Sue does. Mum orders in sushi or dumplings, or if she makes food, it's Italian or English.'

'Boiling fresh pasta or putting frozen food in the oven isn't cooking. And I'm Indian so I tend to make Indian food. You're half-Indian, FYI, so maybe give this a try? You might like it.'

'Why is this for breakfast? It's not a breakfast food,' she says, stalking her way down the stairs to the table.

'Oh,' I reply, 'and what is a breakfast food?' As she lists cereal, eggs, toast, I say: 'That's *Western* breakfast food. The Chinese eat congee. In Costa Rica they have rice and beans. We sometimes eat this.'

Although her expression is scornful, she takes a tiny bit of poori and an equal amount of the bhaji. She doesn't say anything, or make any rude noises, but continues to eat. I'm so glad it's the first proper meal she's had since coming here, and that it's an Indian dish she seems to like, that I don't even make fun of her for eating it with a knife and fork. 'Would you like me to make it again sometime?' I ask gently, so as not to break the temporary peace we've forged.

'If you like,' she replies nonchalantly, as if she hasn't just finished the entire plateful. Some people lure others downstairs with the smell of bacon. It's interesting to know I can do the same with Myra, but with Indian food.

*

She spends the rest of the day in bed, and I allow her this brief reprieve because I know she has her therapy session on Zoom the next morning at ten. The next day, shortly after 11 a.m., while I'm debating whether to take her a cup of tea or not, I smell smoke again coming from under her door.

I'm torn between barrelling in and yelling at her, and wanting to handle things gently, because whatever Daisy says, I think Myra is experiencing some form of mild depression. I knock and push the door open, to find her looking at me guiltily, though with no cigarette in sight. I angle my head and look around.

'The jig is up.'

'What jig? No one's doing a jig,' she says.

'Please give me the cigarettes.' She opens her mouth as if to protest and then thinks better of it. 'Fine,' she says, and hands me a battered packet of twenty Camel Lights. 'I suppose you're going to tell Mum.'

Myra needs a gesture to show I'm on her side. While her behaviour is difficult and chaotic, I have to remember to be the one who is calm and earthed. It makes me appreciate the times our mother *didn't* shout at us because being the bigger person is exhausting. 'I wasn't planning to tell her,' I say. She arches an eyebrow in surprise.

'Did you have a good therapy session?'

I instantly regret asking, because at that her face blanks instantly, as if she's picked up that I'm trying to pry, which I am. I take her water glass and plates from the floor to show I'm leaving, a gesture of surrender. From tomorrow she'll be picking them up herself.

'We're going for a walk by the way,' I say, changing the subject. 'So it'd be great if you could get showered and dressed.'

'No way,' she says, shaking her head. 'I'm not going.'

'Here's the thing,' I say, opting for honesty. 'I know you're having a hard time of it. Believe me, you're not the only one.

But if you don't come with me, and if something doesn't change in the way we talk to each other, we *are* going to have to go back home. Because I can't do five weeks of you refusing to leave the house. Either you come out with me now or we head back.'

My approach is risky because Myra could just say she wants to go home. Or she could refuse to leave her room and then I'd have to get Daisy down here, and that would be an ordeal. I may not be a parenting expert but I do know what it feels like to be a child and so angry at the world you want to burn it all down. And I'm hopeful I've picked the right approach.

It's hard to read her expression. 'And what happens if we go back?'

'You will probably go off to some camp for rich kids like your mother originally planned.'

'You'd really do that?' she says. 'You're really going to blackmail me into having a walk?'

'No. I'm trying to get you out of the house. We've been here nearly a week and the only people I've seen so far are the spotty Deliveroo driver and some hippy lady who lives next door.'

Myra looks at me with a direct stare. 'Fine.'

'We leave in an hour.'

'An hour and a half.'

'An hour.'

'FINE.'

I congratulate myself on my first win.

'Are you going to get changed?' she says. I look down at my baggy harem pants and loose T-shirt with the logo of a pharmaceutical company who were trying to court Wallace.

'I *am* changed.'

Her eyes say everything.

*

The moment we step outside, the smell of salt, thrown into the air by waves crashing in the distance, wraps around me.

The front of the house tumbles down to railings cutting into the hillside leading to the sea below, accessible by two sets of rock-hewn stairs either side. Further along the ridge, the grass at the top is an intense green that hasn't yet been burned off by the relentlessly hot weather. Below, water pulls in and out of the bay, foam speckling white spots across an expanse of blue.

The movement is slow, vast, immeasurably powerful. Somewhere, something heavy leaches out of me and flows towards the tide. We find out the hard way that the coastal path doesn't lead directly into town and eventually double back on ourselves.

It's a good sign that Myra has made an effort in coming out, dressed in a short-sleeved black shirt dress and over-the-knee socks. We still haven't talked about any of it. How she's feeling after coming out of hospital. Maybe that will come with time. But there is a part of me that worries. Is she a grenade waiting to explode? Do I need to be vigilant, keep a careful eye on her? I feel at the very least I should ask her about the sleeping.

'So . . .' I say. 'How are you feeling?'

'Fine.' She shrugs.

'I mean really, how are you feeling? Is there anything you want to talk about?'

'No,' she says, squinting at me. 'Should there be?'

YES! I want to yell. *You're a child and you ended up in hospital. None of your other friends did. Doesn't that tell you something?*

'I mean, I know you've had your therapy session earlier this morning. I'm not prying. But you can talk to me about anything.' We tip our heads back as a kite drops from its position high in the sky, carrying light on its wings as it dips silent and quick into the sea.

'What did you mean when you said you were having a hard time?' she says, pushing her sunglasses down the bridge of her nose.

'When did I say that?'

'When you were giving your inspiring ultimatum.'

'Oh,' I sigh. I'd forgotten how observant kids could be. 'My boyfriend Wallace and I are on a break. It's been . . . tough.'

'Why are you on a break?' she asks, picking at the remains of her nail polish. I don't want to get into it right now, certainly not since she's switched from intermittent grunts into Miss One Thousand Questions.

'It's complicated.'

She snorts a laugh. 'That's what adults say when it's actually very simple.' Now it's my turn to stare at her, at the precise, wise truth in her words. 'Do you love him?'

'Of course I do,' I say, slightly irritably.

'What is it that you love about him?' she asks.

'Well, he's clever and he's a doctor – it's always handy to have one of those in the family. And I . . .' I pause. When I think about the reasons that I love Wallace, it's as if different shades of paint have been mixed over time and now I can't quite discern one from the other. Surely it's normal, however, for the love in a long-term relationship to soften from high, frantic peaks of emotion and desire into something that holds together the parts of your lives? But I can't shake the feeling that I've missed something over the years.

*

At the beginning of our relationship, Wallace's love felt expansive and effortless. But now, it feels measured, uncharted, like trying to navigate through an unfamiliar room in the dark, uncertain of where the sharp edges might be. We fell into the trap so many couples do: working long hours in order to set ourselves up for a life where we'd eventually spend more time with each other. But then our temporary life became our normality, and now we don't know how to escape it, so we stay, using work to distract ourselves from the distance that has grown between us.

We'd met in a Camden bar while trying to buy drinks at respective leaving dos for colleagues, and the bartender was trying to swerve me. 'Wow, what did you do to him?' Wallace remarked. Turns out nothing, except for not being a cute gay man. When I retorted that he wasn't getting served either, he gestured to his five foot eight inches and said: 'Sadly, I don't think I'm tall enough to qualify either.' I laughed, then he bought me a drink and texted me the next day. Would I like to meet him in Brixton market to try some okonomiyaki? he asked. And so I ate Japanese pancakes for the first time, and sat on a wooden bench and drank Negronis while trying to quieten the inner voice that marvelled that someone like him was interested in someone like me. He told me he worked in general practice in the NHS, and had wanted to get into medicine after seeing so many of his family members ignored by doctors because they were Black. That was before he switched to private practice after getting sick of the abuse and endless paperwork.

I remember thinking he was perfect. After the first time we had sex, he didn't rush me out the door. I was woken by the sizzle of a frying egg and the smell of bacon winding a delicious path through the crack under the door. Most of the men I'd slept with before Wallace communicated through sporadic texts, made lukewarm plans and stripped the warmth from their vocabulary in case I got too comfortable. All it ever did was make me feel terrible about myself. When Wallace showed up and didn't make me feel like a kid at the pick 'n' mix who was taking too much, it mattered. He didn't laugh when I was shy about taking my clothes off with the lights on, and I took comfort in his broad shoulders, which I would sleep on at night.

For all the unkind comments that season a long-term relationship, he could be kind. In the first year of us dating, he turned up at my flat with a bunch of tulips on my mother's death anniversary. He didn't say anything but simply sat in silence next to me on the sofa while we watched episodes of *Friends*. I appreciated not just the gesture but the simple physical presence, and that he didn't make the moment about him.

It was one of many small moments that made me love him, but he was not a popular choice with friends and family. None of my friends said, 'We LOVE him!' to me the minute his back was turned. Unlike other people's partners who would initially mount a presidential campaign to be liked, buying drinks for the table or coming to parties as a plus one, he never felt the need to impress.

He knew that I loved him, and he loved me, and that was

all he needed. He didn't understand that people will draw their own conclusions, and what they observed was his absence, or me rushing home to make dinner for him even though I did it as an act of love. In keeping my depression a secret, I also denied them a crucial part of my story with Wallace. That while love should never be built on a foundation of gratefulness, when the bad times approached like a dark planet entering the orbit of my normal life, he was there for me when other partners weren't.

When Myra asks me the question about what I love about him, what hurts isn't just that I don't immediately know how to answer her. It's that for years I have not considered what it is that he loves about me, because I assumed it was a constant. And now the realisation that it isn't feels like a tremor signalling the arrival of an earthquake.

*

'Auntie?' Myra asks. 'You drifted off there a bit.'

'Yeah, sorry,' I laugh, to try and lighten the mood. 'Well, let's see what else. I like how he looks. I think he's pretty handsome.'

'That doesn't mean anything,' she says. 'Remember the guy in *Sex and the City*, the one Charlotte marries, who looks like a hairy egg? If you love someone you automatically think they look good. Looks are pointless.'

As we walk, the sound of insects humming in the grass fills the silence. Where the line of houses merges into the fields, rusted farm machinery sits in the yellowing grass, and the broken handlebars of a bicycle make a perch for two fat and glossy crows.

'Well then,' I say, 'he makes a Trinidadian curry that I love. Oh, and when it's winter, he doesn't mind if I warm my feet against him.' I can feel the judgement rising off Myra like steam. I took too long to answer, and we both know it.

'Are you going to get married?'

'I'm not sure but maybe.'

'Why aren't you sure?'

'That's a lot of questions. When do I get to ask you about your life?' I say, pelting her with a handful of grass. A clod of mud hits her black dress and for a moment, as she stares down at it, I hold my breath, expecting a tantrum. But instead something loosens in her gaze and she dusts the mud away.

'Maybe later,' she says, and thunders down the path away from me, so that she can yell back, 'I WIN, YOU LOSE!' when she gets to the bottom.

6

The trail from the house descends to the main promenade of shops on Beach Road. The sandy bay is preferred by tourists who can step from their Airbnbs straight into the sea, but the locals seek out the quieter beaches further along the coast.

Harkness is famed for its necklace of coves, ringed in golden sand, accessible only via walking trails. There are no lilos, no buckets and spades, nothing to distract from the movement of waves and the stillness of the sky. Beach Road, however, has everything ticked off on British seaside bingo. On the opposite side to the defunct pier is a marina for small boats, and a little channel marked by buoys where people in kayaks and paddleboards can access the water. Considering it's a Wednesday, I'm surprised at how busy it is, but then again, I never usually travel during the summer holiday months.

As we approach the modern café we spotted on the way in, named the Green Goddess, a family of four in shorts and life jackets, holding paddles aloft, are already bickering about who's sharing with who. They stop and stare at Myra, who stares back at them until they continue walking to the waterline in their Crocs.

'I am so hungry I could die,' she says, her words curling into a whine. These hairpin switches between playful and serious make it so hard to know what mood she will be in at any given moment.

Although it is like dragging a storm cloud, when we enter the café I immediately know we are in a place that is loved, despite the fact it is virtually empty. The Green Goddess has high ceilings and is light-filled, and while it reminds me of Delilah's, it has a different personality. Where Delilah is all about minimalism and chunky wood, here there are comfortable armchairs and low wooden tables. It's a place that doesn't hurry people. The frontage is modern and floor-to-ceiling glass, but inside there are long wooden shelves lined with pottery from local artisans. Black-and-white photos hang on the wall, stacks of magazines are piled in a rack, and the counter is crammed with slabs of cake, thick, fluffy doorstoppers of all kinds: rum-soaked, chocolate ganache, yellow sponge fat with jam and cream.

'Hello?' I say, craning to see if anyone is around. Myra collapses into an armchair facing the sea.

'Be right there!' a voice calls from the back. Frantic footsteps, then a big clang as pots clatter to the floor. 'Oh, fuck. I mean, sugar. Whoopsie. Sorry, sorry.'

A thirty-something woman emerges looking like the main character from a rom-com, her brown and gold hair tied in a messy knot at the top, strands escaping to frame her face. She's covered in flour, white marks contrasting with her tanned dark brown skin. Several of her fingers are wrapped in Band Aids. Despite how flustered she seems, she gives me a tired smile before wiping yet more flour across her face.

'Sorry, I'm running things on my own today. It's going horribly.'

'That's okay,' I say. It's impossible not to smile at the scene of chaos unravelling before me.

'Are you here for the day?'

'Actually, my niece and I are staying here for a few weeks. In Hugo Albright's house. Rosemary's house, I guess.'

'Oh, Posh Boy is back?' she says with a grin, wiping her hands on her apron.

'Posh Boy?'

'Hugo,' she laughs. 'He turned up here in his little starched shorts and smart shirt one summer, nose in his books. Oh, wait,' she says guiltily. 'Are you his girlfriend?'

'What? Oh, god, no. He's my brother-in-law's cousin. We're family. Sort of.' I'm betraying my Indian roots here somewhat, where even someone not related to you is referred to as uncle or auntie or cousin. 'I'm Padma.'

'Selena,' she says, tucking some errant hair back into her hairband. 'Want me to get you some menus? The café is vegetarian, by the way. I hope that's okay?' Myra nods and goes back to her phone. While we wait, I text Hugo and tell him I bumped into an old friend of his.

Apparently your starched shorts are still well remembered here.

The minute I send the message, I wonder why I did it. I don't know Hugo, not really. He might think it was overfamiliar. He might send a thumbs-up emoji or, worse, not respond.

If my starched shorts are still the talk of the town, he replies almost immediately, **I shudder to think what else makes the headlines in Harkness.** It makes me laugh out loud. We order jacket potatoes with cheese and beans, and when Selena brings over our plates, I ask her if it's normally this busy in Harkness. 'I assume you haven't met any of the other locals yet,' she says drily. I tell her I've only had the pleasure of meeting Esme.

'Well, Esme certainly is a character,' she says, trying not to laugh as I recount our conversation. 'She's harmless, and her tarot reading is actually pretty good. When she came back from India she tried to insist we all call her Shanthi. It lasted about a week.'

'Oh, dear.'

'But if you had met any other locals, you would have heard about the *Guardian* article. It's all any of them can talk about,' she says, rolling her eyes.

'What happened? Is it a good thing?'

'They ran a piece on Harkness, how it's an "often overlooked gem" that has potential to be the new Margate. The town council are beside themselves with glee. We've already started to see a steady increase in the numbers of visitors coming in, far more than usual. It's a good thing but in some ways I'm sad. I kind of like this little town the way it is. I don't want it to turn into another bolthole for posh knobs, you know? No offence to Hugo.'

'Oh, none taken. And I know exactly what you mean,' I say. 'I live in Brixton.'

'I love that place,' she says. As she turns to walk back to the counter, she angles her head. 'Where are you both originally from, if you don't mind me asking?'

When a white person asks the Where Are You From? question, it feels like the time I was eight and got a mackerel bone stuck in my throat. It's a question that always comes at the front of the conversation – before a hundred others they could have asked to get to know you. It makes you feel you've been seen as a colour, not a person.

'I don't get why it's a bad question,' Henry once said to me when I was visiting them.

'Henry, where are you from?' I'd asked, knowing he was from Stoke-on-Trent.

'Okay, so I don't know anything about Stoke-on-Trent, so it would tell me nothing about who you are,' I'd said. 'I would learn much more about you if I asked a different question, like what you did for a job, what music you like.'

Henry looked puzzled. 'Right, and what's wrong with that?'

'There's nothing wrong with it,' I replied, 'but when a person asks that question before they've asked any others, it's because they are making an assumption about my skin colour, when my skin colour is probably the least important thing about me. When people ask us that, they don't ask which part of the country we are from. They just mine the references their own brain cobbled together from things like Apu on *The Simpsons* and Gita and Sanjay from *EastEnders*. It's assumed that I'm going to have an arranged marriage, I must be religious, must love spicy food. It's just a shorthand – it doesn't make me feel like a person.'

'But you do like spicy food,' he said.

'That's not the point!' Daisy had interjected.

I look at Selena without a trace of defensiveness. 'I'm Indian,' I say, 'and Myra is half-Indian – her dad is white . . . English.' Myra lifts up her head and frowns in silent protest at being labelled so starkly.

'I'm half-Guyanese,' Selena says, undoing the strings of her apron, flourishing it like a matador's cape over a chair. Underneath she wears a red and white vintage floral top and blue high-waisted trousers. 'My mother is white – I grew up around here. When being mixed-race, as you can imagine, was . . .

interesting. But then Mum decided she wanted to move to Bristol and I went travelling. After a horrible break-up, I decided it was time to put down some roots, and this area is starting to develop, slowly. They're incentivising new businesses so the costs are lower than if I'd wanted to set something up elsewhere, plus this is home in a way. A lot of the same people are still here.'

The front door jingles with a customer arriving. While Selena serves them, a boy walks past on the pavement, wearing a plastic horse's head, the kind you might see someone wearing at a music festival. He stops in front of the window, neighs. The customer who came in, a bird-like woman dressed in jeans, heels and pink lipstick, bangs on the window and yells: 'Greg, BUGGER OFF!' He lets out another neigh and trots away.

'Bloody delinquent,' she says to me by way of explanation while Selena works the elaborate coffee machine. 'Sorry about that. I'm Barbara, wife of David Bentley.' Her age is indiscernible because her skin bears the blurred outline of someone who's had filler, but at a guess she's in her sixties. Her hair is like sedimentary rock, grey roots flowing into dark hair fissuring into blonde highlights. A cloud of heavy, musky perfume follows her, the kind that might be labelled 'Dark Orchid' or 'Mystique', the bottle resembling something on the poison shelf of the Queen in *Snow White*.

'David Bentley is head of the town council,' says Selena quickly, in case I say something I shouldn't about Harkness. 'Barbara, this is Padma and her niece Myra, who are staying in Rosemary's old place. They are related to Hugo.'

Barbara sniffs with disapproval. 'You tell him it's a disgrace to have left that place lie empty all these years. And in a prime spot too. I was just telling Esme what a shame it is. Does he have any plans to sell?'

'I'm not sure.' It's not the answer she wants to hear. 'But,' I follow up quickly, knowing how important it is to get on the right side of council folk, 'I can ask.'

'Please do. I assume you've heard all about the *Guardian* article,' she says primly, arching her eyebrows. 'Tell Hugo things are picking up around here. Anyway, Selena, I'm off. Eileen's is packed by the way. Your coffee is better, but you should think about serving sausage rolls. I've always said.' With another deep sniff, she's out of the door. Selena balls her fists in front of her mouth and strangles a scream.

'What's Eileen's?' I ask.

'Eileen's is the much-loved local café, which is owned by the much-loved Eileen, who sits every day behind the counter holding court,' says Selena. 'And I'm told at least once a day how my place is never going to be able to compete.' She sits down and tugs at her hair, depositing more flour onto it. 'It's not supposed to compete! It's a vegetarian café with vegan and gluten-free options! Eileen's serves pies that are so dense they could be used as grenades!'

Myra isn't listening to either of us. 'Who was *that*?' she asks. 'Horse Boy?'

'Oh, that's Greg,' Selena says, getting up and tying her apron back on. 'Barbara has a vendetta against him because she thinks his dad is secretly her husband David. They have the same Dumbo ears, apparently. Greg's mother is a single mum who does a lot of the cleaning work around here, and some people can be snobby about that sort of thing too. He's harmless – a bit eccentric, but he likes to hang around rock pools and look at birds and take photographs.'

'*Is* his dad David?' I ask.

Selena shrugs. 'Probably. No one would dare say it to

Barbara's face as she's his third wife, but he used to be a massive shagger back in the day.'

'Auntie, would you mind if I look around for a bit?' Myra says, while I finish the last bit of potato on my plate.

Although I feel anxious at the thought of not having a visual on Myra, she has seemed better today. From refusing to leave the house to wanting to explore the town – that seems like real improvement. Besides I could hardly keep her on a leash for the whole summer and I'd been looking forward to doing a solo grocery shop for all the dishes I'd planned to experiment with at the cottage – and maybe teach to Myra if she was interested.

'Keep your phone on you,' I say, 'and be home by six for dinner. And no—' I mime smoking a cigarette. She rolls her eyes but says, yes, she will be. When she leaves, the Green Goddess grows even quieter. Selena watches as an older couple let their dog drink from the water bowl she's placed outside. They look poised to come in, but glance at the menu and change their minds. 'Motherfuckers,' she mutters under her breath. 'Sorry,' she says to me. 'It's just tough during the weekdays. A more traditional crowd.'

I feel a pull towards Selena, something I like and trust about her, and I sense her loneliness. I want to help but it's not my place.

*

After exploring the town for just over an hour, it's clear Harkness is undergoing an extremely slow form of gentrification. The modern developments are limited to the Green Goddess, a hole in the wall called Fin & Gill that sells seafood small plates, a clothing boutique called Chic Shack that starts at £150 for vest tops, and an art gallery imaginatively entitled The Space, with a dazzlingly ugly collection of statues with iron spikes radiating from the head. I take a picture of one and send it to Wallace with the caption: **If Pinhead from Hellraiser had a love child with the Angel of the North.** When he doesn't reply, on impulse I also send the same picture to Hugo with a different caption. **Don't worry about your starched shorts – the 'art' here is clearly going to take top billing.** And then, because I feel guilty for texting him, I also send it to Delilah, who replies: **Are you on drugs?**

Behind Beach Road is the real town. Interestingly, there are no chain businesses here. The fishmonger's is a local operation that proudly states they have been in business since 1938. I debate whether to go in, but there's something about the look of the fishmonger when he catches sight of me through the glass that makes me paranoid I won't be welcome. In a fluster, I find myself in a clothing shop called Threads, and immediately feel trapped when I realise it is an odd medley of styles I suspect have never been in fashion, even in the right time period. I exit quickly, making the sales assistant look at me strangely, as if she thinks I might have stolen something.

A few doors down, by contrast, a British Heart Foundation shop has an incredible display, colour-blocking tops, skirts and hats. Drawn in by a pair of flat red mules, I start chatting to the manager, a French lady named Thérèse, who brushes off my protestations about sizing. 'What you're wearing is far too big. What are these trousers? This T-shirt? Why are you hiding?' Empowered by her directness, I buy the mules, a green-striped Cos T-shirt, a flared cotton skirt, a pair of linen trousers with an elasticated waist, and a short-sleeved dress the colour of lemons and purple wisteria. I don't know where I would wear them, but maybe one day.

To litmus-test the diversity, I check to see who's running the local newsagent and it is a large pink man named Clive. There isn't a dark moustache in sight, or the smell of curry from home-made meals eaten in the back of the shop, which always makes me feel strangely homesick. The ice-cream shop is actually selling gelato, run by an English–Italian woman named Bella who only uses local ingredients. Apparently, she says, a positive slew of Tripadvisor reviews has made her life both a blessing and a curse – she hasn't had a day off in three months.

Next I step into the white-and-red shop of Stan the butcher and nervously hover by the sauces, not knowing what the queuing system is. Eventually Stan takes pity on me and talks me through which sausages he'd recommend, how salty the cure is on the bacon and whether I should go for the smaller chicken or the big one. He warms up considerably when I tell him I'm here with my niece for five weeks. 'Tell me if you need any special cuts,' he says, 'and I can order them in.' His warmth makes that tight knot of worry disappear. After visiting two more shops – the local wine shop and the cheese shop (called Gouda Day) – it is a torturous, slow trail back up to the house.

When I reach it, I see that Hugo made good on his promise to get a skip delivered. After a shower and a cold glass of lemonade, I unpack my bags. The wedges of smoked cheese and soft blue go into a Tupperware box at the bottom. From the butcher I unpack richly coloured lamb chops, chicken legs, and chubby sausages with flecks of leeks. Some of it goes into the freezer, and the rest in the fridge for the week's meals. There is nothing more comforting than a full fridge. Once everything is packed away, I start hefting the black bags that I've already filled into the skip.

After a couple of hours of throwing away electricals covered in a sticky film of dust and damp, the house feels lighter, as if it can breathe again. I open all the windows, although some grumble at first, warped stiff with salt and water. The sea air winds its way in, bringing freshness and birdsong. My phone pings while my tea is brewing.

It is a message from Daisy, a list of things she wants Myra to accomplish on a daily/weekly basis because she clearly thinks I am not capable of coming up with one. It is also unhinged.

1. Wake up every morning by 8 a.m.
2. Do some stretches, yoga or take up a sport like Taekwondo
3. Journal your feelings
4. Therapy once a week
5. Learn how to make something – a food dish, pottery, a scarf
6. Wash and iron your own clothes
7. Clean up after yourself during mealtimes
8. Limit TV to one hour per day
9. Read at least five of the books on the Booker Prize longlist by the end of the summer
10. Do at least two household chores a day
11. Do not do any drugs or alcohol
12. Start eating fruit and at least two vegetables a day
13. Clean your face with a proper cleanser, NOT your fingers
14. Shower daily and wash your hair with shampoo AND conditioner
15. Brush your teeth – you are not a child – or you will be left with stumps.

While I am reading it, Daisy messages again.

LET ME KNOW IF YOU HAVE RECEIVED THIS. How fast does she think I can read?

Yes, I text back. **I'll talk through it with her.**

There is simply no way I am subjecting Myra to that list. I know Daisy well enough to understand that this doesn't stem from cruelty but rather a well-meaning attempt to mould her daughter into her own likeness. Because then she'll be happy! And successful! But it is an impossible set of tasks, the expectations are too high, and it makes me wonder if part of how Myra feels stems from this. Maybe I need to be softer, more compassionate towards her.

I start working on dinner and put chicken legs seasoned with harissa and garlic in the oven. I make snacks in case she is hungry when she gets back. While dinner cooks, I turn my phone over so I can ignore the fact Wallace hasn't replied to my message, and secretly I hope that by doing so, it will mysteriously encourage the universe to prompt him to text me back. I decide to clear out more of Rosemary's junk from Myra's room so she'll have space to put her things. Currently, her suitcase is open and the contents are a nightmare jumble. When I head downstairs to put more rubbish bags in the skip, I can't resist turning my phone over. I feel a little flutter in my chest when I see Wallace has sent a voice note. *Thank you, universe!*

I press play. *Padma,* he says in his serious voice, *I hope you are settling in okay. Work has been very busy – one of the practice managers quit, which is a nightmare.* (Sighs) *I need more sleep. I envy you being at the seaside – wish I could take a holiday too. I know it has only been five days but I miss you, and wish you were here. I know I shouldn't say that when we're on a break but – the house is in a complete state and I've been eating a lot of takeaways.*

I went to visit Ola and Michael on Sunday after footie. Their kids are cute. Sorry – I probably shouldn't say that either. Sore subject. Anyway, I've been thinking . . . we've exchanged messages almost every day since you left and that's making it a bit harder than if we had less contact. I don't want to hurt you but I have feelings in this too and I need to take care of my needs for once. Please don't think this means I don't care about you. I do. But . . . anyway. Take care of yourself and we'll speak soon, I hope.

The elation I felt before listening to his message descends into a muddy mixture of irritation, upset and an actual physical pain in my stomach. Since the beginning I've accepted that Wallace's work is more important than mine. He's a doctor, he earns more money. In lieu of me having a big career or ambitions, I felt I hadn't the right to be upset when he could sometimes be patronising about work. But his message makes it so clear what he thinks of me and what I'm doing. Calling it a seaside holiday. Dropping in mention of Ola and Michael's kids. Saying he misses me and anchoring it to the state of the house. *Take care of yourself*, as if I'm a colleague he's saying goodbye to. When did he become this dispassionate and cold?

To try and shake off my thoughts, I go downstairs at 6 p.m. to wait for Myra's return. Then 6.30 p.m. passes with no sign of her. 7 p.m. Her phone goes straight to voicemail. Then 8 p.m. Where is she? I go up to her room to see if I can find anything to give me a clue as to why she isn't here. All thoughts of Wallace are burned up by my worry about whether I have messed up and lost my niece before a week has passed. What if she is drinking? Passed out somewhere and vulnerable? I don't even know the town well enough yet to have a sense of where to look. By 9 p.m. I remember what it is like for blood to feel cold, while the adrenaline washes over me like fire on a lake.

Myra's absence sets off every landmine I thought I'd buried deep after Mum's death. Not just fear of the harm she might do to herself, but the threat that others could pose to her too. Men with dark thoughts, who might offer to buy her alcohol at the local offy and then squirrel her away into a van. The thought makes me feel sick and violent. I am so angry at Myra and her thoughtlessness and fragility.

The anger flickers for a moment, before cooling into upset that I have failed, and guilt that I have taken Daisy and Henry's money knowing nothing about looking after children, and now Myra is the collateral damage of my greed. The sense that I am yet again worrying and caretaking, being thrust back into a role I've tried so hard to escape.

*

Having an alcoholic mother caused untold uncertainty in our lives, and although I would try to detach to establish some sense of order and control, it felt impossible at the time. I didn't know she was an alcoholic then; that wasn't a term people used until after a person had died, usually of cirrhosis, and certainly not when it came to Indian women doctors. The alcoholics we knew were always men of a certain age, who'd drink during the day in the local pub and occasionally shout offensive things at people walking past.

At the time, I didn't think Mum was negligent or relying overly on me; I actually took a warped sense of pride at being her second-in-command. *This house would collapse without me*, I'd think smugly, not realising it wasn't ever meant to be a child's job to keep a household together.

When it was happening, I knew she had her good days and

bad days, but I didn't understand why. Some days she just seemed to sleep more, or would forget things, or be clumsy in a way that didn't seem accidental. She was also in deep denial about her drinking, so on the rare occasion another adult would ask if she was okay or confront her with the truth, she would laugh it off or cut them ruthlessly out of our lives. Given that it was the nineties, and most adults not only drank alcohol but also frequently drove drunk, she felt her behaviour was normal.

I didn't know Mum was an alcoholic but I knew that I had to throw out her empties so that Daisy – Dhara back then – didn't see them. I knew I had to wake up at night after she'd come back from a late shift to check she hadn't left the oven on. I knew I had to double-check the doors were locked after we had dinner. And that any event which involved my twin worlds of school and home colliding sent me into a sweaty panic. What would Mum be like when she turned up? Would she turn up? Would the other parents think she was odd?

The older I got, the more I tried to keep our home as clean and ordered as possible. I played a role in Dhara's life that shouldn't have been mine, making her dinner, helping with her homework. I was the one who dropped her off and picked her up from birthday parties by bus until she was old enough to travel by herself.

When I was twelve and Dhara was nine, Mum announced one Saturday morning that we would be going to Brighton for the day. We had never visited the beach before, and we were expecting Mr Whippy ice creams, sand between our toes, and a sea so warm it felt like bathwater. We encountered a wind that threatened to whip across our faces like paper cuts, and the pebbles hurt Dhara's feet, which were squeezed into slightly too small jelly shoes. I took mine off and gave them to her, walking barefoot on the stones. Mum ruffled my hair and told me I was being a good sister, rather than buying me a new pair.

'Padma, I'm just going to find the toilet, okay? Stay with Dhara,' she said. She handed me a £10 note just in case we got hungry. I didn't understand – surely she'd only be gone five minutes? The pebbles pressed through uncomfortably on the thin towel, and the sun rose higher and higher in the sky. 'I'm hungry,' Dhara said, pulling at her plaits, and I gave her my half-melted Twix, ignoring the rumbling in my own stomach. Children ran towards the sea, the foam dissolving into glossy pearls around their waists. I hugged my knees tightly, every part of me contracted and tense, while Dhara dozed in the sun. What if our mother never came back?

An older lady walking a fluffy brown dog came over and leaned on her stick next to us. She must have seen me frantically scanning the horizon. 'Are you girls all right?' she asked. I pocketed my worry and smiled as widely as I could. 'Yes, Miss. Our mother is returning from the toilet any moment now.' She stared at me with filmy blue eyes as if deciding something, and eventually walked off. I went back to my post looking at the crowds walking by, but still no Mum. When she returned two hours later, the sight of her made me cry. All of that worry found release in the familiarity of her curly hair and green jumpsuit. 'Where were you?' I cried, holding on to her arm.

'I couldn't find the toilet,' she laughed, 'I got lost.' I cried even harder and held on to her tightly. 'Oh, my silly sausage. Look, even your baby sister isn't crying.' Dhara was emerging from her nap, unaware of anything that had happened in the last two hours.

'You left us!' I yelled.

The tone of my voice made my mother frown. 'Well, I'm here now. Did you get something to eat?'

I wanted her to be more penitent, but she behaved as if nothing was wrong. 'No! I thought you would be coming back!'

'Padma, I gave you the money,' she said, sitting down. Her voice was ever so slightly off-key. 'It's your job to look after your sister, why didn't you get something?' Then she curled up next to Dhara and slept, while I spent another hour immobile with fury. I wanted to walk off, get an ice cream, *do* something, but the fear she might not be there when I got back pinned me in place.

'I had such a lovely day, Mama!' Dhara said when we were eventually back in the car.

'I'm glad, baby.' Our mother smiled and kissed her on the cheek. She glanced at me briefly, but unable to withstand the reproach in my gaze, quickly looked away.

Alcoholism, especially in a parent, writes parts of your future in a way you aren't even aware of. It defines your choice of partner, your career, how you raise your children, how you cope with the world. When the components of your life change in any significant way, it makes you constantly vigilant, scanning the horizon for when, not if, the danger comes.

I wonder if I have been holding my breath around Myra, waiting for the terrible moment to arrive. Just as I am about to give up hope, I look out of the window at the dark path running below the house, the only direct way in from the town. I see a torch moving along the alleyway cutting between Rosemary and Esme's houses. Two figures. One is carrying a plastic horse's head.

*

'My phone died,' Myra says, as she approaches the front of the house. I am so relieved to see her, yet so angry, that I want to kick her inconsiderate carcass back down the path. Her shoulders are already rounding defensively. Greg the Horse Boy trails behind her. He is at the age where he is mostly physicality: a mop of mousy-brown hair, an angular nose his face is still growing into, and long limbs that struggle to co-ordinate to get him where he wants to go. 'I got lost.' And with those three words, without Myra knowing, that day in Brighton comes rushing back to me. I don't say anything.

'I went for a walk to the other side of town and got stuck on a coastal trail,' she says. 'Then it became dark and my bloody phone battery ran out. Luckily, I bumped into Greg, who helped me find my way back. I swear.'

Even before the words are out of my mouth, I know they are wrong and stink of unfairness and misplaced anger. But I can't help myself.

'Myra, tell me the truth. Have you both been drinking?'

She looks at me, and the hurt on her face, and the horror on Greg's, punches regret into me. 'No. Of course not,' she says. '*How could you even ask that*?' Shame cascades over her. Especially because I've said this in front of Greg. To Greg.

'Um,' he says, twisting the corner of his T-shirt, 'if it helps, I don't drink alcohol. But I should probably go home now, if that's all right?'

'Yes, of course, Greg,' I say. 'I'm sorry, I didn't mean . . . anyway. Are you okay to get home or do you need a lift back?'

'I'll be fine walking, thank you,' he says, sensing trouble in the air.

'Bye, Myra!' he says and heads back down the path. She doesn't answer because she's too focused on me.

'I can't believe you asked that in front of him.' Her eyes are like emeralds caught by the sun. There is so much fury in them, and now the anger and blame have swung too far to my side. She has yet to say she's sorry, and the build-up over the past few days, her refusal to talk about any of it, irritates me.

'What do you expect me to say? You disappeared. I was worried sick. You were in hospital only two weeks ago for alcohol poisoning. Is it really that far a reach to wonder if you've been drinking again?' I know I will regret these words in the morning but the current of emotion is too strong.

'My friends have stopped talking to me,' she snaps, 'and that's the first person I've met who doesn't treat me like dirt, and you just . . . you know what? Forget it. No one listens to me anyway.'

Daisy told me about her breaking curfew and being difficult about coming home. If one incident like this could tear me apart, I don't know if I have the capacity to withstand more. On the shore of all that departed emotion, a decision had to be made soon about how I'm going to handle her.

'Let's talk about it in the morning,' I say tiredly, trying to broker enough peace so we can both go to sleep. 'There's food in the fridge.' By the time I make it into bed, my anger starts cooling off as the mini-fan propped up on the dressing table whirrs left to right. The reassuring hum reminds me of when I'd lie on Mum's lap in the summer as a child, feeling her flesh surround me, the rise and fall of her chest as the fan cooled us down enough to sleep.

Eventually I hear sounds below of the kettle being switched on and the murmur of the television. I know Myra is probably feeling bad, but I also know that I cannot be the caretaker of all her bad feelings. I cannot keep her under close observation all the time. It's too much responsibility.

Somewhere in between wakefulness and dozing, I realise that I can't work on Myra *and* my feelings for Wallace, and perhaps going home is for the best. Even if we are on a break, at least we can work things out if I am in London. I could 'accidentally' bump into him, request visitation rights with Winston, or visit Ettie to check she's doing okay. Eventually I drift off to sleep, unhooking myself from the present, to visit the rooms of my mother and sit with her ghost for a while.

*

When I open my phone the next morning to text Wallace that I am coming back, I check Instagram on impulse and see several Stories that show videos of him partying with his friends. A mix of men and women boomeranging glasses of champagne at a marble-topped bar in the city. The contrast between his night and mine deadens something in me. If I go back to London, what am I returning to?

While I debate the pros and cons endlessly over the next couple of days, some silent agreement exists in the *froideur* between Myra and me that, although we aren't talking to each other, we aren't going to text Daisy about what has happened. The only noise comes from the TV, or when Myra feels compelled to say out loud how much she hates it here, and how bored she is. Our combined mood seeps through the entire cottage and work on the house halts as frustrations mount in the enforced quiet.

After picking up yet another used plate of hers from on top of a stack of boxes, I fling open the door to her room and ask her to get up and do her chores. She tells me she'll do it in half an hour. Then twenty minutes, then ten minutes. She manages to eke out a whole day under the covers with these fractional promises.

At least when an adult gives you the silent treatment, you can walk away. I could hardly drive off and, if I took her home, Daisy or Henry would probably bribe her with a new iPad or another pair of boots. I can't, and don't want to do that. It has nothing to do with the money I'm being paid. The flashes I've seen of how Myra can be when she is truly herself have been fleeting but precious. They exist. I think about how I actually want to help her, how much she needs my support, and that perhaps London isn't the best place for me either, right now.

In that moment, I realise helping Myra means being something other than her jailer or another person who gives in to her. By the end of a full week of us being here, I realise something has to change, and perhaps first of all it needs to be me.

7

Overnight the sky has switched from a bright blue to a heavy grey. Myra languishes in bed but I take Daisy's advice not to hover and leave her to it. It feels cleansing to be walking through the wet grass and fresh earth – salt from the water catching on the breeze. Drizzle teases my hair into curls around my face. Beach Road hasn't woken up yet, and the shops tucked behind it are mostly empty save for a few locals shopping before the tourists come out. I meander into the local health food shop, and as I enter, there is Esme working behind the counter. 'Padma!' she exclaims. 'What a nice surprise. How are you both settling in?'

I tell her I'm in a hurry and ask if she has any saffron. I left mine at home and there is a prawn biriyani I'd like to experiment with that requires it as an ingredient. As she fetches it, she asks me what the recipe involves, and when I explain, says: 'You should give me a lesson sometime! Maybe we can do a cooking workshop for my mandala girls.'

'Sure,' I reply, having no intention of doing so. The recipes I inherited from my mother are for my loved ones. I don't want to become yet another story in Esme's exotic repertoire of tales. 'Do you have an Instagram account?' she asks. I do, but only to look at other people's feeds and now to spy on

Wallace. When I had tried to post about food on my own account while working for Majid, he told me it would distract me. Now it seems suspiciously like he was trying to snuff out any hint of competition.

'Drop me a note with what you'd charge and I'll share it with the next group I have over.'

I wonder now why the idea of selling South Indian cooking lessons has never occurred to me before. It seems such an obvious thing to do given that it is a more niche form of cooking in England. And if I made a mistake, Esme's rich clients wouldn't know the difference. A rogan josh, a brinjal bhaji maybe, familiar takeaway favourites – but not Mangalorean chicken curry or fish fry.

Besides, Majid offered cooking workshops to people all the time. Hosted dinners for celebrities as a segment on his show. And his cooking was average at best. I always wondered if he knew he didn't have much talent and, looking back, perhaps he did. Maybe that's why he was so quick to pull other people down. When I'd try and run some of my recipes past him, he'd say they'd never work, citing flavours clashing or incorrect cooking temperatures. Mysteriously they'd then appear in some iteration or other further down the line, repackaged as his idea.

Majid hadn't just taken my job from me, he had stolen my confidence. More than that. He had actually *stolen* from me. According to Rekha, he was talking to Paul's Bakery about a possible collaboration regarding chilli pain au chocolat – the recipe I had been first to trial, though he failed to acknowledge that when he passed it off as his. Although Majid had behaved appallingly, I had let this happen. Just like I had let so many other things happen.

'Don't forget, Padma!' Esme says just as I'm about to head out of the door. Although I have been so dismissive of her, she is willing to take a chance on me.

'I won't,' I reply, 'I promise.' And I actually mean it this time.

*

Majid had taken me on after his aunt Naseema, a sixty-something Pakistani woman who lived on the other side of Ettie, told me her nephew was putting together a food channel on 'The YouTube'. No degree required, just a willingness to work. 'You love food, Padma,' Naseema Auntie had said, looking at my stomach. 'You'll be great.' I didn't have a degree or anything that constituted a proper qualification in food. Given that he was mainly looking for someone with a willingness to work, and who would not kick up a fuss about being paid in cash or demand employment rights, it suited both of us.

His entire gimmick was to present himself in the persona of Lankey Pandey, a rude boy from Leicester. He'd wear a tracksuit and gold jewellery, pepper his chat with a lot of 'innits', and would then produce a culinary wonder that was easy for people to make at home, usually on low incomes. He didn't care about sharing recipes with people on low incomes (he called them The Povvos off-camera); he cared that this focus would guarantee lots of views.

I'd been hired as an assistant, and while at first it meant general dogsbody work of making sure everyone ate lunch, picking up Majid's dry cleaning, fobbing off people on the phone, holding camera lights and carrying bags, I slowly found myself in charge of styling some of the food shoots plus helping with the food prep for events. His office was the converted downstairs of his uncle's flat in Forest Hill, and we'd shoot out in the garage, which he'd had impressively converted into a test kitchen. I was so pleased to be there that I over-compensated. I started bringing in food for staff on long shoot days, which gave me catering experience even if it wasn't reflected in the salary. From time to time, Majid let me help with the brainstorming, and then came the breakthrough moment (or so I thought) of featuring my own recipe on his site.

The dish they were going to make had fallen through because some of the ingredients hadn't arrived, and I'd brought along everything to make the pain au chocolat as a snack for the crew. While I was prepping in the staff kitchen, I saw him observing me. I didn't like Majid much – he tended to leer at the young female interns, would take them out for drinks, and then mysteriously they'd develop an ailment or get a new job offer and we'd never see them again. His manager, Buddy, instigated an unofficial policy that all interns going forward would be male, after one of the former interns threatened to sue for sexual harassment. Rekha and I weren't in any danger because, being older, and bigger than a size 8, we were Majid's worst nightmare – women who had 'let themselves go'. While Rekha was on the dating circuit, her preferences were large white men, while I had zero interest in a scrawny Asian boy who looked like he had stolen his grandmother's jewellery.

Majid had been accused of copying other people's recipes before, but his reputation remained intact. When he came up to me in the kitchen and asked if he could borrow the chilli pain au chocolat recipe, his tone was so nonchalant. Afterwards, he was effusive with praise, saying how much I had helped him out, and it made me feel good. Until the recipe went viral and he refused to credit me.

At that point his mood switched. There was no paper trail, no evidence to say it was my recipe, he said, shortly after firing me. I was left with festering resentment. Eventually a mild depression set in, meaning I stopped cooking completely. When I slowly came out of it, I made little things for Delilah, and I cooked for Wallace. But as for actually turning cooking into a business – the confidence to do anything like that had been taken from me.

Esme's words make me realise what I now feel is no longer sadness and defeat, but a deep anger and desire to reclaim my love of food.

*

While walking back up the path to the house, my phone rings. 'How is it all going?' Hugo asks. 'Fine,' I say abruptly, taking myself off the track as two women come careening down on bicycles, one of them losing a Birkenstock to a hedge. 'That doesn't sound fine?' he says, concerned. When I don't say anything back because I don't know where to start, he thinks I'm cross about the state of Rosemary's house. 'I'm really sorry about the mess. I know it must be such a pain to have to empty it. Can I make it up to you? Treat you to dinner?'

I balk at him offering to take me to dinner. I don't think it's appropriate. Wallace might be out partying and living his life, but it doesn't mean there isn't sadness and longing when I think about him and our relationship. When you say 'we're on a break', there should be some sort of pre-drafted agreement as to whether or not you're allowed to go out to dinner with people named Hugo.

'Look, that's not necessary,' I say. 'And it's not you. It's not the house – I don't mind about it, honestly. You're letting us stay there for free . . . tidying up is not a big ask. It's Myra that concerns me.'

'Oh?'

'She . . .' I hesitate.

'I won't tell Daisy or Henry,' he says gently. 'What's going on?'

The pressure of caring for Myra feels huge, and if I don't talk to someone about the situation, I could risk damaging not just her but myself too. I relent and share with him what happened, as well as my concerns about whether she might be depressed, gently skirting around the parts that would require me telling him about my own mental health.

'What do I do?' I say desperately. 'Do I believe her? Or stop her going out? And she still hasn't really talked about what happened to her in London. Is it teenage shenanigans or something more serious?' It's a relief to get it all out.

'It sounds like there are a few things going on here,' he replies. 'The mental health stuff – look, I know she's had a difficult time of it. But you aren't a healthcare professional, and it doesn't sound like it's at the point where she needs medical supervision.'

'But she ended up in hospital, Hugo.'

'Yes, that was bad. Really bad. But we don't know if it's connected to the drinking. I mean, it would be different if she'd just been drinking alone but it sounded like she was with a group of friends. And you've already voiced your concerns to Daisy.'

'About her refusing to get up for most of the day. Not about her coming home late the other night.'

'I wouldn't tell them. If she was in danger, then yes, but it sounds like a genuine mistake.'

'So I just pretend it didn't happen?'

'I think you need to talk to Myra and level with her. You're not her parent but that's a good thing. It means you can be honest with her, and demand the same honesty in return. She's a clever girl, who picks up on a lot more than her parents think. I would try having a conversation with her and see where that gets you. And if it doesn't work out, then you can tell Daisy and Henry and they can find another solution. It's not solely on you to figure it out.'

He's right, but I'm still not convinced she'll listen. 'What if she ignores me and does what she wants?'

'The best advice I can give you is something I heard from a teacher friend of mine. He said that even if a child is behaving like a delinquent, if they genuinely think you have their best interests at heart, that's what will get them onside.'

I feel a pang of guilt because I do want what's best for Myra, especially if I can somehow make a difference to her life. But I am also being paid to be here.

'Padma?'

'It's just . . . I feel bad that Daisy's paying me to do this.'

Although Hugo has been a paragon of patience so far, he lets out a frustrated groan. 'But you care about Myra,' he says. 'You're not just doing this because they are paying you – that side of it is pure pragmatism. They would have paid over the odds for her to go to some camp, and this way it means they actually save money. I don't think it would be fair on anyone to do this without some compensation.'

'Yes, but you wouldn't charge for babysitting, would you?'

'No,' he says slowly, 'but babysitting is a few hours at best. This is twenty-four-seven, cooking, cleaning, making sure she's fine. In what world would it be okay to ask someone to do that for free?' He's got a point, but I suspect Myra wouldn't see it that way if she found out.

I sigh. 'Okay. I'll let you know how it goes.' I feel relieved to have spoken to him about it.

'If you ever need me, I'm just a phone call away, okay?'

'Okay,' I say, feeling warm and comforted until guilt catches in my throat. Shouldn't it be Wallace who's a phone call away?

*

I head straight to the outdoor deck because I'm not ready to deal with whatever awaits me in the house. I want to turn over Hugo's words and feel newly reassured by them. Although the deck needs re-varnishing (a Myra task), as well as new furniture, cushions and blankets, it is already a comfortable suntrap. I expect her still to be in her room, so it's a shock when I find her sitting out there in her pyjamas.

When I sit next to her, her body stiffens, as if she's waiting for me to shout, yell, say something unkind. Although the residual anger is there in both of us, I remember Hugo's words. She is difficult and prickly but I want more than anything for her to be happy and well. I don't want her to go through the same things Daisy and I went through, and that means I need to be the bigger person. We've only been together for a week, but it has felt longer.

'Look, I know you're sorry about the other night,' I say, dusting off a chair and sitting down. 'Do you want to talk about it? Now's the time if so.'

Her silence is infuriating but I try and remain calm. Rather than interpreting it as her being wilfully rude, maybe she doesn't know how to meet a person in the middle. But I'm the adult, and I do.

'I find the silent treatment really tough,' I say, dropping my tone to something softer. 'I once had a boyfriend who did it, and it was . . . horrible. So, I can't do five more weeks of this, and I can't imagine you're having fun either. I'm not saying this angrily or as an ultimatum – but would you like to go home? I don't want to make you do anything you don't want to do, and you should have a say.' Part of me quietly hopes she'll say yes.

She looks up and her face holds less anger than before. Maybe because I asked her what she wanted, rather than telling her.

'Like that's an option,' she says gloomily.

'It's always an option. You have choices – you're not a prisoner.'

'Yeah, right. My parents sent me here. I don't know that they'll be that keen to have me back. No one wants me.'

'They sent you here because they think it's the best thing for you, not because they're trying to get rid of you.'

'And what about you? You obviously don't want me here.' She looks at me sideways to gauge my reaction.

'What – you think I came to Harkness for the sea air? I'm here because I'm trying to help you. Not that you're making it easy.'

She squints at me and says: 'Why *are* you doing this though? I mean, we're not exactly close. I hardly ever see you, and now this grand gesture. Don't you have a job?'

This is a dangerous question, given that Daisy and Henry

are paying me to be here. But I feel less guilty after talking to Hugo and acknowledging that I genuinely do want to help Myra because she's my niece and I love her. She needs me even if she doesn't think she does. Telling her the truth would change things completely and jeopardise her journey.

But I need to give her some explanation. 'I don't have a job – I've been out of work for a while. I got fired and the guy who fired me stole my work. It's been tough.' I hold my breath, waiting for her to laugh or make fun of me, but she doesn't. The silence feels unbearable. She continues to stare ahead as if I'm a mirage, and if she waits it out, I'll disappear. She needs more. An apology.

'For what it's worth, I'm sorry for assuming that you'd been drinking.'

'I hadn't,' she says reproachfully.

'I know. But look, we haven't had a chance to chat properly and you've just been told to go on this trip with me. I can't imagine that's easy. Feeling like you have no control over what happens to you. But, Myra, this is new for me too. And you scared the shit out of all of us when you ended up in hospital. I do think we need to talk about that.'

'I don't want to.'

'We don't have to talk about *all* of it, but I just want to make sure you're okay.'

'And what if I say no?' she says. 'What if I say I feel awful all the fucking time?'

'Well,' I answer slowly, 'I already know that. I don't think people stay in bed all day if they're feeling good. But I do know that talking about it might help.'

'I have a therapist for that,' she says with a mirthless laugh. 'Who I'm now going to be seeing twice a week apparently because she's told Mum and Dad that I could do with the extra sessions, and they were only too happy to agree.'

'Well, therapy can be great, and you're lucky to be able to have it. A lot of people can't afford it. In my experience, it does work.'

She looks at me curiously. 'What did *you* have therapy for?' If she was an adult, I would say it's rude to ask. But she's still a child, and I can't hold her curiosity against her. The truth lies somewhere in my chest, and a rising sense of nausea tries to stop it from coming out. But I pull it through anyway, and the sensation is like dragging the softest part of myself through barbed wire.

'Well, firstly, it's not appropriate to ask someone why they had therapy – just for future reference. But . . . I had depression. Have depression,' I correct myself. I can't believe I am telling her something I haven't even told Daisy yet.

She looks at me with something new in her eyes. Maybe recognition, maybe a reconfiguring: no longer seeing me as just an extension of her mother. 'I didn't know that.'

'I haven't told your mother,' I say, hoping she will understand the unspoken thing between us. That this is something I am trusting her with, and that if she wants to trust me back, I will carefully respect it. Something in her shifts, her gaze being drawn back out to the sea as she digests this piece of information. We both sit there, looking out at the incoming tide, the golden sand slowly turning to burnt caramel as the water pulls in.

'Let's go for a walk,' I say after a while, feeling the need to be close to the shoreline. She shakes her head.

'It's either that or I'm going to tell your mother you want to video-call her right now.'

'You're horrible,' Myra says, but with the ghost of a smile

that reassures me things are moving in the right direction. That something has settled between us.

'I know.'

'Is that what you're wearing?' she says, looking at my Indian uncle-style shorts and crumpled T-shirt.

'You're horrible.'

'I know,' she says.

*

'Have you got the sunscreen?' Myra yells before we head out, just as the doorbell rings. I've endured a lecture about how important SPF is. How does this child know so much about skincare?

Standing outside the door is a committee. Selena is carrying a basket of knobbly carrots, oat milk and fresh bread, with an apologetic expression on her face. She looks radiant in a deep red sundress with a full skirt, dotted in little white flower patterns. I feel embarrassed by my shorts and T-shirt. Standing next to her is Barbara, who has clearly come straight from tennis, judging by the visor and white pleated skirt.

Next to Barbara is a short man in his sixties in an immaculate salmon-pink suit. He introduces himself as Elliot Bentley, 'secretary and tourist relations at the town council', and indicates Yvonne Bentley, 'head of the PTA'. Yvonne has breasts like enormous bao buns, a nondescript bob, and her mouth is pulled into a frown. It's unclear whether they are brother and sister, or husband and wife.

'Am I in trouble?' I laugh.

'We wanted to give you a proper welcome,' Barbara says, looking my outfit up and down. She introduces everyone to me.

'We want you to know that we welcome all kinds of people in Harkness,' Elliot says with a nervous, sweaty smile, which makes me wonder what incident happened here previously to necessitate this intense, strained welcome party. 'And I support Black Lives Matter, of course.'

Selena rolls her eyes and I try not to laugh.

'Right, well, this is so kind of you,' I say, 'but we were just about to head out.'

'Auntie?' Myra comes to the door dressed in a short purple slip dress, fingerless gloves, and has swapped her beloved Chloé boots for a pair of Nike trainers. It's wonderful to see her in something other than pyjamas. She realises too late that there are people at the door and she will have to say hello.

Yvonne waves at Myra standing behind me. Myra does a half-hearted wave back. 'Well, Myra,' she says, 'if you ever feel like helping out with the Youth Volunteer Group, we are always looking for people to clear rubbish off the beach. Our daughter Caitlin is head of the initiative, I'm sure she'll make you feel welcome.' There was that word again. Three welcomes in the space of five minutes.

'Although,' says Elliot, tucking his thumbs into his tan belt and trying to peer sidelong around the door and into the house, 'I imagine you've got your hands full clearing out all the rubbish in this dump! Rosemary really let things go. Didn't I say she'd let things go, Yvonne?'

'You did,' Yvonne says. 'I don't suppose you know if Hugo is planning to sell at all?' She looks hungrily at the house.

'I don't, I'm afraid. But I can ask him?'

Yvonne, Elliot and Barbara share a look. 'We actually have a town meeting coming up,' says Elliot, 'and as someone who owns property in Harkness it would be pertinent for Hugo to attend. I assume you've read the *Guardian* article?' On his sweaty brow he uses a florid purple handkerchief that he pulls out of his suit pocket like a nervous magician.

'We've also got this blasted scooter problem – teenagers these days,' says Yvonne. 'There's a gang of them. They ride up and down the bay – it's a complete menace.' She pauses and looks at Myra with fresh eyes. Assessing her clothes properly, and realising she looks like one of the bad kids in a PG film who smoke behind bike sheds. 'You don't have a scooter, do you?'

'No,' Myra says brightly, 'but it sounds like fun.'

Yvonne is so outraged her skin colour rises to match the pink tones of Elliot's suit.

I sense the need to smooth things over. 'There is no scooter. She's just joking. I will ask Hugo about the meeting.'

Barbara and Yvonne look at Myra with the suspicion reserved for a shoplifter wearing a puffa jacket. As if it's not a matter of *if* she will cause trouble, but when.

'If you haven't read the article,' Elliot continues as if the last few minutes haven't happened, 'I have a laminated copy back in the town hall.' They all look expectantly at me until I verbally confirm that, yes, I have read the article and what a wonderful article it was.

As the rest of them say their goodbyes and troop down the driveway, Selena lingers behind and says apologetically: 'I'm sorry. It was just going to be me and then they ambushed me when they heard I was walking up here.'

'It's okay. At least they're being friendly.'

She raises an eyebrow. 'If that's your definition of friendly . . .'

'Try growing up in 1990s Rochester. This lot aren't too bad. Even if they are hovering over the house like vultures.'

As Selena turns to go, she says: 'Esme tells me you cook?'

'Wow – news really does travel fast here, doesn't it?' I say, dislodging the mud on my trainers by banging them against the wall.

She shrugs, stuffing her hands into the pockets of her dress. 'You two are the most exciting new arrivals at the moment. But don't worry, there's a Nando's opening up in the neighbouring town so your fifteen minutes of fame will be over soon enough.

'We should cook together sometime maybe?' she says, handing me the basket. 'I can make you some Black Cake.'

'What's that?'

'Let's just say it involves cake, my grandma's recipe, and so much rum I wouldn't advise driving home afterwards.'

I laugh. Selena and I may come from different countries, but we both have dishes that make us feel safe, dishes we make as acts of love, and dishes we want to recreate so that for a moment our ancestors might come into the room.

*

Exploration of Harkness's coves requires common sense and patience, advises the local walking guide. Common sense not to become stuck as the tide rises, and patience when it comes to finding the trails that lead down to them. We venture out into the woodland and take a sharp right along a track that is meant to take us over and around the bay. As someone who has the average outdoor skills of a South Asian person (that is, none), I approach our excursion with caution and slowness.

As we walk, we keep the sea to our right. The sun is already high in the sky as it climbs up into the hottest part of the day.

Wild raspberries come into view growing over the fence, tiny red globes hanging in thick clusters. I pick a ripe one, blow on it in a half-hearted attempt to clean it off, and pop it into my mouth.

'Ew,' Myra says.

'What? They are delicious.'

'Yeah, but it's just come straight from a bush.'

'Where do you think they normally come from?'

'Waitrose?'

It's impossible not to laugh, no matter how irritated we've been with each other. Eventually we are both bent over, with tears in our eyes. When we resume our walk, I get up the courage to suggest, 'Can we talk about what happened?'

She looks quietly ahead, as if she wants to switch elements and unfurl fins, diving further and further into the deep.

'Myra, I swear I won't tell your mother.'

'There's not much to tell,' she says, throwing up her hands. 'I went out with some mates, drinking in the park. I had too much, and that's it. I don't know why everyone is making such a big deal. Blaming me.'

Despite her dismissive tone, her body curls in on itself as she walks, as if she is holding the truth close to her chest. I can feel her thoughts spiralling inwards.

'Okay, but your mates didn't end up in hospital. You did. That's not very common, is it?'

'I would have been fine. They landed me in it by dropping me off at home. If I'd just been left to sleep it off it would have been okay, and there would have been none of this . . . shit,' she says, gesturing at the pastoral scene of grass-covered hilltops.

'Do you really think that? That you would have been okay?'

Looking at her face, I know she doesn't think so. Part of

her looks scared at what the outcome might have been; the rest is bravado. 'Because you had a seizure,' I continue gently. 'And if your mother hadn't been home when she was, it could have been really serious. You know that, right?'

Her eyes strain red with the effort of trying not to cry. I don't need to press any further. The doctors have told her all of this.

'I know it must have been tough, to know your friends left you like that.' I hadn't forgotten the outsized reaction that day in the service station when she dropped her phone.

'I don't want to talk about it,' she says, coming to a stop.

'Okay,' I say, trying a different tack. 'Do you feel you've been dumped here?' Her immediate response when asked something she's uncomfortable with, I realise, is not to react at all. Almost to torture the other person with a non-reaction. But I can see her wrestling whether to have a conversation or to be silent. She settles for something in between and nods almost imperceptibly.

It makes sense now. She thinks she's been shipped off because she's hard work, not as a protective measure. 'I get it,' I say. 'But you must know your parents suggested this because they thought it was the best thing for you. There's no way they would have done it otherwise.'

'Oh, yeah?' she says bitterly. 'They care more about work than they do about me.'

'I don't think that's the case at all. I think they work hard so you can have the life you have.'

'And what life is that?' she says, with such disgust. She doesn't know how lucky she is.

'You have a life, believe me,' I say, trying to keep the rising anger at her ingratitude from my voice.

Where I live, we know the tough mathematics most families face, the decisions they make as to which child they can send to university. Who has to do weekend jobs. Who has to go to the food bank. Who showers at work because the electricity bills are too high at home.

'I don't want to sound like I'm lecturing you, but drinking at your age isn't an okay thing to do. Let alone allowing it to get to the point where you need medical help. You know that, right?'

'What, and you never did it as a teenager?'

'Actually,' I say, 'no.' There's something about witnessing problem drinking that nullifies the hedonistic enjoyment that alcohol appears to promise. Although I drink as an adult, when I was Myra's age, the odour of it on a person's breath, the drunken arguments that would never happen sober, the sense that my mind was floating away from the stem, was not appealing.

'Why do you do it?' I ask. 'Drink? Even though you know you're not supposed to?'

She takes her time deciding what to say and how to say it. 'I mean, everyone does,' she says at last. 'Or they micro-dose. Or take edibles.' It's shocking how casual her tone is. I know there is an enormous disparity between what parents *think* their kids are getting up to and the things they are *actually* doing, but Myra looks like a kid. Who's telling me that she regularly drinks – and probably takes drugs – as if she's talking about Swimming Club.

'Okay,' I say, struggling to keep the shock and judgement from my voice. 'But *why* do you do it?'

She stops for a moment and heaves a sigh that feels heavy,

too heavy for a summer's day. We should be out there getting lost in a kayak or terrorising Yvonne with a scooter – not having a therapy session halfway up a hill. 'I don't know,' she says. 'Maybe because my friends do it. Maybe because when I do it, I feel like I'm a different person. And sometimes, that's a relief.'

She looks at the ground, her long lashes shielding whatever truth she holds in her eyes. I want to hug her, hold her, and tell her she is perfect as she is. But I also know for it to count, she has to realise that herself. Whatever happens from now on, Myra needs something that will help her build a sense of self-worth. Because right now, what little she has of it is hidden behind bravado, sarcasm and caustic remarks.

'I think most people wish they could sometimes escape themselves,' I say.

'What, even grown-ups?' She sounds surprised, and I remember that for all her world-weary statements she is still a child.

'Especially grown-ups,' I say with a wry smile.

'But you get to do whatever you want.'

'Exactly.'

'I don't understand?'

'You get to do whatever you want, and yet somehow, you wake up and realise you made the wrong decisions. Or perhaps other people don't agree with your decisions and decide they want to give you an ultimatum and go on a break. And you realise you have no one else to blame but yourself.'

'Do you miss being my age, then?'

'Sadly not,' I say. 'We had very different childhoods. That's what I mean when I say you might not realise how lucky you are.'

She pauses, as if it's the first time she's considered her life might not be as bad as she thinks it is. Her face in repose is so much like my mother's that it makes me think about what it must have been like for my sister that day in the ambulance with Myra.

'Do you know how your grandmother died, Myra?' I ask. She shakes her head.

I don't need to tell her all of it, but maybe enough for her to understand why we are holding on to her so tightly.

'She died at home,' I say, feeling the chill the memory still carries. The soft glow of lights coming on in the neighbours' houses like curious fireflies gathering around the commotion. 'Your mother had to call the ambulance.' Dhara-before-she-became-Daisy had just turned seventeen. Our neighbour Mrs Martinson, although she had gazed disapprovingly over the fence at us over the years because of the unkempt garden, the endless bottles in the recycling, held Dhara's hand tightly.

I had just come back from a friend's house and realised this was not happening to a neighbour, this was happening to us. But whoever was being placed with reverent care in the ambulance, it was not Mum. It was just an empty chrysalis – she was somewhere else, becoming something else entirely. The pink in her cheeks had been replaced with delicate blue. It felt like a scene from a movie, our faces bathed in the flickering lights from the ambulance. But the warmth of my sister's body, as I held her tight and safe in my arms, told me this was real.

Sudden cardiac death, the doctor would tell us later. Mum's drinking had always been heavy, and we came from a family with a high risk of heart failure. I'd known this was likely, though nothing had prepared me for the reality. I was angry.

So angry. With Mum for leaving us. For not trying harder. For making me play the part she should have done, and that I would now be stuck with. I was angry at the physical pain that bloomed in my chest at the thought of never seeing her again. At the shame and guilt of knowing that something heavy had been lifted from me.

'Do you get why, even if you are okay now, it may have been hard for your mother?' I say gently. And there, for the first time since we've arrived, I see understanding written on Myra's face.

*

After a while, an unremarkable dirt track cuts away to a dramatic viewpoint of the curve of the bay, grassy cliffs marking the last line before the vast expanse of water, a bowl of light holding every ounce the sun pours in. In the distance a military ship emerges from the white heat haze. I spot a safe nook cut into the cliffside halfway down, and perch against it, feeling the earth against my back. I motion to Myra, who shakes her head.

'You live in a city with rats and people carrying machetes – and a grassy knoll is too scary?'

I turn back to the view and close my eyes under the sun. I think this is what being peaceful feels like. No moment but this moment. Feeling as if I could come apart in pieces, disassemble into sea spray. A soft thump beside me tells me she has sat down.

When I open my eyes, she's watching the crows overhead soar and zip back into their nests hidden in the rock face. One of them is caught in a strong headwind and is almost unable to move from the spot, suspended in mid-air. Maybe it's seeing the crows out here and not in their usual London habitat, pecking at unmentionable things in the street. Maybe it's that even a crow is beautiful when caught between the air, light and water, feathers outstretched in perfect symmetry, a creature whose essence is the definition of freedom, observed so closely.

'What are you thinking about?' I ask her, willing to be content with whatever answer she gives.

She looks at the birds overhead. We stay like that for a while, observing the line between life and death floating above us. And she says in a voice that sounds far older than her fifteen years: 'I wonder what it feels like to be that free.'

8

Over the second week, we settle into something of a routine. A treaty is hashed out at the dining table, which finally became visible after we cleared off stacks of sticky tablemats, boxes of nails and picture hooks, and Rosemary's favourite things – pieces upon pieces of paper. 'What's a Woolworths?' Myra said as she peered at a yellowing receipt.

We started with the matter of Daisy's list, which was actually useful because we were united in agreeing it was ridiculous. 'It reads like the itinerary from a bootcamp crossed with a ladies' finishing school,' I said. Myra looked at me warily as if she couldn't quite believe I would disobey Daisy, and this must be a trap. But the look disappeared over time. Especially when she realised she could tell me things and I wouldn't tell her mother. That I hadn't told Daisy about the smoking.

In the midst of this fragile peace, we agreed the following. Myra would be responsible for overhauling and repairing the garden. That included painting the fences, weeding and planting. For extra credit, I said, she could also clear out and reorganise the garden shed.

'I don't know anything about gardens,' she complained.

'I can help you,' I replied. 'And so can Uncle YouTube.

Also, it's either that or you help me repaint the inside of the house. You'll have to sugar-soap the walls, sandpaper the skirting boards and help me strip the wallpaper. Which is it to be?'

'They both sound shit,' she said, adding quickly when she saw my expression, 'But I'll take the garden.'

We both needed a routine, so Myra agreed to be out of bed by 9 a.m. on weekdays, but weekends were her own to do with as she wished. General house rules seemed like a good idea too. After once sharing with a particularly bad roommate who never washed up, played loud EDM while doing burpees in their room, and used some kind of oatmeal scrub in the shower that stuck to the tiles like glue, I'd decided it was always best to discuss co-habitation rules.

'Right,' I said using the back of a Life Alert letter to make a list. 'We need a list of rules, music and TV preferences, and no-nos to ensure harmony.'

'Rules?' Myra scoffed.

'I don't mean rules like "lights out at nine p.m.". It's more to make sure that if something irritates you, then I'm aware of it and vice versa. The rules apply to me as much as they do to you. This way we minimise the opportunities to get pissed off at one another and I won't smother you with a pillow.'

She stared at me with her big green eyes before going back to doodling on the back of a yellowing receipt. 'You're nothing like Mum, you know.'

'Is that a compliment or an insult?' I said, pen hovering. She didn't answer.

The list included the washing-up (not to be left overnight), not touching each other's respective yogurts, chocolate and crisps, cleaning the bathtub of hair, and not shoving sweet wrappers down the sides of the sofa. TV overlaps included *Gilmore Girls, The Umbrella Academy* and anything with Kevin Hart and/or The Rock. Film genre overlaps included sci-fi, fantasy, romantic comedies that didn't reduce the female character to wanting to get married, and crime. Music overlaps were much easier because we based it around what was banned: Justin Bieber, ABBA and the Beatles.

It was by no means a perfect system. Although Myra had agreed to work in the garden, she would take ages to get outside, like an old car that needed a lot of coaxing before the engine finally spluttered into life. Her morning routine consisted of eating several bowls of Coco Pops, dribbling chocolate milk down her front while watching the Horror Channel. When her therapy session came around, I excused myself to go for a walk. I knew therapy could be galvanising, but it could also be intense and upsetting. Afterwards, I'd sometimes felt like a melon with the insides scooped out and this was how Myra seemed when I found her, lying on top of her bed, watching anime on her laptop. I didn't ask her how it went. I simply made her a cup of tea the way she liked it – with a lot of milk – put some biscuits on a plate and took them up to her room.

On some days Greg would knock for her.

Since the incident where Myra had almost disappeared, he had returned to ask if she could 'come out'. 'She can't,' I said abruptly, even though I admired his bravery in returning, 'but you can come in.'

She made him lug some bags of compost, after they'd watched TikToks for a bit. Then Greg asked if he could show Myra around the town. When I looked sceptically at him, he said: 'I'm in the Scouts – we won't get lost. And my phone is charged.'

'That was one time,' Myra hissed at me. But as promised, he dropped her back in time for dinner. Since then, Greg had been a regular fixture at the house. I didn't mind him because he was tidy and didn't smell of Boy – a pungent mix of armpits, sweat and hormones.

*

Daisy had yelled at both of us for not replying to her messages, so once a day Myra would send a text, a photo or have a video call with her. Her mother would peer at the screen and ask her how she was sleeping, was she eating properly, had she made any friends and who were they?

'I'm running out of things to say,' Myra moaned.

'Don't look at me,' I replied. I was not the expert in talking to Daisy.

At the beginning, I tried to convince Myra to join me for a daily walk and maybe a swim. 'I don't swim,' she said.

'You can't swim or you don't want to swim?'

'Both,' she said tersely.

I didn't want to force Myra to spend time with me, but one thing I felt strongly about was that we had to eat dinner together. It was the one time when we could talk and I could properly assess her mood.

I would prepare most of our food from scratch, and because our breakfast and lunches were cereals, eggs and sandwiches, dinner was often Indian food – marinated lamb chops, paneer skewers, fresh fried fish and buttery yellow dal. Everyday staples I'd make at home for Wallace and myself. The first time she'd wrinkled her nose at a meal before trying it, I was filled with such outrage, I wanted to frisbee her plate out of the window. How did parents do this? But eventually she would try it and realise she rather liked it.

One day she came down while I was preparing dinner – I'd had a craving for appams. They were gluten-free and vegetarian, and the plan was if they came out well, I might take some down to Selena as a gift. 'What's that?' Myra asked.

I told her appams were pancakes made from fluffy rice flour and coconut milk, and originated from Kerala, the state next to the place we came from. I told her about Kerala's back-waters and coconut trees. I said I'd always wanted to visit, and did she know that the author Arundhati Roy, who wrote *The God of Small Things*, came from there? I ladled the batter into a wok and she looked mesmerised as it bubbled and cooked, and came out perfectly round.

'You love doing this, don't you?' she asked.

I nodded, happy that I was able to share with her a part of my life that gave me so much joy. 'Would you like to make one?' I asked. She looked hesitant but I encouraged her to try it.

Even though Myra ladled in the mixture too slowly and created one that looked sad and floppy, her eyes shone brightly with the achievement. While she ate, I asked her about the kind of things she liked to eat, the flavours she preferred, and wound those into our meals. Things our mother never did with us because to her food was food. *You should be grateful to have it at all*, she'd have said.

When I felt confident Myra was happy enough starting her mornings by herself, and was not just putting on an act, I started to adopt my own routine. I would head out in the early morning into town, sometimes to pick up ingredients for lunch, mostly to walk along the bay and allow the water and light to fill me with a sense of limitless quiet.

*

I called Daisy later that week, after Myra asked me, 'What on earth are you doing?' when she saw me oiling my hair after returning from a walk.

'I asked her if she wanted me to do hers for her and she actually said *ew*. Do you not oil her hair?' I asked Daisy in surprise.

'I can't do everything, Padma!' she replied defensively. 'And besides, she prefers to use a hair mask.'

'Yes, but oiling isn't just about moisturising your hair. It might be a nice thing for you to show her?'

Daisy snorts. 'I can just imagine the look on Henry's face when he sees an oil stain on his antique Versailles armchair!'

'Maybe get a chair that doesn't cost thousands of pounds? What if I buy him a beanbag? That way if she gets something on it, we can just turn it over to a different side.' I am joking but Daisy isn't amused.

'Don't you dare,' she says.

'I'm just saying – it wouldn't be the worst thing if Myra learned more about our culture. She didn't even know what Sanskrit was.'

Daisy hollowing out her Indian heritage and replacing it with whiteness is not a new thing. You see them, the people with truncated names like Bob and Dee, who are the only bit of colour in their friendship groups, who don't keep jars of ginger-garlic puree in their fridge, who only wipe their bottoms with paper. But this is probably why I've never bonded with Henry. I blame him for Daisy's reinvention of herself. Even if he never demanded it, he inspired it. Daisy hasn't just changed her name, she has remodelled her entire culture. There is no statue of Ganesh near the hallway. Italian herbs predominate in her spice rack, and there is no sign of a spice dabba. She allows her child to say the word 'fuck' *and* to sit on the bed in her outside clothes. She buys Mexican mangoes, not sweet-as-sin Alphonsos.

But this thing about the oil – it is one of the worst failings. No matter what my feelings towards my mother, the softest memories I have of her are of the moments when she would rest on the sofa and make me sit in front of her. *Catchphrase* or *Pride and Prejudice* (the proper one, starring Colin Firth) would be on the television. She'd heat the plastic bottle of coconut oil in a pan of water. Tap the bottom and test the temperature of the oil on her hand. Run her hands through my hair, methodically part it again and again, and massage oil into my scalp. One of the most tender, delicate and time-honoured traditions a mother could carry out for her daughter or a sister perform for her sister. A precious, generous act of care and trust carried down through the generations.

'Well, you seem to have parenting all figured out, don't you?' Daisy said in a clipped tone. 'I already feel guilty enough for sending her away, but this is great. The icing on the cake.'

'Daisy . . . I didn't mean to make you feel bad,' I said, trying to mollify her. 'I'm just surprised she doesn't know a few things about our culture, that's all. I can show her. Or not, if you don't want me to.'

She sighed, as if this conversation had already taken up too much of her time. 'You can show her. I mean, good luck trying to get her to do it.'

'Then maybe I will,' I said defiantly, emboldened by Myra's interest in my cooking.

*

As if Daisy's words carried a curse, the wheels started to fall off Myra's routine slightly by the end of the second week. The 9 a.m. wake-up times turned into 10 a.m., which slid into just before 11 a.m. After a few days of this, I started to cajole her into a morning walk. We would mostly follow clearly marked trails along the edge of the cliff. Catch glimpses of the sea rushing in to fill the spaces in the rocks below, curls of white foam forming a long necklace of horseshoes as they met the curving mouths of the caves.

Although Myra did not like getting wet or being wet, I would sometimes bribe her into walking down to the shore and letting the sea touch her feet. She'd always yell as the cold water bit, but would quieten down eventually. Something about being the conducting rod between two elements rooted us in this time, in this place. I'd feel the enormity of Myra's thoughts being transmitted into the sky, and mine starting to settle. By the time we returned home, I'd head out again to run chores or go into town, and she was allowed to watch some TV before heading out into the garden to finish her list of tasks.

Although life felt more peaceful than before, I still started every day with thoughts of Wallace. I would lie in bed with one eye cracked open, scouring Instagram for signs of what he had been up to. Once, when I couldn't find anything, I lowered myself to checking his LinkedIn, but he hadn't posted anything since 2019.

I still felt love and yearning, but in the silent chasm between us, resentment was starting to appear. I wanted to share my achievements around the house – such as the first time I fixed a leaky tap – or a photo of a beautiful sunset, and every time I reached for my phone and saw his last voice note, the little squiggles like the beats of a heart, I remembered the words they contained.

The small child in me just wished that nothing could have changed between us. Why did he have to want kids? Why couldn't we just continue as we were?

But even as those questions arose, I realised the answer I had before no longer fitted. I couldn't go back to how things were, and I knew that this enforced break he'd asked for wasn't fair. A break can be a break from each other, but if we weren't talking or trying to work through things together, I struggled to see how we weren't just postponing the inevitable.

I needed someone to chat to about all of this. Texting Delilah and Rekha wasn't the same. As much as I loved them both, Delilah would often reply hastily with an emoji or 'lol', while Rekha would use it as an opportunity to dump a fresh load of work drama on me. To fill the void, I started dropping into Selena's for coffee and it had become an everyday habit.

When she asked me about my relationship status, I told her it was complicated. 'He wants children, I don't,' I said. 'And now we're on a break, and he's given me an ultimatum.' She didn't ask me why I didn't want them, which I appreciated.

'Ultimatums are tough,' she said. 'They make you feel as if the other person is attacking you, when really they are just desperately trying to hold on.' I'd never thought about it like that before. And deep down, I believed that because Wallace knew I didn't want a baby, he was trying to expedite the end of our relationship. 'What about you?' I asked. 'How's your love life going?'

'Try using dating apps as a dark-skinned brown woman in coastal Kent,' she said. 'Sure, I've had a few one-night stands, some hot and salty sex with visitors passing through, but nothing substantial.'

I felt better after seeing Selena, and with the absence of my usual support system, realised I needed someone to confide in. It wasn't just Wallace stuff. I'd had a real breakthrough with Myra but I was still finding the caretaking exhausting. I naively thought if I talked to her as if she was an adult, she'd follow the routine I'd set for her because we'd agreed it was in her best interests.

But I would still have to pick up her plates and cups that lay around the house, ask her to do the washing-up, and the garden was excruciatingly slow progress. If I asked her to do something more than once, she'd grow monosyllabic. It was getting to the point where I didn't know how to communicate with her any more.

I tested the waters of my friendship with Selena by telling her a bit about Myra and why we were here. It was a great relief when she listened without judgement, and agreed that there might be something more going on beyond regular teenage attitude.

'It's hard to say whether it's to do with mental health,' she said, 'not that I'm saying it isn't. But I remember the thing I found hardest at her age was that I felt I wasn't listened to. By anyone.'

Her expression looked faraway and sad. 'But from everything you've told me, there are things in place to offer her support. Her parents don't sound like the type to be hands off, and she's talking to the therapist. You can't fix her. She's got to come to it herself.'

I was mortified. 'Is that what it sounds like I'm doing? Trying to fix her?'

'Well, no,' Selena said, choosing her words carefully. 'But you've given her this list of chores, and when she doesn't do everything on it, you get worried or upset or frustrated she isn't taking things seriously. It doesn't sound all that different from the list your sister gave her.'

'So what should I do?'

'Maybe ease off if she doesn't get everything done. But not so much that she takes the piss. Offer to help her with things if she's struggling. I mean – could you honestly say you wanted to do gardening at fifteen?'

I laughed. 'I hated gardening.'

'Well, there you go,' she said, flicking a tea towel at me.

Talking to Selena gave me reassurance and a sense of perspective but it wasn't enough. After Hugo sent me a message asking how everything was going, I'd started giving him little updates. Given that he was Myra's godfather I felt it was okay, and he would message me back the same day. Mainly, I told him about how Myra was doing: funny little things she might say in a day like, 'What's a VHS?' Or I'd take pictures of things I saw around town – like the butcher's sign proclaiming 'Get your big sausage!' and Esme's bindi-wearing gnome.

When I told him about my daily walks, he asked for pictures, and so slowly I started sending these too. One morning, I had woken up just before sunrise to see the turning-point between night and dawn. I saw a note from Myra on the counter: *Dear tyrant (or is that tyr-aunt?!!), I worked until late last night so if it's okay I'd like to sleep in.*

It made me smile, because we had come a long way since our drive here, and I carried that smile to the top of the cliff, where I watched the dark blues of night soften into light – a pink glow that began at the horizon and expanded to stretch across the sky. It felt, for the first time in a while, as if things were in balance. It made no sense given that beyond Myra, nothing in my life had changed. But something felt different, and watching the brief moment when the moon and the sun were both held in the palm of the sky, my heart almost couldn't contain it all.

I wish I was there, Hugo had written in response to the photo I sent him, and I instantly felt a sharp bite of guilt. It felt too intimate, too close to the edge of something inappropriate. I should have been sending these messages to Wallace, not him. I went silent for a day or two, and then texted him something jokey like: **Myra has just told me she likes Ready Salted crisps. Who actually likes them? If you say you do, we cannot be friends.**

When he messaged back with a picture of Tyrrell's Ready Salted in his desk drawer, asking what my favourite flavour was, I'd replied: **Nik Nak's Nice and Spicy. Like any respectable Indian.** He'd replied with: **My humble apologies, I didn't realise India had a national crisp.**

*

Despite my conversation with Selena, I couldn't stop worrying that Myra was letting things slide. I bribed her into getting a set amount of work done in the garden with the promise of unlimited snacks and a movie at the local cinema. She'd been in a strange mood at dinner and I felt being outdoors the next morning would be good for her. She came in after a couple of hours, looking suspiciously immaculate, while Greg trailed behind her like a faithful Igor, covered in mud and leaves.

He seemed happy enough. It was clear after the first day he'd come over that he would put up with any number of commands because he was happiest when in her orbit. As her skin grew darker in the sun, her green eyes remained the colour of new leaves and the contrast between the two of them, along with her long limbs, made her beauty almost otherworldly. Unfortunately for Greg, the adoration was clearly not mutual.

I felt sorry for him but he made my life easier. Unlike other teenage boys, he didn't seem to be a creep, and he didn't do stupid things like wheelieing into oncoming traffic or supergluing his extremities to the railings along the seafront. After meeting his mother, Sarah Margaret, it was evident why. She'd obviously raised him with an unswerving reverence for women, and as a single mother simply didn't have the time to deal with a child who was a menace. Sarah Margaret worked as a cleaner all over Harkness and was the best in the whole county, according to Greg. When she turned up to help me wash the curtains and sugar-soap the walls, it was clear she'd worked hard all her life. Her skin was red and weathered, and she had thick, sturdy forearms.

Sarah Margaret didn't talk much as she worked, but what little I gathered was that her love for Greg was a fierce thing. 'He gets bullied,' she said, 'and that sweet boy never fights back. Except when someone says something about me.' At that, she smiled. 'He once lamped someone who made fun of him for being raised by a single mum.'

Usually we only realise the sacrifices of our mothers when we know something of their stories as adults, so for a child to know this in real time added something to his character that I knew would serve him well later in life.

'Looks like you got a lot done,' I say, looking pointedly at Myra.

'Yeah,' she says absently, pouring them both some juice. 'Greg was on clean-up duty while I fixed some of the fences to stop the rabbits getting in.'

'*You* fixed fences?' I say disbelievingly. I don't want to call her out while Greg is still here, not after what happened last time when I accused her of drinking.

'What are *you* doing?' She points at my phone propped up on a makeshift pillar of pots and pans with the screen and video function in full view. 'Nothing,' I say quickly and turn it off.

After bumping into Esme, who yet again asked for my Instagram, it prompted me to finally start taking photos of the food I was cooking and the produce I'd buy in town. I started posting about ingredients, explaining their origin and what dishes they worked in, and how to be versatile with them. Maybe when I had posted enough to establish a following, I could start offering cooking classes to unsuspecting white people, and this could act as my culinary resumé. So far, I had 100 followers, and was convinced fifteen of them were bots in India because they had elaborate names like Ali Kubla Khan and Ram Sita Das, and all their photos looked like they had been taken in the 1970s with the saturation filter cranked up. When I sometimes saw that Wallace had viewed my Stories, it gave me a little rush of dopamine. But it was also terrifying how the small act of seeing someone else observe your life could catalyse into wrongly thinking that they cared about you. I spent a few days smiling to myself because Wallace had thought about me, was involved in my life, until I realised that he hadn't actually messaged or made any attempt to reach out.

When I wasn't thinking about Wallace, I was thinking about food. I'd decided to experiment with my first video after having the idea to make a lasagne with curried ox cheek (and had promised the butcher a sample in exchange for a future discount on meat). However, I hadn't a clue where to start.

'Auntie, give me your phone,' Myra says with her hand on her hip, looking disconcertingly like her mother. I shake my head.

'Fine,' she says, pulling out her own. She taps away and I wonder what exactly it is that she's doing. 'Got it. *Padma Cooks*. What the . . . Are these the photos you've been posting online? For public consumption?'

'How did you . . .'

'It's not rocket science. You have your phone propped up using pots as a makeshift tripod. You haven't the iron stomach for Twitter, I doubt you even have a TikTok account. So, Instagram. All you oldies have it. And you are also the type to call your account the most literal thing. Easy.'

'Imagine if you could use these powers for good instead of evil, Myra,' I say, taken aback.

'The photos are horrible,' she says, frowning. 'Look at the angles. And that one—' She points at my lamb curry. 'That one looks like actual dog shit. And you don't use hashtags.' These words feel harsh, even for her. I don't know if this is bravado for Greg but she's never before shown any inclination to impress him.

'Well then, why don't you help me?' I say hotly. 'If it's so tragic?'

'You may be beyond help,' she shrugs. I turn my back to her because there are some days when I'm able to weather her sharp remarks, but today, when it feels like my very bones are exposed, I can't bear it. I know she had a therapy session yesterday – is that what has prompted this ugliness in her? When I don't turn around or rise to her remark, she hovers uncertainly for a moment, wondering if she has pushed me too far. But she is young and inexperienced, and doesn't know how to comfort a thing when she has crushed it between her hands.

*

After a day that made me feel heavy and alone, I lie on the sofa to watch reruns of *Gilmore Girls*. I have no energy to talk to Myra, and she is old enough to know there is plenty of food in the fridge if she wants to fix something for herself. She has spent the day avoiding me, embarrassed perhaps by her words.

My mind wanders to Wallace and our conversation about children. Even without my own issues, I know definitively after taking care of Myra that there is a motherhood part inside me that is missing, or perhaps never existed.

It's different if it's your own, people say. But is it? If that's true, why are there so many negligent parents? Why was our mother never able to choose us fully, but chose a bottle instead? But even as the thought arises, I know it isn't true. That addiction is never the entirety of a person.

I have memories of lying in my mother's lap when I felt sleepy after a late lunch. Of her taking me swimming.

Hugging and singing to me when my teeth chattered because I'd wanted to stay in the pool as long as possible. Corned beef and mayo sandwiches, which was a punchy move for a Hindu mother.

But the memories of her have diminishing returns. When she was alive, I would lie awake at night worrying about how much she'd had to drink, whether the front door was locked, the hob left on, or if Dhara would accidentally drink the vodka she'd sometimes stash inside water bottles. When Mum died, I would lie awake realising the worry no longer had a home. It opened a different compartment in my grief: all the things I wished had never happened, the things that never did, and the things that now never would. Afterwards, I was surprised by how upset I was. I had spent so long being furious with her that I'd forgotten she was a person. I'd spent so long believing life would be easier without her that I was shocked to find it was harder. Not just because I loved her or missed her. But because I had lost any chance of receiving an apology, or closure around how she'd behaved.

Although I can't bear the burden of bringing a new child into the world, I realise what children represent for so many people. The chance to do things better. A living channel to transfigure the grief that death and trauma have poured into us.

I love Wallace, but I am starting to realise that what he is asking isn't fair. And perhaps Myra isn't the only person feeling exiled.

9

The morning brings rain, sheets of it arriving inland, drumming horizontally against the windows. Although it won't be welcome to everyone, I am glad for the coolness sweeping through the room. For a moment I wonder why my body feels so achy and stiff, until I realise I must have fallen asleep on the sofa.

My phone lights up with a call and I'm too sleepy to realise who it is until her brusque voice jolts me into action. 'Padma,' says Daisy, 'I'm coming to Harkness this weekend. That's all right, isn't it?' A question that isn't a question. In a moment of madness, I wonder what would happen if I say no, and imagine Daisy's eyes bulging in surprise, which makes me laugh.

'Why are you chuckling?' she says.

'No reason.'

'Look,' she continues defensively even though I haven't said no, 'it's been almost three weeks since I've seen Myra and it's the longest I've been apart from her. And after the therapy session yesterday and her kicking off about school – I'm a bit worried about her. I'm not saying you aren't doing a good job but I think she needs her mum.' Daisy thinks I'm doing a good job? I'd keel over in surprise if I weren't already lying down. But wait.

'What do you mean, the therapy session and school?' I ask. This is the first I've heard about either.

'Oh, she didn't tell you? Her school wants her to transfer to their remedial programme for the last year of her GCSEs. With all the troubled kids. It's a fucking nightmare. Basically her shithead friends got into trouble smoking weed on the school grounds during the holidays. They all started crying and said Myra was the ringleader.'

'But I don't understand – she wasn't there.'

'It's not about that. It's about the day when – you know – Myra was in hospital.' Daisy pauses. 'And because there have been a few other incidents over the year, and they all said it was Myra, she's the bad influence. The therapist got dragged into it because one of the parents mentioned it to the school . . . that Myra's seeing one . . . and is saying she's unstable.'

'How does she know Myra is seeing a therapist?'

'Well, this person is – was – a friend of mine,' says Daisy in a heavy voice. 'I thought I could trust her.'

'How did Myra take it?'

'Not great,' she says. 'I don't think it's so much about the shame of being shunted to the remedial class as it is about her friends selling her out. I'm working on it though – I'll have the school board in tears before I let them ostracise her.'

The whole thing seems so unfair, especially given the progress Myra has been making. Although she could still be mercurial in mood, she'd mostly worked in the garden when she was expected to, I hadn't caught her smoking again (yet) and she was usually home when she said she would be.

'That's so rubbish,' I say, feeling strangely emotional at the news. 'She is trying. So hard. She's a good kid. You know what? Those friends of hers don't deserve her. Nor does her school. Fuck them.'

Daisy laughs. 'I don't think I've ever heard you use the F-word Padma. But yes, I agree. Fuck them to hell. Anyway. So I'll come for a night or two?'

Part of me knows that Daisy being here will change the dynamic between Myra and me. We'll revert to the roles we are used to playing. But I have no right to keep her from her daughter, and I am currently feeling out of my depth. This is grown-up stuff I am not equipped for. I say yes, of course, and lie back on the sofa, and find myself falling asleep to the sound of rain hitting the earth.

*

When I wake up around 10 a.m. a mug of tea is standing next to me on the coffee table, with a note next to it.

I'm sorry x

It's an apology from Myra for her behaviour yesterday, which instantly melts the jagged pieces of upset in my heart, but I can't work out why it's there. Myra isn't a people pleaser and hasn't worked out how to apologise for something when she is wrong.

'What prompted this? I say, standing in the doorway of her room. In this short space of time, she has turned it into a cave of nightmares. Make-up strewn across the dainty console table, clothes spilling out of her suitcase, black candles that she bought in town dribbling wax all over the cabinets. She's sitting on the floor with a sketch pad on her lap, and shrugs. 'I was being horrible.'

I take a long sip of tea and remain standing by the door. 'Your mother is coming to visit the day after tomorrow.'

'Yeah, I heard you talking to her.' Ah, so that explains the apology note. She would have heard me sticking up for her.

'You know I'm on your side, right?' In response, she pulls the pad to her chest, protectively.

'I'm sorry about all the school stuff,' I continue gently. 'It sounds unfair and nasty. But one thing I do know is that, whatever happens, your mother is going to sort it out. Okay? I know she is terrifying but sometimes you need someone terrifying in your corner.'

Eventually Myra looks up. 'Am I terrifying?' she says in a tone that, to my relief, is lighter and enquiring.

'No,' I say, trying not to laugh, 'you're just scary. You *wish* you were terrifying.'

'You know what *is* scary? Your Instagram account.'

'Well, help me then. It's not like you have anything better to do . . . like school.'

She looks at me so solemnly, I can't suppress my laughter any longer as she says: 'Too soon.'

*

Lists are my anchor to sanity. When I am depressed, I can't make them because my decision-making becomes fragmented. It's impossible to tell what's important. With Daisy's arrival imminent, I have made a shopping and a house list. It's calming, grounding stuff. I head into town to get the former done, trying to make the most of the freshness of the morning after the rain.

Although it is a Thursday and usually a 'work day' for Myra, she has been given the day off to spend with Greg. The space will do us both good. When I head into town, there is an unusual amount of activity. I see Barbara and a group of workmen in high-visibility jackets standing at the old pier, pointing and taking measurements. At the entrance to the beach, where you can rent loungers and parasols, there is actually a queue even though the sand is slightly damp. While walking to Selena's, out of curiosity, I google Harkness and see it is trending.

Nicole Kelly, a supermodel turned parenting influencer with over 10 million followers, posted a series of photos from her stay in Harkness a couple of days ago. *So good I want to keep it for myself*, she writes before going on to post beautiful photos of ice cream at Bella's, sunbathing on the beach, a shot of the shore from a private charter boat. It had exploded into numerous news articles. *For people who may have struggled to find a booking for the school holidays in the usual haunts, this is a prime opportunity to save their summer*, said a news presenter on an ITV news clip.

The Green Goddess is packed. When I go in for my takeaway coffee, Selena vibrates with frantic energy, trying to take orders and cook them. The number of people indoors is also testing the air conditioning, and almost everyone is using the menus to fan themselves while they wait for their food, which will not arrive unless Selena makes a decision to abandon the till.

'Let me help you,' I say, and point her in the direction of the kitchen. It's surprising how much of it is muscle memory from helping out Delilah. I take orders, walk around assuring people their food will soon arrive. I make iced coffees and wipe tables, gently steer people into buying flapjacks and Selena's special oat and chocolate cookies for afternoon tea. When I clear the last plate, the café empties out as people stream off onto tour buses or head off on the bay cruise that runs once an hour. All that is left behind is the scent of sunscreen and seawater.

I go out to the back and find Selena smoking a cigarette. 'What the fuck was that?' she says, looking dishevelled and haunted.

'That,' I reply, 'was a successful morning.'

'That fucking influencer,' she says, shaking her head. 'They're meeting in the town hall today to discuss it.'

'It's not a good thing?'

'No,' she says. 'It always starts like this for towns up and down the Kent coast. More people. Then Londoners deciding they want to have a different life. Then they move in, snap up all the houses and turn this into a microcosm of the fucked-up place they were trying so hard to leave.' She stubs out the cigarette and puts her head in her hands. 'Some of us need this place to stay as it is. Small. Sweet. And this . . .'

'Look, I can help you,' I say. 'Not just taking orders. I'm not a professional or anything, but maybe think about cutting your menu down and offer more daily specials. That way you feel less pressured and, if something changes, people won't be any the wiser *and* they'll feel like they are getting something special here that they can't get anywhere else.'

'That's actually not a bad idea. I mean, Eileen hasn't changed her menu since 1975.'

I take a gamble on something about Selena, something that being with Myra has made clear to me, as I take in the cute red ribbon tying back her hair, the gold hoop earrings and the vintage heart-covered orange top. She may dress the opposite to Myra, but they have the same goal: to project an image in a world that doesn't make it comfortable for them to inhabit both parts of themselves. 'Maybe try out some of your Guyanese food out on them?'

'What? No – they wouldn't like that,' she says, shaking her head.

'You can always try it as one of the specials,' I say gently. I know why she is scared – she's spent so long surviving by fitting in. 'Use it to test what works and what doesn't. And something like Black Cake – trust me, they'd love it. As you say, it's basically solid booze.'

'Maybe,' she says. 'Oh, I don't know.' The jingle of the door sounds. She sighs and gets up. 'You've done more than enough. Don't worry about me.'

I follow her into the front and, at the counter, spot one of the most beautiful men I've seen in my life. A full head of thick, silver hair. Chin dimple. Slightly oversized ears but a strong jaw like Marlon Brando. Tall and broad, the kind of build you might see on a woodcutter. Even his aftershave is divine: cedar, salt and lavender.

'Ah, Selena,' he says, his voice deep and booming. 'And this must be our new visitor I've heard so much about.' His ice-blue eyes actually twinkle. I thought that was just a thing you read in Mills and Boon novels. I look at him curiously. He clearly expects me to know who he is, but I don't.

'This is David Bentley,' Selena says weakly. 'Our dear leader and head of the town council. And my landlord. David, this is Padma, who's staying in Hugo's place.'

'Oh, Selena,' he says with a jovial chuckle, except it doesn't match his tone. '"Dear leader" – you are funny. We're having an open council meeting later. Four o'clock. With all these new visitors we need to discuss a strategy for how we'll cope. You are coming, yes?'

'I would love to, David,' she replies, 'but we've just had a morning rush and lunch could be as bad. I haven't any waiting staff to help me and I'll need to prep for tomorrow . . .'

'Ah,' he says, placing his hands on the counter and leaning in. 'Well, that is a shame. I might as well tell you that with this new interest in the town, we will have to raise the rent on all our commercial properties.' He looks at her pointedly and I see him for what he is. A bully. 'We can hold off for a month because I'm considerate like that.' Selena's face crumples at the news, and I know tears are probably not far off. It feels like David knows it as well.

'You're welcome to come too, of course,' he says, switching his gaze to me. 'I know Hugo would want to be kept abreast of developments.'

I've done so much to clear out Rosemary's house but I am not Hugo's PA to be taking minutes about a place I'm not sure I'll return to. 'Oh, I would love to,' I say with as big a smile as I can muster, 'but I've promised to do something with my niece.'

He looks at me with a calculating stare. 'May I have Hugo's number?' he asks. 'I could let him know about developments directly.' I can hardly say no. Not just because Hugo is technically invested in the area, but because David is the kind of man whose vengeance comes slyly. I don't want to offend him or refuse in case it has repercussions for Selena.

He leaves with Hugo's number in his phone, and when the door closes Selena breaks down into tears, hiding her face behind her hands on the counter. I stand next to her and pull her into a hug. She eventually cries herself out and lifts her head.

'I am already so in debt, Padma,' she says. 'Today was busy but what if this surge doesn't last? I can't make the rent as it is, let alone if he increases it. And he and his shrew of a wife already own so much of the property here – it's not like I can go anywhere else.'

I look at Selena and realise there is so much I haven't been seeing because I didn't want to. The nails bitten to the quick. The perennially cheery outlook. The red lipstick and cutesy clothes designed to make people think she is jolly and quirky. I hadn't guessed how much of it was a brave face.

'Look, let me help you. If there is one thing I know, it's that Londoners and tourists love being able to get something special and unique that they can't get anywhere else. And, Selena, that's you.'

'But it's a risk and I've already borrowed up to the hilt . . .' She wipes her face dejectedly with a napkin.

'If you continue the way you are, you're in trouble anyway, right?' She nods. 'Well then, why not take a chance on something new?'

She pours herself the last dregs of coffee from the pot and sits down. 'Tell me what you think I should do.' There's a part of me that feels uncertain, an imposter. When I have felt like this in the past, the person I've asked for advice is Wallace, and he has always advised me to err on the side of caution. Perhaps because he's worried that if my expectations are too high, if things crash, he's seen the place of darkness I might one day return to. But he isn't here. He hasn't been for a while.

The anger that surges in me at this realisation, combined with the look I see in Selena's eyes then – one of deep need – tells me that maybe I can help her pull this off. Just because no one is coming to save me, doesn't mean I'm not capable of saving someone else.

So we talk. Selena says she can pay me an hourly rate on the days I want to help out in the café, and a fifty per cent cut on anything I make and sell. I tell her that I think she should do a relaunch of the menu. Make a party of it. She says she can't afford to pay me as a food consultant, but we agree that it's an official position I can put on my CV afterwards, and she will give me a reference. Slowly, it feels like I am being nudged in the right direction.

*

When I get home, I take off my overheating trainers and tip out the stones. On the walk up, I'd felt the change in atmosphere again: the air tasted of iron, the birds swooping into the trees in hasty flight, and in the distance, thunderclouds gathering, their grey shoulders bunching up against one another. There is no point hoping that Myra had taken an umbrella. She may spend hours on her make-up and endlessly debate which over-the-knee socks to wear, but she hates carrying anything superfluous. I pull out some towels and switch the hot water on just in case she needs a shower on her return.

The wave of optimism I felt at helping out Selena evaporates as my thoughts drift to how Myra has been over the past few weeks. In particular, the last few days when she's been dealing with something huge – the ongoing rejection by her friends, now her school – but didn't feel able to tell me. Am I helping her or am I making things worse? I'm tempted to seize the rare opportunity of her being out, to go to her room and find the journal she's been writing in, to find out how she's really feeling. The madness almost catches light, an old flame kindled long ago when I would comb my mother's room for bottles. But just as my foot reaches the second stair, I stop myself. To remove temptation, I head out into the garden, the fresh air providing welcome relief.

Outside I see what Myra has done and it makes me feel proud, and ashamed of myself for doubting her. The fences are fixed and she's begun painting them. The lettuces are covered with wire netting to stop birds from attacking them, and the chilli and capsicum plants have little nubs growing among their leaves.

The shame I feel at believing the worst of her squeezes the air from my lungs. If I am going to help Myra, I am going to have to be able to trust her, and she is going to have to trust me. Demanding her innermost thoughts in order to protect them would be like taking a crowbar to an oyster. When she needs it, I can guide her along the way. The hard part will be how to do it with grace and faith. Faith that she will be the one to save herself. Grace for when she makes mistakes.

*

When the doorbell rings while I'm making tea – Myra likely forgetting her keys – I yell: 'It's open!'

I almost drop the kettle when I see the person standing by the front door.

'Hugo,' I say, and he smiles as if he is the spirit of the summer, bringing warmth and light and hope into our home, when we need them most. His face is so friendly and soft, his beard golden-brown in the sunlight that drenches the kitchen at this part of the afternoon. Seeing him strangely brings up all the sadness and upset I've been trying to suppress around Wallace, and the loneliness I feel. A wave of homesickness even though he isn't a place I call home. But also the guilt around mistrusting Myra. Feeling the dam burst around all the emotions I've been trying to hold in, I burst into tears.

*

'Padma,' says Hugo, looking horrified. His pale blue shirt is crumpled. His hair has a Tintin tuft. 'I'm so sorry – I've been trying to call but I got no answer.'

I wipe the tears from eyes. 'Sorry, this isn't you, it's me.'

'I've heard that before,' he says wryly. When I don't smile back, he says, 'It was a very last-minute thing. I got a frantic message from David Bentley saying there was an urgent town hall meeting. I had the day off anyway, and the drive time wasn't too bad, so I thought I'd pop in to say hello while I'm here.' I clamp my hands over my face like a starfish hugging the seabed because I don't want him to see me crying. 'I can go if you want me to?'

'No,' I say, 'it's all right. Honestly. I almost did something I'm not proud of.'

He doesn't push me to tell him what it is. 'I'm sure whatever it is, it can be fixed.'

'How was the meeting?' I ask, desperate to take the focus off myself.

'Not urgent, as it turns out,' he says, rolling his eyes. 'Just a bunch of blowhards flapping about the influx of tourists, some influencer I've never heard of, and five different people asking me if I'm going to sell the house. Which looks amazing, by the way – I hardly recognise it. I can't thank you enough.'

All the empty boxes, the miscellaneous bin bags full of paper, the rusted cookware, are gone. The electricals, which included five toasters, ten hairdryers, two printers – all broken – are gone too. The kitchen could do with a refit, but the countertops are gleaming, fresh lemons and apples sit in ceramic bowls, and The List that Myra and I regularly add to is pinned to the fridge. The latest addition is *No Air Supply/ Cradle of Filth before 10 a.m.*, which sits under *No Cheese Doritos Unless Windows Are Open*. The living room remains a work in progress, with dust sheets on the sofa and part of the main wall painted white.

'You're welcome,' I reply, and stuff my hands in my pockets to stop them sweating. Although Hugo and I have been chatting easily by text, it feels more awkward in real life. I find myself second-guessing what to say, and I'm acutely aware I'm wearing my lounge clothes. I must look uncomfortable because he jiggles the plastic bag in his hand, like someone about to give a toddler a treat. 'Would you like some crisps?'

'What kind?'

'"What kind?" she asks,' he says, pulling out a bag of Nik Naks Nice and Spicy. The gesture is small, yet so enormously kind and thoughtful it makes me start crying all over again.

'Why don't we go for a walk?' he says, handing me a box of tissues.

*

I'd been taking regular walks to explore the coastline further east, but my limited navigational skills meant I had stuck nervously to the straightest and flattest tracks. Hugo offers to take me to an old spot he loved visiting as a boy.

'Is it the White Sentinels?' I ask.

'No,' he says. 'That's a longer walk and you need to be careful with the tides. We can go there another time maybe. It might rain this afternoon.'

We head off in what seems like the wrong direction through the woodland, until Hugo points to a worn stone marker wrapped in moss and we take a sharp right that takes us back towards the sea.

From a higher vantage point, we see a sequence of small coves, their basins lit to turquoise by the remnants of the sun, gold-daubed at the waterline where sea meets sand. The nearest cove has a small beach with steps cut into the rock leading down to it.

'Come on,' says Hugo, taking off his beige and navy boaters and socks and heading in the direction of a series of flat rocks with pools of water in between, fronds of seaweed skimming the surface.

I roll up my jogging bottoms but the elastic is so loose, they threaten to shoot down at any moment.

The water in the rock pools is very clear and cold. I wonder what we look like to the creatures in the murk: a tall white man wearing a blue shirt and long shorts, and a round brown woman in a loose half-sleeved T-shirt with a frayed collar. Hugo doesn't remark on it, doesn't make a mean comment asking why I'm wearing men's clothes. I should have worn the striped top I bought from the charity shop, but it would have looked strange if I'd changed, as if I was making a special effort.

'Be careful,' he says. 'Technically we should be wearing shoes with a grip sole so we don't slip on the algae.'

'Er, what are we looking at?' I say, because all I can see are jagged pieces of dark brown rock, turning silver in the places where the water pulls in the sky.

'What are we looking at?' he says, mock-offended. 'Only an entire world caught between rock and water.' For a flickering moment I see a young Hugo, hopping between dry bits of rock and peering into a different realm. 'Look here!'

He bends down at the edge to a pool and talks to me about anemones and starfish, then asks if I knew there were seven types of crab? He picks up a strand of seaweed and holds it against the light, thick brown strands with a lightning bolt of yellow running through the centre, pearls of water shaking off and running down his tanned arm. 'And look at this guy,' he says, pointing at a small hermit crab. 'I used to think this was me,' he laughs. 'Just someone looking for a home, any home. I would draw them all the time.'

I look at Hugo as he peers at the water. The expression of delight on his face makes something shift in my understanding of him. He isn't a rich oaf who stumbles around taking things without asking; he's an inquisitive nerd who shows the same passion for sea urchins that others do for Ferraris.

'What's the name of this beach?' I ask.

'It doesn't have one,' he says, continuing his search.

'What if I name it Alva Beach?' I say mischievously.

'Oh, colonising the local beach in your name, are we?' he laughs. After a while, I leave him to it and wade into the water up to my shins. Eventually he joins me. Even the smallest movement of our legs pushes ripples out into the still, calm surface, fragments gleaming where they catch the light.

'So,' he asks. 'Do you want to talk about it? Why you were crying?'

'Not really.' My initial relief on seeing him has been replaced with excruciating embarrassment. I shrink from the memory of him seeing me cry. The line between air and water is all that tethers me to this point. I feel unmoored from everything else, and if that line breaks, I could slide between the cracks in the earth. Hugo is offering himself as an anchor. Maybe I should accept.

'Is it one thing in particular or everything?' he says.

'Everything,' I say morosely. 'I have no job. My relationship is falling apart. And I feel like I am messing up with Myra. I just don't know how to make her happy.'

Hugo stares ahead, and for a moment I am certain he is going to say something like, 'Well, try not to feel that way,' or make a joke, or go for the silent shoulder squeeze.

'That's not your job though, is it? To make her happy? I mean, that's no one's job. Taking that on for another person is a lot. Believe me, I know.'

I close my eyes and for a moment I'm not Padma, I'm just light and thought. The sound of splashing breaks through as Hugo wades out to sit on some driftwood. I follow and pat my legs dry.

'My ex, Elaine,' he says. 'She – we – had a miscarriage and afterwards, I tried to do everything to make it better for her. I removed every obstacle, made her choices easy and soft, but it wasn't enough. I couldn't make her happy, I couldn't be the reason for her happiness.'

'I'm sorry,' I say, and stay quiet. I always feel guilty when I hear about people who have lost children, given my choice not to have them. When I tell Hugo this, he says: 'What do you have to feel guilty about? It's your choice. It's like feeling guilty if you want to break up with someone because you know someone whose partner died. People talk about having kids as if it's a given, a duty. And maybe that used to be true but it certainly isn't now.'

'Try telling that to my boyfriend,' I say glumly. When Hugo looks at me enquiringly, I give him a summary of what happened, and where Wallace and I are at. He frowns and brushes grains of sand off his feet. 'What?' I ask. He clearly has something to say.

'It just seems like an odd tactic for him to use,' he says. 'I mean, I get why you're struggling to tell him your choice, but it also seems like he's not behaving in a way that would encourage you to make the choice he wants you to make. Is he punishing you? I don't get it.'

'He's not a bad person,' I say quickly. 'He really wants to be a dad. That's a good quality – it means he's caring.' Hugo doesn't respond. I think treacherously that Wallace hasn't exactly been particularly caring over the last couple of years. He talks about how stressful his work is, and how tired he is, but he has stopped asking me how I am. While I will bend to his needs – cook him a nice dinner if he's had a long day – when I've been stressed out, there isn't much thought or care shown beyond pouring me a glass of wine from a bottle he's already opened for himself.

'Do you think you might say yes, then?' he says.

I shake my head. 'There's no question of that. I've seen what happens to people who try and fill their own void with children, or use them as a form of validation.' Vocalising it to

Hugo makes me realise I need to talk to Wallace about this soon rather than dragging this out to the end of the summer.

My phone buzzes with a message from Myra. **Where are you? I have a surprise for you.**

I have a surprise for you too, I text back.

'It's Myra,' I say.

'Let's head back. I can buy the little ratbag an ice cream before I drive home.'

For a moment I can't move from the log. I know that when I do, reality will be waiting for me at the top of those steps. 'Are you okay?' he says.

'Myra needs me,' I say eventually. 'And she needs me to help build her self-worth. To remind her that in a world that will tell her she's a piece of shit, she is worthy of love. How do I begin to do that when I don't believe it about myself?'

'Do you believe people deserve love, no matter who they are? And are you someone who gives love to others?'

I nod. He reaches out his hand to help me pull myself up. 'Well then,' he says, 'if that's the case, why don't you think you are someone who deserves to receive it?'

I know why I wear loose clothes that don't fit properly. I know why my haircut is the same as it has been ever since I was twenty. I could blame my mother for the past. I could blame Wallace for the present. But I am like this because part of me has given up on the future. And for that, I can only blame myself.

10

While Hugo takes a work call outside the house, Myra reveals her surprise for me: a tripod and a ring light. 'Look, I know I gave you a hard time,' she says, 'but this is going to change how you post on social media.'

I'm confused about why I need it. 'Auntie,' she sighs as patiently as she can. 'Your pictures are terrible. Some of them have the flash on, making them look like a serial killer's last meal, and others just . . . the angle is unflattering. Indian food is not the most photogenic so you have to work harder at this.'

'But it's just a little account for when I start doing cooking classes,' I reply. The idea of putting my recipes out there feels too exposing. Food has always been a safe place for me – I don't want some troll leaving mean comments about a recipe or even what I look like. And after my experience with Majid, I definitely don't want my ideas being stolen by anyone else.

When I tell her this, she has a comeback for that too. 'Even more of a reason to start staking your claim to your recipes. If it's on your feed, it makes it harder for someone else just to steal something and pass it off as their own. Have you told Mum about this by the way? She could probably help you.' She starts pulling ingredients out of the fridge: the loaf of bread, cheese, potatoes, to show she means business.

It hadn't occurred to me to ask Daisy about any of it. She has always expressed her disappointment in my choice of career in an exquisite brand of passive-aggression: references to my salary, to the clothes I wear. I know it all comes from a good place – Daisy wanting me to have the life she does – but it is also deeply irritating and means that I have completely shut down talking to her about my finances or what I do in my job.

'Think of it this way,' Myra says as she sets up the tripod. 'Cooking classes are great but this is a way of sharing your recipes with a much wider audience. You don't just cook, you explain things. Thanks to you, I can't get rid of the knowledge that the nutrients of coriander are mainly in the stem, which everyone usually throws away.'

'But they are!'

'See what I mean?' Myra laughs. 'If you do this right, you could make money from it. One of my classmates – her dad lost his job during lockdown. He started making videos of himself making bread and this guy now has sponsorships and earns six figures.'

'I don't know, Myra, I think I'm too old to change.'

'No one is too old to change,' she says, crossing her arms. 'That's just something people say when they don't want to or they're too afraid.'

'No one is going to want to see me cooking for them,' I protest. 'They want a sexy lumberjack cooking out in the woods or someone who looks like Priyanka Chopra cracking eggs into a bowl.'

'So? We'll make it fun, play around with it. I can moderate any mean comments. Plus you do a lot of hybrid food too. You could call it something like *Not Your Auntie's Kitchen*. Keep the captions real. Maybe tell people your story. First we grow engagement, then we get subscribers, and then we do collaborations. Now come on, I want a Bombay chilli cheese sandwich like you've been promising to make for ages and I'm sure Uncle Hugo will like it too.'

'Fine,' I grumble, and start chopping onions. I don't understand most of what she says, but the fact Myra thinks it's possible germinates something in me that resembles hope.

*

On Saturday, there is another break in the weather, which means I get a decent night's sleep. Daisy is due to arrive sometime in the afternoon, so I wake up early to finish cleaning the third bedroom. My phone buzzes with a WhatsApp from Myra: **Don't want to get up, just want some quiet time before Mum gets here. Is that okay?** I stare towards the crack in her door, knowing she is awake on the other side, and I could just barge into her room. But maybe this is how we break the cycle between my mother's generation and mine, by respecting that she wants space, by listening to what she is saying.

I text her back and tell her to take her time, but to be ready for when her mother gets here. What I don't want is for Myra still to be in bed, and for Daisy to wonder what I've been doing the past three weeks. It's like an Ofsted inspection, but worse. There's no grading, only cutting comments that will season the next ten years of family dinners.

After cleaning, vacuuming, and changing the guest-room sheets for an extremely fetching yellow floral pair plus a frilly orange valance, I go downstairs to check everything is in order. There are still some boxes piled in the larder, and the sofa has had to be covered with a ratty yellow blanket after Myra tipped a bowl of ice cream on it by accident, but it mostly smells of bleach, lemon and fresh air.

I slip on my trainers to head into town for the rest of the food shop. Shopping for food for other people always gives me a happy fizz in the back of my teeth. Even though she gives the impression she's all caviar and blinis, I know Daisy still loves Skips, Mr Kipling's French Fancies and a cup of builder's tea (now with oat milk). Her favourite dish is a Keralan chicken curry, which came from an old recipe belonging to one of Mum's colleagues. I used to make it for her on the days when food was the closest thing we had to comfort and routine.

My phone starts to ping with a few notifications, which means Myra must have uploaded the Instagram video of me making chilli cheese sandwiches for her and Hugo. I grudgingly admire the job she has made of it. It actually looks beautiful, like something I would bookmark if I was scrolling. Towards the end, I see Myra has accidentally caught a shot of Hugo in the background, wiping chutney from his beard and somehow managing to get more chutney on it. I send it to him with the caption **The pinnacle of sophistication**! and he replies back with: **For use of my image I'd like to be paid in sandwiches until further notice.** It makes me laugh, a wholesome, deep-belly laugh that rises up and colours my cheeks, until I realise if he's in the video, it means Wallace may have seen it too. My phone pings again, making me jump.

But it isn't Wallace. It's just Daisy telling me to buy oat milk.

*

I'm running late, having somehow spent an hour mindlessly scrolling, gathering bags and keys, when I open the door and yell. Esme is on the other side of the front door, hand poised to knock.

'Oh, gosh, I'm so sorry – is this a bad time?' Esme says, her voice as melodic as the blasted wind chimes in her garden that tinkle all day, driving us to distraction, to the point where Myra has sketched out a plan to steal them in the night and throw them into the sea.

'No, it's fine,' I say, even though I'm worried Stan the butcher will run out of chicken if I don't get there soon. 'What can I do for you?'

She's wearing a long blue chiffon top that floats on the breeze and soft beige trousers with dark brown elephants printed on them. The way she presses her hands together as if in prayer, the reddish hair tied up in a big bun, gives her the look of a kindly elf coming to enquire as to how the hobbits are doing.

'A little birdie told me that your sister is coming today and we haven't had a chance to properly catch up. I know you said you were busy when I asked you to the mandala workshop, and it is such a shame you are allergic to turmeric and couldn't come over for my special latte! But I would love to have you over for my full moon event tonight.' The turmeric thing was a lie I had completely forgotten about.

'The thing is, Esme . . .' I say, trying to find a polite way to say no.

'I insist,' she says, smiling but with iron behind her eyes. Perhaps it's because I'm distracted, or more likely that I want to keep her onside in order to sell my cooking classes. I say yes and wearily accept the argument Daisy will have with me about it later. The moment I do, Esme's countenance changes and she opens her arms to embrace me. 'Oh, namaste, Padma! I shall see you both later,' Esme says. As she's about to whirl off to her house, I say: 'You do know what namaste means, right?'

She looks at me, the smile dropping for a moment. 'Of course,' she says haltingly. 'But I'd better run!' *You'd better*, I think, as she scoots over to her side of the fence.

*

By the time I come back from town, which took longer than usual due to the number of visitors streaming in for the weekend, the coolness of the early hours has evaporated into the start of a long, hot day.

Already, the beach is filling up and although I have rolled my eyes at the 'emergency' town meeting to discuss the influx of extra tourists, it seems the worry isn't misplaced. In the past week, the Nicole Kelly effect has become clear, and after the ITV special, other networks are featuring the town too. The butcher's is almost empty of food – I had to plead my case for the last chicken – and all of the seafront shops and cafés are full, people queuing up outside, waiting for a free table. I wave at Selena, who has finally managed to hire some help in the form of Yvonne's daughter Caitlin. She first offered the job to Myra, who said truthfully: 'I appreciate the offer but I would be a bad employee. I don't need the money and I don't care about serving people and you seem like you should have someone who cares.' Selena laughed and said she appreciated the honesty. While Caitlin has the same sense of humour as her mother – e.g. none – she understands commitment.

By the time I return, the enormous bulk of a black Land

Rover Defender is parked outside the house, its burly presence incongruous against Esme's wildflower garden heavy with bees.

The car door is open and I peer inside to see reusable Waitrose bags stuffed with food.

'Padma!' Daisy says, emerging from the front door and making me jump. She's wearing what city people think they should wear to the countryside. Hunter boots (even though it's summer), a crisp white shirt, jeans and a Louis Vuitton bum bag. 'Where were you?'

'I was in town – I didn't expect you to arrive for another hour.'

'Oh,' she said, 'I texted but didn't get a response.'

'The reception here is terrible. Hugo said he . . .' I trail off, realising I hadn't told her about his visit, and now it looks suspicious. Like I'm hiding something.

'Yes?' Daisy says expectantly. As if she already knows but is waiting for me to say it.

'Hugo said he had the same problem when he came over a couple of days ago,' I say resignedly, knowing what is going to happen.

'Well, you two seem to be getting cosy,' she says, trying not to laugh.

'It's not like that,' I sigh.

'Yes, yes, I know, you're madly in love with Wallace,' she says, and stops when she sees my face drop. 'Is everything okay?' I can't bring myself to tell her we're on a break.

'It's fine,' I say, brushing it off. 'I'm just hot.'

'You look different,' she says, running her eyes over me. I am wearing a T-shirt dress and trainers. The last time Daisy saw my legs exposed was when we lived together in

Rochester. 'You're dressing better. I'm sure this is nothing to do with Hugo, of course,' she says, winking. It is infuriating. Not just because of the inference that I'm dressing differently for a man (which isn't true), but because regardless of the shaky territory my and Wallace's relationship occupies, it feels disrespectful for my sister to be implying that there's something between me and Hugo. I remain quiet as she rattles through the details of her week as we walk into the house.

Myra is sitting at the table eating a bowl of cornflakes, dressed in a long-sleeved Beastie Boys T-shirt and over-the-knee socks. Her face is like a mask – expressionless.

'And of course,' Daisy continues, 'I missed my baby. I'm dying to hear how she is.' She pulls Myra into a hug. Myra frowns and slides the sleeves over her hands a bit more tightly. 'I know it's been rough with all the school stuff. But some good news on that front. I've got a meeting with the headmistress and we're going to work something out.'

'Great,' Myra says with her mouth full of cereal. 'Spiffing. Tip-top.'

Daisy frowns. 'Why are you being sarcastic?'

Myra looks at her. 'You really don't get it, do you? It's not about whether I go to school or not. It's what everyone thinks about me. And it's not true. You know it's not true.'

'I do, sweetheart, but right now it's important we just get you off that remedial list and deal with the other stuff later. Don't you think? We've got to start choosing A-levels and then . . .'

'Mum, stop,' Myra says, getting up. 'Please, stop.'

'There's no need to get so upset, Myra!' Daisy says hotly. 'I'm doing all of this for you. And you can't even . . .'

'How long are you staying?' I ask quickly, to change the subject. She has brought enough stuff to indicate several days.

'Only until Monday morning,' she says. 'Your father wanted to be here, My-My, but he had to go to Singapore. He sends his love and kisses. And this brand-new camera! Apparently there was a six-month waitlist.' She brings out a very expensive-looking Fuji camera.

'What am I supposed to do with that?' Myra asks.

'Well,' Daisy says uncertainly, 'Daddy thought you might want to try photography. He loved it when he was your age. It's one of the extra-curriculars that helped him get into Cambridge.'

'Well,' Myra says, flatly, 'I've got things to do. So I haven't the time.' She gets up and puts her bowl in the sink.

'Wait – I've got some amazing clothes for you from Selfridges. I think you'll love them,' Daisy says. I empathise with her, hearing the desperation in her voice, trying everything to curry favour with her daughter but not being able to win. When she holds the yellow bags aloft, Myra says, 'Maybe later' before walking out of the room, and Daisy's face falls.

'You've managed to get her to take her dishes to the sink?' she says, changing the subject.

It has taken Daisy's arrival to show me the little world Myra and I have created, through new eyes. Although we fight, it is a bubble where we mostly don't pick at each other. I don't judge her film selections, and she doesn't judge my music choices. I enjoy making food for us, and she eats the food I make without asking for something different. Peace treaties have been settled with less.

When I bring the rest of Daisy's things inside, I find her

running a finger over one of Rosemary's sideboards. 'This place is kind of a dump,' she says. I want to tell her how hard Myra and I have worked on it, and what it looked like before. But I know she's taking her upset at her conversation with Myra out on the house and, by extension, me.

'Right,' she says, 'let's head into town.' Daisy doesn't ask other people what they want to do, she decides on a plan and announces it to everyone.

'I think Myra has plans to meet up with Greg.'

'Greg? Who is Greg? Are you dating someone named Greg, Myra?' she hollers up the stairs.

'It's not what you think, Daisy,' I say, exasperated. If every conversation was going to go straight from zero to stratospheric, this was going to be an exhausting weekend. 'He's actually quite sweet – this local kid. He's helped us out a lot, and especially in the garden . . . you might want to take a look actually. Myra's done a good job out there.'

Daisy frowns, dismissing the garden tour as Myra comes thundering down, eager to leave. 'I want to meet this Greg,' she says. I know Daisy is being protective and means well, but she doesn't consider that Myra is lonely, and that maybe interrogating the one friend her daughter does have, after her entire friendship group ghosted her, might be an unwelcome prospect. 'He can come and have lunch with us.'

'Mum,' Myra says with her arms crossed, which is her battle language, 'I'd rather not go with you and Auntie. I made plans before I knew you were coming.' She had agreed to go with Greg to the rescue shelter to see if there were any dogs he could adopt, after his mother had finally said yes to having one.

'Well, change them,' Daisy says dismissively. 'And maybe

change your shoes – platform boots could be a bit OTT for the village.'

Myra's face drops, but there's no room for discussion.

'What if we all walk into town,' I say, 'and Myra, you can get Greg to meet us there quickly maybe? Daisy – we can head off and do our own thing and meet up with them afterwards?'

'I was hoping we'd get to spend some time together, My-My!' Daisy says, her mouth puckering with frustration. 'Why can't you meet Greg some other time?'

'Because I gave him my word, and unlike some people,' she looks directly at her mother, 'I keep my word.' Daisy rolls her eyes. I don't know the history of this particular exchange, nor do I want to.

'Why don't I give you both the whole of tomorrow to spend together?' I say, stepping in again. 'I promised my friend Selena I would help her out at her café anyway.'

'Oh, Padma,' Daisy says, 'before I forget, let me give you money for all the groceries.'

'What groceries?'

'You know, the groceries you had to get for me.'

The embarrassment I feel at having this conversation in front of Myra, the dragging anchor of my own lack of money, and the memory of that day Daisy loaned me her black Amex card, is so sharp it almost burns.

'I think I can afford to pay for your oat milk, Daisy,' I say tightly. 'Let's go or Myra will be late.'

My niece looks at me gratefully and with some measure of empathy. It is the start of our alliance to survive Hurricane Daisy.

*

I've not had much opportunity to observe Myra around her mother over the past few years. It is hard to discern if she's quiet because of her mood, or because Daisy is so garrulous that she uses all the oxygen in the nearby vicinity. But eventually even she slows down. She doesn't have meetings to attend to, people to see, contracts to sign – the only thing her agenda holds for her today is pottering about town.

In the quiet, I notice Myra. How she looks down at the ground. How she fiddles constantly with her sleeves.

Daisy starts telling Myra about the people who've been asking about her. 'I hope you didn't tell them what happened?' she says sharply, referring to her stint in hospital.

'Of course not,' says Daisy. 'We don't want people knowing that.' Myra's head snaps back under the weight of this judgement, as she realises she can't have it both ways. She might not want everyone to know but doesn't want it to feel like a shameful secret. Everyone wants their parents to love them for all of who they are, especially the bad parts.

Greg is waiting for us outside the Green Goddess, and the minute Daisy sees him she relaxes. He isn't like the teenagers she normally associates with trouble. His hair looks like it has been cut by his mother, and he's so nervous that sweat runs down his face and soaks the neck of his T-shirt. After the briefest of introductions, Myra pulls him away so they can go and catch the bus to the animal shelter.

The door jingles and Selena comes out, looking like a sunbeam walking the earth, in a pretty yellow sundress and a green headwrap. 'Hello, hello!' she says, smiling broadly. 'I'm Selena,' she says, 'so nice to meet you, Daisy. I've heard so much about you.'

Daisy gives Selena her appraising stare, which I know

consists of wondering how much she earns, how old she is, is she single?

'We're friends,' I put in quickly before Daisy can ask an invasive question.

'Yes,' Selena replies, 'Padma's been helping me experiment with some of the food at the café. You're so lucky to have such an amazing cook in the family!' Daisy angles her head, as if trying to figure out if Selena is competition for my affection and time. I'd forgotten she could be territorial like this, especially because we haven't been in any setting for a long time that would mean she'd meet or socialise with my friends.

Eventually arriving at some conclusion, Daisy replies: 'Yes, we are – I am – very lucky to have Padma. She's the best cook I know.' The comment is so unexpected and kind, I am unsure how to respond. I tell Selena we'll be back for coffee after we visit the beach.

'What do you feel like doing?' I ask Daisy as we walk onto the sand and carefully pick our way through the upturned pink bums and scattered bottles of sun lotion. The number of sunbathers is five blankets deep from the shore, and when enough Prosecco and beer is consumed, arguments will break out around umbrella configurations, sand flying into someone's sandwich and rogue beach balls landing on the wrong person.

She shrugs. 'What is there to do in this tinpot town? Go shopping? Get a drink?' The line to the beach bar, which is actually a van, is so long, neither of us can bear it. Then her eyes light up. 'Or,' she says, pointing at a sign, 'we could do that.' One of my worst nightmares is being stuck in a car with Daisy, where I'm trapped and she's telling me everything that is wrong with my life. (This happened once when she helped me move my things into Wallace's house.) The only thing worse is being in the same scenario, but on water. As Daisy marches towards the sign that says 'Pedalos For Hire', my heart sinks.

*

Pedalos seem great in theory, but in practical terms there is always the prospect of one person doing perceptibly more than the other, and this triggering all kinds of deep-buried grievances, bringing them to the surface. Daisy loved them because she had the fondest memories of them as a child.

'Do you remember when we went on one with Mum?' she says excitedly. 'We had the best time, didn't we?' Perhaps you could have the best time on one if you were not the poor donkey doing all the hard work. But I was that donkey, and I remember feeling so overwhelmed by trying to pedal, steer and get us all safely back to shore, I burst into tears in the toilets. Daisy had been eleven and I was fourteen at the time. The only adult present, Mum, had thought it was something Daisy and I would be great at because we were children. She pedalled half-heartedly at the beginning but quickly gave up. 'You kids will enjoy it more than me,' she said, and put her feet up. I don't think she realised how hard it was, and Daisy's chicken legs couldn't help much.

'The good thing,' says Claire, the pedalo lady, 'is that there is no wind, and so you won't get blown off course.' The one bad thing, however, she adds, is that there is no wind, so coming back to shore may feel hard depending on when the tide comes in.

'It's fine,' Daisy says breezily, 'we've done it before.'

It starts off promisingly. We use the same channel as the kayaks, so we don't end up bruising any swimmers as we forge our way out. At sea, the water is calm and peaceful. We've manoeuvred ourselves away from the kayakers, who are paddling towards a small uninhabited island to the east of the bay.

The view back to the land is humbling. Behind a crescent of gold, the whole of the town sits cradled in the bay with green fields stretching inland, rising upwards into the hills. It looks so small from out here, but ashore so many lives are threaded together. Daisy trails her hand through the cold, clear water, her diamond ring sparkling in the sunlight, her pink nails washed clean. The only sound out here is the swish and wash of the water that gently nudges the bottom of the pedalo.

'How long do you want to stay out?' I ask.

'We only just got here! I thought you liked this too? I remember you loved doing it when we were kids.' For a moment I think about lying. But if I keep agreeing with Daisy, how are we ever going to have a real relationship?

'That's not how I remember it,' I say, turning around to face the expanse of water and sky, feeling how it provides scale for my problems, and how vast it makes me feel, remembering I am part of a planet, not just a small inner-city borough or a seaside town. Our little pedalo sits on water threading to a droplet beading alongside the Panama Canal, joining the white powder shoreline of the Whitsunday Islands, spouting from a blowhole in a beluga whale in the Canadian Arctic. Allowing myself to dream that I may see them one day makes me feel hopeful, even when my past pulls me back.

'Oh?' says Daisy, pulling out some cans of gin and tonic

and handing me one. 'How do you remember it?' I look at the tin and wonder if this is a good idea. 'Don't overthink it, Padma,' she says. I almost laugh at being told not to overthink something by my control-freak sister. 'I'm on holiday and life lately has been . . . stressful.' She opens the ring pull. We bob around for a while, taking a few sips, adjusting the pedalo to face out to sea.

'It wasn't like that for me,' I say. 'I was the one who had to pedal on my own and it was scary at that age. Mum was always so . . . unpredictable when we went on those trips.'

Daisy looks at me from behind her Christian Dior sunglasses. 'I remember her being so much fun though. It was the one time she wasn't busy with work and actually spent time with us.'

I sigh. How much of this do I tell Daisy? We haven't examined it for so long – do we need to do it now?

'It was awful, Daisy,' I say, deciding to come clean. 'She was awful.' I see her open her mouth but I cut her off. 'I know she was our mother, and I will always love her, but it was difficult. She would be drunk half the time when we did those road trips. She'd slur her words. Forget where she'd parked the car. Once she left us on the beach for two hours and I didn't know if she was coming back. And I would never say this to you because what I did, I did out of love, but there were so many times I had to hide what she did from you.'

She looks shocked. 'That can't be true?'

'What do I have to gain by making it up?'

We're quiet for a time. Although Daisy stares ahead at the horizon, her eyes are not looking forward. She is caught up in the past, looking back at what she missed.

'I mean . . . I did know something wasn't right. But I just thought she was difficult,' she says eventually. 'She wasn't that bad – was she?'

Daisy is no longer a child, and I have to stop protecting her feelings all the time, because the collateral damage of that is to our relationship. 'Do you remember when Mum left us? For two days?'

She looks bewildered, so confused and hurt I almost wish I could take it back. But instead I start to tell her about it. In part, because I think she should know. But also because I am tired of carrying this burden for both of us and I think I have earned the right to put it down, even if it's just for a little while.

*

When Mum left us for two days I was twelve and Dhara was nine. Mum was wearing her favourite navy suit and polka-dot top. She kissed Dhara on the cheek and patted me on the shoulder. 'You're a good girl,' she said to me, and it sounded odd. Like someone saying goodbye, not giving a compliment. She carried her brown leather bag, which made us think she was going to work. Dhara and I went to school. I was distracted because I had a history test about Henry the Eighth and I was angry that we never seemed to learn modern history, unlike the boys' school.

After school, my friend Claire came over, and I made us potato waffles and turkey drummers while Dhara did her homework. Claire and I played Would You Rather and when it was nearly 8 p.m. she reluctantly went home. I remember checking the door wasn't double-locked and that the hob was off. Mum's bedroom door was open – it was only ever closed when she was at home.

In the morning, I woke up and followed my morning routine as normal. I showered with my Body Shop Dewberry, sang to the radio while I got ready. Checked Dhara's toothbrush had been used and popped my head into Mum's bedroom. I stood frozen to the spot when I saw her made bed. Where was she? Had she come home? This was before people carried mobile phones, so I couldn't call her, and it was too early to phone the office. I fixed on a smile and dropped Dhara off at school. Then I caught the bus to Mum's office at the hospital. Bernice, her secretary, hadn't seen her. Besides, Dr Alva had the day off. 'Is she okay?' she asked, a worried wrinkle between her eyebrows.

I checked the local shopping centre. Every pub near our house, then the ones near her workplace. Attracted the inquisitive stares of middle-aged men nursing 10 a.m. pints.

The rest of the day passed by in a state of hyperreality. I sat in the living room, in the grey armchair nearest to the telephone. I didn't want to turn the TV on in case I missed the sound of the door opening. I learned that day that a house talks in the daytime. An unexpected clank in the pipes; an answering groan to the wind outside. Then time stretched and passed, and the street filled with the noise of children coming home.

'Where's Mum?' Dhara asked around 9 p.m. I said something about her working late, but I couldn't think, couldn't breathe. I oscillated between worry and anger. I went to bed at midnight, rigid, staring up at the ceiling. Wondering if she was dead, if she was drunk, if she was both. The next morning, I was less sprightly. I couldn't fake it any more. Dhara asked what was wrong and I snapped at her. I remember the hurt expression on her face, I remember adding that to the list of grievances I nursed against my mother. Because back then I didn't take responsibility for how I behaved, how I felt. My whole being was dictated by my mother's shortcomings and lack of care.

I didn't go to Mum's office again but I called from a urine-soaked payphone near school and put on an accent. Bernice told me Dr Alva was off sick but should be back at work tomorrow. I made it to school and drifted through my lessons. Declined an invitation to go to McDonald's afterwards and went home. Waited. Prayed. Cursed. Daisy was still cross with me from the morning and went to her room straight after dinner. I spent the second night the same way, staring up at the ceiling, listening out for the front door. The third morning was a blur. School was painful. Listening to girls drone on about their pointless problems. This time, I went with my friends to the local mall, and burst into tears outside Our Price. They gave me a hug and asked me what was wrong, but I couldn't tell them. I said, 'PMS,' and went home.

I heard Daisy's excited voice through the door. My heart soared for a moment. The key turned and there she was. Mum. As if she had never left. Daisy was surrounded by a pile of toys and new clothes. 'Look, Pads!' she said excitedly. 'Mum got stuff for you too.'

I looked at my mother, who met my gaze, then looked down, embarrassed. 'What about this one?' she said to Daisy, picking up a sparkly top for her. This was how it always was: never acknowledging what had happened, never apologising for it.

'Glad to see you're alive,' I said to Mum, before going to my room and slamming the door.

*

'I don't remember that at all,' Daisy says. 'Are you sure it happened?' I don't answer because whatever Daisy thinks of me, she knows I don't lie.

'She . . .' Daisy starts to say as the truth sinks in, rewriting what she knows. 'I remember her being so loving. There was this one time I was so angry about not having a dad. And I was awful to her. I said it was her fault. That if she'd made a better choice, we would have a father who'd take us to tennis lessons and buy us ice cream. I think it was because of some comment from a boy I liked at school – about how he'd never go out with me because I didn't have a dad and that made me a reject. And Mum . . . she just held me. She told me that one day I would love someone who would love me back with all their heart. 'It's okay,' she said. 'This boy you're crying over isn't the one. That person is waiting for you and they will make your heart feel whole.'

My heart feels so full for Daisy. Our mother had found the right words to ease the pain that coiled in her daughter's chest, and she was the only person who could have given this reassurance to her.

'It wasn't all bad,' I say. 'She loved us more than anything. I truly believe that. But she wasn't well, for a long time. I think she did the best she could, and we did the best we could. But that doesn't mean we aren't affected, or that we don't have scars because of it.'

Behind her sunglasses, Daisy starts crying. 'Jesus Christ,' she says after a while, 'and to think I suggested we should hire a pedalo because it would be a fun thing to do.' It makes me laugh, and that makes her laugh too.

*

Here's what no one tells you when a loved one who has led a life of addiction dies. When you think of them as the years go past, you mainly think of the moments their addiction touched your life or changed you. You trace back your anger to the edge of a memory, and that memory contains mostly the bad parts of that person. When you have the self-awareness to notice your patterns – how you communicate, who you fall in love with, what makes you feel unsafe – and you see how inextricably they are tied to this mess, there is a part of you that doesn't know how to deal with the grief of that. Who you might have been if the circumstances were different. That then leads to the issue of truth. What is true about them? And crucially: what is the truth about you?

When Mum died, I deferred my last year of university and moved back to Kent to stay with Dhara for her final year of school. I stayed in the house, soaked in all of the poisonous memories of our last few years. I didn't know what to throw out because I didn't know what I wanted to keep, and because I had waited too long. If I had done it in the first month, it would have been fine because my nerve endings were numb with grief. But after that first month, all of that delayed pain returned, and it was impossible to do anything. My decision-making was shot to shit, and when I stood in the aisle of the supermarket, unable to choose what cereal to buy, what hope did I have of dealing with my dead mother's things?

When Dhara left home for university, I told her to keep what she wanted – which, in the end, wasn't much. Mum's spectacles. Her doctor's bag. Her favourite nightie – inexplicably, pink polyester and shaped like a sack. I binned everything else apart from the photo albums and her gods. The house went on the market, and all of the money from the sale went to pay for Dhara's tuition fees.

I was twenty when Mum died. My brain hadn't finished growing. I wonder sometimes if her death pressed a pause button so deep inside me that I've never really moved past that age. There has been very little in my life since that has been new or different, because everything I have experienced has come from a desire to stay within my comfort zone.

Myra is very much outside my comfort zone. Seeing myself reflected in her eyes is unique. She can't see any of the barriers that I've put up and while they may have been built to protect, it's clear that somewhere along the line they started holding me back. The truth is I've stayed angry with Mum because I didn't want to let her off the hook. I don't know why some people end up in sobriety and some don't. I do know that we distil it down to a laughably simple choice of wanting it enough.

I don't know what my father leaving did to her emotional chemistry. I don't know how she managed the sadness in herself, or even how much sadness she was managing in the first place. But being with Daisy has made me reconsider. I don't think Mum trying to escape herself also meant she was trying to escape us. Although I was dreading Daisy's visit, it allows me to put down something heavy, and perhaps make room for something else.

11

Back at the house, I start prepping dinner before we have to head out to Esme's. We had returned to see a handwritten note from her taped to the door, telling us to be there at 9 p.m. with three exclamation marks.

Although I thought she would balk at the idea of a full moon event, Daisy is agreeable. 'I did once try ayahuasca, you know,' she says, 'and it changed my life. These days I've learned to keep an open mind.'

Myra sent a message saying that Greg had found a rescue dog, and asking would it be okay if she stayed to help get him settled in? Daisy said it was fine, as long as she was back by 10 p.m.

While she pours herself a glass of wine and opens a bag of Skips, I wash some dal in my trusted Prestige pressure cooker that I've brought from home and set it to boil. It's nice to see Daisy loosen the tight control she usually exerts over herself when it comes to her diet back in London.

'I cannot believe you have brought your own pressure cooker like some old-school auntie-ji,' she howls. Myra hates the pressure cooker and its shrill whistle, and stomps upstairs whenever she sees it on the hob.

Cooking reduces the volume of noise in my head; the ritual

of it is like swimming through cool water during a heatwave. Selecting the vegetables, chopping them, picking out the parts lost to age. Feeling the cold, heavy texture of the chicken, the rustle of cinnamon sticks and cloves scenting the ghee, the fragrance of cardamom pods as they crush under my knife. While the dosa batter rises in the warmth of the airing cupboard – a trick to help the ground rice ferment quicker – I fry the onions. When the fenugreek and mustard hit the pot, the whole house billows with the rich fragrance of spice. 'It already smells so delicious,' Daisy says. 'I can't use fenugreek at home, unfortunately.'

'Why not?' I say, frowning.

'It makes everything smell,' she says ruefully. There's something about the 'poor me' tone of her voice, and the insult I feel that Daisy considers our food too pungent to sully her home with, that makes me snap. It is this shame she feels around our culture that has prevented Myra from accessing a part of herself that should be hers. Daisy should have considered it her duty to teach it to her daughter.

'I didn't realise how much you hate being Indian,' I say, stirring the spices so they don't stick to the pot. I gather up my chopped tomato and lower the heat a minute after it hits the pan.

'What? No, I don't,' Daisy says defensively. But I see it in her eyes, the guilt, the times she has erased herself from her own home.

This time, I don't look down or away, but give her the full force of my gaze. *Tell the truth,* it says. The power balance is different here because for the first time in years, we are not in Daisy's domain. We are not in the townhouse, where I am overwhelmed by the money and grandeur, and feel as if I have no legitimacy to advise her or comment on her choices when our lives are so different. I have found my words and this conversation has been coming for a long time.

'You changed your name, Daisy. Your actual name.'

'That's none of your business,' she snaps.

'I'm your older sister. I know you've forgotten that, but I do get to have an opinion if you stop using the name I've been calling you since you were a baby. The name that Mum and Dad gave you.'

'Don't you *dare* mention him!' Her eyes are bright with anger at the conjuration of our father. But Daisy isn't scary here. Without her poise, her sleek hair, her clickety-clack heels, she is just my baby sister.

'I'm not saying this to hurt your feelings. But your daughter doesn't even know the half of her that is Indian. Is it so bad that you want nothing to do with it?'

It is the burden of immigrant parents and children that a rejection of our culture from one of our own feels like a rejection of us as individuals. We see them cauterising parts of themselves and worry this will include us too. We wonder what that person will use for an anchor, for a sense of belonging, and who or what they will call home.

'Of course it's not that!' Daisy yells. 'How on earth could you think that?'

'Then what is it?' I raise my voice in return, slightly surprised and empowered by the return of nineties Padma who had no problem telling someone to back off. I was so used to being yelled at by her that I'd forgotten how satisfying it could be to yell back. 'What conclusion am I to draw from it? We've never spoken about it apart from that one day. I don't understand why you don't cook our food in your home. I don't understand why you're trusting me to take care of your daughter when you don't even seem to *like* me very much!'

Daisy is usually so focused on what she wants to say that she has a habit of not really listening to people. She doesn't listen to Myra trying to tell her how she's feeling, and she doesn't listen to a thing I say about my life. But now she is listening because she isn't distracted by her phone, or what Myra is up to, and she is shocked.

'How can you say that, Padma? You're my sister.'

'That's not really an answer,' I reply.

She massages her temples with her hands. 'Can you put the kettle on? I need a coffee. Please. And a paracetamol.'

I flick the kettle switch with as much vim as I can muster. When it boils, I make her a coffee the way I know she likes it. I've never been able to deny someone what they need if it's food or a drink.

'It's not about you, okay?' she says after a few sips. 'I didn't change my name because I wanted to distance myself from you. It's just . . . I wanted a change, Padma. I didn't want to feel so weighed down and sad, and that name, my name . . .' Her voice breaks. 'That name felt like it belonged to someone I wanted to forget. Like a bad dream.'

Hearing these words from Daisy unmoors me. I try and focus on the small things. Grains of sugar on the counter. The smell of coffee filling my nose. But still I find myself floating in a sea with no recognisable markers, no sense of north and south. Was everything I did for nothing if my sister still felt her old life was something to escape from?

'But I tried to protect you from a lot of stuff,' I say, struggling not to suffocate under the weight of her words. Trying not to remember the enormous sacrifices I made to shield her, to keep our household running. To learn none of it helped, in the end, almost winds me. 'I took care of everything after Mum died.'

'Yes, you did,' she says, a bit more softly. 'You really did. But you were also a kid, and you couldn't protect me from everything. It's easier for me to remember Mum being fun, or to focus on her loving us. I know you tried, but there were still things I saw, things I felt. Things I never got a chance to learn. I mean, take the cooking thing. You learned because Mum taught you, right? Who taught *me*?'

She's right. Of course she's right. I didn't teach her because I felt I needed to do it *for* her. I didn't think about the day when she'd need to do it herself. And how could I? I wasn't a parent – I was a child myself.

'I don't know if changing my name was the right or wrong thing to do,' she says. 'I just know that I was young, and it was this small thing that helped me to leave some of the more painful stuff behind. Helped me reinvent myself.'

Sequestering something that is a part of you, that is so deeply yours as to be categorised as soul stuff, has its consequences. I know this. I know why she was so flippant all those years ago when I asked her about it. It belied her true emotions: shame about who she was, guilt about wanting to let it go.

'Dhara was such a beautiful name,' I say sadly, knowing the day will never come when Daisy changes her name back.

'I know,' she says, with a brief flicker of grief and longing.

The whistle on the pressure cooker screeches so dramatically we both jump. 'I still can't believe you cook with that thing,' she says. We sit in each other's company for a while longer. I wash the chicken to put into the coconut mixture that has become silken and rich, while Daisy quietly sips her coffee.

*

Although the full moon hangs crisply outlined in the cloudless sky, the air feels humid and thick. The night-time insects buzz, saw and chirp, as we walk over to Esme's for her full moon event.

'Is that gnome wearing a bindi?' Daisy says. Before I can answer, Esme appears and joyfully says: 'Namaste!' I can't look at Daisy or I will burst out laughing. 'Welcome to you both. Please come in.'

In the entryway is an enormous geode, purple and white crystals catching the light. 'We have a wonderful group,' Esme says as she leads us through the kitchen, 'mostly from London.' Daisy shares a look with me, because we both know exactly what type of Londoner would do something like this. 'They're *dying* to meet you.'

Esme's house is the opposite of Rosemary's cottage. Not a net curtain in sight but white wooden plantation shutters. The grey and white palette reminds me of certain influencer Instagram accounts, but I forgive it because of the kitchen, which has an enormous solid oak countertop, cream cabinets and a copper pan display.

The other women are a mixture of Sarahs, Claires and Beths – who are at senior levels in their careers, mostly in their forties and fifties, talking about how calming it is out here, and how they are considering big life changes. They've been foraging for berries, paddleboarding, doing yoga, and now they know the true meaning of life. These women will return to London and within the first twenty-four hours, any acquired serenity will be burned off by their inbox and the demands of their children.

'Esme,' I say to give us an out, 'we can't stay too long because Myra will be back home soon.'

'Well then,' Esme pouts, 'you can stay for the group circle of full moon healing. We're starting now. Ah! Here comes my husband, Derek.' A bald man with brown skin enters the room carrying eye masks on a tray. He is wearing only a lungi, the piece of cloth that Indian men tie around their waist, like a sarong. Before Esme asks us to close our eyes, I look at Derek's skin closely and realise he isn't mixed-race or Indian; rather, he's extremely aggressive with the Bondi Sands Ultra Dark tanning solution.

*

When the ceremony begins, it is clear why we've been invited. We are the token browns, whose presence adds legitimacy. Esme starts tapping a round bronze bowl, which releases a rich, deep sound, and as the frequency of it hums through us, she starts talking about the importance of the full moon and what it means in Hinduism: fullness, abundance, prosperity. 'It is an auspicious time,' she says, 'for new beginnings.' Daisy and I are in a silent pact not to look at each other or we may laugh again; we are hardly believers who light the incense of the home shrine, but the incongruity of having Hinduism parroted back to us is almost too much.

We are seated on cushions in Esme's living room, with three fans rotating in the corner to cool us down. Several of the women are menopausal and they're still sweating through the breeze.

Derek sits in front of a collection of bowls, using a short wooden stick to circle the rims and tap to release the sound. Everyone takes that as the sign to put on the eye masks.

'I want you to feel the light of the full moon coming through the room to wash clean the past,' Esme says. 'I want you to think about the future. What you hope for yourself. What you want your future to look like. Don't hold back. You deserve to feel all that happiness. All that love. All that peace.'

To my horror, the laughter I felt bubbling in me previously drains away and my mind starts to float, very loosely tethered to Esme's voice and the sound of the bowls. I think of Wallace. I think of what I want from my life. I want to feel loved unconditionally, and I don't think he can offer that. Even if we stay together, if I don't give him a child, he will hold it over me.

I want to travel. I want to try the food in every country I visit. I want to eat pastel de nata on the streets of Lisbon; thick, honeyed barbecued ribs in Texas; fresh crab in the Caribbean. I want to see where Mum grew up, walk underneath the arches of the university she studied at. I want to run my own business so I never have to ask someone what time I can take a lunch break or fetch them coffee. And the things I used to believe to be impossible obstacles, I now realise aren't obstacles at all.

Esme continues to speak in a soft murmur, and then the crying starts. Soft little sobs, one by one, as the women confront themselves and realise they have denied themselves softness. That they have sacrificed and made other people's dreams happen, but didn't give themselves permission to dream. I wonder what Daisy is thinking about, and whether she feels moved by this too.

I don't know whether it has been half an hour, or an hour, but by the time we are finished, I feel empty and full at the same time. The emptiness is a relief because I know it represents what I am going to get rid of. The fullness is terrifying because I have to be brave enough to take chances and pull new things into my life until they fill up every part of it, so that when I die, I can say I led a life I loved.

Eventually we take off our eye masks, and I see that Daisy has been crying. A lot. She looks so small, my sister. Like she has taken off her armour and now she doesn't have the energy to put it back on.

*

After we get back to the house, Daisy pours us both a glass of wine and we sit on the wicker chairs, looking out to sea. The moon casts a trail from the shore to the horizon, a silver shimmer snaking through the dark.

'Well, that was unexpected,' she says, draining her glass.

'Are you okay?' I ask. Her shoulders are slumped. I'm not sure what the ceremony has brought up for her, what secret worries she is now acknowledging.

'What if it's my fault?' she says miserably.

'What do you mean?'

'My fault that Myra is like this.'

'Because of her having to go to hospital?'

'Not just that. I spoke to her therapist and it's early days but she seems to be doing okay. I was worried . . . about the drinking and whether it was a sign of something bigger. But the therapist thinks it isn't.'

'That's a good thing, isn't it? And from what I can tell, she hasn't been drinking here.' I don't tell Daisy about the cigarettes or the false accusation I made about Myra drinking because it wouldn't be helpful. But I know what Daisy is alluding to, because I've seen it in Myra, that heaviness she carries.

'She's still got a lot of stuff to work through,' Daisy says, pouring more wine. 'I just don't get *why* she ended up like this. What compels her to do these things that seem so . . . contrary to Henry and me. She's been raised with so much money – so much privilege. She doesn't want for a single thing. And still she has this void in her. I see it. Maybe I had it. I think Mum had it and that's why she was the way she was. And I am terrified for her.'

I think of my own void, the one I have kept hidden from Daisy. I didn't connect that to Mum or to her until just now. But perhaps there is something like that inside all of us, and we deal with it in our own way. Our mother had her way; mine is to hide it and keep myself safe, and never venture too far from myself or take risks.

But Myra is still working it out. Given that Daisy experienced post-natal depression, I'd have thought she'd recognise the signs better. But perhaps she felt it was specific to motherhood. I want to tell her what I think I know about Myra, but the way ahead feels fraught with quicksand, and I don't want to get pulled into something between Myra and Daisy, who have their own language even if they pretend not to understand each other most of the time.

'Wait a minute,' Daisy says, checking her phone, 'where is Myra?'

*

We'd asked Myra to be back home by 10 p.m. and 10.30 arrives with no sign of her. At 11 p.m. Daisy starts pacing and calling her phone. Unlike when she went missing a couple of weeks ago, this time there is a dial tone.

'ARE YOU FUCKING KIDDING ME, MYRA, YOU'RE PULLING THIS SHIT – AGAIN?' she yells into voicemail. While Daisy calls Henry, I send Myra a furtive message.

Where are you? I think you should come home. Your mother is REALLY angry.

I see her typing and then, all of a sudden, it stops.

Daisy gestures at me furiously. 'Henry wants to talk to you.'

'Has she ever done anything like this with you before, Padma?' Henry isn't angry or upset but sounds remarkably calm. He's trying to gather all the data before deciding the scale of panic.

'No. I mean the phone reception around here is terrible, and there was one time when she got lost but she was back by 9 p.m. And she's been doing well. Gets up in the morning, has a routine . . .'

'And this friend of hers – Greg. Is he . . . okay?'

'I'd say so. He's round here a lot. He helped Myra when I gave her the task of sorting out the garden. He isn't like the little shits around here who drink Strongbow and throw stones at pigeons, if you know what I mean.'

'Myra has been doing stuff in the . . . garden?'

'Well, yes. Daisy asked me to give her a task, and I thought it would be a good project.'

'And she actually did it?' He sounds shocked.

'Yes. You'd be proud – she set up a whole homemade irrigation system with a barrel of water and some hose because the weather has been extremely dry. Saw a video on YouTube and just did it. Hasn't she told you any of this?'

'No – I mean, I've been travelling for work, and she doesn't say much about her life anyway. You know what teenagers are like – monosyllabic at best.' He pauses, 'What do you think has happened? Do you think she's off drinking or is doing something with this boy?'

My phone pings with a message. Greg. He's with Myra, but there's more. 'Henry,' I say slowly while reading it, 'I don't think it's to do with either of those things.'

*

I don't believe in God, but if I did, I would fully accept there is a god of mischief. Not only does Daisy have a flat tyre, but she's blocked me in, so we can't take the BMW. 'I can't believe this,' she says. 'Now I have to call a mechanic. Where am I going to find one at this time of night!'

'We can do it,' I say calmly.

'What, you know how to change a tyre?' she scoffs, pulling out her phone.

'Not exactly, but we can watch a video of how to do it. I've fixed loads of stuff around the house that way. Leaking tap, dodgy toilet, fuse, pulling out a splinter. You don't need men for this stuff,' I say sagely.

'All right, go on then.' After watching the video a few times, we open the boot of the car to see there is no spare tyre. When I look enquiringly at Daisy she says: 'What? This is a rental.'

'We'll never get a taxi on a Saturday night this late. Myra is at Greg's,' I say, 'let's just walk there, all right? You can get your steps in or whatever.'

'Fine,' she snaps.

'Daisy,' I say, 'you promised you wouldn't lose your temper.'

'Yeah, well,' she says, without a trace of humour in her voice, 'promises can be broken.'

*

Greg's house, a cottage on the other side of the town, is a thirty-minute walk away. After we pass the crowds clustered on the beach around bonfires, laughing raucously in the beer garden of the local sea-facing pub, I make Daisy stop for a moment. For a small woman she can certainly get her march on, sweat beading on her upper lip as she mutters loudly about how she *CAN'T BELIEVE IT* and *Myra is coming back to London tomorrow MORNING* and *fuck summer camp, it's MILITARY CAMP.*

Using Myra's phone, Greg texted to let me know what the situation was. He had got a rescue dog from the shelter and so had . . . Myra. Except while Greg had been through the whole process in advance with his mother and had already been approved by the shelter, Myra had stolen hers. The rest of the details were still unclear, but when they returned to Greg's, reality set in for Myra and she'd been too scared to go home.

'Look, is what she did really that bad?' I ask.

Daisy's face shakes with anger. 'I know you think you have a handle on things because you've turned her into Alan Titchmarsh, but this is what she does, Padma. She pushes and pushes to see how far she can get away with things. And this time she has gone too far.'

'Just listen. Give me a minute. Three weeks ago, your kid would have been doing god knows what, god knows where. We've passed tons of teenagers just now, drinking and smoking behind their parents' backs. Worse even. And look, I don't know what I'm doing – not really. I'm not a parent. I can't imagine how hard this has been for you . . .'

'No, you can't,' she says sharply. 'She's my flesh and blood, Padma. I'm the one who worries about whether she's dead in a ditch somewhere. I—'

'I know,' I say, squeezing her shoulder. 'She came from you – you literally created her from breath and bone. I cannot imagine how it must feel, the weight of that love! But, Daisy, do you trust me?' She looks at me across that gulf we have allowed to grow between us. Maybe she wants to say yes but doesn't know how to reconcile the complicated love between us.

'Whatever has happened in the intervening years, I have loved you longer than I have loved anyone on this planet,' I continue. 'If you need something to trust in, trust in that. But I am telling you, this kid needs to be heard, to be understood.'

'She *knows* how I feel about this, Padma,' says Daisy, her voice strained. 'She's been asking for a dog forever. We've always said no because we have a ton of art in the house. And she doesn't take responsibility for anything – how is she going to take responsibility for a living creature? And rather than talk to us about it, she *steals* a dog? Does that sound like a normal thing to you?'

'I don't agree with how she did it but I think we need to find out why she did it,' I say, refusing to give in. 'And this may be an inappropriate thing to say . . . but think about when homeless people have dogs, Daisy. They can provide love, routine and purpose. Maybe this will be good for Myra.'

'Well, how do you suggest I handle this?' she retorts. 'Just say, "Hey, kid! Congratulations, you're now the proud owner of a dog!"'

'I wouldn't say anything tonight. I would tell her you can talk about it tomorrow. But I think if she shows she can take care of a dog, then let her keep it. I'll help. Okay? Because I don't think any piece of antique furniture is worth the price of your child's broken heart. Have some fun with her tomorrow. Go shopping together. Have some food. Watch one of her awful horror films with her. Ask her to show you what she's been doing in the garden. Do your make-up together. Walk the dog.'

She grunts and eventually motions me to keep walking. 'I can't *believe* you said that about homeless people,' she says.

*

'Her name is Tara,' Myra says softly to us when she opens the door. In her arms is a small, wriggling caramel ball of fluff. I catch sight of one enormous dark brown eye under a frizz of fur. The other seems to be permanently closed, an accident, maybe. Tara's tail wags so hard it beats a tattoo against Myra's arm. I hold back to give Daisy centre stage. She doesn't shout or yell. Something softens in her gaze when she sees Myra, but anger holds her back from saying anything loving.

Sarah Margaret drops us all back at the house together with a plastic bag of dog food to tide us over until the morning. When the front door closes, Tara shoots off to inspect the rest of the house. 'She's a year old and house-trained,' Myra says, her body language submissive and small, trying to reduce the surface area that will receive a verbal lashing.

But there is none. 'What happened?' Daisy says wearily. 'Why did you . . .'

We sit in the living room, the two of them on the sofa, and me in the oversized armchair covered in blankets. 'Mum, I know . . .' Myra begins, and then stops. Takes a deep breath like I taught her and gathers herself. 'We went to the shelter and everything was fine. I promise, I didn't plan this. But while Greg was sorting out Lucky, I overheard that they were going to put down another dog. She only has one eye – I don't know if you noticed? No one wanted her because of that, even though she's the cutest thing. When I said I would take her, they laughed and said I needed to have all this paperwork. They *laughed*, Mum. And she was going to die because of what? Not having the right paper?'

Daisy leans over and holds her hand. The confusion and hurt on Myra's face are painful to see. Witnessing someone's first steps towards understanding how brutal the world can be sometimes, the lack of value placed on a life. And, I thought more proudly, how sometimes you need to find a way even when other people won't make one for you. And Myra had. 'While they were on a lunch break, I just – snapped. If I hadn't taken her, she would've been . . .' She starts crying and Daisy pulls her into a mother-bear hug.

I go to get up from the armchair to give them some time,

but Daisy gestures me over. I gingerly sit on the other side of Myra.

'Hello, trouble,' I say, hugging the other side of her.

'Hello, Aunt,' she says back, her face muffled in Daisy's neck.

'Why did you name her Tara?'

She lifts her head and turns to face me. 'It means "star" in Sanskrit. Did you know that?'

Daisy's face behind her fills with emotion, some of it pride, some sadness, all of it love.

*

The next morning just after dawn I make myself a coffee and open the back door to see Myra leaning half-asleep against the wall in a Pokémon hoodie, watching Tara sniff the flowers, selecting a spot to pee. I've never seen her awake this early. I'm not necessarily a dog person, but she is undeniably cute. A mixed breed with some poodle in there.

'Good morning, dog-napper,' I say.

'Ha-ha,' Myra yawns.

'I put my neck on the line for you yesterday,' I say. 'You have to show you can look after this dog, and if you can, then you can keep her.'

Myra looks at Tara, shaking her bottom in the air as she digs between the fence posts, and love is already written in her gaze. There is no question of them being parted.

'Whatever it takes. I'm amazed Mum let me bring her home at all. Although if she'd tried to separate us . . .'

I sip my coffee and we listen to birdsong for a while. 'Your mum is wondering whether you should just go back to London with her. But I said you might want to stay. Do you want to be here with me? Or would you prefer to go back?'

She takes such a long time to answer, it makes me nervous. 'I should probably stay. After all, who else would look after you? Besides, Mum just talks endlessly about school and A-levels and *you're lacking in direction, Myra*. I'm only fifteen, for fuck's sake.'

'*Language*. Have you ever spoken to her about it?'

'She doesn't listen. She barely listens to you – and you're a grown-up.'

It won't help anyone if I take sides. Daisy needs help in softening towards Myra, and Myra needs help understanding her mother.

'Did your mother ever tell you about your grandmother? What she was like?'

'Not much. We have that picture of her hanging up and that's it. I know she was a doctor.'

'There's a lot about your mother that can be explained by the type of person your grandmother was. I know it's hard at your age – it feels like everyone has a say in your life or tries to control what's in it. But I think maybe understanding your mother can make that stuff a bit easier, you know?'

'Why – what was she like? What was different about her?'

'Your dodda – that's the word in our language for "grandma" – came over from India. She was a brilliant doctor but she always had to contend with being an immigrant and never fully being accepted. I think your mother saw how hard it was for her, and for me, and tried to make sure things were different for you. But it also means she puts a lot of pressure on . . . everything, and that can be really difficult. Especially if you don't know why she's being like that. What you think is a criticism of you – or you not being enough for her – isn't really about you. It's about her.'

I look at Myra to see if any of it is sinking in. She seems to be absorbing it, for now at least. I can tell the idea that her parents have had different experiences of safety and belonging has never occurred to her.

'Your video is doing well, by the way,' she says, changing the subject. 'Let's record some more this week.'

Tara bounds over for attention and Myra reaches down to give her a treat. Already in such a short space of time, Tara knows Myra is hers. I leave them in the sunshine, feeling the warmth of our shared plans, and this new life that has come into ours, needing both of us.

*

Before I walk down to the Green Goddess, I make a detour across to the beach Hugo and I visited. Alva Beach. I love this part of the morning, the softness present in the sky that is smudged pinks and blues, dew gathered in the grass as I walk past. There is only silence, too early for the hum of jet skis in the distance, and too late to catch the birds tidying up their nests or stalking about for worms.

I think about Daisy, and how tangled our love is. I've been avoiding conflict with her for so long, I failed to see that this is a vital part of how we measure our love for each other. That we cared enough to fight or disagree, and that love isn't just agreeing with what the other person wants for fear of losing them or being banished. That daring to disagree is in fact an expression of certainty.

I make it to Beach Road just in time to help Selena with the morning service – plating up, chopping, making coffees – and Caitlin smoothly moves between tables, taking orders and handing out plates. Selena has been banished to the kitchen and told not to come out, which has alleviated a lot of the pressure she feels to talk to her customers while panicking that the fake bacon is burning.

Once the morning rush eases off, we sit down at a table with tea and a veggie sausage sandwich to discuss the two specials I'll be making for her lunch service, but more excitingly, the relaunch of her menu in three weeks. While she'll still be serving some local favourites, she'll also be offering gluten-free and dairy-free options in the pastry and dessert cabinet. Eileen, who owns the only other competing café on Beach Road, is someone who believes gluten-free is 'hipster bollocks', and I think it will give Selena an advantage being the only place in Harkness to do it well.

'This is cute,' she says, gesturing at my striped top and loose parachute trousers that are tapered at the ankles. Given how meticulous she is about her clothes, it is a compliment that warms me.

I start working on the two specials I'm trialling at lunch, both hybrids. One is a macadamia nut chaat and the other a tikka masala vegetarian pie. I prep the chaat, chopping boiled potatoes, coriander, washing chickpeas, so all Caitlin has to do is scoop some in a bowl and drizzle on some tamarind and mint chutney, while the pie filling is already cooked. As I roll the pastry out for it, my eye catches Myra and Daisy peering through the window. I gesture at them to come in.

'Why are you being so weird?' I ask.

'We didn't want to disturb you while you're working,' Myra says, trying to rein in Tara, who is going berserk at the new and interesting smells in the café. As she snuffles her way over to Selena, who is putting out a bowl of water for her, Myra follows.

'I see presents have been bought,' I say to Daisy, referring to Tara's new lead and the shopping bag that says Pups N Stuff. 'Does that mean the dog is staying?'

'For now,' Daisy says, glaring at Tara wagging her tail. 'She's on probation. I'll have to sort things out with the shelter but I'm sure we can reach an agreement.'

'And are you going to take Myra back to London now or let her stay?' I try to act nonchalant but I'm hoping Daisy will let her stay. I have no desire to return to London either, given that it will mean having to piece together my life.

'She seems happy here and there's only another three weeks to go so I've decided she can stay. How do you feel about that?' she asks. 'Wallace okay with you being gone this long?'

'It's fine with me.' I roll out the dough, coloured a deep yellow from the turmeric I have folded into the flour. When I raise my head Daisy is looking curiously at me. 'Oh, yeah, and Wallace. He's fine.'

'Mum! Let's go,' Myra says.

'More shopping,' Daisy explains. 'We'll see you back at the house. Let's continue this chat later, okay?' I nod and start pressing the filling into the pastry, eager for her prying gaze to be somewhere else.

'Padma?' Daisy says, and I look up from my work. 'You look . . . happy. Right now. Like you're in your element, you know?'

It's the first time she has said anything like this to me. An observation that isn't stapled on to a piece of advice about what she thinks I should be doing. Maybe it isn't too late for people to change. For me, and for her.

12

The next morning, I wake just before the dawn. It feels as if something from the beyond, the dream or the death realm, is shaking my shoulder. With a blanket wrapped around me, I make my way out to the back of the house and settle into the new outdoor sofa, a mug of coffee held between my hands. Witnessing a sky full of stars transform into dawn makes it seem reasonable, possible even, that the loved ones we have lost sit in the space between the horizon and the earth.

I think of Mum, and that makes me think of Daisy and our histories, which are the same and yet so different. Daisy and I aren't best friends, or even best siblings, but when it came to Myra, she listened to me. It made me feel like I mattered. That she needed me. I hadn't realised how much I had needed to feel that from her.

The patio door scrapes open and Daisy steps over the threshold, her tiny body wrapped in a thick cardigan, like a piece of glass in cotton wool. She sits on the sofa, her knees pulled up to her chest like she used to do when we were kids. 'Couldn't sleep either?' she says.

'Something called me out here,' I reply.

'Careful,' she says, 'you're starting to sound like Esme.' I smile and continue to look straight ahead. We sit in the silence for a while until she gathers the right words. 'Pads . . . it's been brought to my attention that I don't really ask you about . . . you.'

This must be the work of Myra.

'I'm fine, honestly,' I say.

'Yeah, she said you'd say that. But are you fine? How are things with you? How are things with Wallace?' She sips her coffee and looks sideways at me. For years, I have stopped telling Daisy anything about Wallace. She asks how he is, I say he's doing well, neither of us talks about his absence from various parties, and he remains a distant satellite in her life. But now she isn't asking how *he* is, she's asking how things are *with* him.

I don't know if it's because it's too early in the day to manufacture lies or because I've recently realised just how wearing it is to carry around a different version of myself for Daisy. But I tell her about how things have been, our conversations around kids and his ultimatum.

'I don't understand,' she says, 'why don't you want kids? You'd be a great parent.'

I sigh. 'See, this is why I don't talk about this kind of thing with you.'

'What is that supposed to mean?'

'Isn't it enough, Daisy, for me to say I don't want kids? That maybe I have given it some thought and it wasn't something I just decided on a whim? Why is it that people cannot wrap their heads around the fact that not everyone wants a child?'

'I didn't say . . .' she begins, but my repressed anger spills over.

'I don't want kids. I never have. It doesn't mean that I don't love Myra, or that I don't admire what you do as a mother. Believe me, I do. But I don't. Want. Them. I am not going to change my mind. And no matter what I say, no one seems to listen to me, least of all my boyfriend!'

The word 'boyfriend' rings out in the silent dawn. I hate losing my temper and Daisy doesn't say anything. She knows the anger isn't for her and for once she doesn't rise to it. We watch the morning sky and wait for the sea air to carry away the heat of my words. Eventually she says: 'I'm sorry.' I cannot believe she has said that. The last time those two words came out of her mouth, she was a teenager. 'That must be shit. Especially if you've been given an ultimatum.'

'You've always hated him,' I say. Not accusingly, just a statement.

'I don't *hate* him, Padma, but . . .' She tries to search for the right words, aware that she's in danger of saying the wrong thing.

'I hate that you don't seem happy with him,' she says, with a sigh. When I don't respond, she angles herself round to look at me and puts her hand on my knee. 'I mean, are you happy?'

I can't look at her. It's one thing to know that you are not and mostly be in denial about it, and another to see the full reflection of your unhappiness in another person's eyes. The upset that I carry around Wallace not being in touch feels so big, as well as the growing feeling that I won't be able to forgive him or look past him asking for a break, that I'm worried if I offload that onto Daisy, I will never stop crying.

'I've lost my job, and if I don't say yes to Wallace wanting a child, I'll lose him and my home,' I reply. 'It's a stressful time. So maybe I'm not my happiest right now.'

'No, Padma,' Daisy says patiently. 'I'm not talking about now, or the last year. I'm talking about most of the time you've been with him. I've seen you get smaller and smaller.'

I laugh. 'I'm not exactly small.'

'No,' Daisy says, shaking her head. 'Don't do that. Don't do that thing where you make a joke, or laugh it off, or stay quiet. You know what I mean.'

'I mean, who truly is happy?'

'You know,' she says after a long pause, 'I used to think happiness was this complicated thing – always out of reach. But there are people who wake up, have a coffee, look out at the ocean, do the things they love in the day, go for a walk, have a good dinner and go to bed. And that's it. That makes them happy.'

'And what about you? Are you happy?'

'No,' she says, looking out to the horizon, as if the answer lies in the soft pink band beyond. 'But I'm working on it. And sometimes, that's the best any of us can do.' The alarm on her phone goes off. It's Monday morning and she needs to shower and leave before traffic on the motorway gets too heavy.

She stands up reluctantly and pats the dew off her bottom. 'The only thing worse than not being happy,' she says, looking at me, 'is thinking you're a victim and that nothing can change. We are so often the architects of our own sadness, Padma. Maybe it's time to change your blueprint.'

After she leaves to go inside, birds of prey take to the sky and scour the sea, which flows in a smooth silver line towards the shore, making the air smell of salt and change.

*

Myra and I spend the next week decompressing from Daisy's visit, allowing the new bond between us to settle. Her routine changes significantly with Tara's arrival. Although I'd anticipated having to cajole Myra awake or nagging her to walk the dog, she takes Tara out first thing in the morning, and for a longer walk in the afternoon – usually with Greg and Lucky. I wonder what these two must look like to people who encounter them: Myra, beautifully made up with eyeliner and hair in mini-braids, walking around in her over-the-knee socks and chunky black trainers. Greg dressed like a small off-duty accountant in high-waisted beige trousers and a polo shirt.

I mostly spend my time working in the Green Goddess, walking and swimming. Selena's grand opening is in two weeks – a few days before we are due to go back home. The afternoons are hot, drawing every ounce of moisture into the sky, and during the hottest hours, I sit next to the new air-conditioning unit whirring in the kitchen.

The garden has fallen off as a Myra project – but I can't press something onto her that she finds boring, and then use that as a measuring stick for her progress. Besides, with a lot of the work in the house done, I find it peaceful to potter about planting things and pruning when I'm not at Selena's. My mind is constantly drawn to Wallace, a weave of memories from the past and questions around what he is doing in the present. Every night, I sit outside with a cup of bedtime tea and look up at our corner of the cosmos. I start by wishing hard upon a star that he will call. That somehow he will feel me looking up at the night sky. But then my mind drifts from Wallace, and the cosmos connects me to something indescribably vast: the sight of a thousand stars, each one a pinpoint of light against the darkest night. He used to feel like the centre of my solar system, but the more I reach for it, the more I realise it has shifted. My centre is no longer another person.

It helps that Myra's mood is more even. I'm not sure if it's

Tara or the cumulative benefit of therapy, but she is less tempestuous. She has a lot to occupy herself with. Her interest in my social media accounts went from zero to sixty – now she has a 'strategy'. Myra insists I post something on TikTok and Instagram every day or I'll 'lose engagement'. Her focus is terrifying – she checks analytics, course-corrects when she thinks I've not explained something properly. Although I've never been particularly confident in front of the camera, she will ask me questions to draw something out of a story, which keeps me distracted long enough to forget I'm being filmed. I still find it mostly baffling, but her work is paying off and she seems to take great enjoyment from it. Even in just a few days, she's increased my following.

Towards the end of the week, we are having a lazy day, trying to avoid the weekend rush of people, which has not abated since Nicole Kelly fever enveloped the town. Myra is in her cubbyhole upstairs, near the skylight, with Tara dozing next to her in a pool of light, and I'm sprawled on the sofa downstairs, reading a book. I'm settling into a peaceful sleep after a cheese toastie when a scream spears downwards like a lightning bolt.

I run up the stairs to find the cubbyhole is empty. The noise comes from Myra's room and I burst in, only to find her excitedly bouncing up and down on the bed while Tara barks and nips at the bed covers.

'Auntie – you will never believe what has happened!' she yells. There's no emergency, she's perfectly fine.

'I don't care,' I say, trying to catch my breath. 'Never scream like that again unless you are actually being murdered, okay?'

'*Nigella flipping Lawson* has reposted your cramosa video on her Instagram page. Have you checked your follower count?'

The last time I checked it, we had hit the 500 mark, which I found impressive. I scroll to my page on my phone. Oh my god!

'*Ten thousand followers*? How is this possible? Why – *how?*'

'And counting,' says Myra, beaming. 'I just kept tagging chefs on your videos and she must have liked what you posted. Also she famously loves helping out people. Look, I've already updated your profile with an email address for paid partnerships and opportunities, and I've invented your agent's name. I called them Pinky Dishwallah.'

'*Pinky Dishwallah?* You've been watching too much Netflix India.'

'We need to work out what your next post is going to be. It's got to be something phenomenal.'

*

While Myra goes into mad media guru mode, trying to narrow down which dish I should make – it's a tie between masala mac and cheese or butter chicken pizza because 'Nigella is a queen who loves a carb' – my phone pings with a text from Hugo.

I hear congratulations are in order. Nigella is as big as it gets!

How did you find out?! I text back.

Myra had apparently sent her mother a message about the news, Daisy must have passed it on to Henry, and Hugo was visiting when she arrived home. I debate whether to call him. It feels like good news that I want to share, but am I just making excuses so that I can speak to him?

I feel foolish and self-aware. What if he had been nice to me because he saw me as some sort of project? Another voice said treacherously: *Why does it matter if he is just a friend?* With things still in limbo with Wallace, it feels wrong to call, but then again – it shouldn't feel wrong to call a friend, should it?

Unless, I reasoned, I called him and he *also* spoke to Myra. Then it was *completely* harmless.

'Myra,' I say, 'if I call Uncle Hugo, do you want to speak to him?'

'Whatever,' she murmurs and continues scrolling. Taking that as a resounding yes, I call him on speakerphone and he picks up immediately. 'Well, well,' he says, 'if it isn't Instagram sensation Padma Alva. To what do I owe this pleasure, madam?'

Myra looks up and raises an eyebrow. I hastily move to the next room and talk to him about the post and what we've been up to in the last few days. 'Sounds like you and Daisy made a lot of progress,' he says.

'It's so hard to tell with her,' I sigh. 'We talked about a lot of stuff we haven't done in . . . years. Our parents. How absent they were. It was tough but I do feel better for having talked about it, you know?'

'Oh, yeah,' he says. 'That stuff never goes away. It just sits in a closet and leaks out into everything anyway. My dad was absent all the time. It's why I spent so much time at Aunt Rosemary's and at Henry's. And I thought – well, I don't know what it's like to really have a dad anyway, so how can I miss what I didn't have? But it turns out I do, and I have. It's been this void that has impacted the kind of partner I choose, how self-sufficient I am – all that stuff.'

'Do you find it hard to let other people help you too?'

'All the time,' he laughs. 'I'm guessing you're the same.'

'Yes.' I laugh back wryly. 'Listen, let me hand you to Myra.'

'Wait – before you do, there's something I need to check with you,' he says. 'This weekend I need to come back out to Harkness. Is it okay if I stay the night? I can drive back in the same day but Saturday night traffic will be horrendous.'

'Er, sure,' I stammer, not expecting this at all. It's one thing to talk to Hugo, another thing to spend time with him. And although Wallace and I are on an enforced no-contact break, should I tell him?

'I've been thinking about putting the house on the market and I have a meeting with the estate agent. With the sudden renewed tourism interest, I think I can get a good price. And I mean – I'm not exactly using it.'

I feel slightly deflated. Not just because I've spent hours and days clearing the house and making it a living space that felt like a haven for myself and Myra, but because I've got used to being here. The idea of never coming back, or someone else living here, hadn't occurred to me.

'Of course,' I say, tucking my feelings away, 'it's your place. Let me know your dates.' After I pass the phone to Myra – who raises one eyebrow in the same way Daisy does – my head is crackling with so many thoughts, I need something to ground them. Wallace is going to hit the roof when I tell him.

When Myra is off the phone, I tell her to put her shoes on. We're going for a walk. I need space to think and walk, but I don't want to be alone, and Myra has had way too much screentime.

'But we have to work on the recipe!' she groans. 'Where are we going?'

'We are going to visit the White Sentinels.'

Tara yaps excitedly, sensing the prospect of a walk in the air.

'*You* are not coming, I'm afraid,' I say. 'There are nesting birds,' I explain to her, 'and I don't know if you're allowed on the beach.' She doesn't care for my explanation and trots upstairs in a huff to Myra's room.

*

Chalk is compressed life: plankton and marine creatures turned into rock. It is what mostly makes up Harkness and a lot of the basins and downs in Kent. The White Sentinels, we learn from a tourist brochure, is a stunning geographic formation called a sea stack. At one point in time, they were part of a larger cliff, until erosion wore away parts of the cliff face, leaving three imposing pillars of chalk rising up from the sand.

Unlike the Needles, the chalk stacks near the Isle of Wight, they are accessible by foot at certain points in the tidal range, but aren't easy to access from the town. Google Maps goes haywire and usually tips people out by a crumbling old shepherd's hut further inland, and locally produced maps are incomprehensible as they were written by David Bentley, peppered with flowery language and historical anecdotes. It takes detailed instructions from Selena and Hugo to identify a proper route that is around an hour to walk. By the time we work our way to them, we have consumed two Snickers bars, a bottle of Lucozade and half a ham sandwich. There have been three stops and two monologues about sore feet and needing the toilet, but as we approach the stacks, a quietness settles over us both.

'Be mindful of the tide', a sign hanging off a rusted post

reads. Myra can't swim, and I don't know how confident I feel in a bay that looks so wild, with unseen currents waiting to hook around my ankles and drag me further out. But maybe it won't hurt to get our feet wet.

'Come on,' I say to her. She shakes her head.

'We're only going to go in a little way, you wimp.' I roll my joggers up and stand in the shallows. Occasionally I see shoals of tiny white fish moving in a ball and darting around as one. In the time it takes for a kite to join its mate circling overhead in the updraught, a soft splash tells me Myra is approaching. We stand there for a while, feeling the delicious contrast between our cool feet and the hot sun on our skin that floods through our bodies, carrying with it light and hope and clarity.

'Auntie, can I ask you a question?'

'Always,' I say, with my eyes closed, not thinking or searching, just in the moment.

'Why do you think you get depression?' Myra asks. My eyes fly open, unprepared. It feels strange for it to be brought into the sunlight, to be talked about so freely. What has made her think about it now?

'I don't know,' I say slowly. 'I've spent so many hours wishing I knew, because then maybe I could stop it from happening. But I don't . . . know.'

Daisy's visit has stirred up things that have sat quietly in the murk. Did our mother have depression? Was that why she drank so much? Was it a reprieve from the hollow silence inside her own head? Daisy and I had processed our father's absence differently, but we had almost exclusively viewed it through the lens of how it affected us. I had never considered how it must have affected our mother, and what abandonment of the heart did to a person. How much it must have made her question her own worth, and how much she must have blamed herself.

'Do you wish you could be . . .' Myra bites her lip and stops herself from speaking further. 'Never mind.'

'Normal?' I hear the word anyway, even though it is unsaid. She looks down, unable to meet my gaze. I bend over to dip my hands in the cool water and dab the back of my neck.

This is the moment I should tell Myra there is no such thing as normal. That we see and think and feel the edges of the world in a way others don't, and sometimes it is too much and bruises our skin, but other times it allows us to feel the humanity in things. Maybe the price we pay for the dark and the muck is the ability to see the full brightness of things. But thinking about it only makes me remember what I've lost, and who I've become.

I want coffee brought to me in bed in the morning; for someone to wrap their arm around my shoulders and pull me close as we look at the sunrise arriving. I want work to fill me up.

I stand as still as possible, feeling the tears roll down my face, my toes pinching into the sand, my hands in tight fists by my sides. I don't want Myra to see me crying, but when I eventually take a breath, it comes out in a gasp, all of it, and she looks at my wet face, concerned.

*

'Auntie, is this because of what I said?' She speaks in a small voice. We're sitting on a dry dune some distance away from the shore, our feet dusted in sand like doughnuts. Behind us, long grass whispers in the soft breeze that ripples down the coastline.

'It's not you,' I reply. 'I'm just so—'

I want to say: *My heart is broken. Whatever path I choose, the pain that lies ahead is unavoidable. I know I should choose me, but I don't feel able. I don't know how to. It's not as simple as leaving Wallace. I don't want to be alone. I wish I was stronger than this; I know how many women fought for us to be stronger than saddling ourselves with a mediocre man.* But how can I tell Myra about any of this when she is already stronger at fifteen than I seem to be at thirty-nine?

Something shifts in her gaze. Instead of losing respect for me because I'm crying, something equalises between us. I suspect she's spent so long with a mother who goes to great lengths to appear perfect, that there's something new in the vulnerability I'm showing.

'Okay, tell you what,' she says. 'I do this thing sometimes in therapy. You tell me a feeling, and I'll tell you a feeling.'

'That sounds nuts.'

'Nuts is not a word you should use in that context, Auntie,' she says solemnly. 'Tell me something you're feeling and why you're feeling it, and then I'll do the same.'

'Okay, okay,' I say, dusting small granules of salt from my ankles. 'You know Wallace, my boyfriend?'

'Yes,' she says, studying the dirt beneath her nails. She also is not a fan of Wallace, especially since she overheard me telling Selena he hadn't been in touch recently.

'Well, I've been struggling with my feelings towards him. We've been together a long time. He wants children, I don't. And he's told me that unless I change my mind, we have to break up.'

'Why don't you want children?' she asks curiously. 'Don't you like them?'

'It's not that.' How do I answer this without offending her? 'I've just never had the urge. And it seemed to me like it was an enormous responsibility that people just didn't talk about truthfully. It's like you're expected to want kids, but no one really talks about how hard it is. People always say, "What if you regret not having them?" Whereas I think it must be awful if you have them and regret them. And there are plenty of people whose parents were terrible. That's the thing. People act as if situations like this don't exist when they're trying to pressure you into having kids.'

'Hmmm,' she replies, rolling down her leggings over her shins. 'I wonder if Mum regrets having me.'

'I can tell you one hundred per cent she does not,' I laugh. 'She loved you from the moment she had you, and even if she tests your patience now, or yells at you, you're everything to her.'

Myra looks down before asking: 'But if you don't want kids, why don't you just break up? You could find someone else, easy.'

I smile at the innocence in her words because she doesn't know, just yet. She doesn't know the currency women have in youth, how it diminishes in the eyes of men as they age. That at the beginning, your newness gathers in the mouth like the juice of a peach that everyone wants a taste of. That as you get older, what society values in a man – wisdom, achievement, learning – is not what a man values in a woman, because they are looking for someone to be their backlight, not someone who will match them. My friend Rekha is constantly fending off men twenty years older than her, while men her age want to date women twenty years younger.

I stare into the distance as if the sky holds the answer, but all it contains are clouds and contrails.

'I'm not sure. I've spent so much time with him, on our relationship, that I am worried if I end it, it will mean I've wasted ten years. And if I am being honest, I don't want to be alone.'

'Why not?' she asks.

'Well, because human beings want to be needed, they want to be around other people, and more than anything, they want connection,' I say.

'But you have me and Mum,' she says. 'And Dad. And you have friends. You're not alone.'

'And what about you?' I say, trying to change the subject. 'How are you feeling at the moment? After the hospital, and being away from your friends?' When she doesn't answer, I gently poke her in the side. 'I answered a lot of your questions, Myra . . .'

She sighs and throws up her hands. 'Mum has really high expectations, you know? She's worried I'm going to end up down a bad path, and so she's doing so much – too much – to try and keep me on track. Yes, I was drinking a lot and worried her and Dad, and that was a dick move, but sometimes . . . sometimes I feel like there is this weight that presses down on me. Like a rock that just sits on my chest. Sometimes I can carry the rock. I go to school, and I do my homework, and I play video games with my friends . . . but sometimes the rock is too heavy.

'I told one of my teachers about it and they told me to fucking meditate or google mindfulness! Sometimes it's hard to leave the house. Sue covers for me and doesn't tell Mum I haven't left for school, but then she gets a note saying I've missed class. And she yells and tells me I'll never get into

Cambridge. She's never even asked me if I *want* to go to Cambridge. And all the while *there is a rock on my chest.*'

'Do you want to talk about it?' I say softly. 'About what happened? The seizure? That must have been scary.'

'What's there to say?' she asks. 'You know what happened. You saw me . . . it's so *embarrassing*.' I hold my breath, cultivating a silence for her to fill. But then something shuts down inside her.

So we wait. We watch a bird turn its brown-and-white wings towards the sun, then pivot and hurtle into the sea, neatly slicing the surface with its beak before exploding upwards in silver, wings, light and fins.

I remember what youth was like. The sense of self so raw and new, it felt like everything. First love, first angst, first rebellion.

'Sometimes I just think . . . why bother?' Myra says. 'Why are you bothering with me? With this? I'm not worth the effort.'

Myra wears her swagger like a pigeon puffing out its chest, but with it removed, what remains is still a child. Her small hands, the little charms that hang off her shoelaces, the weight of everything bowing her down, and she doesn't yet have the strength to push it off. 'Is that what your friends said?' I ask, knowing these words haven't just appeared from nowhere. She doesn't answer but looks down at her feet. She's unlike anyone I've met before. A little latte-coloured goth girl who listens to music about death and killing and pain, who stole a rescue dog, is surprisingly good at gardening and will painstakingly edit a video for her aunt's cooking account.

'Myra. Would you say that the four of us – your parents, me and Hugo – are similar people?'

'No.'

'Okay. Logically, the four of us are very different people. We can barely agree on the proper way of making tea let alone our opinion of someone. And yet we all think you are a bright, incredible girl, one we love and want to see flourish. So either that's true or each of us is completely wrong. Which is more likely?'

She stares ahead in silence.

'What I'm saying is, however you feel about yourself, there are people who love you more than anything. Who have seen you come into being. And whatever choices you make, our love is not conditional on that. Do you understand? You are worth *every* effort. I know that. Hugo knows that. Your parents know that.'

'What about Grandma Ida?'

'Yes, even that racist old bag.'

'Auntie!'

'What? Who says the British empire was a "good thing" to an Indian person? Seriously?'

We both laugh and sit in that bubble of warmth for a bit. Sharing laughter, feeling that connection between us like a light beam. Out in the distance, the tide changes direction and starts to creep slowly back up the shore.

When we reach the house and I finally check my phone, I almost drop it in surprise.

There's a message from Majid's assistant, Akaash.

Good day, ma'am. Majid sir would like to schedule a phone call. When you have availability?

I stare at my phone for a moment. He hasn't responded to any of my previous messages about work so what does he want now? Does he want to apologise? Is he going to offer me my job back? It doesn't matter. Whatever he has to say, I'm not interested. I don't know who or what I am becoming, but my mind is not the same shape any more and I can't squeeze myself back into a box that was always too small for me. I delete the message. I am tired of men having a say in my life.

13

The atmosphere in the house is like the aftermath of a storm. It feels cleansed, renewed, after a necessary emptying out and letting go of things.

The one thing I won't let go of, however, is the anger I feel towards Majid. His text spurs me into being more proactive with my social media, especially when I get a message from NTR Spices asking if I'd like to do a collaboration.

I ask Myra what it means. 'This is how people make money. You could make *money*. Subscriptions, cooking classes, sponsorships.'

'That sounds completely beyond me.'

What Myra knows about the world already is so impressive. At fifteen I was fixated on which boy liked me, not thinking about business strategy. 'I don't know,' I say, 'I don't think anyone would want to see *this* on their phone.' I gesture at my body and laugh.

She doesn't laugh back. 'You know, Auntie, you're always on at me to believe in myself, and love myself, but you talk about yourself in a shitty way. You need to stop, it's getting old.'

She's right, but part of my self-deprecation comes from an unpleasant side-effect of the jump in my followers: the increase in trolls. My most recent post attracted a few comments about whether I had put on weight since the first video I'd posted a couple of weeks ago, the state of my eyebrows, and how badly I need to get my nails done.

'So?' she says. 'That's just the internet. People will always have an opinion – it's YOUR choice whether to believe that opinion and give it power.' I'm so taken aback by the wisdom coming out of her young mouth, I'm speechless.

For all the negativity, there are some wonderful messages from people saying how they love the combination of flavours in the post, how they might try it out on their kids or serve it as a buffet when their mates come over. It's strange to feel warmth and validation from people I don't know, but it feeds into a small well of confidence that has steadily been growing in me over the last few weeks. I show the world snippets of our garden – the runner beans growing rapidly in the heat – and share the delight of finding a newly ripe strawberry underneath a bushy cluster of leaves.

When I'm not getting schooled by Myra about body confidence, I'm agonising over whether to tell Wallace about Hugo's visit.

One afternoon as I'm keeping Selena company while she tries out a recipe for Guyanese pasties with fake chicken, I tell her about my feelings of guilt. 'Why do you feel guilty?' she says. 'Do you like Hugo?'

'No!' I say, blushing furiously. 'Hugo is just a friend but . . . if Wallace had someone to stay over, I think I would want to know.'

She crimps a pasty and groans as the stuffing spills out from the top because the pastry has been rolled too thinly. 'Real talk: are you trying to use the situation to justify being able to message him? Or to make him jealous? No judgement either way.'

'I don't know,' I say. 'I'm confused about what we actually are. He said we should take a break until I get back. So are we together or not together? Does he want to break up or not?'

'Well, that's a toughie. If you are together, then yes, you should tell him about Hugo coming over. And if you aren't together, then no, you don't owe him shit. Even,' she says before I can interrupt, 'if you have been together for years. If you weren't out here, you'd be sleeping on some mate's sofa in London, and from what you've told me, he didn't seem overly concerned about where you'd be staying while *he* figures things out.'

'He's not a bad guy though . . .' I say miserably.

Selena scoops the stuffing out and starts again with the pastry. 'Is that a reason to stay with someone though? Does anyone have the words engraved on their tombstone: "Here lies Steve: Not a Bad Guy"? Think about why you want to be with him. Not why is he with you – but why are you, Padma, with him?'

'I don't know!' I'm frustrated and defensive because Selena's words are cutting too close to the truth.

'You *do* know,' she says. 'I mean that as gently as possible, but you do know.'

I bite my lip, unsure of whether to tell her about my depression and how it ties me to Wallace. I start telling her about it, and when I finish, I brace myself, waiting for her reaction.

'I get it,' she says calmly. 'It's not the same, I know, but I had chronic fatigue for about two years. My partner at the time was amazing. He helped me through it, was an absolute rock. Then I recovered and, as time went on, I realised our relationship wasn't right. Nothing terrible or dramatic, just that we wanted different things. I wanted to travel a lot to make up for time I felt I had lost, he wanted to build his business and stay at home. But I felt I couldn't leave him. He had been there for me when I was at my worst. He sat with me in the darkness and held my hand, and I felt it was something I owed him.'

It's exactly how I feel about Wallace.

'What happened?' I ask.

'He ended things,' she says, 'because I was so distant, and refused to make a decision about anything. Whether that was moving in with him . . . having a joint bank account. After we broke up, he moved on quickly, and it made me think about so many things. I had projected what I thought our relationship meant to him, without even talking to him about it.'

'How do you mean?'

'I stayed with him because I felt I owed him for what he had done for me when I was ill. But he had never asked that to be the price. In fact, he had asked for nothing at all. And when I flip the situation – if I knew the reason someone was with me was because they felt it was a debt they had to repay, I wouldn't want that for myself. Love thrives on freedom, Padma. It cannot be built on gratitude, and it can't be held hostage.'

'I just . . . I don't want to lose him. And I don't want to hurt him.'

'Procrastination or inaction isn't any better than purposely hurting someone. It just hurts them anyway. And holding on to someone because you're afraid to lose them . . . you'll lose them anyway.'

Taking action, being direct, isn't my strong point. And so, before I call Wallace to tell him about Hugo's visit, I ask Selena if she'll come over for dinner while Hugo is here. That way, it won't appear as if he and I are playing happy families.

'I'd love to,' she says. 'I saw him briefly when he came for the town meeting but it'd be good to see him properly.' She places the reworked pasties on the tray and laughs. 'Ah, Posh Boy,' she says with the kind of nostalgic tone that suggests History. When I ask about it, she says: 'We had a fumble when we were kids. By the lobster cages. A fisherman caught us and told us to bugger off.'

'You had something going on with Hugo?' I say, shocked.

'It was barely anything, let alone something,' she says with a smile.

'Oh,' I say, flustered, 'I had no idea . . .' I feel jealous, and I don't know why. And I shouldn't feel jealous if Hugo is just a friend. And I shouldn't feel jealous of my friend Selena, who has been nothing but warm and loving since I got to Harkness. Besides, her words of advice have clarified some of my thoughts about Wallace and our relationship.

Although I was shocked at first that he'd wanted a break, I'd now had time to think. It's normal for couples to evolve and change their minds about what they want in life, especially in a long-term relationship. The problem wasn't so much that Wallace had decided it was important for him to be a father, it was the *way* in which he'd communicated it to me. It didn't feel like he was using our break to figure things out, it felt like punishment, despite him saying it wasn't. And it was impossible to work through any of this without speaking to him.

I didn't know if I was using Hugo's visit as an excuse to

call Wallace, but I did know it was more than time for us to settle things between us.

*

Back at the house, I call Wallace. The ringtone is unusually long, as if he is abroad. Eventually, he answers.

'Are you away?' I ask after our initial hellos.

'I had to go to Stockholm for a couple of days, for work,' he says, a touch too dismissively for someone who hasn't spoken to their partner in over three weeks. 'What's up?'

I feel so disorientated by him being in a different country without my knowing. Most couples would text each other when they leave and when they land safely, at the very least.

'You didn't tell me.'

'Well,' he says, a bit more uncertainly, 'I didn't know whether I should. You know, what with things being a bit . . .' Here I am, worried to tell him about Hugo's visit, and this berk leaves the country and doesn't feel the need to tell me? Sadness turns to rage.

'You *left the country* and you didn't message me? Is that what we are now? We've been together ten years and we don't tell each other crucial information like when one of us leaves the country? *You're* the one who set these rules, Wallace! I wasn't the one who suggested this whole texting ban, remember? So if you wanted to text me, you bloody well could have! Don't act as if you've been captured by guerrillas and your phone has been confiscated!'

'I—' He's taken aback by the fury in my voice. I've never spoken to him like this before, and he knows he's made a mistake because to my surprise, he says: 'You're right. I'm sorry. How have you been?'

I don't know where to begin, so I return Wallace's coldness with some of my own. 'I'm fine. Myra's fine too, by the way, in case you were wondering. Anyway, the reason I'm calling is to tell you that Hugo Albright – you know, we're staying in his house – is coming to stay over on the weekend. He's got some house stuff to sort out, but it didn't feel right not telling you.'

'Hang on,' Wallace says, 'who the hell is *Hugo Albright*?'

'Myra's godfather. I told you we were staying at his place.'

'You didn't,' he says with a raised voice. And before I can reply, I realise I haven't told him about Hugo. I merely said we were going to Harkness, and because things had been so strained, I hadn't elaborated.

'There's nothing to worry about,' I say, trying to move the conversation away from who told who and what. 'Hugo is just Hugo – he's harmless. He's literally family. Besides, if something was going on – why would I call you and tell you about it?'

'I'm not very happy about this, Padma,' he says sullenly.

'I can tell,' I say, knowing that it's important I don't use the S word. If I say sorry, it will validate Wallace's sulkiness and I have nothing to be sorry for. I can hardly stop Hugo from visiting his own house. 'I'm not happy about you leaving the country and not telling me, but here we are.'

'Which is where exactly?'

'I don't know, Wallace. You tell me. Are we still together?'

'Of course we are,' he snaps, 'we're just on a break.'

'And what exactly does that mean?'

'It means I'm not happy about some random toff staying in the same house as you overnight.'

I know this is the point in our argument when I am expected to make Wallace feel better, as I usually do. But this time, I don't.

'Well, there's nothing more to say, is there?'

'Padma . . .'

'We don't talk for weeks,' I say, unable to hold back. 'You don't seem remotely bothered by it. Do you even love me any more?'

'What kind of question is that?' he says. 'Of course I love you! It's just easier . . .'

'Easier for *you*,' I snap. 'Not once have you thought about how hard this might have been for me. Have a safe flight back.' Even as I disconnect the call, I cannot believe I have spoken to him like that.

Wallace and I have never really done jealousy. While there is a horrible thrill at hearing it creep into his voice – because it is the first time in a while I've had proof that he still cares – there is another part of me that wonders if his reaction is less about losing me, and more about another man taking what's his.

14

Nervousness builds in my stomach ahead of Hugo's arrival on Saturday. I place a little vase of yellow and purple wildflowers on his dressing table, then pick it up in panic that it might say too much. 'It's a nice touch,' Myra says drily, watching me fuss about the room, placing fresh towels on the bed and plumping the pillows. 'Why are you being so weird and frantic?' she says.

'Why are you so dressed up?' I say to deflect. She has selected a black tulle miniskirt and has braided her hair into two Princess Leia buns. It is possible to detect Myra's mood from how she dresses, and today is a good day for her.

'Well,' she says, 'seeing as you asked . . . could I invite a new friend over for dinner tonight?'

'A new friend?' I ask, surprised. 'When did you make this new friend?'

'While out walking Tara, actually. Her name is Violet, and I feel bad for her. Most of her friends are away for the holidays and she's sort of been left behind.' I imagine this Violet, a sweet kid with dungarees and plaits, walking her dog and searching for a friend. My heart goes out to her.

'Yes, of course,' I say. 'Greg's still coming, right?' I'd asked him to beef up numbers and make the Hugo dinner seem less strange if I needed to explain any of it to Wallace at a later point.

She nods and bounces out of the door.

*

A few hours later, about thirty minutes before Selena and Greg are due to arrive, my phone pings with a text from Hugo. My nervousness picks up speed, a long wave that pulses through powerfully from a wellspring of anxiety, barely pausing before the next one arrives.

Still stuck at the estate agents. Am so sorry.

Greg arrives at the house dressed like an American nerd: hair parted to the side and slicked back, bow tie, neatly pressed trousers, with a box of Dairy Milk Tray and the other holding Lucky's lead. Lucky, a mix of sheepdog and poodle, is a soppy sweetheart, a black and white shaggy ball of fur who pads and huffs around Greg, waiting to be unleashed. The minute the dog senses Tara, he runs around Greg, trussing his legs with the lead until finally the catch is released. As Greg topples over like a rotisserie chicken, Myra jumps on him and drags him over to the sofa. I need a lie-down just from looking at them.

Shortly after the doorbell rings, and Selena is standing in the doorway without her apron and the usual cooking stains. Her make-up is artfully minimal – a bit of blusher, dabs of highlighter on her high cheekbones, and a smudge of pink lipstick. Her skin is so richly brown and flawless, she doesn't need any foundation. 'Pretty dress,' I say, admiring the pattern of a rainforest twirling around her knees. 'You're welcome to borrow it any time,' she says. 'We're probably the same size.' When she tells me her size I'm shocked to find we are, except she carries herself so differently.

She hands me a hamper of bread, cheese and chutneys.

'Can I help with anything?' she asks. Normally I would tell her to take a seat and not to worry, but Selena feels familiar and close enough for me to ask her to chop some onions. It's as if we have known each other for far longer than four weeks. 'How's everything been since the announcement about the relaunch?' I ask. There had been a small announcement in the local paper, mentioning that a Guyanese band would come and play on the day.

She rolls her eyes. 'Oh, the banshee brigade dropped by. Barbara and Yvonne. *Will the music be too loud? What will be on the menu? Oh, I do hope this works out for you, dear,*' she mimicked.

'Oh, what do they know?' I snapped. 'They read the *Daily Mail* and tut about the number of tourists at the same time as moaning about the number of places that had to close because of lack of business. Don't listen to them. You're amazing, the menu is phenomenal, you're going to blow them away.'

'Thank you.' Selena has tears in her eyes – although it could be the onions. We work in silence for a while until she looks up and says: 'I'm so grateful you're here, Padma. I don't know if I've ever said that to you. But you give me the confidence to be myself.'

'Oh,' I say, slightly shocked because I don't see myself that way at all. I see that quality in Selena, Delilah – even Hugo. They seem to know exactly who they are. 'Well, thank you.'

The doorbell rings and I jump, thinking it's Hugo. I wash my hands and check my reflection in the small hallway mirror.

Selena looks at me curiously, wondering why I'm taking such care. I open the door, with Tara straining behind my legs to push through, but it isn't Hugo. A slim girl, with sallow skin and silky blonde hair so fine her scalp shows through, is standing in the doorway. Her blue eyes are heavily ringed in purple eyeshadow, and she's wearing what amounts to lingerie with heavy boots. She pulls at the stack of bracelets on her left wrist. Tara abruptly turns around and trots back to her basket, which is odd because she is usually friendly to the point of love-bombing.

'Yes?' I ask.

'I'm Violet,' she says. I'd completely forgotten about her, and this version of Myra's new friend certainly didn't fit the image I had in my head of a lonely country bumpkin wandering the wilderness.

'Oh, please come in! Sorry, Violet, I was having a senior moment,' I laugh. She looks at me so witheringly, it makes Myra's stare look like a sunbeam. Myra comes over to give her a hug while Greg hangs back, showing the same kind of jerky hesitation one might affect upon encountering an aggressive dog.

'Oh, Victoria, it's you!' Selena says, waving from the kitchen. 'How's your horse doing these days?'

Victoria – Violet? – glares at Selena and says: 'My name is Violet.'

'Let me give you the tour,' Myra says, and pulls her by the hand. Greg leans into Lucky for comfort, cuddling him close. Like the two dogs, he's clearly not a fan.

I look at Selena for an explanation and she shrugs. 'As far as I knew, her name is Victoria and she used to have a horse named Muffy. Used to be friends with Caitlin, who works in the café. Maybe she's had a Madonna rebrand.'

The doorbell rings again and this time it is Hugo. Tara shoots out of her basket to investigate, sniffing and wagging. He apologises while trying to give her a cuddle. For being late, for being here at all.

'Posh Boy!' Selena yells behind me, and my heart sinks as they give each other a big hug. I'm not a jealous person, but something dark clutches my heart.

'Uncle Hugo!' Myra says, giving him a hug too. 'Where's my present?'

He rolls his eyes. 'Here, you vulture,' he says, and gives her a bag filled with expensive chocolate from Godiva. Greg looks crestfallen and glances at the Dairy Milk he brought. 'I LOVE Dairy Milk,' I say to him.

'So do I,' says Myra and squeezes his hand.

'Food is ready,' I say, checking everything is hot. Hugo slots in next to me at the counter, under the warm glow of newly fitted spotlights, and starts uncorking a bottle of wine. Myra starts filling up glasses with Coke and water, and I close my eyes for a moment. It all feels so natural and comfortable – too comfortable. *Snap out of it, Padma.*

'This is a feast,' Selena says warmly as we all sit around the table. Serving bowls filled with steaming rice, chicken, green beans, grilled spicy mackerel, dal, an aubergine curry and a raita sit in the middle.

'We don't plate up, in Indian culture,' I say. 'We all serve ourselves. Dig in.' As everyone serves themselves, I ask Violet what she likes to study in school. She shrugs and says she hates school. She wants to quit and do art.

'I'm not sure I want to do my A-levels either,' Myra says. 'Being a make-up artist sounds cool.' Hugo raises an eyebrow and I cock my head at her, wondering where this has come from. I know Myra is unsure about studying, but I've never heard her voice this before. Daisy would go ballistic.

'Yeah,' says Violet, 'I was telling Myra that make-up artists get to go to the coolest places. They can work for themselves. My aunt Lydia – she does the make-up for TV shows, London Fashion Week, and she gets to meet a lot of famous people.'

'I mean,' Selena says, 'life is more than just meeting famous people though? Surely you want to do something you're good at. What is it you like doing, Myra?'

Before she can reply, Violet excuses herself to go to the toilet, and when she comes back her eyes look a little red as if she's been crying. I make a note to ask Myra if everything is okay once we've eaten.

'Myra,' Violet says, her plate piled high with food that she's served herself and which remains untouched. 'Is it possible to have something else? I don't really *do* spicy food.' If Violet hadn't taken so much before she says this, perhaps I would feel less murderous, but if there is one thing guaranteed to make an Indian cross, it's food wastage.

'Oh.' Myra's face drops. 'It's so delicious though – do you want to at least try a bit?' Violet shakes her head. 'Okay, what if I make you a sandwich?'

'Too fattening. Have you got a Cup a Soup? It's only ninety calories,' she says, patting her flat stomach. She excuses herself to go to the toilet again. 'My stomach is feeling a little funny,' she says.

Hugo, Selena and I don't have to make eye contact to know what we are all thinking. While I feel sorry for Violet because she is calorie-counting at fifteen and has learned it from someone – her mother, an aunt, maybe another person at school – and it will be an emotional tapeworm that sits inside her until she digs it out, I don't want her infecting my niece's thoughts.

'You know what, Myra,' I say, 'you continue eating and I'll get Violet something, okay?'

While I empty a tin of soup for her, I hear Selena say: 'So, Greg, how's life – I haven't seen you for a while. How's your rock-pool project going?'

'Oh, it's amazing,' he says, happy to be asked about something that interests him. 'I've started doing a project on the geology of the area too – Myra's been helping. She sometimes comes pebble hunting with me.'

'Pebble hunting?' Violet says, trying not to laugh.

'Shut up,' Myra hisses at Greg.

'You know who used to love rock pools?' Selena asks. 'Hugo. You should ask him about it.'

'What do you mean, used to love them?' Hugo says mildly. 'I still love them.'

'Seriously?' Greg says. 'I would love to talk to you about that.'

'Sounds like a good idea, Greg,' Violet says almost too sweetly. 'I mean, it's not like your dad is around, is he?' It doesn't take a genius to work out she lives locally and so likely knows all about Greg and the rumours of him being the illegitimate child of David Bentley. For the first time, however, Myra looks at Violet oddly. Greg may be a dweeb, but he's her dweeb, and she knows how much he has ached to have his father in his life.

'My dad isn't around either,' I say, wanting Greg to know he isn't alone or weird or wrong in yearning for a father who doesn't care. Myra looks up in surprise. 'I thought Ajja was dead?'

'Ajja?' Violet says.

'Yeah, it's our word for granddad,' Myra says irritably.

I know the truth may lead to a confrontation with Daisy, but for the moment I don't care. Greg's feelings seem more important right now.

'No. He left when your mum was a baby, and never came back.'

Myra looks shocked. 'Do you think about him?' Greg asks me.

I could lie. I could say it doesn't hurt, it doesn't matter. But there is a difference between a parent being dead and a parent being absent. The possibility of seeing him again is both hopeful and sad, all at the same time. It is still better than that possibility being wrenched away forever, but it is hard in a different way.

'All the time,' I say.

*

After dinner, the kids barrel upstairs to play video games. Hugo helps me with the washing-up even though I've told him not to. He starts to take out from under the sink what I call the white people's tub – where the washing sits in soapy water and is then taken out and dried without being rinsed off with fresh water – and I veto it immediately.

As he washes each dish individually, water splashes onto his linen shirt, his broad, thick hands working methodically. Selena heads home with two gulab jamuns in a Tupperware box as she's opening the café early in the morning. 'I'm sorry to hear about your dad,' Hugo says after a while. 'You said he was absent but I didn't realise . . .'

I think about the fragments we are left with, and what we cling to, of the parents who didn't stay.

'The thing is,' I say, 'as angry as I am with him, if he wanted to come back into my life, I would say yes. And I don't know if that makes me pathetic because I'm yearning for a love and a person I don't even know.'

'It's not pathetic,' he says. 'You get only two people in life, who represent that love. You can get stand-ins, chosen family – all that stuff – but nothing can ever replace those two people. I get it.'

'I don't think everyone is cut out to be a parent,' I say. 'That's what I have a problem with. The lie that everyone should be. And the damage it creates.'

'Is that why you don't want children?' he asks.

I look out the window at the sky that is finally darkening, the thinnest slice of orange on the horizon being consumed by the night. 'I don't know. Maybe,' I say, not realising there is sadness and grief behind my words, being surprised to find it there. Maybe if I'd had different parents, it would be different for me. But then where does that end? Wishing away our reality, placing so much weight on the different outcome if we'd been dealt different cards, can only lead to madness and resentment.

At that moment, we hear yelling from upstairs. 'You're both so BORING!' Violet yells. Then we hear a door slam and she runs down the stairs and almost tumbles at the bottom. 'WHAT?' she says to Hugo and me as she staggers off the step.

'What's going on?' I say, bewildered. Myra comes running down the stairs after her. 'I think Violet needs to go home now,' she says tersely. 'Right now. This is her mum's number.'

As I start dialling the number Myra has given me, Violet stomps over to the sofa and puts in her headphones. 'No, I'm not going ANYWHERE,' she says. I talk to Violet's mother and give her the address as Hugo motions that he's going to drop Greg home.

'What happened?' I ask Myra sharply under my breath. Is she involved in this too?

'She brought vodka with her,' Myra says flatly. 'We told her not to drink it. She threw up in my room. And she was vaping cannabis in the toilet too.'

Every cell in my body wants to ask if she took part in any of it. But if I do, if I allow that trigger of the past to take control of my words, I will be repeating the same pattern again. Myra looks at me, expecting me to ask. Steeling herself for the interrogation. Almost resigned to her fate.

'Okay,' I say calmly. 'Don't worry – her mum is coming to get her. Hugo and I will take it from here, don't worry.'

'Oh, okay, thanks,' she says, slightly surprised she isn't the one being blamed. 'It's . . . horrible seeing it from the other side of things, you know? Watching someone lose control?'

I look up from spooning leftovers into plastic boxes and reply: 'I know.'

'Violet reminded me of one of my friends back home,' Myra says. 'But she's kind of awful. Actually also like my friends back home.' Violet starts singing loudly from the living room to whatever she's listening to on her AirPods.

'I think your dog knew before you did,' I say, laughing.

Myra laughs back. 'You're right. She did.' Something has taken root in her, something that I hope will continue to grow.

*

The next morning, I wake to the smell of pancakes. As I go out onto the landing to investigate, Myra's bedroom door is still shut, while Hugo's is slightly ajar. As I debate my next move, Hugo spies my feet through the gap in the banister.

'Why are you creeping around?' he says from the kitchen, making me jump. It's odd to see him in blue-and-white-striped pyjamas, his hair slightly mussed and flopping over his brow. Tortoiseshell-rimmed spectacles instead of his usual contact lenses.

Maybe food doesn't have to be a political act. Maybe I can just enjoy breakfast with my friend. That's who Hugo is. A friend. Even if I did harbour feelings for him, an online investigation of his ex, Elaine, demonstrates I am not remotely his type. Elaine is elfin. She dresses in tight power suits and works as the head of marketing at a FTSE 100 tech company.

He's set the table. A sprig of blue hydrangea balances in a small glass tumbler. Technically, it's not just the two of us – there's a place set for Myra too. 'I hope you don't mind me making breakfast,' he says, 'but I wanted to do it as a thank you for yesterday's incredible food. And I thought we could do with a reset after that unexpected drama last night.'

'It's your kitchen,' I say, pouring myself coffee from the French press. I don't want to talk about Violet or to think about her. When her mother came to pick her up, she had to be dragged out. Then the mother actually blamed me for not being watchful enough. If I believed in spiritual cleansing like Esme, I would light up some sage and waft both of their bad vibes out of the house.

'I know, but . . . this place feels like it kind of belongs to you both, now. Not a chintz pillow in sight. I love the white and blue – you've done such a great job with it. It's almost a shame to sell it.'

'How did that go? The estate agents?'

'They could barely contain their glee. I won't start the process until you guys go back to London because you don't need people under your feet in the last two weeks of your trip.' Two weeks doesn't feel like much time, but it is also the measure of how far Myra and I have come.

'Thank you,' I say. Even though I'm sad to leave, I appreciate Hugo's considerate nature, his softness. 'You don't want to keep it?'

'Maybe if I had someone to share it with,' he says. 'But I don't.' He looks at me, and for a moment there is something in his eyes I can't quite place.

'Uncle Hugo?' Myra says sleepily from the top of the stairs. The moment passes.

'Breakfast in ten,' he says.

'Can you stay tonight too?' she asks. 'We didn't really get to hang out.' He looks at me and I nod.

'Sure,' he says, and she pads back up to her room.

'She's different around you,' I say. 'Softer, more like a child.'

'Are you jealous?' he says, smiling.

'What? No.'

But I am jealous. Myra didn't hesitate to hug Hugo. I'd had to work for that. If Wallace and I stayed together, it struck me she would never be like that with him.

'She told me she was embarrassed,' I say. 'You know – about when she was admitted to hospital. I can't stop thinking about what a terrible word that was for what happened. This big, enormous thing . . . and what she's most worried about is looking silly?'

The smell of frying bacon fills the house; there's a soft pop and sizzle as he flips it over. 'I haven't spoken to her about any of it, but I don't think that's what she meant. It's that you saw her like that. At her lowest point. And now she must deal with the consequences of that. But for what it's worth, she seems content. I haven't seen her like that in a long while.'

'You think she's happy?'

'Happy is a strong word. I think she feels like she can be herself.' He calls Myra down.

When she eventually joins us, as we eat, I look at her more closely. The shadows under her eyes are lighter, and she hums while she serves herself food. Her long skinny arms stick through a cut-off Evil Dead vest and she looks so young without make-up. Every time she bends down to feed Tara a bit of bacon, her expression turns molten with love.

After breakfast, I start washing up, feeling the slipperiness of suds on my hands. I allow my mind to relax and blur with the motion of rinsing out the pans, scrubbing away at caked-on rice grains. Fresh air and birdsong ribbon through the open back door. It's already a beautiful day – cloudless and warm. I turn my head so that my eyes close against a bright beam of sunlight.

It is a peaceful moment that I could live in forever. Until my phone rings.

It's Daisy.

'Why is Myra asking if she can meet her granddad?'

*

'I didn't realise you hadn't told her,' I say defensively. 'It just came out.'

'It's now created a situation I really could have done without,' Daisy snaps.

'I'm sorry.' I genuinely am. Siblings may grow up in the same household but experience things so differently. I was only three when Dad left but he is still a memory, a faint coming together of smell, sound and emotion. A will o' the wisp, but a presence nonetheless. Daisy has none of that because he didn't leave on a random day, but the one on which she was born. When you are told that your birth is generally considered to be the best day of your parents' lives, and yet one of them took it as an opportunity to escape, it must rip a hole in your existence.

'I know it must have brought up some difficult stuff,' I say. 'I know we've never really talked about it . . .'

'It's fine,' she says brusquely, in the decisive tone of someone who has scooped all her feelings into a box and snapped the lid shut.

'I'll talk to her.'

'Don't. You'll just make things worse. Just . . . don't tell her anything more.'

'Hugo is here,' I say, keeping my voice light, trying to change the subject.

'Oh, is he?' Daisy says with interest.

'Stop.'

'What?' she says innocently. 'I'm just saying . . .'

Hugo calls from the kitchen with epically bad timing: 'Padma, shall we go blackberry picking? There are some bushes just beyond the back of the garden.'

'Ooh, blackberry picking . . .' Daisy croons down the phone.

'Daisy, STOP!'

'Is that Daisy? Let me say hello.' He takes my phone off me and they chat, about putting the house on the market, about Henry's trip to New York. Not so long ago I couldn't even remember who Hugo was, and now we are at his seaside home about to pick blackberries while he talks to my sister on the phone. Deep guilt floods through me.

When he's done, he hands my phone back to me and coughs awkwardly. 'You've got a message from Wallace.'

It's a text asking if I have time for a chat. I let out an elongated groan and run my hands over my face. 'He's slightly jealous of you coming over.'

'Oh. Oh, dear. I'm sorry, I wouldn't have come if I'd thought it would create problems.'

'No . . . it's not you, Hugo. Stop being so . . . Hugh Grant about it all. He's doesn't have the right to say that. Or to be jealous.'

As he's about to say: *Are you sure it's fine, I can leave, honestly*, I open the door and head into the garden. He follows. The back garden gate opens onto a path that meanders into the woods. The temperature drops slightly. When we reach the line of bushes, thick thorny brambles with tiny black jewels growing from the remains of their bright white flowers, he wordlessly hands me a basket to put berries into. It's a good blackberry season, round dark globes thick with juice, the skin breaking against our fingers, staining them purple.

'How long have you been together?' he asks eventually.

'Ten years,' I reply. 'Daisy can't stand him, so there's that.'

'Do you and Henry get on?' he asks. I don't answer and pretend to examine the bushes for berries. 'It's okay, I won't tell him.'

'It's not that we don't get on,' I say. 'I just didn't think he should have married my sister when she was that young. And I think he looks down on me.'

'I understand,' says Hugo. 'No, really, I do,' when he catches my glare. 'An eleven-year age difference is odd. But I also remember your sister when they decided to marry. I'd never met anyone so sure of what she wanted.'

'Really?' I'd always viewed Daisy's decision to get married young as weakness – showing her as someone too afraid to be alone and so she chose the rich white man. I hadn't considered there may have been strength and certainty in her character that made her choose Henry.

'Oh, yes. She was young, but so determined. You're actually more similar than you realise.'

I laugh. 'I don't know if anyone would describe me as determined.'

'I would,' he says with a smile. A comfortable silence settles between us. 'Henry's not all bad, you know.'

'I know but . . . it's complicated.'

Perhaps it is because Hugo looks so amiable, and his features so soft in the sunlight, that I don't at first register how sharp and insightful his next comment is.

'Do you feel like he took Daisy away from you?' he asks.

'I feel like my relationship with my sister would be different if it weren't for him.' It's the most I'm willing to admit. 'She changed her name when she met him. And then everything else changed too.'

'What was her name before it was Daisy?' he says, surprised.

'Dhara.'

He exhales loudly. 'Oof! It's such a beautiful name.'

'I know. A daisy is a flower that grows in the earth. Dhara is a god of the physical cosmos, and represents the entire Earth as an element.'

Something about Hugo's presence makes me feel as if I am held in balance. Around him, the walls soften. For the first time in a long time, I feel like myself. But with things still unclear with Wallace, this feels like dangerous ground to be treading. 'We should go,' I say abruptly. Hugo nods and pops the last berry into his mouth.

'I know this might be hard to hear,' he says as we walk, 'but Daisy made the choice to marry Henry. He may not be the easiest and he can sometimes be pompous . . .' At that I snort in agreement. 'But he cares about her, a lot. He doesn't have affairs, he loves Myra. He constantly thinks about what will make them happy. What I'm trying to say is – she chose to go. And . . . the choice she made could have been worse.'

We walk towards an opening in the trees, becoming aware of long, pearly strands hanging from the branches. The trees are covered with them. A light breeze lifts them in a soft wave that catches the light, turning them into a curtain of white and silver.

'Caterpillars,' he says. He looks at me and stands so close, the smell of lime shower gel rising from his skin. I'm aware of the architecture of his body, how it is framed against mine. He lifts his hand slowly and cups my face. For some reason I can't remember how to breathe.

'See?' he says and plucks something off my cheek, holding it up. It is so small, barely a centimetre across, bright green and wriggling.

'AUNTIE! UNCLE HUGO!' Myra yells in the distance,

with Tara sprinting ahead towards us. 'Why didn't you tell me you were heading out?' she says, huffing with the effort of trying to keep up with her dog.

'You are way too young to be this out of breath.' Hugo affectionately ruffles Myra's hair as she says 'ugh' and smooths it back down. 'I'm planning to head into the village – would you both like to come with me?' he says.

I hold back awkwardly. 'Are you sure you two don't want to spend some time together?'

'Don't be weird, Auntie,' Myra says, and seizes a handful of berries before Hugo can snatch them out of her reach.

'Yes, don't be weird, Auntie,' he says.

I look at him square in the eyes. 'Don't ever call me Auntie.'

*

Myra abandons us the moment we hit the Beach Road, saying she's going to find Greg and Lucky. It's late Sunday morning and already people are streaming in for another hot, cloudless day on the beach, carrying enormous rattan bags with parasols and towels poking from the top.

Selena waves to us from the door of the Green Goddess. She is wearing a 1950s fuchsia-coloured dress with a full skirt. Her skin is dark bronze and shiny with cocoa butter, and her smile is broad and welcoming, the kind that makes you feel warm merely witnessing it. Hugo gives a small wave back.

'Thank you for dinner last night,' she says, kissing me on the cheek. 'That Victoria-Violet kid, though – what a piece of work!'

When I don't follow them into the café, she looks at me.

'Why don't you both catch up, and I'll meet you back here?

I should make a call. Honestly – it's fine,' I say. I need time and space to speak to Wallace and find out what he wants. I hated how we had left things the last time we talked.

A short walk takes me to a quiet bench on the concrete walkway, where I sit staring out at the tide as it gradually recedes.

Wallace answers on the second ring. 'Thanks for calling me,' he says. 'I'm back in England, by the way.' Even his tone irritates me. Clearly the anger I felt the last time we spoke hasn't fully abated.

'Good to hear,' I say. 'What's up?'

'I'm just finding out how you are. That's what you wanted, isn't it? To have contact again?'

I sigh, deeply, madly, exhausted to my bones. He just doesn't get it. I want him to *want* to call, not call me because he's afraid of the repercussions if he doesn't.

'And this has nothing to do with the fact that Hugo is visiting this weekend?' I ask.

'Of course not.'

'So you don't mind that he's staying more than one night?'

'What? He's staying two nights? Padma . . .' Wallace is indignant, his voice rising an octave.

'It's his house, Wallace. And Myra asked him to – she's his god-daughter.'

'Oh, that again,' he snaps. 'I'm not happy about this at all.'

'Why?' I snap back. 'What exactly is the situation with us? One minute you're giving me an ultimatum, the next you say we've been together for ten years. Yet you can't seem to name a single reason why that is.'

'I don't know what's going on with you, Padma,' he says slowly, 'but this doesn't sound like you. You've changed.' It's true, I have changed. Or am changing. But the things that are changing aren't hurting anyone, and they are long overdue and are all in the name of happiness. Anyone who loved me, in that pure way Myra does, would want this for me.

'Well then,' he says, galled by the fact that I'm not rising to his comment. 'What about you?'

'What about me?'

'Why do you want to be with me?' he says.

'Because . . .' As I search the list of things I love about Wallace, I realise most of it has been struck off and all that is left behind is the fear of being alone. Even that is lessening. I do love him, but by instigating this break, he's forced me to confront my fears, only for me to realise there is love in my life in the form of my family, and a sense of purpose if I want it. And it has shone a light on the long-time neglect in our relationship. We don't champion each other, we don't witness each other's joy. We are each merely vessels into which the other pours the inventory of their day.

'You can't think of one thing?' he says incredulously.

'I love you,' I say, 'isn't that enough?' Anger threatens to sweep over me. Wallace is the one who issued the ultimatum. He is the one who asked for a break.

'Padma!' Hugo says from across the road. Is he some sort of homing pigeon for bad timing?

'I'd better go,' I say.

'Yes,' Wallace replies tightly. 'You'd better.'

*

On the walk back home, Myra and Greg dawdle in front of us at an excruciating pace while the dogs take their own time sniffing every flower and twig they come across. As Hugo and I overtake them, I ask how things were with Selena, as nonchalantly as possible. 'I hear you had quite the romance back in the day?'

'Romance?' Hugo snorts. 'We were very young, in a place where nothing happened and we were bored. Why do you ask?'

'Selena is an amazing person, so if you wanted to . . . you know. You should.' There. I'd said it.

'Thank you,' he says, trying not to laugh. 'I'll bear that in mind.'

I look at him out of the corner of my eye and take a sip of my coffee. 'Are you dating anyone?'

'Not really,' he says, frowning, trying to figure out what has inspired this line of questioning. 'Why do you ask?'

Before I can reply, he says: 'Please don't set me up with Selena. I get enough of that from Daisy and Henry.'

'They do that?'

'Daisy set me up with a colleague of hers. Defence lawyer. Had a few too many martinis and then told me she wanted me to tie her up and whack her with a paddle.'

'Oh, wow,' I say. 'And did you?'

'Did I what?' he laughs. 'Whack her with a paddle? No, Padma, I did not.' At that moment, an elderly woman walks past, her head snapping back to look at Hugo as if he is a deviant.

'Sorry, madam,' he says to her, 'it's not what it sounds like.' It only makes her glare even harder, and I can't help but laugh.

My phone pings with a message from Wallace. **I'm sorry. I didn't mean to snap. I'd love to send you flowers – what's your address?**

I start typing that he doesn't have to send anything, that we're fine and we'll talk when I come home. But it's too hard juggling my coffee and constructing a nuanced, sensitive reply. It's easier to send the address and leave him to it.

*

In the early evening, the smell of pepperoni, herbs and cheese fills the air as Hugo takes out pizzas, requested by Myra, made by Pizza Express. He burns his hand on the edge of the baking tray, and while he runs it under the cold tap, I wrap a few ice cubes in a kitchen towel. 'How's the movie selection going?' I ask Myra.

'I don't want to watch *The Goonies*,' she says, padding into the kitchen. 'I've looked it up and I think there are some bad things in it.'

'What?' Hugo yells. 'It's not scary, you wimp. It's a classic.'

Myra rolls her eyes. 'I eat horror for breakfast, Uncle Hugo,' she says. 'I'm talking about Sloth and Chunk – it doesn't seem right.'

Hugo and I look at each other. 'Oh, god,' I say to him in a low voice, 'she's right. Remember truffle shuffle?' Hugo wiggles his torso ever so slightly. 'Stop it,' I whisper, trying not to laugh.

'Okay, okay,' he says to her, 'pick whatever you like. NOT horror.' I hand the ice cubes to him and set the table with some inoffensive IKEA plates. The sun is softer now, turning the sand-coloured flagstones in the kitchen to gold. 'I just need to change,' he says, wiping his hands dry.

'Into what? This isn't Downton Abbey.'

'I can't wear shorts while eating,' he says apologetically. 'Boarding-school thing.'

'Is it okay that I'm wearing shorts?'

'You can wear what you want,' he says. 'A budgie smuggler, if the mood takes you.'

'Hmm, sadly my budgie smuggler is in the wash,' I say, laughing.

Just as Hugo sets foot on the first step, there's a knock on the door. This had better not be Greg. Or Esme. I volunteer to get it while Myra sets up the TV. I open the door and gasp. I know then the answer to something I have been avoiding. This is not the reaction anyone should have to seeing their partner for the first time in four weeks.

15

'Hello, Pads,' Wallace says. He is carrying a bunch of station flowers in his hands, chrysanthemums wilted under fluorescent lighting. The last time I saw him he was clean-shaven; now he is sporting the gentle fuzzy start of a beard. He looks good with it. He's wearing a half-sleeved white T-shirt that shows the lean muscle he has gained through playing football. The sunset catches the hazel in his eyes against the warm brown of his skin, and as he pulls me towards him, the flowers are crushed between our bodies, staining his shirt pink. I'm still angry at him, but there is also relief at seeing someone again who represents home and comfort.

It would be a nice-enough embrace if I couldn't feel his gaze fixed on Hugo for the duration of it.

For a moment, Wallace and Hugo stare at each other. Even Myra stops scrolling on her phone long enough to look up. Tara launches herself at Wallace's legs, playfully nipping at his shoes.

'Whose is it?' he says irritably, as if I should have told him in advance that we had a dog, even though this is a surprise visit.

'Mine,' Myra says, scooping Tara into her arms to calm her down.

'Myra, you remember Wallace, don't you?' I say, using a high pitch, trying to defuse the situation.

'Not really.' She shrugs but it has been a few years since they have seen each other. 'Why are you here?' she asks abruptly. All she can see is the derailing of her evening. Wallace raises his eyebrows – both of us were raised by women who would not have tolerated a child speaking with such disdain.

'Myra,' I say warningly, while also trying to be certain of why he is here. Wallace has never been jealous up to now because somewhere, even if we are in the trenches, he's always known that I love him. But betrayal can be a slow process. It can appear in the paper cuts of seemingly insignificant comments and the smallest actions, a current pushing you further away from the shoreline until the other person is indistinguishable from the landscape.

Hugo is not just a potential threat to Wallace. It is what Hugo represents: private education, whiteness, privilege. Wallace has had to earn his validation in society. He lives in a house bought at great personal sacrifice by his grandparents, who pushed through in a world designed to push them down.

My heart aches for him, but it is the ache of compassion. From the moment I saw him at the door, I knew the fire of love and loyalty I should feel towards him as my partner is barely a flicker.

'Don't you have to open the surgery first thing tomorrow?' I ask.

'I wanted to surprise you – I've got someone to cover me for the morning.' He turns to Hugo and says: 'I hope I'm not interrupting anything?' His tone is polite, restrained, but what it is holding back feels enormous and accusatory.

'If anything, I'm the one interrupting,' says Hugo apologetically. 'It's good to finally meet you.' He is genial, but I realise I still don't know enough about him to be sure if this is genuine or part of his customary charm.

'I thought I would surprise Pads. She loves surprises,' Wallace says, laughing. An in-joke because he knows I hate them. The one and only time he'd arranged a surprise birthday dinner for me, I'd had a panic attack in the toilet because he'd misguidedly invited a friend I no longer spoke to, who had only turned up for the free food and to berate me.

As Hugo places the plates on the table, he says almost as an afterthought: 'Have we met before? Would I have seen you at one of Daisy and Henry's things?'

'Unlikely,' I reply, 'Wallace doesn't come to those – well, not for the last nine years at least.'

'Easy, Padma,' he laughs. 'Anyone would think you'd been counting.'

Myra gets up off the sofa to pile her plate with pizza and then sits back down. 'Are we going to start this film or what?'

'Does she always dress like that?' Wallace whispers to me.

'Like what?'

'Like something from a horror film?'

'Yes, she does,' I say, daring him to say something more. I know what he's doing. He's trying to furtively undermine Myra in my eyes so that if it comes to a choice between them, I will choose him over her.

Hugo looks at us all. 'Myra,' he says, 'why don't we have dinner at the table, and then we can decide what to do after that?' She groans long and loudly, while he pulls out another plate for Wallace. Wallace – who has brought nothing – takes four slices of pizza, leaving Hugo and me four slices between us.

'It's cheat day, babes,' he says with a grin, chewing on a slice. He has never, ever called me babes.

'So, Wallace,' says Hugo, trying to change the subject, 'what made you want to surprise Padma?'

'I've missed her,' he says. 'It's been over a month and I get that it's for a good reason, but it has been hard without her.'

I'm embarrassed. Not just because it's clearly a lie. We haven't seen or spoken to each other much in four weeks because of boundaries *he* set. And now he's here because of jealousy, I'm certain of it.

Wallace will say later that Hugo had been polite, but I know he's being formal. And I know the version of Wallace I am seeing is not *my* Wallace.

And yet a comparison point is drawn. I didn't have the full measure of my feelings for Hugo until I saw him and Wallace in the same room. Hugo's love for Myra is something to behold. He isn't perfect, but he strives. He makes room for me to be myself. He doesn't ask me to shrink so he can expand.

I know how much I owe Wallace for all the time he took care of me and didn't judge, and I don't want to hurt him. But his presence here makes me feel like I'm trying to wear a dress that doesn't fit any more. We don't want the same things. Even beyond the decision about children, what we value and how we want to experience the world is different.

But perhaps the biggest reason is not just that I have finally found the confidence that has eluded me for most of my thirties – a decade I was led to believe would be soaked in wisdom and self-acceptance. It is that my life now has Myra in it, even when we leave Harkness. And I don't see Wallace wanting to be a part of that.

After we eat, Myra heads to the sofa to watch TV with a big bowl of ice cream in her hands. 'Wait,' Hugo commands. He scatters in some of the blackberries we gathered. 'Ugh, fruit,' she says, but begrudgingly accepts them anyway and stalks back to the living room.

Wallace observes the whole thing and comments: 'She's a bit of a handful, isn't she?'

His comment has an Effect.

'She grows on you,' Hugo says with a polite smile.

'I'm sure she does,' Wallace says. 'Well, Padma, shall we . . .' He points upstairs. As he does so, I see Hugo's expression change just for a moment. He thinks we are going to go and have sex (we aren't) and he seems . . . bothered by it? Interesting.

'Sure,' I say, trying to turn the mood to lightness. 'Hugo, are you heading out in the morning? Will I see you before you go?'

'Actually,' he says apologetically, 'I might head back tonight.'

'Oh, I'm sorry to hear that,' says Wallace, not sounding remotely sorry at all. 'I hope I haven't driven you away?'

There is something unreadable and dark in Hugo's expression, which he replaces quickly with a rueful smile. 'Not at all. It'll be one less person in the bathroom and it'll give you both a chance to catch up.'

After Hugo leaves, there is a strange sense of melancholy in the house. Myra watches TV by herself, and after several unsuccessful attempts to engage her in conversation, Wallace gives up and goes upstairs. I sit for a moment in the kitchen, wrestling with an uncomfortable anger that Hugo is gone and my boyfriend is upstairs.

I'm angry at myself for not feeling what I should be for Wallace, and I'm angry at Wallace for tearing a hole in an evening that started so peacefully. Soon afterwards I join him, but he taps his ears to indicate he's listening to a podcast on his AirPods so that I don't interrupt. I poke him on the shoulder and he says irritably: 'What? I'm at a really good bit.'

I look at him and say: 'You're on my side of the bed.'

'What? But you always sleep on the left,' he says, making no attempt to move.

'No, *you* always sleep on the right,' I say. 'I prefer to sleep on the right but I wasn't able to tell you that when we started dating, and then it just stuck.' He stares as if he has never met me before, wondering what other things I've kept from him. Do I really like sugar in my tea? Do I actually judge him for going into private practice?

'Fine,' he grumbles, moving over. 'It's not a big deal.'

Somehow Wallace has brought with him the loneliness I hadn't realised I'd felt in our Brixton home. That it is here, in a place I feel seen and loved, with Myra, Selena and Hugo, makes me realise that loneliness isn't always in the absence of a person, but can sometimes be caused by their presence.

*

The least contentious activity I can find for the three of us to do the next morning is to go to the Green Goddess for breakfast. Now that he has successfully driven off Hugo, Wallace is keen to return to London quickly, but I've asked him to spend some of the day with us. In part to punish him, smoke him out into confessing the real reason he came down here. 'It's the one thing I'm asking,' I say when he starts protesting about his workload. 'It's important to me that you get to know Myra.'

The mornings are getting slightly cooler as the unpredictability of August lays the groundwork for summer winding down. As we walk there is a heavy quiet between the three of us, until eventually Wallace asks Myra: 'How are you feeling now?' referring to her time in hospital.

'Fine,' Myra says in a clipped tone, putting her AirPods in. She trails some distance behind us, with Tara on a lead investigating every tuft of grass along the way.

'Well,' he says sarcastically, 'seems like Myra is doing a great job of wanting to get to know me.' Wallace and I walk alongside each other but it doesn't feel like an amicable silence. It holds within it the emptiness of two people who don't have anything to say to each other.

'I don't get it,' I say. 'You seem so sure about having kids but you don't have any patience with her. She's a child, Wallace, not a robot – she doesn't just automatically do what she's told. She asks questions. She has opinions. And she's learning. How would you cope if we had them?'

He rolls his eyes as if I have just said the stupidest thing in the world. 'It'll be different when it's our own,' he says. 'Because we'll be raising them from a baby. We'll do everything right.'

'That's not how it *works*, Wallace,' I say sadly. And I realise why this is so important to him. Wallace was raised by his grandparents – his father died when he was young, and his mother spent her life in a psychiatric institution before she died. He wants to change his past by creating a future that allows him the power to make the choices for someone else that he couldn't make for himself. 'Children aren't our clones. They aren't a proxy for the childhood we wanted to have but didn't get. They're meant to be better and the only way they can manage that is if they are allowed to be themselves.'

'Look, we should discuss this another time,' Wallace says coldly, which is what he always does when he feels the debate slipping away from him.

I'm not sure what Selena sees on our faces as we stand outside the café, but it makes her come out and say a breezy hello. After I introduce them to each other, she squeezes my hand to let me know she is there.

'Coffee?' she says. We both nod gratefully, although our heads are still full of our conversation, unable to tidy all those emotions away. Finally Myra joins us after tying Tara up outside.

'Myra,' I say, 'take your AirPods out.' She scowls but puts them away. Heaves a deep sigh. Then sinks further into her chair. I can't deal with her being difficult as well as Wallace.

'What's wrong?' I ask her.

'Nothing,' she snaps, picking the raisin off a Danish. I don't want to look at Wallace only for his look to say *I told you so.*

'Come on, tell me. We don't keep things from each other, right?' I bend my head level with her eyeline. She looks at me solemnly.

'I don't know if you want me to say it in front of . . .' She gestures at Wallace. Now he sits up, looking interested. What is it that she might not want him to know?

'It's fine,' I say. 'I don't have anything to hide.'

'You received a message on Instagram, from that guy named Majid. The one you used to work for. He said you're not replying to his messages.'

'That's right, I blocked him.'

'Well, he says he's going to out you for ripping off his content if you don't take your account down,' she says miserably. Finally it sinks in. Myra isn't being moody or angry at me, this is directed at herself. For what she perceives to be her responsibility.

'Well, I didn't rip off his stuff, if anything he ripped off mine. That counts for something, right?' I say.

'It doesn't matter,' she says morosely. 'If he does a video about you, you're finished. That's how it works on social media. It doesn't matter if it's true. He has the bigger following. All that work we did . . . I'm so sorry, Auntie.' She looks so shamefaced, I feel compelled to go over and hug her.

'Hey,' I say, rubbing her shoulder, 'it's okay.'

Selena keeps a tactful distance.

'I don't get it,' says Wallace, 'isn't this just some Instagram thing? It's not a big deal, surely.'

We both stare at him. 'We were going to leverage it into a business, Wallace,' I say. 'I was thinking about starting my own thing, and this was an important way to do that.'

'But . . . it's not a proper job, Padma!' He laughs in disbelief. 'I mean . . . you're probably okay for money now what with . . .' I shoot him a venomous *shut up right now* look, because he's about to blurt out that Daisy has been paying me to look after Myra. He looks at me in understanding and detours, but still keeps up the pressure. 'I've tried to be patient about you finding work but this is just a hobby for you surely. Don't tell me you really expected it to turn into a business?'

'Well, yes,' I say, 'it was supposed to be my new job. There are ways I can make money through it.' Until that very moment, I hadn't realised how much I'd been counting on it to pay my bills when I got back to London.

At this point Selena comes over with our drinks and bends down to give Tara a scratch around the ears. 'Sorry to eavesdrop but . . . Padma has been amazing helping me with my business here. She's helped me rework my menu, shown me a few shortcuts. And I've taught her a bit about the buying and budgeting side of things. She could make a real go of it if she wanted.'

I feel so much gratitude for Selena's support. It feels like there is someone to get my back, to be my advocate. The only other person who makes me feel like that is Delilah.

'I'm sorry,' Wallace says, feeling outnumbered by the three of us. 'I didn't realise you could make a business through "Instagram".' He uses air quotes as he says the last word.

'Instagram is actually a thing,' says Myra, 'so if you're going to air-quote something, it should have been the word "business".' Selena laughs, but although it's funny, I can't bring myself to join in.

'You know what,' says Wallace, getting up, 'I should probably head back to start packing. I don't want to miss my train.' He's furious, and while I want to calm the situation, I'm also upset that he is dismissive of what I've been doing, not to mention worried about this potential fallout from Majid. He looks at me, expecting me to get up too. And when I don't, he picks his wallet up off the table and angrily flings the door open.

'I'd better go in a moment,' I say to the others. 'I'm sorry.'

'You don't have anything to be sorry about,' Selina says.

I rub my eyes. 'Selena, I'll come and see you tomorrow about the relaunch, okay?' She nods and heads back to the kitchen.

'Can I go over to Greg's?' Myra asks.

'Of course. Just be home by dinner.'

'Auntie,' she says hesitantly as I stand up to go. 'You love romcoms even when the sexism in them drives you mad. You listen to Air Supply when you are sad, and you listen to Whitney Houston when you are happy. I know you. You want the kind of love that burns and blows out the entire world.'

I press my lips tightly together, forbidding them to quiver. I leave to face my present, and my future.

*

I don't want to return to the house just yet, I need some time to think. As I start walking to the far end of the beach, the part no one goes to because it is shaded by the pier, I spot Wallace sitting on a bench.

He can't see me, and as the path curves upwards, I study the side profile of his face, noticing the amount of space his body occupies. His expression when he thinks he isn't being observed.

Every inch of him should feel familiar but all I see is how much I don't know. I will never observe him again like this, as if he is a statue, a piece of art. It is this, the finality and rarity of the moment, that stops me from calling out to let him know I am there. Instead, I carry on walking.

When I reach the end of the beach, I stand by the shoreline for a long time. Sunlight shoots through the rolling pipe of water that is the incoming tide, lighting it briefly into a portal to a heavenly world, right before it breaks apart on the sand. I look at that molten doorway created within it, wondering what lies beyond. Maybe a different version of my life.

When I look upwards, blue sky fills every angle of my gaze.

For a few minutes, I think of nothing. But eventually, in that quiet, something comes through.

*

When I get home, Wallace is packing his things in a huff, waiting to be mollified.

I love this man but I am not in love with him. And I am certain he is not in love with me. None of this is really about us having children, it's been about finding a way to continue a relationship neither of us was ready to end.

Perhaps he feels guilt, knowing the depression that hangs over my past, feeling the spectre of his mother around him even though we were nothing alike. Perhaps I've always needed someone else to make me feel safe because I haven't trusted myself enough to be the bricks and mortar in a relationship. But I do trust myself now. Even if I have spent the last decade or so hiding from my life, there was a time when I held my mother and Dhara close and kept them safe.

I sit on the bed while he stuffs things into a bag. 'What?' he says.

'Wallace,' I say softly. 'I think we need to talk.'

16

'This isn't working, is it?' I say. He continues to pack, rearranging his toiletry bottles for the twentieth time. 'What do you mean?' he asks gruffly.

'You know what I mean.' I place my hand on his bag to make him look at me.

He sighs. 'I just think if you change your mind about . . .'

'Stop! Just stop. Stop saying that if I change my mind about kids things will be different. It's not okay, it's not fair.' Finally, I have the words I need to say.

'What do you mean, "not fair"?' he says. 'I'm not the one who . . .'

'Wallace, I don't owe you children. Okay? No woman does. Ever. If I don't want them, it's okay. It's not okay to make me feel guilty about that. And this isn't the only thing wrong with us. Can you honestly say the last two or three years have been good?'

'Well, they haven't been bad.'

His refusal to admit the truth would make me laugh if it didn't show how low our expectations had got for being in a functioning relationship. 'Let's face it,' I say, 'we don't see each other. You work long hours . . .' I hold my hand up as he opens his mouth to protest. 'I'm not blaming you. I know you're building up your practice. But I also know if things were okay with us, you'd want to prioritise our relationship.'

'But I do,' he says.

'Do you know that in the last few years, you have never suggested a date night? Or said that we should spend time together?'

'That can't be true,' he says uncertainly.

'Wallace, I'm not saying it to blame you or say it's your fault – I think we both let it happen. But somewhere along the way we just stopped trying, and stopped evolving with each other.'

We sit side by side on the bed and I can see it finally: the fight has gone out of him. I rub my hand against the stubble on his head, an old gesture. 'I love you,' I say. 'You were there for me when I needed you. And you showed me how love could feel unconditional. I owe you so much . . .'

'I didn't do it for that,' he says roughly, his voice filled with emotion. 'I didn't do it for you to owe me.'

'I know,' I say gently. *That's why I have found it so hard to let go.* 'I think we love each other, but I don't think we love each other the way we want to be loved. I don't think we are right for each other. Maybe we were once, but not now. And I think you deserve to be a dad.'

Maybe it is the softness with which I say it, but he starts crying. 'I've left it too late,' he says. 'You saw what the fertility test said.' It is so strange seeing Wallace without his invisible doctor's cloak, the self-assurance he wears almost constantly.

'Well, what do doctors know anyway, ay?' I say, squeezing his arm. He looks at me as if to counter-argue, but when he sees the small smile on my face, it makes him smile too. 'I know plenty of women who have been told they can't have children because they have polycystic ovaries – and then, bam! They get pregnant. I know it's not the same thing but trust me when I say, you are not going to find a shortage of women who want to be with you *and* have a baby with you.'

It doesn't hurt me to say this, and it doesn't feel like sacrifice. I am sorry for holding on to him out of fear and loneliness, and he is sorry for making me think I didn't know my own mind, or that there was something lacking in me because I didn't want children. It is done now.

'I'll be back soon,' I say. 'I can come and collect my things.'

'I suppose this clears the way for Hugo,' he says.

'Nothing was ever happening there,' I say, rolling my eyes. 'Be honest. Did you come here because you missed me or because you were paranoid something was happening with him?'

He hesitates and then realises he doesn't need to lie any more. 'It was Hugo,' he says. 'It's not that it wasn't good to see you but . . . that's what made me come.'

'And do you not think that tells you everything about our relationship?'

Wallace doesn't answer. When the taxi arrives to pick him up, I feel a sense of relief at not having to manage his feelings. That although I feel the enormous shifting of tectonic plates, the sadness of something huge moving out of my life, I'm only feeling like this because it's the right decision.

*

After I say goodbye to Wallace, the finality of him leaving hits me. I have to find somewhere to live. I have to start all over again, and the prospect of being single and dating is a void that yawns below my feet. I have to find a job because from the sounds of it, my fledgling cooking career is about to be torpedoed.

As if the universe has been listening, my phone pings with a notification. I've been tagged in a video. Posted by Lankey Pandey aka Majid. I know I shouldn't look, I should wait for a moment when I am less fragile or when Myra is home, but I can't help myself.

The video is called 'Auntie's Takedown'. Majid is wearing a red velour tracksuit that is ever so slightly tight around his crotch and the camera pans out to show new red Everlast boxing gloves on his hands. He is pretending to shadow-box in front of the camera. 'It's come to my attention that a certain auntie is trying to rip off your man Lankey's hard work.' The video switches to some deeply unflattering behind-the-scenes footage of me at one of his shoots. I almost don't recognise myself. My shoulders are rounded. I'm wearing such baggy clothes it's impossible to tell there is a body under there. It's a hatchet job. He says I'm a bitter ex-employee who has stolen all his ideas. I could sue him for slander but he peppers the word 'allegedly' throughout – and uses finger quotes whenever he says it.

The clips make me seem dowdy and uninteresting. As if someone who looks like me couldn't possibly come up with all these new recipes.

I wish Myra was here, but she isn't. And then slowly it starts. A trickle of Majid's trolls come through onto my page, filling my posts with comments about my appearance, how fat I am, how I dress like an auntie who's given up on life and love, how my recipes aren't real. The more they comment, the more it encourages others to do the same.

These people are strangers but somehow they have found a chest filled with all the worst things I think about myself and are repeating them back to me. I reach for an anchor, something to keep me tethered to myself, but the chain has been cut and I can feel myself floating further and further away. I know I should call someone – but who? Selena is working, so is Delilah. Rekha has been out of the loop for too long. Esme will probably want to cleanse my aura. Hugo . . . things are awkward with him after Wallace dropping in unannounced. Daisy would only say: *I told you so . . . and would you like that application to Leiths*?

The relentless waterfall of comments sets something off inside me. *I knew all of these things were true about myself.* It feels like tar has been poured on all the bad parts of my brain – the depression, the anxiety, the paranoia, every insecurity I have acquired since childhood. It extinguishes the hope that I might be able to cook full-time and make a living from it. Daisy's money will only go so far, and all it would take would be for one potential employer to google my name and come across this video. Even I wouldn't hire myself after this – how could I expect anyone else to?

When I try to fill the time by watching TV, my gaze is slippery. I feel something darken and loom in the corner of the room, but if I try to look directly at it, it moves away. Myra won't be home yet for a few hours. I want to call Wallace, to text him, and realise I can't. That for all my confidence and bravado in getting us finally to talk about breaking up, the grief that gathered at the door is stepping through. I am so tired. I manage to get into my bed and close my eyes.

*

At some point I fall asleep and when I wake up, it's dark and the house is quiet. I know I should get up, but I can't. It's safe here in the bed. I can hear Myra moving downstairs so at least I know she is home. But getting up means having to talk to her, and then explain Wallace. And Majid. I pull the covers over my head. As the distant high-pitched whine of night insects filters through, I drift off back to sleep.

*

I wake up the next morning to find midday punching its light through the curtains. When I turn my head away, I nearly scream at the sight of Myra's head hovering over me. 'Are you dead?' she demands.

I can't reply; my throat is the texture of gravel. I shake my head. 'Are you okay? Have you eaten?' I can barely whisper a reply.

'Is this because you're mad at me for turning up late for dinner?' she says. 'Or is it the Majid video? Look, that's being taken care of, don't worry.' When I don't answer, her defensiveness shades into concern. 'You've been in bed since last night. Have you even gone to the toilet?'

I know I should be concerned about Myra being on her own. I know that somewhere a part of me finds her indignation funny. She's behaving like a harassed dad, hands on hips, but I can't find the part of me that laughs.

'I just need to sleep,' I say. My voice is a croak, a papery rustle.

'Are you not feeling well?' she says, a bit more uncertainly. I nod. She doesn't know what's going on, but neither do I. Maybe I'm coming down with a bug.

'Okay, let me get you some water. And some tea?' All I can do is nod again.

At some point, there is water and tea. Later, when the moon rises, a film of oil sits on the surface of the untouched cup, now a death trap for a fly.

A creak of the door. 'Auntie? Do you want something to eat? Sausage sandwich?' she whispers. I am exhausted. The kind of tiredness that makes me feel as if my blood has been leached, and my bones have been removed and neatly packed away. I am now a jelly, a starfish, pressed into the bed as if it is coral. My eyes are fiery puddles of underwater magma. How is it possible to be so tired, after so much sleep? At some point, the door closes again.

*

The next evening, two days since Wallace left, I wake up to the sound of chanting. Esme is in the room, wearing a yellow top with long, draping chiffon sleeves that wave about her like a sail, while a worried Myra stands in the doorway. 'What's going on?' I ask. Every word is an effort. It is not a bug, unless it is in my brain. Bugs in the brain.

Esme looks at me kindly, placing her hand on my forehead. 'I'm cleansing the room. It can help . . . lift the mood.'

A lot of people think people with depression can't laugh. Or rather, if you laugh, then you don't have depression. But I laugh at the idea of my mood lifting because a white woman is mispronouncing Sanskrit scripture. Esme looks approvingly at Myra and mouths the word: 'See?' As if I am miraculously cured. She turns to me. 'What do we think about getting out of bed?' *We?*

I pull the bedsheets more tightly to my chin, which causes her euphoria to fade slightly.

'Some people believe a low mood is caused by an imbalance of the chakras,' Esme says in a concerned tone. 'Would you like me to do some reiki?' I know she means well, but her sing-song voice makes me feel unsettled. Still, it can't hurt. In the past I've had medication, journalled, gone for cold-water swims – maybe the problem was that I didn't have someone waving their hands over me. 'Sure,' I say.

While she goes next door to collect her things, Myra says: 'I'm sorry. I would've got Selena but she was working and Esme was right next door. I didn't want to leave you for too long.' She looks at me worriedly. 'Auntie, are you okay? Do I need to call Mum?'

Maybe Myra should call Daisy. On the other hand, I might feel better in the morning, and then we'd have to deal with the fallout of getting Daisy involved. I look at her mutely because I don't have an answer.

'What about Wallace?' she says. 'Should I call him?' I shake my head.

'We broke up.'

'Oh,' she says, processing the news. I can see her wondering if this is why I'm in bed and maybe it's not depression but basic heartbreak malaise. 'I am sorry. That must suck, even though you didn't seem right for each other. So maybe it is for the best?' It is for the best, I want to tell her, but I am still sad about it, and I feel like it is yet another thing I failed at. Right now, there is not much in the column of things I have got right in my life.

Esme returns and lights some joss sticks, placing them next to the bed, the fumes overpowering me with heavy coils of jasmine and sandalwood. 'Shanti, shanti, shanti,' she says.

Although it takes more energy than I think possible, I pick up the incense and drop it upside down in my glass of water. It's bad luck to douse incense before it burns itself out, but I'll take my chances. Esme's mouth pinches tightly. 'I'll take that as a sign you don't want the reiki then, shall I?' And she leaves.

At some point, a kite flies on an updraught from one side of the window to the other. It seems impossible for me to think of freedom and wings and air, so I look away and leave the sky to the birds.

*

A few hours later, Selena arrives wearing a pair of very flour-covered dungarees. 'How are you feeling?' she asks, taking a seat by the bed. But I can't answer her. When you're ill and someone asks you this question, it's like trying to number all the galaxies in the universe. It is too big, some parts are disappearing even as others are arriving, and some of it is entirely unknown. 'Do you think it's a virus or should I call someone?' she asks.

I shake my head. 'I'll be fine. Just under the weather. Need to rest.' I realise Selena's launch is coming in just over a week and I offered to help. 'I'm sorry,' I say, hoping she'll know what I am apologising for.

'It's okay,' she says in such a soft, compassionate way I think she understands what's actually going on. 'Most of the work is already done. You don't need to worry, all right? When you feel better, maybe tomorrow or the day after, we can just pick up from there.'

She doesn't understand. She thinks this is a virus, and I am going to be better tomorrow. And maybe I will be. Or maybe

I will be better in a month. When I think about this, I start crying, because I have less than a couple of weeks left here. I must find somewhere to live. Earn money. And my only prospect has been destroyed by some tracksuit-wearing man-child who is insecure about anyone else being successful even though there is plenty to go around. Selena leans over and hugs me, but I can't hug her back. It takes too much effort. Eventually she lets go.

At some point, she stops talking because I stop responding, and then I fall asleep. When I wake up in the morning, I have watched three moons travel across the window of my room.

*

On the fourth day, Myra is sitting next to the bed. I know she's worried, and I hate it. I want to get out of bed. I want to shower and take her to the shops. I want to do whatever it takes to make her feel okay.

But when I grope around for the other half of the cable, the one that holds all the electricity to jolt me into action, it's not there. I feel everything, the worry, the guilt, the shame, the self-loathing. But I'm not worth anything, and I can't do what I need to do for my loved ones.

Myra tells me that I'm not to worry about her and that she's doing okay. She's been keeping her Zoom appointments with her doctor. She's been eating leftovers and even tried making some samosas. They tasted like barf, but hey, at least she tried. Selena has been dropping off food. I shouldn't worry about the Majid thing, she says, as it is being handled. The video will be taken down imminently. Teflon have contacted us about a sponsorship deal, isn't that amazing? She demonstrates the voice she's invented for the fictitious agent Pinky Dishwallah, which sounds like an Indian Lady Grantham, and then says we should probably think about getting me a proper one. Tara is doing fine although she keeps scooting her butt on the floor, which means she might have worms. Myra forgot to water the lettuce and now it looks like crispy seaweed and she's sorry, but at least the chillies are thriving in the heat.

She tells me that she called Wallace, who sounded concerned then merely wished her 'good luck'. As sad as I am about the end of our relationship, part of me wonders why I wasted a quarter of my life on someone who is such an unfeeling idiot.

Before she gets up to leave, she says she doesn't want to rush me but if I don't get up soon, she will have to call her mum, and she really doesn't want to do that. Right now, however, there are things happening in my brain that are scarier even than Daisy.

*

Depression, like grief, turns time into more than just a measurement. At one remove, it passes slowly, turns all your negative emotions to the consistency of elastic. At the other, it moves so fast that minutes, hours and days blur.

As far as I can tell, we have just one week left in the cottage, but I also don't know exactly how much time has passed. Myra won't let me near my phone in case I feel the temptation to check Instagram. I don't leave the bed beyond needing to use the toilet.

Although I can't feel much, what I do feel is bad. My brain

likes to create lists that it will then run through repeatedly. An all-time favourite is the I Can't Believe I Said That list, and includes all the times I embarrassed myself, ranging from what I said as an eight-year-old at the local swimming pool to commenting unfavourably on a colleague's outfit at a Christmas party. Other lists include: People Who I Allowed To Treat Me Like Shit and the perennial: Things I Grieve But Can't Do Anything About:

1. My relationship with Daisy
2. Her not being Dhara any more
3. Wallace
4. My lack of a career and spending my life working for people I hate
5. Not travelling the world when I was young
6. Being around more when Myra was younger
7. Telling my mother I loved her more when she was alive
8. Forgiving my mother
9. Wanting to be a size smaller
10. Not being secure enough to not say 'Wanting to be a size smaller'
11. Dad

After insisting I have my phone back, I open it to see Myra has deleted Instagram and there is only one message, from Delilah.

> **Hey gorgeous girl! When are you back? I have some news . . . I am thinking of selling the café and moving back to Oz. I know it's huge. Let's meet for dinner when you're back. Miss you and love you more. Xxx**

Delilah is a part of what makes me feel at home, and now a future yawns ahead of me that doesn't have her in it. Brixton won't be my home any more. The prospect of finding a new place, job, and packing up all of my stuff, overwhelms me once again. I put my phone down and pull the blanket over my head.

*

On the night of the fourth moon, the clink of plates downstairs tells me it's dinnertime. Sometime after that the house grows quiet and I fall asleep again. When I wake up, it is because Myra is gently shaking me. 'You have a visitor, Auntie,' she whispers, and the softness of her voice almost makes me cry.

'Padma,' a voice says, and I close my eyes. I don't want him to see me like this.

*

'You don't have to open your eyes,' Hugo says. 'I'll just talk to you and you don't have to say anything.' His voice is low and deep. It threads around the blankets, tucking me in.

I'm in the place suspended between realms, the halfway point between reality and the Beyond. Hugo sits and talks to me. He tells me about growing up, and his only memory of his mother being a white hat, gloves and the scent of roses. She'd died when he was young and at boarding school, and that's when he and Henry bonded as brothers. After that he spent every Christmas with Henry, and when he started secondary school, every summer with Rosemary. His father saw him about four times a year, when he was required to give a progress report on his studies.

Unlike Henry's father, who would beat him with a strap if the report was bad, or buy him an extravagant present if it was good (I didn't know this about Henry), Hugo's father didn't seem to care much about the outcome either way. He had a new wife and son and planned to correct all the mistakes he felt he had made with his firstborn. Left to his own devices, young Hugo took an interest in nature. He examined the ponds in their stately home, spent time with the gardeners to learn about different varieties of trees and plants and what made them thrive. He travelled in the Amazon and was duped out of £500 for an antidote after a local told him a parasite had swum up his penis and was the cause of a rash. (It was simply heat rash.)

Encouraged by the small puff of laughter that escapes me at this point, he tells me about the Pantanal, the tropical wetland that has lily pads so broad they look strong enough to cradle a baby. He brings the birds of the rainforest into the room, their colours and the sound of their feathers – *whomp whomp whomp* – in the canopy above. He tells me about Elaine, and how they met: she on an archaeological dig, he trying to negotiate access to land on behalf of the fuel company he worked for. He tells me about the almost baby they'd had, miscarried after five months. That when the baby died, it took the kernel of love between Elaine and Hugo with it, and after that they couldn't bear to see their loss reflected in each other. He tells me about the moment he walked into the sea, his life in the balance, and the moment he walked back out. He whispers the reason why, and I hold it close to my chest and vow never to tell another soul.

He tells me that life is hard and unfair, but there are gilded moments: people whose lives we change, not by doing anything spectacular, but just by being in them. He tells me that the moment we are here is a moment in which everything is possible. 'I am scared of so many things,' he says, 'but I am most scared of the moment when everything ends.'

He tells me about the first time we met, and how he was intrigued to meet me. This person who made the light come on in Daisy's eyes when she talked. He saw how angry I was at the wedding, with her and with Henry, and decided to stay out of my way until I allowed him nearer. He said that at the hospital all those weeks ago, I had seemed so different from the person he remembered, even though I yelled at him and accused him of being a racist. He saw how carefully I moved around Daisy and Henry so as not to upset them, but he also saw the rage that lay below the surface. He noticed how, although I was snappy with him, I seemed more like my real self and he was interested in why that was. He says how lovely it has been to see the real me in the last few weeks. That I am funny and passionate and I care. That I make a difference. That I shouldn't give up hope, because there is a girl who is worried about me and loves me very much, and that girl doesn't love many things.

And at the end of all this, when Hugo has drawn me to a place where I am safe, he tells me that today is a supermoon, and did I know that supermoons are thirty per cent brighter than ordinary ones, and that woo woo folk say emotions are more heightened on these days? I could listen to his voice forever. Then he says: 'Padma, would you like to come out and see the stars?' I look at the ceiling and try not to cry because I would like nothing more than that. But I can't. I can't move – it is impossible, unfathomable, that I could attempt such a thing.

He sees the tear rolling down the side of my face. I nod, to tell him, yes, I would like to see the stars, but I can't, I just can't. He pauses for a moment. He is going to leave. I know it. Then he reaches a decision and scoops me up with the blanket and holds me tight to his chest. He smells like cologne and sweat and earth and sanity. A wisp of my real self winds its way through a crack in the glass, the iron gate, the dead space between my eyes, and hooks itself around the part of Hugo that feels safe. 'Are you okay?' he murmurs.

'Yes,' I say, muffled within the sheets.

17

Hugo carries me down the stairs and onto the deck to look at the night sky. He places me gently on the outdoor sofa. I hear feet run then halt. Hugo waves his hand for Myra to join us.

Squeezed between them, I am still so exhausted. But there's a part of me that is content to be there.

We sit for a while, looking at the stars, sparkling clusters that look as if a celestial being has pressed a thumbprint of glitter against the blackness. I wonder if the solitary bright stars are lonely.

Hugo tries to explain the constellations to us. 'Er, that one is possibly Aquarius . . . and maybe that is Venus? Possibly the Horseshoe Nebula . . .'

'Good grief,' Myra says, pulling out her phone. 'Horseshoe isn't a nebula – you mean *Horsehead.*' Her phone has a stargazing app, and as she points it towards the sky, it unlocks our universe. She sketches her hand across the Orion Nebula, and then the different constellations – Cygnus, Ursa Major. 'Jupiter is there, see,' she says, jabbing a finger at a bright speck Hugo said might be a satellite. 'Saturn is there.' I've never knowingly seen the planets of our solar system before. I didn't even know we could see the outer planets from our own. It expands the sense of wonder I feel. And after days of feeling nothing, feeling something feels like . . . everything.

'But where is the moon?' Hugo says.

'Behind us,' Myra replies. We crane our necks back, and the biggest moon I have seen drops into view. It is the kind of moon you could imagine reaching out your hand towards, touching the craters on its surface, poking a finger into the Sea of Tranquillity. We sit bathed in its light, and for a moment, I don't think about anything else. I am where I need to be, and Myra is next to me and is safe. I readjust the blankets and my left hand brushes against Hugo's. As I pull away, his fingers lace with mine. I am not ready to look him in the eyes and see what is held there. I lift my face to the moon and silently give it my wish.

*

At some point, I fall asleep again. In the morning, Hugo leaves and Daisy arrives. I hear her voice downstairs and burrow further into the bed. I can hear her and Myra talking, but because Daisy doesn't know how loud her voice is, I can only hear her side of the dialogue.

'What do you mean, Wallace isn't answering his phone any more?'

'What? They broke up! Why didn't she . . . oh. Is that why she's . . . Okay, okay, don't yell at me, how was I supposed to know?'

Whatever Myra then says catches Daisy's attention, long enough that she seems to be listening.

'Why didn't you call me sooner, Myra? Oh, Hugo? What does Hugo know! I'm her *sister*!'

There is a long wait. If Daisy comes up to shout at me, or

tell me that I shouldn't have left all of this to Myra, I might never, ever get out of bed again and then Hugo will have to sell the cottage with me in it. I don't have any defences. My skin feels so raw and thin, I don't have it in me to push back or converse with her the way we normally do.

Eventually, the door eases open and Daisy cranes her neck around it. 'You're awake!' she says as brightly as she can, and sits down on a chair next to the bed. 'How are you feeling?'

I can't do this now. Daisy doesn't understand that I can get like this. Given how infrequently we see each other, how carefully I curate the version of me she knows, it hasn't been too hard to keep my episodes of depression from her. I've either dealt with them alone, or with Wallace. The person I need most isn't Daisy, but Dhara. Dhara would understand. Dhara would hold my hand, or crawl into bed with me while we listen to the radio so that we don't have to talk. I look at Daisy, her fresh white shirt and expensive haircut.

'Do you want to come down and join us for lunch?' she asks. Her kindness is harder in some ways because I don't expect it. I imagined her saying I was being dramatic or chiding me into getting up. Or, as she would be right to do, admonishing me for making Myra look after herself. Really, is forcing her into a caretaking role any different from what my mother did to me? The final layer of the onion falls away and reveals the core of my fear. My tendency to depression means I don't trust myself to look after a child, but also that I have felt afraid of passing it on. Yet seeing all the wonderful things that exist in Myra has made me realise not everything is predetermined because of the hard things we experience. The tears fall even though I will them not to.

'Oh, Pads, what's wrong? Tell me.'

'Everything,' I say, and pull the covers over my face because I don't want Daisy to see me crying. I must look like an exceptionally sad ghost quivering underneath a sheet.

At some point, she returns with a sandwich and a cup of tea and sits down in the chair next to the bed. 'It's got ham and hand-cut slices of cheese in it,' she says, 'I know you hate it when the cheese is grated.' It is a small gesture, but it feels big. I take the plate from her and when I hesitate, she says, firmly: 'Padma, you need to eat something. Come on. I know my cooking is bad but even I can't mess up a ham and cheese sandwich.' Something in her expression makes me sit up and take a small bite. It tastes like sawdust in my mouth.

After a while, she says: 'I spoke to Wallace.' I silently implore her not to say anything more.

'Why didn't you . . .' She stops and shakes her head. 'I wish you had told me, Padma. I wish I had been there to help.' But I didn't want Daisy's help, I hadn't wanted anyone's help.

'How long have you had this?' she asks.

I put the sandwich down. Normally I spend so much time preparing my reaction to Daisy that I never truly see her. There is worry on her face. Her facial features are fine and her body delicate, but I can feel how big her heart is despite that. I know she came the moment Myra told her what's been happening, despite her busy job. She is the type of person who wants to fix everything, for everyone, and doesn't understand how sometimes that can be a hard thing to be around. I haven't kept her close. Maybe we don't see each other as much as we should, but that isn't all her fault.

'Since Mum,' I reply. I'm sure she wants to ask me why I'd never told her but she doesn't. Instead, she asks me what depression is like.

Sometimes, I say, I step into a pocket of darkness that opens up in the ground below me. Sometimes it's just one foot, and I can wiggle my way out after a struggle. Sometimes it's both feet and when that happens, I just have to wait.

'I didn't . . .' She shakes her head again. 'I'm sorry.' For the first time in a long time, it feels real, our bond. 'I'm sorry I wasn't there for you, I'm sorry I was caught up with my own stuff. Especially when . . .' She trails off. Especially when I was there for her when she'd had post-natal depression. We both know what she is remembering. But it's not about that. I didn't help Daisy then because I wanted something in return.

'MUM!' Myra yells from downstairs. 'Phone call.'

'I'll be right back,' says Daisy, patting my hand. 'Have another bite of your sandwich.'

I hear voices murmur in the distance. *'Who is it?'* Daisy asks. Myra says a name I can't hear. There is a brief silence and then a furious barrage.

'No, Mr Akhtar, YOU misunderstand me. If you do not take that video down right now and issue a statement of apology, I am suing you for loss of earnings, slander and defamation . . . No, I don't care you used the word "allegedly" . . . Yes, I am a lawyer. I work for one of the biggest law firms in London and I can drag this out for months. And I'm sure it will make for a nice news story that you have tried to take down the woman whose recipe you stole in the first place. And maybe we should also look into some of the allegations she mentioned about your behaviour with the interns at your company . . .'

A long silence. Then: *'I don't care. I do* not *care. Stop talking! Take the video down, issue the apology within twenty-four hours. We are done here.'*

After that the soft burble of Myra and Daisy talking, presumably about the phone call, drifts upwards. I close my eyes and feel the strength of Daisy's love. It is solid, protective. I've felt this before from my mother, but only ever in fits and starts.

But this – what Daisy is doing for me with Majid, and in coming here – it matters. It makes me feel that whatever I become, and whoever I am, there is someone who will love me through it all. I fall asleep in a pool of sunlight, feeling the warmth and concern of my loved ones all around me.

An hour or so later, Daisy comes back and sits down in the chair. I look at her enquiringly.

'You don't need to know,' she says. 'But it's all taken care of. That video thing.'

'Tell me,' I say. 'Please.'

She starts tidying the room, picking up bits of laundry, stacking mugs. 'Myra told me what happened with that idiot Majid and the video,' she says. I wait for her to tell me it was stupid of me to listen to Myra and to do this whole Instagram thing. 'Reading those comments must have been horrible. You know they aren't true?'

I sigh. 'I mean, aren't they? They said I looked fat and old. And I do.'

She snorts impatiently. 'You don't, Padma! Look – I don't know a single person who is completely happy with how they look, okay? But what matters is what you think of yourself. If there are things you want to change about yourself, change them! No one is making you wear Wallace's old clothes. But don't change them because of what some shitheads online say.'

'Okay,' I say meekly, realising how strongly Daisy feels; I am warmed by it.

'For what it's worth,' she says, 'I think you and Myra have done an impressive job. I mean, I want to make everything on there and I don't even cook! And I spoke to Selena – she told me how much you've been helping her.'

'Thank you,' I say to her, not realising how much I needed that reinforcement from my sister.

'I think you could do this, Padma,' she says gently.

'Do what?'

'Set your own thing up.'

'Oh, god, Daisy, I don't want to go to Leiths!'

'Who said anything about that?' she asks, bewildered. 'And what's so wrong with Leiths anyway? I've been offering to help you with that for ages. If you can accept the responsibility of looking after someone, why can't you accept that sometimes it's okay to let another person look after you?'

'Because with you, there are always strings attached.'

'I don't ask you for anything . . .' she says.

'No, you don't. But giving help makes you feel that you can comment on my life. You make me feel like I'm never good enough, Daisy! You send me job recommendations, and if I don't follow up on them, you assume it must be because I'm lazy. Or unambitious. You don't *ask* whether I want what it is you're offering.'

'I only do that because I want to make sure you're okay, and you haven't missed anything. I'm not saying you're not . . . capable.'

'But it does make me feel like I'm not. You make a comment about what I'm doing, and then you suggest a "solution" without asking me if I want to change or if I am in fact happy. And then if I don't do what you say, somehow it's my fault when things go wrong.' I lie back in bed, feeling exhausted. But I don't have the spare energy to worry about whether

Daisy is upset or will get angry. It's not that I don't care, it's more that my feelings have no extra give.

'I don't mean it that way at all. I'm just trying to help you,' she protests.

'Sometimes, Daisy, it makes me feel like I'm not good enough to be loved. And I can take that from anyone else – but it is hardest when it comes from you.'

'I see,' she says quietly. I've probably ruined any chance of us becoming close again. She leaves the room carrying the stack of crockery and I know I've gone too far. That soon I will hear the sound of her car engine and she'll be away. But shortly afterwards, she comes back upstairs with a fresh mug of tea.

'Look, I'm just going to say something, and you might not like it,' she says, sitting down.

That sounds ominous, I think.

'When I suggest these things it's not because I think I'm better than you. It's because I want to help. I feel guilty – all the time – about how much I have. It doesn't seem right that . . .' She breaks off. In her face I see it is the truth. She doesn't just feel guilty about the differences in our circumstances. She feels guilty about what I gave up for her, and worries that it has altered the course of my life for the worse.

'Padma, I don't mean to make you feel bad about your life, I really don't. But I want to be able to help. I think you should open your own place – there, I said it. And if you need money to do it – if that is the only thing standing in the way – then why can't you let me help you? I'm not saying this because I think you're weak or you can't cope by yourself. It's because we're family and we're supposed to be able to support each other.'

'I get you want to help,' I say eventually. 'But have you

stopped to consider that while I respect and admire what you've built, I don't want your life? I'm not perfect. I've made some poor decisions, and maybe I haven't been as ambitious or brave as I should have been – but it's my right to make those decisions.'

'I know,' she says reluctantly. 'And maybe I could have been less patronising about how I've offered my help in the past. But you have a real talent, Padma.'

The idea of opening my own place feels too big. I don't know anything about catering. What if it goes out of business?

You'll learn as you go along, a small voice says. *The worst thing to do would be not to try at all because you're too proud or worried you'll fail.*

'Will you let me help you, Padma?' says Daisy, squeezing my hand. And I see her, for a moment. I see Dhara coming through. 'You took care of me for so long,' she says. 'Can you, just this once, let me help you?'

In the past fifteen years, I've never known Daisy's love not to come with conditions. I've been wary not just out of pride, but because I never want to owe or feel owned by her. Perhaps Daisy has felt that her love has needed to come with conditions, or else people won't want her. Maybe I need to give her a chance too.

*

Myra has created a nest on the sofa, a comforting ball of blankets and cushions fashioned into a mountain cave. They both asked if I'd like to come downstairs to watch a movie, and it seemed like something I was able to do. Although I still feel a dull drag in my head, something about my conversation with Daisy has lifted the weight off. We're watching all of Spielberg's greats, starting with *Back to the Future,* although *The Goonies* is still banned.

We're watching Marty McFly and Doc Brown argue, when Daisy turns to me and says the thing I least expect. 'Would you like me to oil your hair?'

When I'm feeling like this, I usually recoil from anyone touching my skin, so it's a good sign that I don't mind.

As I settle in front of her, she says: 'Don't look so surprised, I remember you doing mine. I always preferred it. Mum was so hardcore.' We both laugh at the memory of how the roughness of Mum's oiling depended on how well contestants were doing on *The Generation Game.* If someone got an answer wrong, a yank. If someone got it right, a gentle rub. Daisy looks like another person who'd work out their catharsis on someone else's hair follicles, but her hands are surprisingly gentle. *Comb, pat, rub. Comb, pat, rub.* Myra looks curiously at us, tied together, lost in a tradition that goes back to our mother, and her mother, and further back than we could imagine. The care and love imbued into such a ritual, looking after one another in lieu of words we cannot say out loud.

'Can I try it?' Myra asks both of us.

'Why don't I do it for you?' I say. I haven't had time to thank her for looking after me when I should have been looking after her. I pat the floor in front of me. I brush her long hair, softly and gently, and part the middle. I pour a little of the warm oil into my hands and work my way through, section by section, rubbing the oil into her scalp, not the hair, gently working my way all around. It is such a vulnerable undertaking, allowing someone to feel the shape of your head.

To allow them to treat it with infinite care. When Daisy is done with my hair, she gets up and goes to the kitchen to wash her hands. While she's getting a round of tea for us and a Lucozade for Myra, I continue. Slowly, and with care.

*

Over the next couple of days, I drift between my bed and the living room. Sometimes I visit the kitchen at night, open the fridge and stare into the light, my gaze unseeing, past the artisanal cheeses Daisy has brought with her from London, the stick of yellow butter bought from the local butcher.

Wallace hasn't checked in. I cannot pretend it doesn't hurt – it makes me wonder if he'd really cared or if he was doing relationship-by-numbers and pretending to because it was expected. That may be unkind, but I am not in a forgiving mood. Hugo checks in daily, and I send him small messages back, or when I feel too tired, a little emoji.

Although I'm relieved, and surprised, to be feeling better so soon, I feel very angry about the time lost to this small depressive slump. It feels as if someone has stolen grains of life from my sand timer. I usually emerge from an episode to a ton of messages, a list of chores, and people who require appeasing because they think I've ignored them. I realise with a jolt that Selena's relaunch is in two days.

I feel my energy returning somewhat. While I still find it hard to talk for long periods, I'm able to move about a bit more. I take walks without a destination in mind. I pass fields of cows, meadows growing wild now that summer is almost over. On the third day of Daisy being here, eight days after I first felt like this, I remember Delilah's message and call her back.

She answers on the first ring, and her voice is so familiar and warm, it helps a layer of my skin to grow back. She tells me how she's been, gives me updates on all the people we know locally, and for a brief moment, Brixton is carried on a crosswind in colour, smell and sound.

'You're leaving,' I say reproachfully.

'Not yet, but yes. It is getting so gentrified here, Padma. I can't bear it. I will miss you so much, but I think it's time to go home.'

'Are you going to sell the business?'

'Yeah, but I want to sell it to a person who will love it, and that's hard to find. I don't suppose you harbour any secret ambitions of running your own place?'

'Hmm,' I say, 'have you been speaking to Daisy?'

'No,' she laughs, 'why – should I have been?'

'She thinks I should do that,' I say. 'But it's so daunting. I don't know the first thing about it.'

'What are you talking about?' she retorts. 'You've spent enough time with me that you know a few things, and I've loved watching what you've been creating on your social media.' I had almost forgotten about Instagram. Although Majid had taken down his video, I hadn't felt ready to re-engage. 'Look, think about it,' she says. 'I didn't know anything about running a café either. I just wanted a space where people could feel at home, feel comfortable. And where I'd be able to bake and think.'

'But, Dee, you're different – you're so talented. I still have a long way to go.'

'Think about it,' she says, 'that's all I'm asking. Anyway, how're things with your niece?'

'How much time have you got?' I laugh. It's good to laugh.

I tell her everything. It is the most I have said in a while. 'She's doing okay, I think. Or at least, she's at ease with herself.'

'That's huge. How many teenagers do you know who feel at ease with themselves?' Delilah replies.

I hadn't expected it when we drove down all those weeks ago, but Myra has been the most surprising thing of all. She makes me see everything is not fixed. To quote *Terminator 2*, which she watched last night, laughing at the special effects: there is no fate but what we make.

What she gives to me, I want to give to her. I want to protect her from anything that might harm her, and I always want to be her safe harbour. Our time together has awoken something in me. Not the desire to be a mother, but to be there for her, standing next to Daisy, a protective arm around them both.

*

When I get home, Daisy is ready to go back to Wimbledon. Her bags are packed and she asks me if I want to return with her. We had originally agreed to be back in London just before the August bank holiday, and are in the final countdown for when we are due to leave the cottage: three days' time. I shake my head. I've made a commitment to Selena about helping her with the launch, and I want to see it through. I tell Daisy about Delilah's offer and watch the delight spread across her face but she doesn't say anything more or offer to loan me the money.

When we all eventually go back to London, I know we won't get time like this together again. There will be her work, Myra, Henry, a thousand other things jostling for her time. 'I know you have to leave,' I say, 'but can I take you to my favourite spot first? Hugo showed it to me – he visited it as a boy.'

Daisy raises an eyebrow. 'Oh, did he now?'

'It's not like that, he's not interested in me.'

'But you're interested in him?'

'Daisy . . .'

'Okay, okay.'

I take her by the shortcut and she grows quiet when we walk through the fields of long grass, golden and green. Soon enough, we are seated on the driftwood, looking out at the calm waters ahead. I don't know why but a thought suddenly comes into my mind. 'Do you ever think of Dad?' I ask.

Daisy and I have never really spoken about him.

'No,' she says, and pinches her lips, in a way that tells me she does. Rather than forcing her to tell the truth, I decide to offer up a part of mine.

'I think about him often,' I say. 'Even though I don't want to and I try to forget. But I wonder what life would have been like with him in it. I wonder if it would have been better. I still do.'

A heron picks its way across the shoreline. Ripples radiate from its long legs through the clear, cold water. 'I hope,' Daisy says eventually, 'whenever he sees two little girls together, he feels darkness inside and never, ever gets over it. I hope that on his deathbed, he wonders where we are and that it is a void that is never filled for him.'

The ferocity of her words, the rawness and pain within them, take me aback. I seize hold of her hand, even as she flinches, and hang on tight. 'He didn't deserve us,' I say.

'Neither did Mum, really,' she replies. 'But at least she stayed.'

We sit in silence for a while, our emotions floating like icebergs in front of us. So much of it held beneath the surface.

I feel like the last historian left in the library, marking time. Even though I have done some work around understanding Mum, understanding how she changed me, and us, I don't know if Daisy has. Maybe she thinks that if she never talks about it, it won't be true. But the past is always here; its long fingers have already moulded her present and will continue to do so if she doesn't properly confront it.

'I know we don't talk much about her,' I say, 'but Mum did affect how we are today. I'm too scared to step outside of my comfort zone, too scared to travel in case I get a phone call telling me something bad has happened. And I want to change that. I don't think it's healthy to be always waiting for disaster.'

'Because you got the phone call when Mum . . .' she says, finally understanding. 'Yeah, I get it. I mean, I was there when she . . . you know. I try and control every outcome, what people are doing, that intense pressure to do everything perfectly – maybe it's because of her. Myra's therapist says her main issues are me and Henry so I can't win either way.' She laughs at the sorry irony of it all.

We sit there until the last possible moment. 'We need to get back if you want to beat the school traffic,' I say finally, with a shade of regret that it's ending sooner than I would like.

'How often do you feel like this?' she says, getting up. 'So bad that you can't get out of bed?'

'I don't know.' I shrug. 'I've lost count, but it's not so

regular any more. And the periods get shorter. At the beginning, it could sometimes last for months.'

'I can't believe I didn't know,' she says.

'I was really good at keeping it from you. You'd invite me over or want to chat and I always found ways of fobbing you off. Besides, it's not like we saw each other all that often.'

'That isn't my fault,' she says, a touch defensively.

'I know.'

'Do you see a doctor for it?'

I don't say anything, because I haven't for a while and I know I should have kept on top of it. But I've been fine without antidepressants for a long time – I've had the odd episode here and there but it has always passed without much fuss. I just didn't like the idea of having to be on medication all the time.

'Oh, Padma,' Daisy groans because she knows the answer just by looking at me. '*Why* don't you see a doctor about it? Wallace *is* a doctor, why didn't he do something?'

'I've been fine for a long time,' I splutter, 'and it takes ages to see someone through the NHS, and then when you do it's never the right person. Or they want you to come into the surgery when you physically can't. It doesn't work and it's easier to do it alone.'

'*Please* will you let me help you? I can add you to our private healthcare – you'll be seen immediately.'

'I'm not a charity case, Daisy.'

'No one's saying you are! It won't cost anything to add you – Henry has his own plan with work, I can just add you to mine.' After a while, I nod ever so slightly and she looks relieved.

*

When we get back to the house, Myra refuses to leave me behind. 'It's only for a few days,' she says to her mother. 'And we can definitely keep Tara, right?' Daisy had asked me how Myra had been with the dog, and I said she'd passed her probation. Even though she was far too lenient with the treats, she did the most important tasks such as walking her and picking up her poop. Besides, they were now so fully symbiotic, there was no chance of separating the two.

'Yes,' Daisy says. 'But if I have to pick up your responsibilities, she's going straight back to the rescue centre.'

Myra clamps her hands around Tara's ears. 'Cruel woman,' she says. 'Auntie, have you had to pick up a single poop since he's been here?'

'I'm not getting involved,' I say, picking up some of Daisy's bags to take to the car.

As she starts the engine, she leans out of the window. 'Myra is doing well, Padma,' Daisy says. 'Maybe she'll never be all sugar and sweetness, but I've never seen her this talkative or willing to spend time with me. With us. That's a good sign, I think.'

I don't voice my worries about what will happen when Myra goes back home. That none of this is real life, and real life is harder. But perhaps the biggest lesson learned is that we cannot keep our loved ones safe. All we can do is keep showing up for them, even when we get it wrong. Especially when we get it wrong.

18

The day before Selena's relaunch the weather turns into a vengeful, mercurial creature. After a stretch of hot, unbroken weather, storm clouds gather in the distance. The light is unnaturally bright on the yellowing grass as I make my way down to the café, through cow pats roasted to thin hard discs. The air is heavy with electricity and the promise of rain. In my basket are a couple of the green peppers that didn't get eaten by snails, and the last remaining strawberries I found in the vines. An apology to Selena for being so absent, a thank you for the care she took of Myra while I wasn't well.

Along the beach, red flags sit starkly against sand the colour of bronze, after the overnight rain. A lone swimmer who has chosen to disregard the warning is floating in the middle of the bay, being nudged back to shore by the swelling current. A speck of life shining brightly on dark waters. I stop for a moment to watch them, taking a long slow breath on what will be one of our last mornings here. I think about how much has changed since we first drove down this road and what we will return home with. And without. I feel I should be leaving this place a new person, but I have more questions than ever, more uncertainty. I have lost an entire person from my life – Wallace. At the same time, there is something shaky and new when I think (guiltily) about Hugo. I wonder if my relationships with Myra and Daisy will withstand the differences of our lives in London. I'm still worried about my job, the decisions I have made so far, and whether it is too late – to travel, to succeed, to find love again. I push it down, deep down, and cross the road to the café.

It's the first time I've seen Selena since her visit, although I'd texted her to tell her it wasn't a virus and I was struggling mentally. 'I'm sorry,' I say, when I push the door open and see her bent over the counter, methodically crimping some pasties. The café is technically closed for the day while she preps for the launch so it's clear of customers. She looks up and comes around the counter to scoop me into a hug. 'What are you apologising for? *I'm* sorry. I was so stupid – I asked if it was a virus when I should have known it wasn't . . .'

I shake my head. 'No, you didn't do anything wrong. It's me.'

I don't know if I will ever come back to Harkness given that Hugo is planning to sell the house, but I know Selena is someone who I want in my life forever. Somewhere in her kitchen, I pieced together my sense of self. Having my deepest love of cooking being witnessed by other people made it real.

'Coffee?' she asks. I nod. While she flicks the switch on the bean grinder, she asks if I want to talk about it. I say no. 'Not because I don't trust you,' I say, 'but it tires me out to talk about it. I would much rather discuss tomorrow, and if you have everything you need. And what I can do to help.'

'You don't have to, Padma,' she says. 'Honestly, I know what it's like trying to handle too many things at once. Just focus on getting better.' I've always found that a strange phrase. Focus on getting better. As if your illness is the sun and you can outstare it.

'This is me focusing on getting better,' I say, gently but firmly. 'I'll let you know if it gets too much.'

We talk through the details. While Caitlin can help with waitressing, Selena will need more help on the day. 'Greg and Myra might be able to bus tables?' I say, and we tick it off the list. There's artwork that needs to be put up – Selena has sourced retro posters of Cassareep, the Guyanese sauce that is used in so many stews, and she's blown up some beautiful landscape photographs of Guyana as well as Harkness. A framed photo of the Kaieteur Falls, an enormous single-drop waterfall that looks as if it emerges from the jungle and thunders over a cavern of rock into a green-lined basin, sits alongside a study of the White Sentinels in jagged formation.

We work through the menu. Unlike Eileen, who has a hundred things on offer, Selena has stripped out a lot of the mains and settled on just six choices, mainly British with Guyanese twists. They're all brunch-type dishes, which means they can stretch out across the day, and for anyone wanting something more hearty, there's always a mixed vegetable curry. Selena wants the counter to shine too. Amazing pastries, but also treating it like a testing ground for things she wants to experiment with. She'll serve pastry with spiced cheese piped through for the first time, and I'd planned to make some of my favourites for the counter. The cramosas, the paneer quiches, and tiny little chaat bombs – a mixture of tamarind, mint and coriander, sev, chickpeas and spicy yogurt, which were easy to make but complex in flavour.

After we write it all down, she shivers at the long list of things to do. 'Selena,' I say, putting my hand on her arm, 'it's going to be okay. You're launching something amazing, and that's scary but whatever happens you are going to learn from it. The *Harkness Horn* is coming to cover it, right? And I can post about it too.' I laugh. 'I can't believe that is a sentence that just came out of my mouth. What a wanker!' She laughs in reply, for the first time since I got there.

'Also,' I say reassuringly, 'Myra is a genius at this stuff. She can help you with your social media, maybe tease a few things out.'

'What if they don't like the food?' she says in a small voice.

'Then they can eat somewhere else.'

'It's not that, it feels like . . .'

'Like they are saying they don't like you?' I finish for her. 'Most people are scared of what they don't know. The idea of sushi, for instance, was terrifying to me before I tried it. I know this isn't London or Bristol, but there will be people who will want and love to try it. And think about all the out-of-towners – you can make a deal with Esme maybe to host lunch for her retreats. Let them find out, and they'll love it. Anything, anyone, who is true to themself can't help but be successful.'

'That sounds like something I might read in an Instagram post,' she laughs, and I poke her in the ribs.

Just then, Greg comes barrelling through the door, his mint-green polo so sweaty it's turning emerald. 'We're closed, Greg,' Selena says wearily. He's at the age where he is a gawky combination of endless limbs and it takes a moment for him to come to a complete stop.

'Myra has gone missing,' he says. 'She isn't answering her phone.'

Selena and I look at each other. Greg's worship of Myra has frequently been a topic of conversation between us. We've discussed what kind of man he'll grow into, and whether he'll mysteriously gravitate towards brown women because of this one girl who broke his heart when he was young.

'That doesn't mean much, Greg. No offence,' I say.

'No,' he bursts out in frustration, jerking his arms wide so that they accidentally knock my coffee off the table. Selena gets up to fetch a cloth. 'Sorry,' he says. 'You don't . . . I was at the house. We were playing *Legends of Zelda*. She was checking her DMs – your DMs – for your social media account.'

'And?' A flutter of panic ripples from fingertip to heart, but from memory there's nothing untoward in my DMs.

'She saw a message you and your sister had sent each other. About the final payment? About you being paid to be here? To look after Myra?' He looks at me, hoping the message will sink in.

'Oh, fuck.' This is the problem with messaging across so many different platforms. Daisy had responded to one of my Instagram stories, and we'd segued into general admin chat about when we were leaving. She'd last sent a message saying the final amount of money would be paid into my account early in case I needed to make a deposit anywhere on a rental apartment.

Selena looks sceptically at me. 'You were paid to look after her?'

'Well, yes,' I say, unsure now of the ethics. It doesn't look great, admittedly. 'But if I had been working, there's no way I would have been able to stay here with her. And I needed the money.'

Greg glares at me. 'You should have told her, maybe?'

'But then it would have been like I was her caretaker and we never would have bonded the way we did,' I say helplessly.

'But you *were* her caretaker. It wasn't like you came to Harkness because you wanted to,' he says. 'And even if you did want to, how is either of you ever going to really know now?' He's right. It is a truly humbling moment to be schooled by a fourteen-year-old.

'Where is she?' I say irritably, more to myself than to him.

'I went to use the loo. When I came out, she was gone.'

'She was *gone*. What do you mean, gone? Did you check everywhere?'

'Yes,' he says, rolling his eyes. 'I checked the whole house. I even checked the beach though – you know – she doesn't love sand. I came here in case she'd come to confront you. But she hasn't. And normally I wouldn't be that worried – I mean, you know what her moods are like. But she's been dealing with a lot. She tried to reach out to her mates in London again, to say she was coming back, and they told her they weren't interested. That the summer had been better without her around.'

I had naively thought Myra was back on track because she'd been able to look after me. That her loneliness had been helped by the arrival of Tara. But clearly not.

'We all fight at school though,' Selena says. 'Maybe it will blow over when she goes back?'

Greg looks at Selena as if she's an idiot. 'They told her to do the world a favour and disappear. Said if she didn't stop bothering them, they'd post drunk pictures of her online.'

This is bad. I had no idea about any of it. If Myra had been going through this sort of bullying, then finding out I'd been paid to stay with her might have been the final straw. If I were in her shoes, I might be thinking I was all alone. That there was no one I could count on. My relationship with Daisy was just taking its first steps towards becoming something solid and good. Now it's in line to be demolished because of my carelessness and cowardice.

I call Myra but she doesn't answer her phone. Then I see three dots typing and my heart jumps. At least she is okay and has her phone with her.

Go away.

Myra – I am sorry. Let me explain. Where are you?

Are you asking out of concern or because you're being paid to?

It's late in the afternoon and the clouds that have been threatening rain all day finally release it. Fat drops pepper the ground, preparing it for the earthy sweetness of petrichor.

She isn't in town, because I would have seen her walk past the café – it's the only route to reach the warren of streets tucked away behind the main road. Which means she's gone in the opposite direction.

I don't think Myra is genuinely running away, but she wants to make us worry. She wouldn't have chosen Hugo's beach – too near, too obvious. But she might choose a place further out, somewhere known to be treacherous depending on the tides, and particularly in a storm. She might choose somewhere such as the White Sentinels, and she cannot swim.

MYRA WHERE ARE YOU?

This isn't funny.

*

The rain is unrelenting, the air tense and charged with ions. I have only ever really known Harkness under a blue sky. Surrounded by greyness and wet, even the paths I've come to know well seem strange and unfamiliar.

When Myra doesn't answer her phone, I make a plan.

Selena suggests enlisting a local fisherman named Bill, who also doubles up as an unofficial coastguard, to scout around the coastline, but first he will require tracking down. She leaves to go and find him, while Greg offers to go back to the house in case Myra returns there.

Meanwhile I am going to the White Sentinels to see if she's decided to go that way. And if she has, with any luck, Bill the fisherman might be there to help us.

I approach the narrow path that runs along the edge of the cliff, connecting the woodland at the back of our house to the long necklace of coves that finally open out into the White Sentinels at the very end. The baked earth is not ready for this kind of downpour and, in places, water collects in puddles, waiting to be absorbed. The poor visibility makes me uncertain of the path. I was sure it forked to the left but now everything looks different and strange. One thing I remember from the maps is that while it seems intuitive to follow the line of the coast, if you take the wrong fork, it will overshoot the path leading down to the White Sentinels entirely. If I get this wrong, I could be picking my way through scrub for hours, and if Myra is in trouble, the implications don't bear thinking about.

My mind is fragmenting. Out of desperation, I cry: 'Mum, help me, please!'

A grasshopper jumps across the left-hand trail. Good enough. I start walking down the path.

*

I know I'm getting nearer when I see a man and a woman in yellow rain jackets heading towards me, hurrying back in the direction of the town. 'I'd head back if I was you,' the woman yells. 'The weather is getting worse.'

'Have you come from the White Sentinels?' I ask desperately, peering out from under the hood of my jacket. They shake their heads and carry on.

I say goodbye to them and see the track curving downwards ahead of me. I wish I could pray to God, say *I will do anything if Myra is there and if she's okay,* but I dig deep for that belief, and all I find is emptiness.

*

Most people who visit the White Sentinels wonder why there are so many signs warning about the tides, because they imagine it must be easy just to climb back up the same way they came down. But the topography means that when the tide comes in, the stairs can be cut off. For unsuspecting tourists looking at rock pools at the other end of the bay, it can happen quickly and quietly.

I can't see the beach clearly because of the rain, but at least the staircase ahead of me is visible. The tide is coming in fast, however, so I don't have much time. While I pick my way down, it's as if the sky has heard my strangled prayers. *I know that you know I don't believe, but if you could do me this one favour* . . . And the rain eases off. The sky is still bruised and swollen, but for the moment it is holding back. Against the dark grey and purple, the chalk behemoths look stark and menacing, crows circling the grassy tops like a bad portent.

I walk along the coast, keeping as close to the rock wall as possible, yelling Myra's name. All I can smell is sea salt and the wind. I was so sure she'd be there – how could I have been wrong? And then I see her. The side of the cliff facing the beach has an almost vertical drop, except for a small ledge raised up from the sand by two or three feet. A small, bedraggled form occupies the ledge, trying to shelter from the rain under the thinnest of overhangs. She doesn't have a rain jacket on, and her black hoodie is likely soaked through. This isn't the warm rain of tropical rainforests but carries the chill of the North Sea. 'Myra!' I yell in relief. She looks over to me, scared but still very angry.

'GO AWAY!' she yells. 'I hate you. I never want to talk to you ever again.'

'I know,' I say desperately, aware we need to move away from this spot. 'I'm really sorry, more than I can say. But we need to get out of here – the tide is coming in and we might be cut off.'

She just shrugs. 'So what? What makes you think I didn't come here knowing that?' I'm shocked by how casually she says it.

'Because you wouldn't do something like that,' I say. 'That isn't you.'

'And you'd know? You've never felt like that, right?' She says this with such vitriol, referencing what I've told her about my own most troubling thoughts.

'If you feel like that,' I say as calmly as I can, 'let's go somewhere we can talk about it. Safely. And if you never want to talk to me again after that, I get it. I really do. I just have to text Selena and tell her where we are, okay?'

'If you want to go, you can go,' she says. 'But I'm staying here.'

In front of us, the sea pulls from deep within and sets the dark waters into a churn that whips up waves with enormous white-tinged peaks further out. The sky is grey, the horizon misted into the colour I imagine oblivion to be. All around us is the crash of water hitting the rocks as it comes closer and closer.

'I'm not going anywhere without you,' I say firmly, sending a quick message asking Selena to send Bill to the bay. I don't know if it's already too dangerous for his boat to reach us. I consider my other options, but they involve bodily dragging Myra up the stairs, and I can't risk her falling if she decides to resist.

'Why do you give a fuck? You've been paid – that's all you care about, right?' She pulls her knees closer to her chest. And when I don't answer – because what can I say to excuse myself to her? – she says: 'I thought you were doing this because you cared. But you're just like everyone else.'

'Myra, of course I care. I love you – you're my flesh and blood.' The words are genuine but they must sound so hollow to her.

'Yeah, right – like that means anything to you. You don't know a fucking thing about me or my life! Be honest – would you have done this if Mum wasn't paying you?'

It's a simple and yet incredibly complicated question to answer. Before coming to Harkness, I loved Myra because she was my niece, in the way you're supposed to love blood relatives even if you don't spend much time with them. But now, I also love her as a person – with all her contradictions. How she can be breathtakingly dismissive but also soft and enquiring. How her room is a pile of nightmares, and yet when it comes to helping me with the cooking, she's meticulous in her preparation of vegetables. How she mostly watches horror films but also cries at *Encanto* – particularly the part when the sisters sing 'All of You'. There is a part of me that was asleep for a very long time before this – and the part that has awoken would protect her to the ends of the earth.

It's now or never. That water is getting so close it is abreast with the first White Sentinel. 'You've always wanted to be told the truth,' I say. 'So here it is. I wouldn't have done this if your mum hadn't been paying me. We hardly spoke before this, I didn't know anything about kids and I wasn't sure I was equipped to take you on. I mean, she'd just had to call an ambulance for you. Seeing you in hospital scared the shit out of me.'

She looks at me, the storm mirrored in her eyes of glass green, emotions cracking against the shoreline, but at least she's still listening. 'It's not black and white though,' I continue. 'If I'd had a job, I wouldn't have been able to come here with you. But I didn't, and your mother asked me to do something for her. And for your mother to ask for help . . . it's a big deal for her. Then I got to know you. And you were . . .' I search for the right words, try to anchor to something bigger than this.

'You are the best thing that has happened to me, Myra,' I yell over the wind. 'You are one of the bravest people I know. You make me think, you challenge me. You have enormous heart. You aren't perfect – so what? No one is – but I see you, okay? I see you, little one.'

'I'm not little,' she says, but her heart isn't in it.

'It's metaphorical,' I yell over the deep bass of thunder that cracks and rolls around the hills above us at a volume that sets our teeth rattling.

*

When I told Delilah I was leaving Brixton for Harkness to go look after Myra, and was wringing my hands at how bad I would be at it, she told me a story about elephants and their herd being matriarchal. I went down an online rabbit hole and came across a viral video about a baby elephant that needed rescuing. It fell into a muddy watering hole, and the sides were too slippery for it to climb back up. At first, the matriarch thinks it isn't a big deal and the baby will use her trunk to shimmy back up. But the baby panics, and it becomes a harder task. Another female elephant comes to help the mother, and they both get into the hole and hold the baby up using their trunks in unison, helping it to clamber up and out. There are a lot of videos like that and what strikes me is how, in all of these scenarios, the baby wouldn't have made it with just one elephant trying to rescue it. But also, how instinctive it is for these creatures to come together to help, how they have evolved to protect and rescue each other.

Some more googling told me that elephant herds are predominantly female. Males leave the herd around the age of five and lead mostly solitary lives. The females walk, bathe, eat together, share their lives and are interconnected in every way. If something happens to one of the calves in their herd, they fight for its life as hard as they would for their own offspring's.

I don't expect the world to understand why I don't want children. But I don't think I need it to. I understand my own purpose in all of this. Myra is Daisy's, but she is also mine. And there is simply no world in which I wouldn't fight for her life, even if it meant giving up my own.

*

We have spent so long talking that the water has surrounded the bottom part of the staircase. If we want to get to it, we will have to clamber down the side of the rockface, and wade through up to our waists. The water is so cold, it almost dulls the feeling out of my legs. My teeth chatter and I fight to stay focused. The water is coming in, but it is also pulling out again in strong surges. Every ounce of energy is precious. I turn to Myra – we don't have time for any more talking. 'We need to go, *now*,' I say. But she's frightened and unable to move – I can feel the fear pulsing from her.

'I'm so sorry,' she whimpers in a small voice. Whatever compelled her to come here, she regrets it now.

'Myra,' I say as calmly as possible, 'it's okay. But we must go. Shall we do that? Shall we go home, and have some hot chocolate and watch a film?'

'I can't,' she whispers.

I remain patient. 'You can. I'm here. You don't need to be scared.'

'Auntie, please,' she says, closing her eyes. 'Please just leave me here. Please go, I'm begging you.'

We are running out of time. 'My darling girl,' I say, taking both her hands, 'there is no universe in which I can do that, okay? I'm sorry but I can't. So either we go now, or I'm staying with you. I'm so sorry I made this happen. I never meant to hurt you.'

She buries her face in between her knees because whatever is happening to Myra right now, she would never put me or anyone she cared about in danger. But she knows I'm not moving.

'It's such a mess,' she says. 'It's not you. I'm just so tired, Auntie. I put on a brave face, I thought Tara would fix it, but there is still this void in me that needs filling.'

I've spent most of my life pouring my love into other people, in the hope they will be able to alchemise something that will fill the empty space inside me. But I also know that empty space is not always a bad thing. Even the cosmos has black holes and dark matter where nothing exists, and still, stars are born, they explode and life continues.

I take her hand and squeeze it. 'Myra, there is nothing that has happened that is so bad it can't be fixed, okay? I know you're tired. I know it's not fair you've been dealt this hand so early in life,' I say, wiping her tears away. 'But, Myra, this is not the answer. And I know it's hard now, but it will get better. I promise you.'

'You don't know that,' she says.

I keep my voice as level as I can despite the sound of water rushing in behind me. 'I *do* know that. Believe me, if there is one thing I know, it's that. I'm not saying it will be easy. But it will pass and I promise that, whatever happens, I will be here for you. Okay? I swear that on my life. I am not letting you go.'

She looks at me with eyes so big and deep, they contain an entire universe. I look at her and see what she represents. She is everything Daisy and I are not; she has so many choices ahead of her, so much potential. With both of us in her life, she could be anything she wants to be. But she has to choose. If I drag her to safety today, it will just be the same thing all over again. She has to find that point inside herself – the one that wakes up and chooses life, the hard bits as well as the good.

'So which is it to be?' I ask. 'Are we going to stay or go?'

She unwraps her arms and says: 'I can't swim.' I turn around to see the water has come in so high, we will need to swim some of the way. In that moment, there is no room for fear or doubt. There's no time for endless procrastination. We either do or we don't.

'Hold on to me,' I say, 'I've got you. But we have to go now. Right now. Okay?' She nods and we step into the water.

*

I was taught a lot of useless stuff at school – javelin, algebra – when what would have helped was outdoor smarts. I might have been able to swim, but what made it so much harder was the extreme coldness of the aerated water and the tide that pulled in different directions. It would have been difficult enough just to manoeuvre myself, let alone another person holding on to me. And especially while trying to move parallel to the waves, which keep trying to pull us further and further away from the wall.

At some point, I realise I don't have the strength to get us there. Saltwater stings my eyes and freezes my bones. Myra is holding on so tightly I almost can't free my arms enough to swim. I feel her heart beating fast against my back. It makes me fight harder but every time I feel us getting closer to the stairs, a wave comes and drags us away.

In that moment I swear to take swimming lessons, never to be a coward again, to travel, to say what I think. But it isn't enough. An enormous wave hooks our feet and drags us further out. I wonder if it is there, in the horizon line, that I will see my mother again. And I think of Daisy, lost to me, and the thought fills me with so much grief and longing.

Just before the moment of release, a voice yells: 'MYRA! PADMA!' It's Selena, but how could it be her? Then an unfamiliar, no-nonsense man's voice yells: 'Oy – girl! Grab the rope. Now! GRAB THE ROPE!' Without thinking, I reach out my hands, with Myra's arms still clasped around my chest, and grab the rope as Bill the fisherman and Selena pull us aboard the little motorboat.

19

At some point, perhaps thirty minutes later, we are sitting on the pier by the lobster cages, wrapped in foil jackets, being shouted at by Bill the fisherman. It's something along the lines of: *WHAT were you thinking, you could have DIED, idiot Londoners, you're LUCKY I was here.* I feel exhausted and empty but relieved we are safe. My hands clasp the big mug of hot tea Selena has placed in them, but I feel so waterlogged from the dousing we have had, I fear I will never be dry again. Somewhere in my ear canal, storm water still sloshes.

Myra is clamped to my side, covered in blankets, her long hair plastered to her scalp. She has no make-up on because of the hurried manner in which she left the house, and looks much younger than her fifteen years. While sea salt has made me look bedraggled, weathered, crusted in brine, she looks like a mermaid, with perfect skin. With the storm over, a burning sun pierces through the veil of low cloud, making us squint in the glare.

In the boat, I'd pressed her hand and said: 'We think life is something that just happens but it's something we choose every day.'

She looked at me and said: 'And does that apply to you too?'

'Touché,' I said. 'That darkness . . . it passes. That's the only gift I can give you, to tell you that it passes and just to hold on until it does. You have so much ahead of you, so much goodness and love, even when things seem hard.'

I see how deeply she feels things. I know this will weigh heavily on her. How, when the lights go off at night, she will think about that moment on the beach and how it could have gone very differently. For both of us. But maybe it will be something that changes her life for the better. I look at my niece and wish it was her despair, and not her hope, that was carried out to sea. But I have to know.

'Myra, were you really going to . . .' I can't finish the sentence.

'No,' she says after a long pause. 'Not really. I just wanted to feel like I could, and then I didn't care if I did. But I didn't actually want to. I need better ways of handling things when it all gets a bit much. And besides, Tara needs me.'

I take her hand again. 'I'm here. I'm sorry I didn't tell you about the arrangement I made with your parents. I need you to know it doesn't change how much I care about you.'

'I know,' she says. 'I think it's shitty you didn't tell me, but I know.' She doesn't shake my hand off this time.

We sit there for a while, until Selena rushes over and tells us that Daisy, Henry and Hugo are driving down. I'd asked her to call them and tell them what had happened, and say that when we had recovered enough, I'd call them too.

'*And* Uncle Hugo?' Myra says, raising an eyebrow.

'Well,' I say, my heart beating faster than my ribcage can contain, 'he's your godfather. I'm sure he wants to make sure you're safe.'

'Er, yeah,' she says in a voice that says: *How stupid do you think I am?* 'He can do that by text. I don't think it's me he's coming to see.'

'Oh, shut up,' I say and elbow her. 'Do not say anything. To him. Or your mother.'

'Why don't you play him some Air Supply – that song you always like and sing along to when you think no one is looking? The one about someone being all out of love?'

'*Stop*,' I laugh. 'What are you – five?' There's a part of me that is held afloat in a bubble of warmth.

'You like him,' she says, seeing the truth in my smile. Not a question, a statement.

'Well, I don't know about that, he may not be free and I just broke up . . .'

'Auntie,' she says, placing her mug down. 'He likes you. Anyone can see that. Life is short. You just said it. Stop messing about.'

'You're horribly perceptive for a fifteen-year-old, you know.'

'I know,' she replies. We both dissolve into laughter, our foil jackets rustling against each other, feeling the sea and the possibility of the future ahead of us, and our past, our land, no longer looming, but firmly under us, raising us to where we want to go.

*

Daisy, Henry and Hugo arrive in one car approximately three hours later, and the atmosphere is tense. Daisy hides her feelings behind big sunglasses, while Henry's normally immaculate hair looks askew. Hugo holds back to allow the two of them to come into the house first. They all look angry and scared. I'm terrified Daisy and Henry will shout at me, but they just hug me tight and murmur, 'We'll talk later.'

Then they hug Myra for a long time, and although their faces are solemn, they go to the living room for The Big Chat while I motion for Hugo to come outside with me to the sun deck. There is some awkward coughing, some polite thank yous when I hand him a cup of tea and a plate of biscuits.

'Thank *you*,' I say. 'For what you did. Last week.'

'I didn't do anything,' he replies and sips his tea. 'Or rather, it's nothing you wouldn't have done for someone else.' Someone else. *So not specific to me and him then?* I think, confused. His body language is guarded, and the general way in which he's speaking makes me almost think I must have hallucinated our hand-holding. Perhaps what I feel is one-sided, an embarrassing crush built on imaginary connections and shared looks. Or maybe now that he's seen me ill, he's decided it is something he isn't attracted to. Either way, it makes every defence inside me slam down and retract the drawbridge.

'Oh, well then, thank you,' I say again politely.

'How are you?' he asks, breaking off a bit of Hobnob. 'You must be feeling shaken after that entire ordeal. It's good that you are both okay.' He's talking like a robot and I don't understand why, or what it is that I've done wrong. The old Padma would have continued with this conversation until it petered out, and then plan never to talk to him again. The new Padma, however, still has enough seawater in her body to say: *Life is short and I want an answer now.*

'Hugo, why are you being so weird? No – don't say you're not. You're behaving like we're strangers.'

He opens his mouth then shuts it. I can't bear to look at his flustered expression. I need to weed something or dig a hole or bash a rock. As I turn to go to the garden, he says: 'Padma, stop. I'm sorry,' he continues, 'it's just . . . you could have *died*.'

'But I didn't. This isn't a ghost standing in front of you. And also, aren't you meant to be nicer to people who have just had a near-death experience?'

'I *am* being nice! I'm trying to be respectful. It's just been . . . a lot to process.' He runs his hands through his hair.

'Respectful?' I look at him doubtfully. 'This isn't a Jane Austen novel, Hugo. Just be yourself. Be a friend.'

'And that's what we are, friends?' he says irritably. And then the truth of it finally dawns. Hugo likes me back. Except because he doesn't have access to my thoughts and feelings, he's been left to wonder whether I feel the same.

'You think I only like you as a friend?' I say, trying to keep my feelings in check because of the shock of the realisation. 'Or you like me as more than a friend?'

'I mean . . .' he replies, unable to look me in the eye. 'I know we held hands when I came over last, but I didn't know if that's . . . because you needed me, or that you just needed someone. Anyone.'

I shake my head. 'You are such an idiot. Do you think I let just anyone sit in my room and talk to me like that? Do you think I tell anyone half the stuff I've been telling you?'

And then the truth arrives for Hugo as he realises what I am trying to say.

Before he has the chance to answer, Daisy comes out and asks if we can chat. 'To be continued,' I say to him with a look that is still worried but now holds something different, more certain.

'What?' Daisy says in what I consider to be far too interested a manner. 'What needs to be continued?'

'Nothing,' I say and followed her inside, smiling at the fact that little sisters never seem to stop wanting to know your business.

*

'Padma,' Daisy says, 'Henry and I would like to talk to you about something.' Hugo has been despatched to keep Myra and Tara occupied somewhere out in the garden.

Henry is generally a serious man even in the midst of a joke, but now he looks positively funereal with his hands clasped in front of him. Both he and Daisy appear drained. I take a deep breath and prepare myself for a telling-off. *I should have taken better care of her, I should have dragged her up the stairs instead of trying to reason with her, I wasn't fit to take care of her, they didn't want me coming round.* If they were going to tell me I couldn't see Myra any more, I couldn't bear it.

Henry clears his throat. 'Padma, the first thing you need to know is . . .' *you're never seeing my daughter again* '. . . it's not your fault. You've done a great job with Myra.' Shock fizzes through me. Henry is not a man of many words, and those he did utter usually had a practical purpose. 'We made the agreement to pay you. You have nothing to feel guilty about. It's unfortunate that Myra saw the messages. She's been through a tough time and Daisy and I underestimated how much it has affected her.' He coughs to indicate his talking time is over.

'Thank you,' I reply, my stomach churning with guilt – at lying to Myra, and failing Daisy and Henry. 'But I feel like I let her down, and both of you too. I mean, she started her summer in hospital and ended it needing to be rescued by boat. I'm not sure how much I've helped.'

'Nonsense,' Henry says gruffly. 'What Myra chooses to do with her life remains to be seen. You gave her a space that was comforting and safe. That is all we could have asked of you.'

'None of this is a quick fix, Padma,' Daisy says. 'It was horrible, driving out here. A real shock. But Myra has issues and we're working on them. We had a good chat with her just now and it was completely different from the chat we had when she was in hospital. Henry and I can see the difference in her. We're not back at square one.'

I start to get up just as Daisy says: 'That's not all that we wanted to talk to you about, however.' I sit back down with a feeling of dread.

'Padma, I need you just to listen,' Daisy says earnestly. 'I think you would be great at starting your own business. I'm not saying what that should be – it could be your own YouTube channel (although I still don't understand how that works), or a café . . . whatever you want. But one thing I do feel strongly about is that I want to give you some money.'

'I don't want to borrow from you, Daisy.' *How many times do we have to have this conversation?*

'Not borrow. Give.' My eyes widen. I open my mouth, preparing to tell them both yet again that I am not a charity case. 'Padma,' she continues, 'when Mum died, all the money from the house went towards supporting me at university. You didn't take any of it – in fact, you dropped out of uni. I'm not saying I am going to give you this money and then hold it over your head. I do think it would be amazing if you used it as seed money for a business, but I'm also saying: this is your money. Spend it however you want.'

'But I didn't do that because I wanted you to give it back to me!'

'Who cares?' she says frustratedly. 'Who cares if you did it without expecting something in return? You did it because you love me and you wanted me to have my best shot. Didn't you?'

I nod again and meet her gaze so she can see what is there. Love. Guilt. Regret. 'Then why can't you let me do the same?' she says. 'Why can't you let me give you your best shot? You have never once thrown it in my face or asked for anything. This isn't charity, this is what you're *owed*. Do you understand the difference? I don't want to be in debt to you any more than you want to be in debt to me.'

'If I take this money, will it change things between us?' I say hesitantly.

'Yes,' she says simply. 'It will mean I can stop feeling guilty about what I've always felt I took away from you. I hope it will make our relationship better. Because I need you in my life.'

Maybe what Daisy also needs from me is to know that, from time to time, she can let someone else carry the load.

'And Myra?' I ask.

'Especially Myra,' she says so ruefully, we all laugh. Then finally, after a long pause, I say yes, I'll take it.

*

The next day is the day of the Green Goddess relaunch. Henry and Hugo have decided to drive back to London, while Daisy has offered to stay and drive us back the following day. 'I'll call you,' Hugo said to me, which was the only thing he could say given we were a full house and there was nowhere quiet for us to talk. Daisy has insisted that I come and stay with them while I find a new place, and though the thought of living with the rules and regulations of the Wimbledon townhouse was concerning, she assured me I could stay in the guest annexe, which had its own separate entrance and bathroom. They'd built it for when Myra got a bit older and might want her own space. As someone who grew up in a house where we could hear the next-door neighbour passing gas, and suitcases had to sit above every wardrobe, it was mind-blowing they had that much space.

The café is already gleaming by the time I arrive. Sunflowers, the last of the summer blooms, sit in a big bunch on the counter; single stems on each table. The menus in cursive and on recyclable paper are stacked, waiting to be handed out. The weather is crisp and clear after the storm, not the kind for sunbathing but for pottering, reading, spending the morning curled up in a café. Caitlin has just finished making the last of the green and berry smoothies that line the drinks cabinet, and Myra is doing a final check of all the tables. One bears a 'Reserved' sign. Greg rushes in, limbs gangling and jangling, with Lucky bringing in mud. 'You'll never guess what?' he says.

'GREG!' Myra yells, 'you're bringing loads of mud in. Tie Lucky up and get the mop NOW!'

'But . . .'

'NOW.' If Myra is this commanding at her mere fifteen years, she will be unstoppable when she's older. He obediently ties a reluctant Lucky up outside. Myra has the mop waiting for him with an outstretched arm. He takes it, chastened, but is clearly still vibrating with the news he's desperate to off-load. 'What's your news, Greg?' I ask.

He visibly sags with relief. 'The reason the town is so busy is because Nicole Kelly might be visiting today. *Imagine* if she came to the café?'

'It's unlikely, Greg,' Selena says doubtfully. 'Let's just stick to the plan. When you finish mopping, put some water in the dog bowls outside, would you?' He troops off dejectedly.

The plan is that Selena will come out and welcome the first ten tables – who will also get free coffee. There is already a queue, and the minute Myra opens the door they rush in. 'This is a good sign,' I say, squeezing Selena's shoulder.

She hugs me so tightly it takes me by surprise. 'Thank you. Whatever happens, thank you,' she murmurs.

As a gentle Brazilian bossa nova plays in the background, and light from across the sea streams through the large windows, I realise this is exactly how I wished it would be for Selena. It is the kind of place you come across while on holiday. Maybe you were out walking and something about it caught your eye. It becomes a daily highlight, the place you think about at the start of your day, where you always come to for coffee, a pastry, maybe a special dish you could only find there, and every time you returned, that same indefinable magic made you feel warm and welcomed.

The customers settle in, murmuring their plans for the day, discussing the menu, issuing little reproofs to children putting things where they shouldn't. There is the clink of cutlery, the smell of frying from the kitchen. Everything a beautiful symphony. Some of them stand up to look more closely at the photos on the wall, many of them a window into Guyana.

Selena and I have talked about maybe travelling together there one day.

Daisy comes in with Tara and takes her seat at the specially reserved table. She watches Myra take orders and smile – actually smile – at people. I place her coffee down, just how she likes it – a skinny cappuccino. Especially for her, I'm making a one-off dosa, with a potato curry and some coconut chutney from the dish in Selena's fridge. She watches me arrange everything on the plate and when I place it down in front of her, there is such undiluted love on her face.

'What's that?' a beaky-looking Englishwoman says, pointing at Daisy's plate as if she's been duped by not being told about this special dish.

'Oh, that's just for her because she's my sister,' I say.

'I want one too,' she says with the sense of entitlement rarely seen outside of the super-rich and the aristocracy. 'I'll pay whatever. If she's sitting in the café and eating it, we should be able to have it too, you know.'

I look sceptically at her, and then sigh as if I doubt she'll be able to afford the dish. 'It's not cheap though – it's a special dish so it's £20 per plate.'

'Fine,' she says, and waves her hand. Others overhear the conversation and whisper among themselves. By the time I go to the kitchen, five more people have ordered it, and I tell Myra to prep the plates with the accompanying sauces.

'You charged them *how much*?' Selena asks disbelievingly while trying to mash avocado with garlic and chilli.

'That's a profit margin of about £17. What? She was very insistent.' We both laugh. Normally, the most a dosa would cost in London would be £7. In India, it would be about fifty pence.

'Are you sure you haven't done this before, Padma? Run your own café?'

'No,' I say, ladling out the batter in a neat swirl onto the frying pan. As I watch the dosa settle, small bubbles rising to the surface, I realise I can do this. Daisy thinks I can too. The worst thing would be not to try at all. 'But maybe I'd like to.'

The doorbell jingles and one of the most beautiful women I've seen in my life enters, carrying an almost hairless dog. Her blonde bob is glossy, her eyes are bright blue and she has a number of delicate tattoos on her hand. A group of young girls hover nervously outside the front window, while Greg looks like he's about to pass out.

'Oh, thank god you allow dogs,' the woman says. 'And you do vegan food!'

'Nicole . . .' Greg sputters. 'Nicole Kelly.' She looks at him kindly, as one would a village idiot who has just tripped over their own shoes. I don't know who she is beyond that she's famous online, but I know it will be a big deal for Selena. The café is packed, but Daisy smoothly gets up and offers her table. I love her for doing that. 'I'm heading out anyway. You should order the dosa,' she says to Nicole, 'it's limited availability and delicious.'

'Looks like I'll have one of those then,' Nicole says with her soft Irish lilt. Myra takes her order, adding with a cheeky smile: 'If you do happen to take a picture of it, the chef is my aunt. Her Instagram is *NotYourAuntiesKitchen*. Auntie with an "i.e.". No pressure though.' Myra winks at me as Nicole makes a note of the name. Pinky Dishwallah has certainly earned her commission.

While I get Nicole's food ready, I pause for a brief moment to take it all in.

If someone had asked me how things were going a few weeks ago, I would have said: *This is fine.* Little phrases we use to wash down our discontent, even though *fine* is an adjective that has moved so far away from its original meaning of things being excellent or good, that it has become a piece of tape hiding the cracks in a life. I only know that because life feels different now.

I don't think about what will happen in the future, I focus on this small point in time. Selena humming in the kitchen, Myra's head captured in silhouette against the bright morning sun. Daisy struggling as Tara's lead gets caught on a table leg. The slow warmth of whatever is happening with Hugo, alongside the grief of what will never happen with Wallace. The gratitude of being able to feel it all.

Epilogue

Three months later

The handover of seasons can be a disorientating time, but strangely I love the change from autumn to winter. The sky is encased in a crispness that snicks under the collar and around our exposed feet while we sleep. The night takes on a burnished glow, streetlights encircled in a halo of mist. The first exhalation of clouded breath. Trees heavy with golden leaves and ready to let go of everything they've carried through the year.

The door jingles ahead of the late-afternoon rush, and a thirty-something woman comes to the counter and says: 'May I have a Pumpkin Spice Latte?'

Myra leans over and points to the board that reads:

We do GOOD coffee
We make GREAT food
Because of this, we don't do . . . Pumpkin Spice Latte

'Why not?' the woman says, looking mystified. 'Everyone else does. They're delicious. You're losing out on good business.'

'If I may answer in order,' Myra says, putting her hands

together as if in prayer. 'One, we are not everyone. Two, it tastes like pumpkin jizz. And three, I think we'll be just fine.'

'MYRA!' I say from the back.

'Sorry, sorry. What about a – oh, she left.'

I make myself look as scary as it is possible to look while wearing an apron covered in neon-pink bindi-wearing gnomes – Myra's private little joke. 'You are honestly the world's worst waitress. Stop scaring customers away.'

'She was never going to order something else. Plus, you aren't paying me to be here. My skills lie in other areas, remember?'

The door jingles again. 'May I speak to the proprietor of . . . Alva Beach?' I come out from the back of the kitchen and give Daisy a kiss on her cheek. Behind her is a group of women all dressed more or less the same way. Bodycon business dresses in grey or navy, sharp pumps and designer handbags held tightly in their manicured fingers. 'I thought I would mix things up and bring the ladies here – they're all part of the women's recruitment steering group at the firm. Plus . . . the chaat!'

'Hi, ladies,' I say, waving to them. 'Please, get comfortable – we'll take good care of you.' Daisy beams.

An entire world can change in a season. Harkness wasn't the only place that Nicole Kelly's fairy godmother wand helped. Although she had looked bemused by Myra's sales pitch while being upsold a dosa, she'd posted a photo and tagged me in it. It likely wouldn't have made an impact except she wrote a caption about how it was one of the best things she'd ever eaten. Overnight, I checked my phone to find out I had 20,000 new followers. I still have difficulty believing any of it is real.

*

After we came back, Wallace didn't feel the need to say goodbye while I gathered my things. I stayed at Daisy's for two weeks – the first was fine because they were on holiday in Greece; the second week she was so high maintenance I decamped to Delilah's sofa. We got to talking. Delilah suggested that I take over the café for three months, and if I liked it, I could take it over permanently. If I didn't, she'd sell the business so there'd be minimal risk on my part. I didn't know anything about ordering, local permits, how to run a menu, hiring wait staff . . . so she gave me an immersive induction in everything I wasn't sure about. A lot of it, she assured me, was learned on the job.

I said I didn't know where I'd get the money from for the start-up costs, but Delilah told me it was obvious. I must take Daisy up on her offer. 'The money is yours anyway, like she said. Don't be a martyr, Padma.' When I asked Daisy, she didn't give me statistics about failed small businesses or tell me what to do, she asked how much and when. And she looked . . . proud.

Myra had started life in Daisy's body, and now she felt like an extension of mine. After all the drama with her school, she asked her parents if she could be home-schooled. It wasn't just that she didn't want to face her friends, it was that she felt the school was not on her side and she couldn't trust them. Daisy and Henry agreed so long as she promised to go on to higher education, to which she said yes. In part because I told her one of my biggest regrets was not finishing university, and also because she saw that it might be a good way to figure out what she really wanted to do.

She had a tutor who, in addition to being great at academic work, was also really into the outdoors and taught her about trees and foraging and how to swim. When I had the time, Myra and I fell into a routine of spending her lunch break together or on evening hangouts where we'd walk Tara together. When she heard about the café, she suggested a ton of ideas about how to market it, and how to make dishes get lots of clicks. I'd make hybrid creations like dessert chaat or kale pakoras and she would create so much hype around them on social media, we'd sell out within the hour. During tiffin time – which was inspired by the afternoon snacks served in Mumbai offices – we sometimes had a queue down the street, waiting at the takeaway hatch.

*

Although the cash injection from Daisy was wonderful, I spend most of my time working, wondering if my lucky streak will end. But even with those worries, even while barely upright after a long day, I am happy here. My travel plans haven't been shelved either – I finally have a trip to Brazil planned during the two quietest weeks in December. I had forgotten what it felt like, to be excited about life. But here I run my hands along the wooden counter-top and think: *Mine*. I see the way my staff talk to my customers, how they make every single one of them feel special. That's what I wanted. To create a space where no matter what happens in your day, you can come here to feel safe and cocooned.

After Daisy and her colleagues leave, and Myra runs me through the video edit for a Hallowe'en-themed masala chai recipe, I finally have some time to switch off. I spray the round discs of pilea and the little succulent corner with water. I say hello to all the new leaves on the monstera. I wipe down all the menus and tidy up the Indian snack-box stand that offers horribly overpriced banana chips and sev. The oven pings and I take out an apple and blackberry crumble, the sugar glazed a rich golden-brown.

The door jingles and in walks the person who is fast becoming my first home.

'Hello, my love,' he says and walks towards the counter. We lean over the pan, the scent of blackberries rising up, sweet and earthy, as it did not so long ago in the woodland behind the cottage. 'Hello, my love,' I say back, and kiss Hugo deeply, as I always do, as if it is the first and the last time.

Acknowledgements

I do not know that this book would have been possible to write without the life I have lived, nor the people who are in it. Because of them, especially my family, I know who I am, whose voices I want to write into being, whose voices matter. Padma is someone who grows up without that, and I wanted to give her back her voice.

Thank you to my parents for always making me feel as if my voice counts, and that it should be used especially to speak up for those who can't. To my sister, Priya, for showing me the brightest and strongest parts of a sibling relationship, and what it feels like to have someone who is a literal Amazon fight in their corner, and be someone I can talk endlessly to. Thank you to my mother-in-law, Prue, whose love stretches across oceans. To my best friend, Mal, for making me believe I can do anything. To my incredible friends who share so much love and support my work – my brother-in-law Shabby, whose inventive food skills are a match for Padma's, my boy pals Niaz, Kumaran and Ahmed, my school pals Alice and Sonia, my girl gang Zehra, Zekra, Shabana and Kudsia, my darling Tania, Aga for all the jiu-jitsu and badassery, Jack for keeping me strong and sane. Thank you Martin, for your home and your friendship.

In no order, thank you to my New Zealand family: Gaby and Felicity, John, and all my loved ones there, and to my friends Yumi, Karen, George, Jesse.

Thank you to the incredible team who worked on this book. My agent, Rowan, who is the best of the best for a thousand reasons, including listening to my many wobbles about the book, and to Eleanor for keeping things afloat from The Soho Agency. Thank you to my patient and brilliant editor Emily Griffin, who saw this book through many transformations, and the amazing Penguin team who worked on it, including Jess Muscio, Laurie Ip Fung Chun, Issie and Izzy, and Ceara Elliot. To my 'men in black' – my fantastic management team Siren – Grainne and Sarah, thank you for helping me to keep life on course while writing this book.

Finally, to all of those lost in the mists of addiction, whether struggling with it themselves, or if they are a loved one caught in the chaos of it. There are many of us who understand you, and you are not in this alone.